THREE MOONS RISING

THREE MOONS RISING

Sheila N. Eskew

Writers Club Press
San Jose New York Lincoln Shanghai

Three Moons Rising

Writers Club Press
an imprint of iUniverse, Inc.

For information address:
iUniverse, Inc.
5220 S. 16th St., Suite 200
Lincoln, NE 68512
www.iuniverse.com

Any resemblance to actual people and events is purely coincidental.
This is a work of fiction.

ISBN: 0-595-22487-3

Printed in the United States of America

In Memory of my mother Grace K. Norman

With sincerest thanks to my husband Frank, my daughter Jessica, my Aunt Jean, and my dearest friends Bell, Pat and Jeannie. Who have given me all their love, support and encouragement and have poked and prodded when needed, with out which this would not have been possible.

Escapism is the first stage of imagination.
SNE

Introduction

*T*error! Never had he experienced so much pure terror. Another light beam scorched the hood of his tan Mercedes and Karl Kirk smelled the burning paint as it bubbled from the intense heat of the ray. Behind him a cone shaped aircraft flew firing beams of pure light energy at his car. Karl knew only time stood between him and a fiery death. Now he wished he had never found the alien's base, or that he had not gone back to take pictures. However, he knew the aliens building the base were planning an invasion, and Karl wanted to warn his government. He had been in government service for thirty years and held a strong sense of loyalty to his country.

A bright beam lit the car's interior, Karl screamed. Then to his horror another craft appeared in front of him. A different light came from the second craft, blue and wider. Upon making contact with Karl's Mercedes the beam did not explode, instead it was as if a giant hand took hold and pushed his auto over the mountainside. Rolling and falling, Karl's only thought was of his daughter, his world erupting with a final beam from the first craft.

Warm and dry, out of the miserable weather just outside, the local Sheriff sat in his patrol vehicle writing the final report on the strange accident that he had investigated. He well remembered the intense red glow over the cliff's edge that had alerted him to the accident, and staring in horror at the car totally encased in flames. Radioing back to his base for help he then tried desperately to get to the automobile, but the cliff's edge had been to jagged and steep. Frustrated and feeling helpless he turned his gaze toward the black velvet sky. So serene was the view, he had allowed his gaze to remain praying the fire trucks would come soon. However, any peace he had found was short lived as he realized two of the stars were growing larger and getting closer. The stars became luminescent cones that hovered over the valley as if they too were watching the auto burn. He continued watching the crafts as they held their position over the car. To his disbelief a red ball descended from each craft and slowly fell on the dying flames, within seconds the car again burst into a bright red-hot blaze. Flames illuminated the mountainside and his patrol vehicle. Apprehensively he backed away from the side of the mountain, both objects moving toward him threateningly. In the distance he heard the sirens of the fire trucks coming closer. The crafts stopped advancing as two fire trucks and an ambulance came into view, all coming to a screeching halt upon seeing the two crafts. Seconds later the two objects had silently flashed away. The lawman shivered the events of four nights ago still fresh in his memory.

Only one person had been inside the burned automobile, a retired government diplomat, but the cause of the accident had been officially resolved and his part of the investigation was over. Now the excitement would fade. He signed his last report glad it was finished.

"Strange," the Sheriff wondered aloud, "I've never had government agents investigate an auto crash before, but then the victim was a retired diplomat." He shrugged. "The agents were more interested in the mysterious craft than the victim of the fire."

CHAPTER 1

Darkness crept silently over Flaming Gorge Utah, filling the gorge with damp mists and obscuring the full moon's silvery light. Sounds became muffled in the heavy still air, echoing back and forth across the canyon walls and fading into eerie and distorted whispers.

Dancing over the western mountain ridge, lightning illuminated the low hanging clouds in a shower of electricity, reflecting an iridescent purple glow of electric blue and red from the canyon surface. Even as the front rumbled closer the wind rose to whip the mists through winding passages of time sculptured sandstone silencing the eerie whispers. Cold rain began to fall, making the twisting, steeply graded roads even more hazardous. Braving the icy conditions, a speeding sports car expertly navigated the winding mountain roads, the driver seemingly mindless of the danger.

Conditions worsened and the rain turned from drizzle to sleet in the dropping temperatures. Catherine drove the car instinctively, her troubled thoughts making her heedless of the road. Ahead she saw the beginnings of a small town, but overlooking the lowered speed signs she sped onward toward a destination unknown even to her.

Leaving the sleeping town behind Catherine glanced skyward into dark clouds that seemed to hang on the mountains. Without seeing the Sheriff's Jeep parked just off the shoulder of the highway, Catherine's gaze once more returned to concentrate on the wet pavement ahead.

The patrol jeep's radar speed detector beeped, the car was coming on fast. As it neared the Sheriff could hear the roar of Catherine's Mustang Cobra. She sped by and falling in behind he gave chase.

Up the twisting road they raced, Catherine way out in front, losing sight of him in her mirrors. Ahead she saw a turn-off, and making a sharp turn onto the small road she did not see the chain across it until it was too late. Old and rusty, the chain broke and Catherine sped several yards down the lane before she could stop. Switching off her lights, she waited, moments later the Sheriff drove past. Catherine drew a deep breath, switched on her auto lights and slowly made her way down the dirt road. Reaching the end, Catherine was surprised to find it ended in an overlook and relieved she had not raced down the road.

Even in the dark it was obvious the area was seldom visited, the benches were broken and tall weeds had scraped the side of her car as she drove in. Switching off the engine and her lights, Catherine got out to stretch her legs, the drizzle had stopped and the clouds were beginning to clear. Breathing in the cool pine scented air her troubled and tired mind also began to clear. She allowed the movements of the light clouds playing hide and seek with the pale moon to soothe her confused soul. Absently, as she had done since it had been given to her, Catherine played with her grandmother's necklace, her eyelids drooped, exhaustion took its toll, and she stumbled to her car. Inside the warm interior she fell asleep for the first time in three days.

Catherine woke just before dawn when the stars were at their brightest. A strange stillness and quiet had fallen over the area and opening her car door she stepped out to breathe in the cool air. She stretched her muscles stiff and sore from the few hours she had slept in the reclining car seat. Yawning, Catherine stretched again. Gazing up into a now cloudless sky she enjoyed the brightness of the stars and walked around to sit on the car hood.

A cold blue light seemed to radiate from just over the scenic edge, in the still air she thought she was dreaming. Cautiously Catherine approached the edge and dared to look over the sheer embankment. Astonished at what she saw there, her mind reeled. Catherine knew she would never forget the spectacle below.

Dominating the floor of the remote canyon, obscured partially in mist, a glowing blue dome provided the source of the unearthly light. Around it hovered three cone shaped craft alternately firing a white light at the dome and forming an opaque glass structure, with each beam the dome enlarged.

Held by the awesome spectacle below, Catherine watched the three alien crafts fly and maneuver in perfect triangular patterns. For a long time she watched until the center craft began to rise out of the canyon. With the pattern broken the other two also began to ascend. Catherine backed away from the edge and ran to her car, she knew they had detected her presence. Looking behind her, Catherine saw them rise above the cliff's edge. Getting inside her car she started the engine and it roared to life, spinning around she raced down the rough dirt road she had driven in on. As she neared the main road Catherine thought the Sheriff's Jeep had returned and for a moment breathed a sigh of relief. A white light beam whizzed past her and incinerated a nearby pine tree convincing her it was one of the craft, it's red and blue lights had fooled her, in the canyon she had seen them only glow blue. Again she spun around, speeding toward the edge with nowhere to go. The cliff was coming up quickly and one craft waited for her there, the other two were close behind her, light beams exploding the trees around her. Catherine was trapped and escape did not look promising. But a strong sense of survival had been born in Catherine and on some unknown instinct she jumped from the car just as it went over the edge. Rolling and tumbling with the sound of her car exploding in her ears Catherine fell a short distance and landed on her stomach. The world went black and she lost consciousness.

Dawn and the aliens were caught! Their anti-detection device only functioned at night, but today in their pursuit of the earthling spy they had unintentionally become vulnerable. Already they were being pursued. One craft had managed to get inside the dome and to safety, but Captain Quar's ship and a second ship Red Star, had not been as fortunate.

Five earth fighters were closing fast. Captain Quar ordered Red Star to change course, splitting Earth's forces. Only moments after they had parted company Red Star was in trouble after taking a direct hit by one of the Earth fighter's missiles. A second missile hit Red Star severely damaging the ship's self-destruct devices leaving it vulnerable to capture.

"Hold out as long as you can," Quar ordered, and he knew if the earthmen took the crew alive their operations would be in even more serious jeopardy.

"Sir!" one of his crewmen informed him, "we have hit one of the Earth's ships with lazzer fire, it is going down and the pilot has parachuted. Shall we terminate him?" the crewman asked hopefully. Zerion were cruel and enjoyed sadistic sport of their victims.

"No. Concentrate on getting back to space." Quar ordered. They were not yet ready to take on the Earth's defenses.

"Yes sir." The crewman said, disappointed. "Space orbit in one minute." In seconds they obtained orbit high enough above Earth not to be followed or detected by the Earth's fighters.

"Find Red Star!" was Quar's immediate command.

Finally they found the downed craft. Unable to destroy the damaged craft from space, Quar ordered the crew to destroy all records and take their termination drug provided to the crew of each vessel. It enraged Quar to think the Earthmen would get the ship, but it would do them little good when the Zerion invaded in force.

Down on the planet, the crashed ship had become surrounded by military police from the near by Air Force base. Only moments remained until the explosive charge placed on the door would force the portal open. Inside the crew prepared to do their duty, all but three of the crew took their suicide pills, these three waited patiently until the door blew open, then walked calmly outside. Quickly surrounded by security people the three were whisked away for Top Secret, government interrogation.

Commander Quar was angry one ship had been lost, possibly for nothing. He was not positive they had eliminated the spy. Even more frustrating, Quar was aware that he must patiently sit in orbit until darkness on this side of the Earth. Calling the Earth base he was in command of, he ordered a ground search of the area where they had encountered the spy. Quar shook his head, 'so close to the base.' he thought, hoping the spy had been killed before he had the opportunity to relay information to others. After the previous incident four nights ago, Quar had ordered tighter security.

If the ground search did not prove fruitful, Quar had decided to make one last scanning search after sunset using his ship's sensor devices. These sensors were delicate enough to determine if someone had died in the car crash or lived and escaped. If the spy could not be found, and was not dead, their base completion plans would have to be advanced further. This area had become too busy.

Vital to the Zerion's plans, this breech of security would have to be carefully explained to his superiors. Before he did this, he would inform the network of Earth agents perhaps they could locate the spy and terminate him. Quar did not achieve his rank by disappointing his superiors, and he would not now. Zerions were a warrior race and did not tolerate mistakes. They could not afford too. Zerion was a poor planet. From the dawn of their history as space travelers they had stolen from other worlds as they were preparing to do on Earth. Earth's oceans of water and fertile land would provide an excellent colony to support their home world. Earth's populace would provide slaves to do the menial jobs, and many of the women of Earth were beautiful. They would give Zerion fresh blood in their inbred society. As always, when the planet was decimated, it would be destroyed.

Quar knew the importance of his part in the subjection of Earth. Already they controlled the planet's one natural satellite, the moon, which served as a lookout for their old enemies, the Creasions.

※   ※   ※

A leaf tickled Catherine's nose. She rolled onto her back and hearing a groan realized it was her own. Slowly she became aware of the ache in her head, worsened by the piercing light from the late afternoon sun glinting into her face. She shaded her eyes with her hand. Groggy and stiff Catherine sat up squinting at her surroundings, her tired mind clearing quickly as the frightening events of the past early morning came flooding back. Luckily she had landed on a slight ledge just over the cliff's edge. If it had not stopped her fall she would have been killed. Looking gingerly over the side, she paled and turning on shaking legs Catherine could see the top of the overlook. Hearing voices nearing she dropped back down. As the voices drew nearer she knew them to be aliens. Panic hit her in waves. There was not time to run and very little room on the ledge to hide. Quickly she lay down and worked herself into the slight crevice just under the overlook. Catherine could clearly hear the two alien searchers talking and to her total amazement she understood what they were saying. Catherine held her breath as they looked over the edge but they did not see her. It seemed like hours before their voices trailed off in the distance as they went to look for her in other places.

Cautiously, Catherine rose upward until her eyes were just level with the overlook, she scanned the area and gratefully did not see the two aliens. What she did see astounded her already overloaded sense. Several trees still smoldered, blackened reminders of the power of the alien ships. Catherine turned and looked down where her car had burned, only charred grass remained, the car totally disintegrated. Over the western horizon the sun was setting, and Catherine knew she would spend another night in the mountains.

Shivering, hunger gnawed at Catherine's stomach reminding her she had eaten little since before her father's funeral, two days ago. 'Strange,' Catherine thought 'with all that has happened, this is the first I've thought about how Dad died.' Tears clouded her vision, Catherine forced them back, later she would think of it, now she had to concentrate on getting to safety, if that was possible.

Standing on the ledge, the top of the overlook came to just below her shoulders, placing both hands on the overlook she vaulted upward and rolled. Catherine stood brushing off most of the leaves that still clung to her clothes.

Looking around the overlook she was further amazed at the damage done by the aliens but relieved not to see anyone. Finding her knit hat where it had fallen in her leap from the doomed auto earlier that morning, Catherine placed it over her loosely braided hair and tucked in a few stray strands. A chill passed through her as the cold wind swept the area and she began walking down the dirt road toward the main highway. Thrusting her cold hands inside her pockets Catherine wished she had worn a heavier jacket but resolutely she trudged on.

Dusk sent hues of lavender and mauve through the evening atmosphere followed by the first stars to appear in the clear sky. Seeing them Catherine quickened her pace, the aliens had sent a search party after her, so they knew she was alive, after dark she knew they would be back. As the moon rose it illuminated the burnt trees along the road giving them a ghoulish appearance, dusk turning to darkness.

An owl screamed making Catherine jump and causing the blood to pound painfully in her temples. She drew a deep breath, steadying herself.

Ahead she could see the main road; suddenly it was filled with bright white light. Catherine froze, her eyes moving dreadfully skyward. They were back! Somehow, she had known they would be, and they had found her.

Hovering just over the main road was one craft, red and blue lights revolving slowly around the silvery hull. From underneath the triangular body came the white light that lit the area. Going ahead to the main road was impossible she heard them coming on foot from that direction. Turning Catherine ran through the under brush in a vain attempt to escape.

Desperation seemed to smother her, they were very close now, Catherine glanced over her shoulder. Pain shot up her left leg and she was falling. Green light spots whizzed by her head as she fell, her skin tingled from them and she hit the ground.

Stunned by the fall and dazed by the pain in her ankle, Catherine lay still. She could hear them getting closer, their feet snapping twigs and small bushes in their hurry to get to her. Catherine's head cleared with a sharp intake of air and the urgency of her position blotted out the pain. She tried to move. Above, she heard the craft hovering over her now, seconds later she was bathed in white light. Fear swept through her and Catherine tried again to move but found a boot placed squarely in the middle of her back.

"Do not move Earthling or your life is forfeit!" Catherine did as the gruff, strangely accented voice demanded.

"Sir," the man with the gruff voice was saying, "We have captured the Earthling." he paused. "Sir, it is a woman. What are your instructions?"

"Bring her." Catherine heard a voice over a radio say as the craft moved toward the overlook.

Removing his foot from her back the alien told her to stand. Slowly Catherine did as he instructed trying not to put her weight on her injured leg. Catherine became aware of their eyes on her. She met the eyes of the one with the gruff voice.

"Captain Quar, will be pleased with you." He smirked. "Had you been a male, my instructions were to terminate you."

Catherine said nothing, affixing the alien with a cold stare as they started back toward the overlook and their ship. She was determined not to show the aliens any weakness. Mentally preparing herself for the pain, she forced herself to walk without a limp, grateful for her tightly laced hiking boots.

Six aliens, if they were aliens, surrounded her as they proceeded toward the overlook where the craft had landed. Walking through the sparse underbrush she studied these creatures. They appeared as human as any man from Earth with the exception of the hard look in their eyes, it did not seem to change or soften. All were uniformed the same, which did not surprise her, it was obvious they were a military unit. Ahead Catherine could see a lone man emerging from the center steps of the craft. He stopped on the bottom step and watched her approached.

Catherine stopped in the area of bright white light just beneath the ship, blinking she focused on the man. Her guards halted as she did and when he approached they snapped to attention, the group's leader stepping forward.

"You have done well, Stx." The man said to the group's leader, then turned to their captive, "So, you are the spy!" Quar laughed. His voice cold and humorless. "I am Captain Quar of the Zerion Imperial Advanced Guard, and you?"

Catherine, though her knees threatened to buckle, looked him square in the eyes and for a brief moment the Captain wondered if she would speak. "My names sir, is Catherine Kirk, and I am not a spy!" she said simply but firmly.

Captain Quar glared down at the small Earthgirl before him. She dared to defy him, "Your guilt or innocence in this matter is moot. You have seen too much and caused one of my ships to be captured. You will come with us to Zerion." he turned to Stx. "Have her brought to my cabin." Quar turned and walked toward the ship.

Catherine stood unmoving, stunned, until a rough shove on her shoulder nearly sent her sprawling in the dirt. Somehow she kept her balance, but it caused her leg to throb badly. Her mind was in turmoil, Catherine knew she must escape. She looked up the steps into the spacecraft and froze, a Lieutenant forced her up two of the steps, but on the third step she desperately kicked backwards causing him to fall. Quar, who was only a few steps ahead of Catherine restrained her before she could make good her escape, twisting her arm painfully until she was forced over his arm backwards, his face very close to hers.

"Lieutenant, are you harmed?" Quar called, glaring down at Catherine.

"No, Captain." the alien stood up.

"After I tire of this little spy, you may have her." Quar told him with a sly smile and forced Catherine the remainder of the way up inside the craft.

The Lieutenant, once inside, guided Catherine through the ship, not allowing her time to study the maze of ship's instruments in the dim light before reaching Quar's cabin.

Blocking her entrance to the cabin, he pulled her roughly to him. "Soon I will have you, and you will pay for humiliating me." He smiled and shoved Catherine through the door. "Until then, Captain Quar will enjoy you." The door closed leaving her in the shadowy cabin, his gruff laugh echoing in the halls.

Slowly Catherine managed to sit up and lean against the wall. In a daze she wondered if she had gone mad. Surely this wasn't happening. It was nothing like the many abduction stories she had read, but she was forced to believe the reality of her senses.

How long Catherine sat there before she felt the vibrations and heard the rumble, she did not know, but it shook her out of her trance. The ship lifted off. With speed she did not know she was capable of, Catherine moved to the small window next to the bunk. Catherine clung to the porthole and watched the ground darken as the white searchlights were extinguished and the vessel hovered briefly.

Below them, Catherine saw the two searchers who had failed to find her during the day. They stood beneath the ship, bound together. Catherine gasped as a blinding white fire flowed from the ship, engulfing the two men and they were gone. Moments later the ship cleared the treetops and quickly the atmosphere of Earth.

Catherine watched the Earth for as long as it was visible. In shock she marveled at the swirling beauty of the clouds that played upon the green, brown and blue globe, the sun shinning on the planet making it almost glow. A deep sob escaped her, and an awful agony threatened to shatter her heart, Catherine wondered if she would ever see home again.

CHAPTER 2

*F*inally glad for the time away from the pressures of his high position and his six councilors, At'r sat before the large cathedral viewing windows behind his desk. His view was extraordinary. Looking down At'r saw only the nose of the massive ship that lay behind him, otherwise his view was unobstructed. The vastness of space lay before the Emperor of the Three Houses of Creasion.

In the short time of two Creasion weeks that At'r had spent on his new flagship he had been more than impressed. Tos-hawk One, meaning Star Hawk, had proven to be the fastest ship in it's class in either his fleet or the Zerion's. Tos-hawk One was maneuverable even at her great size, and the sensor detection filter afforded her invisibility from other ship's sensors. She could close in on an enemy vessel without detection until they sighted her visually and then it was too late. Tos-hawk One's weaponry consisted of fore and aft lazzer cannons, v-ion torpedoes and a newly constructed sound beam that could render another vessel powerless without destroying it.

Tos-hawk One was the first of four. Each ship was designed to be a battle station, but only Tos-hawk One had the elaborate quarters for their Emperor. The other three ships would use the extra space for storage, or scientific studies.

At last At'r felt capable of successfully defending his Empire against invaders, mainly the warlike Zerion. Not since the day the

Zerion had launched a surprise attack against the capital city of Crea had At'r felt secure.

A festive mood permeated the City on that day, people laughing and celebrating At'r's twentieth birthday. Then had come the attack. At'r had lost his parents, and his fiancée'. Creasion had lost many aristocrats as well as much of the population they served.

It had been a devastating attack. But the Zerion had only angered the Creasion people. They did not know that the planet's main defenses were underground and the blow they dealt while killing the populace and the Emperor barely damaged their space force. In the confusion the Zerions had scrambled back to their home world before the Creasions were able to mount a counter offensive.

At'r had become Emperor on his twentieth birthday. His coronation had been brief, witnessed by High Priest Betus, his close friend and Betus' youngest son, Kron, and Admiral Qur. Broadcasts were also made to Metem, Konas and Tross, Creasion's three populated moons. Moments after the ceremony At'r vowed he would make Creasion safe again. With his people watching on their viewer screens, At'r lead the space fleet toward Zerion to avenge the attack on Creasion.

Zerion paid a high price for their deceit, but the evil Emperor had managed to escape and reports from their agents told stories of massing fleets preparing once again to attack. At'r would keep his vow, so he had commissioned these battle stations. However, that was not his only precaution. In four years he had brought the Creasion defense system to a highly advanced state. Most major cities now had the capabilities of sinking below the planet's surface, large doors slid over them to protect and hide the population and structures. On both Metem and Konas the cities were small and the planetary energy field would keep them safe. Tross, the third moon in the system was a cold moon, and it's orbital path made it difficult to secure and difficult to attack.

Now with the positive factors of Tos-hawk One, the others would be quickly completed and tested. At'r felt hopeful for the first time in four years, in the future the Zerions would have a much harder time carrying out a surprise attack. One of the first matters At'r had given priority was the completion of the early warning system begun by his father. A series of well-hidden detectors in the meteor belt between Creasion and Zerion. If the system had been functional when the disastrous attack had occurred, the Zerions would not have so easily damaged them. The next time they attacked would be their last, and finally the old feud would be settled. Zerions had stolen their women, even an Empress, and had attacked them without provocation. At'r would not let it happen again.

A low tone beep alerted him to someone requesting entrance to his outer chambers, he sighed and turned back to his desk. Commander Kron stood outside the large double doors of the Emperor's formal chambers, At'r was not surprised to see him on the viewer.

"Enter Commander." At'r told him. He and Kron were cousins and close friends from childhood. At'r watched Kron's progress through his formal receiving room on the series of security viewers on his desk. From here At'r could monitor any room in his chambers, the surrounding hallways and most of the ship. With a hiss the doors to his private chambers slid open and Kron walked in.

"Sire," he said stopping and bowing slightly.

"Would you care for a glass of wine, my friend?" At'r asked cordially.

"Thank you my Lord, yes." he accepted the glass.

"Can you stay, or is this business?" At'r asked.

"Business, sire, the Zerions are up their old tricks." Kron told his Lord. "Long range sensors have picked up a Zerion construction craft leaving the Sol system. Probably from Earth since they have what appears to be an Earthwoman on board, her life readings are very strong, but not entirely Terrain." "They have violated the neutral area." At'r stated what they both knew, war was drawing closer.

"Not only that, but their present course will take them through three hundred domars of our territory, they seem to be in a great hurry, and I can not keep from being curious about what a construction craft would be doing on Earth." Kron knew what his Lord would instruct him to do.

At'r smiled slyly, "We have caught them, finally. Set an intercept course, I want them as soon as they enter out territory. What type of weaponry is the craft equipped with?"

"Minimal lazzer guns and self-destruct system, it shouldn't be a problem to capture the craft." Kron informed At'r, "They were not expecting us to be here."

"I want the Earthwoman as unharmed as the Zerion have left her, and hopefully all computer records intact."

"That should not be problem either. We will be waiting under the cover of the sensor filter when they enter our space, and before they can communicate any information to Zerion, we will disarm them and neutralize their controls. At that point they will have one minute before the sonar tranquilizer hits them." Kron paused, "As you know, sire, to use the tranquilizer we will become sensor visible, it should be a startling surprise for them."

At'r grinned, "Very soon Kron, I trust you to see to the details. Notify me as soon as they enter our trap." Kron finished his wine and bowed, exiting the way he had come.

At'r sat in the large comfortable desk chair sipping his wine, the grand finale to the perfect test run of Tos-hawk One would be the capture of the Zerion ship. His return to Creasion with the Zerion vessel in tow and all records intact should quiet any disagreeable and discontent voices in his court. But that brought to mind one of the more recent complaints registered by council. They wanted him to marry, and soon, an heir to follow him was becoming their biggest concern and his least.

Most of the available women of his court were either old widows or eight years his junior. Thanks to the raid the Zerions had carried out four years ago there was not a woman in his empire he wanted to wed. According to their strict laws he could only wed a daughter of one of the Royal families of the Triangle. Among the few remaining daughters, the oldest was sixteen, a mere child.

Before the Triangle was formed, Creasion had a long history of war. Although they were descendants of the same race of humans, they fought. Eventually they split into three separate groups and each group came to be ruled by one distinct family.

When space travel became possible, many generations ago, each family had fought for total control over the planet and the three moons. The house of Konas won and choosing the forest moon for their family home, declared the planet neutral ground. The other two families took up residency on the two remaining moons. Still, control and power of the system was split three ways, and when the first Zerion attack came it had almost totally wiped out all three realms. They destroyed everything in their path and took many slaves back to Zerion, leaving behind only a handful on each moon to re-populate. Finally the system of one planet and three moons had become one people again by means of the House of the Triangle.

Blood was a stronger bond than a signed treaty. From that precept, the High Conqueror and Lord of the House of Konas took for his wife the daughter of the family of Metem, and to equally honor the house of Tross he gave in marriage his beloved sister Ena to the first lord of that moon. From then on the High Conqueror ruled from the planet Creasion, which was set up as the seat of government. From these original-ruling families came all future Emperors of Creasion. Each heir chose his wife and Empress from one of the two families, soon the three families became intermixed and each family was able to claim a certain heritage to the Throne. Each family had control over their moon, ruling by the consent of their people and by the grace of the Emperor, his word and wish were law. But his life was dedicated to not only rule but to serve his people. His education was closely monitored from childhood and in the thirty generations of Emperors and a few Empresses, only two had proven to be corrupt. So At'r grew up as his father and his grandfather had. To rule with a firm but just and wise hand, doing the job he had been trained to do.

Now At'r must choose a wife when he returned to Creasion, even though he did not really want to marry. A wife would mean children and family, and the one thing the High Lord Emperor of all of Creasion feared, love. Once again he would be vulnerable to the pain of losing a loved one, as he had with his parents and fiancée. Now his people were his family and his conscience was heavy with their loses, he needed no further pain.

Again a low toned buzzer drew his attention away from his meditations. He depressed the button to receive the incoming message on his private channel.

Kron's face appeared, "Yes, Commander?" At'r inquired.

"Sire, the trap is set and the Zerion ship should enter our territory in just a few moments. I thought you might enjoy watching the capture on your viewer, since the burst shields are covering you windows."

"Thank you Commander, I would." At'r agreed. At'r switched on his main viewer and settled back to watch.

Three hours had passed since Catherine had been taken from Earth and placed in the alien Captain's cabin. Her nerves grew tenser with each passing second, she feared the Captain's return. Catherine had searched the disorderly cabin for a weapon and luckily found a knife that had been discarded or forgotten from a previous meal the Captain had eaten. It was now well hidden in her sleeve, point down, and ready to drop into her hand if needed. Catherine knew even if she killed the Captain it would not help her position, but she could not think of another course. It was clear what he intended to do with her, and the least she could do was to fight him.

With a serpentine hiss the cabin door opened and Catherine stood as the Captain entered, ready for any move the alien made.

"No need to stand on my account Earthgirl, that bunk is where you will spend most of the remainder of this journey." He laughed, his eyes devouring Catherine.

"Go to hell, alien!" She threw at him.

His speed was astounding. Suddenly he had her gripped by the shoulders, his fingers bruising her as he crushed her to his body, his thick lips covering hers, forcing them open, only to draw back in pain seconds later when Catherine bit his lower lip.

"I see Earthgirls will be interesting to train." the alien said, dark, blue-red blood oozing from his lip.

Catherine saw the fury in his eyes as he briefly released her, she spat his blood out and carefully let the knife drop into her hand.

His hands were on her waist now, picking her up almost off the floor Quar dragged her toward the bunk. Catherine swung at her only available target as he ripped her high collared shirt from her shoulders, grabbing a bit of flesh in his grasp. With a howl of pain Quar released Catherine causing her to fall onto the bunk and the knife to fly from her hand, leaving her to face the enraged alien, defenseless and half naked.

More of his blue-red blood poured from between his fingers, the knife had missed his throat, but cut a long gash in his cheek. Slowly he looked up at Catherine, her ripped shirt revealing not only her breasts but the necklace her grandmother had given her. Captain Quar's eyes became fixed on it.

"You lying Creasion slut!" He screamed and lunged at her grabbing the necklace, giving it a yank with all his strength, only to release it with another howl of pain as the medallion burned his hand. The chain held and the seared imprint of the necklace on his hand infuriated him more. Enraged, Quar screamed then struck Catherine with the back of his hand, smashing her to the floor. Dazed from the blow she could not move, Catherine felt his weight cover her and his hot breath near her ear.

Bells began ringing and the lights were flashing, Catherine thought she was losing consciousness. She heard the Captain mutter something, a curse, and he rose leaving her lying on the floor. A voice boomed through the room declaring a first stage alert, requesting the Captain's immediate presence on the control deck.

"I will finish with you a little later Creasion." Quar told Catherine, and holding his cheek the alien Captain hurried to the control deck.

Moments after he left her, the ship gave a violent lurch, as if it had been hit by something. The jolt motivated Catherine, weakly she pulled herself back on the bunk and looked out the porthole.

Gathered around the Zerion craft were five smaller ships and they reminded Catherine of the new Stealth Air Force fighters in design. As they drew closer to the now disabled Zerion ship she could more clearly see that they were, by far, more advanced. In a blur of blue-white light they flew by and out of her limited vision.

Where there had been a gossamer cloud, a ship appeared and rapidly took shape obscuring the stars and blocking any light save what reflected from the ship's metallic black body. Moments after it had appeared, a piercing sound permeated the Zerion ship. Catherine clasped her hands over her ears trying to protect them from the deafening noise, but she could not block the sound out.

Catherine felt as though she could not breathe, the room danced before her tired eyes and a strange man's bearded face loomed over her. She screamed. As if her screaming extinguished the piercing sound, it stopped, her breathing returned to normal, the room once again became stable, and the mysterious face faded. Catherine sat very still trying to recover.

An ominous silence had fallen over the ship causing Catherine to jump at the loud metal clang that echoed through the ship as the Creasion fighters docked on the Zerion craft. Twice more she heard the sound not knowing the cause.

A voice boomed through the silent corridors of the tranquilized Zerion ship. Unknown to her, only Catherine was conscious to hear it.

"Attention aboard the Zerion construction craft! You have violated Creasion boundaries. All of your weapons have been neutralized. Prepare to be boarded!"

Long moments of expectations became longer still, she wondered what these new aliens would be like. Catherine decided if the Creasion were enemies of the Zerion they must have some redeeming qualities, still in the past few hours she had learned to fear the unknown. It came to her that the Zerion Captain had accused her of being Creasion, so she assumed they must be human, like herself and the Zerion. Again she looked out the porthole at the giant Creasion vessel, it had turned and she could now see part of a silver emblem.

Her attention was drawn away from the ship to the scuffle of feet in the hall just outside the cabin door. Sliding open the door was blocked by three formidable figures. Two male Creasions uniformed in dark blue one piece uniforms stood behind a female who dressed in tight dark blue pants, a silver-blue blouse and short cape. Each person wearing ribbons designating rank, the young woman obviously in command, her ribbons holding back the right side of her cape from her shoulder. Catherine stared in amazement at the group, the sight of another woman causing her a sigh of relief.

Lieutenant Kara's quick insight had served her well during her short career. Quickly she appraised the situation, first noting Catherine's torn shirt, then the necklace and chain burn. Kara recognized immediately the Royal necklace of the house of Crea, this was no ordinary Earthgirl before her, but a daughter of Royalty.

"Holster weapons," Kara told the two guards. Then she instructed one to summon Commander Kron, the other guard she instructed to admit no one other than Commander Kron and to face the hall in deference to Catherine's modesty.

"What is your name?" Kara questioned.

"Catherine Kirk, from Earth." Catherine replied simply.

"I am Lieutenant Tari Kara from the Creasion system."

Tari said removing a small triangular shaped pin from her uniform. "Commander Kron will be here shortly, maybe you could use this to repair your garment." and while the tattered girl repaired her torn shirt, Tari studied her.

Behind her moments later Tari heard the door guard move aside and as she turned she drew to attention, standing in front of Catherine and saluted Commander Kron as he entered the dingy cabin.

"Lieutenant Kara, I was all but dragged here by the crewman you sent. What have you found?" Commander Kron stopped in mid sentence as Tari stepped aside and revealed a somewhat calmer Catherine than she had found.

"This, sir, is Catherine Kirk," Tari paused and looked meaningfully into her superior's eyes, "from Earth."

Catherine forced herself off the bunk to face this alien on her feet, blushing slightly at his close scrutiny as his gaze came to rest on the necklace she wore. Catherine saw the perplexity in Kron's eyes and wondered why?

"Are you harmed Ms. Kirk?" the Commander politely inquired.

"Nothing major, Commander." Catherine said evenly. "I would like to return to Earth, if that is possible?"

"That," he said "can only be authorized by our Emperor." the Commander turned to Lieutenant Kara, "Take Ms. Kirk to my fighter and see to her comfort, I will take her back to Tos-hawk One myself." Leaving the Lieutenant to carry out his orders, Kron went directly to communications and called his sovereign.

Kron saluted the video screen image of At'r, "Sire!" he said formally, "We have found someone." he paused then pushed a button on the control panel causing Catherine's image to appear on a viewer on At'r's desk. "This is Catherine Kirk, from Earth, this is the girl we monitored as both Terrain and Creasion. Sire—" he stopped again, "she wears the gold Royal necklace and our medical scanners are blocked by it."

At'r sat in stunned silence for a few moments, just as his great-uncle had prophesied, the Zerions had, without knowing, returned the direct descendant of the Empress they had kidnapped.

"Bring her directly to me when you arrive and bring the Zerion Captain to Tos-hawk One also."

"Ah," Kron cleared his throat and laughed, "the Zerion Captain is in sickbay with a knife wound and a severely burned hand."

"What happened?" At'r asked amused.

"She laid his face open with a knife, from here to here," Kron said running his finger along his cheekbone, "and on the palm of his hand is the burned imprint of her necklace."

"Was she hurt in the scuffle?" At'r wanted to know.

"Minor injuries are obvious, but then, as I said the med-scanners will not register on her. Also she is requesting to return to Earth."

"Very well Kron. Keep me informed should anything else occur. At'r out."

While final preparations were made on board the Zerion craft to tow it back to Creasion, At'r sat pondering the arrival of the woman that would become his wife if the necklace she wore proved to be authentic. Her face was beautiful, although he could read strain and exhaustion even in the still picture that had appeared on his screen. He wondered what the rest of her looked like. Kron had said she had fought with the Zerion but he had said nothing of hysterics, only that she had requested to be taken home.

At'r ordered the crash doors opened and he stood to gaze out the windows at the captured Zerion craft. Now he would not have to choose a bride eight years his junior, now the council would have very little claim on his wife or their heirs. The triangle would remain in tact and an ancient prophecy would be fulfilled. At'r smiled ruefully thinking of how the sour stuffed face of his senior council would look when he presented this alien Earthgirl as his new bride.

When he did there would be no disputing her position, for in the time they would voyage home to Creasion from their present observation point of this solar system he would see to it that she would be pregnant. Then even if they did not believe Catherine was their lost Empress' granddaughter she would be carrying his heir, and that they could not dispute.

Gritting her teeth against the pain in her leg, Catherine followed Lieutenant Kara through the Zerion ship, finally stopping before a set of double doors that opened onto a dock like platform on the outside of the vessel. It took Catherine completely by surprise, and she drew back slightly, awed by the spectacle. Before her lay open space unobstructed by the walls of a ship or any visible atmosphere. Docked along side the wide clear plastic docks the Creasions had attached to the Zerion vessel were several smaller ships.

Lieutenant Kara gave her little time to look them over before she hurried Catherine up the steps to the first fighter, following behind her. Catherine stopped suddenly on the top step. Gazing about, she inquired of Lieutenant Kara, "How do we breathe? I see no enclosures, what contains the atmosphere?"

"A magnetic field around this area of the ship gives us minimal gravity and creates an air lock." Lieutenant Kara explained, then motioned Catherine inside. Once inside Kara indicated a reclining couch in the small bay behind the ship's control center.

"I must return to my other duties, so please sit here." Kara indicated the couch.

Complying, Catherine did as she was asked, and as she expected, buckled in.

"Are you comfortable?" Lieutenant Kara asked.

"More so than on the Zerion ship." Catherine replied, Kara smiled at her knowingly.

"Well," Kara said, "you are safer." She turned and left the way they had entered.

As soon as Catherine was alone she tried to unbuckle the belts that held her snugly to the seat. As she had suspected the seat belts were locked. They did not trust her and she did not trust them. For the first time in days she smiled slightly, and rested back in the chair to wait.

Heavy footsteps alerted Catherine to Commander Kron's approach as he walked up the stairs and entered his ship. Catherine turned slightly and looked up to find the Commander's gray eyes on her.

"Ms. Kirk," he addressed her stiffly and it amazed her still that these people seemingly spoke the same language she did.

"Yes, Commander," she answered.

Leaning over Kron unbuckled her seat belts, "You will come with me, please." he said and with a wave of his hand he opened the hatch to the ship's cockpit control center. Turning, he beckoned her to follow.

Standing slowly, Catherine followed him putting as little weight on her lame leg as she possible could. Kron was turned away from Catherine and she hoped he did not see her pain. Entering the cockpit, Catherine was astounded at how advanced the Creasions seemed over the Zerion. She sat on the small couch recliner next to what was obviously the control center, curiosity plain on her face at the instrumentation and monitoring green and red lights.

"Please," Kron asked of her, "do not touch any of the ship's controls. They are very sensitive," he paused as if uncertain, "I must leave you once again and this chair has no locking belts, I trust you will not leave your chair or this compartment. Unfortunately the Zerion Captain must come back to Tos-hawk One in this vessel, he will ride in your former seat." Kron turned to leave, "Again, please do not tamper with anything."

After visually satisfying her curiosity inside the ship's nerve center Catherine began watching the busy crew on the floating docks outside the ship's front windows. From this vantage point she had a clear view of the main doors that she and Lieutenant Kara had come through, most of the forward portion of that dock and if she turned, Catherine could see most of the rear of the ship's starboard side.

Crewmen and women came and went, but when an armed guard of six, each with a large lazzer rifles, came through the double doors led by Lieutenant Kara, her attention went totally to what was happening there. Three guards stood shoulder to shoulder across the width of the dock, the other three did the same, but facing the opposite direction with their backs to the first three, so that the dock was completely secured. Again the doors opened, and the Zerion Captain entered followed by six more guards in the same formation as the first.

Remembering too clearly her struggle with the Zerion Captain, Catherine smiled at the large white bandage on his cheek, pleased she had been the cause. It also pleased Catherine to see the Zerion's hands tightly bound behind him and leggings restraining his legs. So intense was her stare that the Captain stopped. Looking up slowly he saw Catherine and said something. Although she could not possibly have heard him, so venomous was the manner he said it, Catherine knew he cursed her. Catherine smiled coldly back as Commander Kron backhanded the Zerion Captain across the uninjured cheek, causing Catherine to wonder why Commander Kron would react in such a manner. The Captain could only stare back in anger.

With a firm push from the butt of her lazzer rifle Lieutenant Kara told the Zerion to keep moving, Catherine watched as he calmly entered the same vessel she was in. Six of the guards accompanied by Lieutenant Kara and Commander Kron escorted the Captain until he was safely strapped in the chair with locking belts, afterwards all but two guards left with Lieutenant Kara to attend to other duties. Catherine turned as she heard the hatch opening and Commander Kron came through the door securing it behind himself, locking them in the cockpit. Before saying anything, he scanned the surrounding controls then looked at Catherine.

"It is good to see you did not allow your curiosity to overrule your good sense." he said, a little irritated. "Sit back, we are leaving for Tos-hawk One, you may expect a quick acceleration and an even faster braking when we land." he explained while energizing the ship's systems.

Looking again out of the front windows Catherine could see the busy crew clearing the docks. A loud horn sounded a warning that the magnetic field was about to be dropped to allow their Commander's departure. At a distance of a hundred yards, space began to turn shimmering blue as the magnetic field dissolved and the air rushed out into the vacuum of space. Catherine had leaned slightly forward watching the activity but suddenly found herself pushed back in her seat as the ship roared away from the dock toward the mother ship and Catherine' meeting with the Emperor of Creasion.

A feeling of weariness came over her as the events of the last few days seemed to catch her all at once. Before her, stretching out to infinity, space called as it had when she was a child lying under the stars on Earth. Catherine saw space as it had never been seen by anyone on Earth, but because of the throbbing ache in her ankle, accompanied by exhaustion, she could not enjoy it. She felt cheated. For as long as she could remember space had intrigued and beckoned to her.

Many times for sneaking out late at night from the European girl's school Catherine's father had insisted she attend, she found herself in trouble. Her father had shook his head, unable to understand, but her grandmother had.

Becoming so overcome by the peaceful tranquillity of space, Catherine felt her thoughts begin to wander, only the sudden braking of the fighter enabled her to rouse herself. Catherine watched Commander Kron from beneath her lashes hoping her lapse wasn't noticed, she decided he was too busy with the ship.

Now they were close to the mother ship Commander Kron called Tos-hawk One. Catherine could see why he had said the name with reverence. It was the same ship she had seen through the porthole, but her view had so limited. Now she could fully appreciate its magnificence and size. All navigational lights were on and so were the lights on the landing decks, ready to receive the incoming fighters. Unlike the clear plastic movable docks Catherine had seen on the Zerion's ship, this ship had four large bays, two on each side, one on top of the other with a tunnel like opening at each end. As Kron swung around to enter the tunnel of the top right deck Catherine caught sight of the large silver emblem that adorned the front bow.

Something so familiar struck her about the emblem's design that her eyes became transfixed on it, although more than half of it was obscured. Breaking herself away she shook herself mentally failing to recognize the same symbol she wore around her neck.

'You must keep your wits about yourself.' she chided silently.

Inside the landing deck the blue white light was blinding to Catherine's tired eyes, she closed them until she felt the ship stop, then reopened them slowly.

"Stay put." Kron told her as he opened the hatch to the back compartment. Catherine heard the outer hatch open and looking out the side window she saw a dozen or more armed guards waiting as the Zerion Captain was led off the fighter and through a set of doors to disappear into the colossal ship.

Of the waiting guards only four remained, she realized they waited for her. Catherine looked away from the bright lights, suddenly more afraid than she had been on the Zerion ship. Kron came back to the cockpit and she shuddered.

"You will come with me now Ms. Kirk." Kron beckoned her to proceed him from the ship.

Unconsciously she straightened her ripped shirt, stood and walked through the ship and down the stairs to the landing pad where four formally dressed guards stood.

Turning she asked Commander Kron, "Do you fear I will try to escape?"

"No, they are only an honor guard." he replied stepping out to lead the party to the Emperor's private chambers. Catherine knew by his tone that Commander Kron did not like being questioned.

Walking down the long, brightly-lit corridors of the overwhelming vessel Catherine tried to remember as much as her tired senses would retain. What impressed Catherine was the way the crewmembers looked at her and the necklace around her throat, a few had all but stopped in their hurried paces.

Keeping step with Kron became increasingly her main concern, the long trek was making her ankle more aggravated and try as she might, Catherine could not totally hide her limp. She prayed it would go unnoticed.

Commander Kron's ship had already landed when At'r switched on several of his monitor screens, curious to see how this mysterious girl from Earth would conduct herself. At'r watched Catherine's face on the second camera as she watched the Zerion Captain depart, Kron entered the picture and At'r saw her shiver. Bravely she descended the stairs from the ship and looking Kron square in the eyes questioned the guards around her. At'r was astonished, Kron did not like to be questioned about his directives, but he had given her an answer.

"She might just be my great aunt's granddaughter." At'r said to the empty room and frowned, "My future wife."

With interest he watched the six make their way to his chambers. On the screens the girl's exhaustion was evident along with a well-hidden limp favoring her left leg. At'r had to admire her courage, for although he could see pain in Catherine's beautiful hazel eyes, she kept pace with Kron without complaining, her gaze, forward and steady, undisturbed by the astonished looks the crew gave her.

Catherine's clothing had become torn and soiled, her shirt held together by only a small pin that did little to cover her full breasts or the Royal gold necklace. Tight pants outlined her shapely hips but hid her long slender legs and injured ankle. Beneath the knit cap

Catherine wore covering her long auburn hair At'r could see stray stands that had managed their freedom, for now he could only wonder about the rest. They were in his outer receiving room now, here Kron instructed their guards to wait.

Finally, with Catherine almost at the end of her endurance they stopped in front of two traditionally, but sparsely dressed Creasions. Reminiscent of ancient battles fought by the three houses of Creasions each guard held an weapon called a Symaka but also wore a lazzer pistol on their hips.

Behind the guards painted by talented hand on the mammoth double doors was a an ornate and haunting design but before she could discern the scheme the doors slid back into the wall. Following Kron, Catherine found herself in a receiving room large enough to accommodate thirty or forty people with a small informal dais at the far end.

Kron's pace did not falter as he lead Catherine down a hallway with accent lights on various works of art decorating the walls. Silently, yet another door opened in front of them and no light issued from that portal.

Following Kron into the darkened room was like walking into a bottomless void to Catherine's tired mind and she found in unnerving. Seconds after she entered, the door silently closed leaving her instantly in darkness, Catherine stilled the scream that threatened to burst from her throat.

Blinking to adjust to the darkness, her eyes were drawn toward the ceiling to floor windows made from what appeared to be plate glass and provided an unobstructed view of space. For long moments she stared at the cold beauty of space displayed before her until the chair behind the huge desk in front of the windows began to turn. All her senses became alert, her eyes glued to the turning chair. Catherine knew the occupant was the Emperor of Creasion and she suddenly felt stricken with overwhelming panic, realizing the power this alien controlled. She dared to hope their Emperor would send her home, but her intuition told her differently.

Catherine glanced at Commander Kron. He had bowed from the waist as she remembered her father doing when as a child she had accompanied him on a diplomatic assignment.

Catherine knew she should do something, but she felt frozen feeling the Emperor's eyes on her.

Amazed, At'r stood his eyes drawn to the slight glow of green fire around this strange girl's neck, he turned the knob on the panel subtly brightening the lights until the room seemed to be lit with candles.

Catherine's feeling had been right, At'r's eyes were bodily scrutinizing her. She felt as if he noticed every detail of her tattered clothing, but she would not allow this alien Lord to see her embarrassment. So Catherine bravely withstood his scrutiny, her chin high until their eyes met. At'r's emerald eyes took full possession of Catherine's, holding them captive as he tried to read her thoughts, but he could sense this would not be an easy task.

'Her will is strong,' At'r thought, 'and she is lovely.' He found himself picturing her in bed. She amazed him standing there, not bowing, not shivering in fear but bravely returning his appraisal with cool demeanor. Her necklace gleaming, proclaiming her Royalty and her innocence of the fact apparent.

Catherine found At'r's appearance overpowering. Just over six foot tall, his wide muscular shoulders were encased in a midnight blue leather tunic without sleeves that covered the top of his matching trousers, his pants legs disappearing inside polished black leather boots. Draped across At'r's powerful shoulders and held by a large silver pen, a cape of rich midnight fabric obscured the silver version of the Royal necklace. At'r's dark honey colored hair and beard framed his tanned face, and his piercing emerald eyes tried to bore through to her soul.

Turning to Kron, who was no longer bowing. At'r spoke, "You have done well," he paused, "as always. The Zerion Captain has been taken care of?"

"Yes, my Lord, he is in a maximum security holding cube and has also been put in suspended time. He will be held ready for your personal interrogation." Kron replied competently.

"Thank you, Kron, now go, see to your crews." At'r dismissed Kron. Kron bowed again and giving Catherine a quick glance left.

Glad for the respite from his perusal when he turned to Kron, Catherine began to breathe again, but her break was brief when Kron was dismissed, leaving her alone with the Emperor.

Catherine watched At'r closely as he walked around the desk. Inwardly she shivered. She had expected, no, hoped for, an older monarch, instead of this young, masculine and powerful Lord. Even with the Zerion she had felt less threatened.

"So!" At'r's voice broke the deafening silence that threatened to engulf Catherine, "You are the Earthgirl who spies on Zerions." He laughed, still astonished the Zerion had found her.

"Do you always laugh at ones less fortunate than yourself...Your Highness?" At'r's manner made Catherine feel reckless, and she did not understand it. She almost challenged him with her tone of voice, adding, 'Your Highness' as an after thought.

At'r's amusement ceased, his eyes turning to emerald fire, inwardly Catherine recoiled, she had acted foolishly to hide her building panic.

"You are fortunate you still breathe." He told her icily, and pouring two glasses of wine from a decanter, allowed the electrified air to tingle a while longer. It seemed to Catherine that he was enjoying her predicament. "The Zerion usually do not take prisoners, but in your case, I can see why they spared you." At'r's burning eyes raked over her; somehow, although she felt singed, Catherine kept her composure. "Come," he said more congenially, "you must be exhausted, sit, relax and we will talk." He indicated the sofa.

At'r was correct, she was exhausted, but Catherine hoped he did not know how close to the end of her endurance she was.

"Thank you," she said turning to sit on the couch hoping her legs would still move. After Catherine sat, At'r handed her a glass of the royal blue wine which she took graciously but eyed with distrust.

At'r sat next to Catherine, seeing her apprehension assured her, "Catherine, the wine will not harm you, we are as human as you." He smiled, a full sensuous mouth with a taunting gleam in his eyes. "It will soothe your nerves."

Gingerly at first Catherine sipped the liquid finding it as At'r had promised, soothing, "Thank you," she said, "It is pleasant."

"Did the Zerions harm you?" At'r asked touching a remote panel on the couch's arm, again causing the light to brighten. This time to peer more closely at Catherine.

"No!" Catherine answered a little to sharply.

At'r was not fooled and Catherine knew it, but he did not press her.

"Tell me, where on your planet did the Zerion find you?"

"If I tell you," Catherine said carefully, "I will have nothing to bargain with in return for my trip home."

"Catherine, the Zerion ship was taken all records intact. It is only a matter of hours before I have chronicles of their entire operation. If you do not wish to tell me," he shrugged, "it is of little importance." At'r watched as the words took effect, and when she turned her head the light reflected on her bruised cheek.

Lightly he ran his finger along the bruise. His touch felt like an electrical charge raced through her, and Catherine jumped. "How did this happen?" At'r demanded angry anyone would damage such beauty.

"Sir," she said quietly, not knowing how she should address him, "it is really nothing and unimportant." She looked away afraid of the passionate anger she saw in his eyes.

At'r gently turned her face back to his, "Catherine, if I ask it, it is important. Now, I want to know how this," he again ran his finger over the bruise, "and this," he touched her chain burned throat and black and blue shoulder, "happened, and how your shirt came to be torn?"

Feeling the Emperor's charismatic power and hearing the command in his voice, Catherine had no strength to deny him. "The Zerion Captain," she said in a low, barely audible voice, "tried to…ah…" she stammered, feeling a red blush cover her face.

"Is that how you came to cut his cheek?" At'r inquired further, he knew how the chain burn had occurred.

Amazed he knew of the incident, she answered, "Yes, I…found a knife, hid it in my sleeve and when he tried to." Shakily, she briefly closed her eyes, then finished the glass of wine and sat the glass on the dark rosewood table in front of the couch, not finishing her sentence.

"You are brave, Zerions are rough." At'r replied, his eyes wandering to the knit cap she wore. Time stood still for Catherine as he reached to pull it from her head.

Catherine dared not move as her long auburn hair, now loose, fell midway to her waist. Wearily Catherine closed her eyes and she felt a gentle hand behind her neck drawing her toward the alien Lord. Sudden panic possessed her and Catherine stood, forgetting everything but escape, until the pain in her injured ankle reminded her with blinding clarity, standing or walking had now become impossible. Her exhaustion and pain proved to be too much, if At'r had not caught Catherine, she would have fallen on the floor. He eased her unconscious body to the sofa.

CHAPTER 3

*H*igh Priest Betus was preparing for bed when a sharp knock on his chamber door delayed his sleep. His servant opened the door and admitted Betus' oldest son, Casso.

"Father," Casso bowed slightly in respect, "you must come, the Diamerald Tower has begun to glow." he said excitedly.

Betus stared at his forty year old son who was his chosen successor finding what he was saying hard to comprehend. "Casso, you have been dreaming." he stated rather flatly.

"No father, I have just come from the Tower and there are two guards outside who saw it also." Casso explained.

"Very well Casso, you are not known for jokes so I will come." he turned to his servant, "Please ready my clothing."

When he had dressed, Betus followed his son to their transcart. Casso expertly piloted their conveyance among the other elevated free flying vehicles. Speeding past the Emperor's massive palace that had been re-built around the Mystic Tower Betus could see what his son had said was true, the Diamerald Tower had begun to glow a brilliant, luminous green. Its renewed luminescence causing the normal smooth flow of elevated traffic to become chaotic as people slowed to stare in awe at the phenomenon. Normal communication channels were becoming jammed with bewildered chatter from excited voices of the people of the City of Crea theorizing about the meaning of the sign.

Betus was amazed. Vividly he remembered his older sister Iza. She had been so happy and full of life and love when she married Emperor Tor. But their happiness and love was not meant to be, shortly after their wedding the Zerion kidnapped her and sparked a terrible war. After the war was won, Emperor Tor searched for her fruitlessly. From the limited information he found out little; it was suspected that the Zerion craft carrying Lady Iza had crashed on a small planet called Earth. Rescue attempts were impossible at that time. Creasion just did not have the resources.

Emperor Tor had been so heartbroken he had turned his responsibilities over to his brother, devoting his time to construction of the Diamerald Tower. There, Tor had lived until his death, carefully keeping historical records and compiling data to be passed on to a future heir. Shortly after his death, the Tower had stopped glowing. He had left only one legacy behind, a prophecy;

From Creasion, the Zerion stole a Royal daughter,

to maroon her on a barbaric planet.

To Creasion, they will return her heir, a Royal

bride from Earth.

United again with her sovereign, their children

will vanquish the Zerion, and command the

galaxy with justice and freedom.

Betus had been twenty years old when the glow had ceased. Now it was beginning to glow again, he could only hope it was signaling the fulfillment of the prophecy. His sister, Iza had been a physic and it had been a long time since they had a physic in the family. He hoped her heir would be similarly talented.

Arriving at the Tower the two guards snapped to attention before the glowing front doors. Betus reached for the door latch hoping it would open and finally reveal its secrets. Instead, he had received a mild electrical shock when he grasped it. Drawing back sharply Betus stared in amazement at the doors. Perplexed Betus stepped back to gaze at the top of the lofty tower. The door had always been locked but never had he received an electrical shock. Since the day Emperor Tor had sealed himself inside and died the Tower had been a mystery, it seemed it would remain so a little while longer.

Betus turned to his son, "We must return to the temple to notify His Highness, Lord At'r at once."

❧   ❧   ❧

At'r looked down at the fainted girl on his couch, her face was ashen, her beautiful features seeming even more fragile, as though they were made from fine Metem porcelain. Already he felt protective toward her and contemplated the Zerion Captain's fate if he had succeeded in harming her worse than was apparent.

Placing a cool damp cloth on her forehead At'r poured two more glasses of wine and sat next to Catherine on the edge of the couch. He started to unpin the torn shirt as she became slowly conscious.

Catherine felt someone tugging on her shirt, wearily she covered the tear with her hand. Becoming more alert, pain radiated through her leg and Catherine heard a voice calling her.

"Catherine." At'r said firmly, "Where are you hurt?" Still dazed she did not answer, "If you do not tell me I will find the problem myself." He brushed her hand aside and tired again to unpin the shirt.

"No," she groaned "please!" and again covered the tear with her hand, "My leg." she admitted.

At'r suspected as much, drew the crystal handled knife he always wore and slit her pant's legs up the side, then pulled them off, leaving Catherine in only underpants, a ripped shirt and winter boots, these he unlaced. After sliding the right one off without difficulty, At'r immediately tried to remove the left boot in similar fashion. This boot did not come off easily, and he slit the leather on each side and drew it off. Her ankle was badly sprained and swelled. At'r marveled at how she had hidden the pain.

Catherine was almost totally conscious now and At'r left her to summon his physician. When he returned, he quickly unpinned the shirt before she could object. When that failed to allow the garment's removal, he drew his dagger again, silencing any protest Catherine might have made to stop him. At'r carefully slit the fabric from her, stopping to place a light kiss on her bruised shoulder, his eyes briefly held hers.

Completely overpowered by the situation Catherine found herself in and the throbbing pain in her leg, she lay still on the couch, shivering more from fear than cold. Much to her astonishment, At'r seeing her condition took his cape from his shoulders and spread it over her. Unable to any longer bare the bright lights that At'r had turned up when she had fainted, or the fire she saw each time their eyes met, Catherine kept her eyes closed and did not see the necklace At'r wore, uncovered when he removed his cape. Moment's later Doctor Trentos came in without a knock.

"At'r!" he called addressing his Emperor on a familiar note, "Are you ill, sire?"

"Not I, Trentos, but our guest could benefit from your skill." At'r answered.

Never had At'r seen his physician and great-uncle so shaken as when he saw Catherine. Trentos' normal composure vanished the girl could have been his sister-in-law as she was when the Zerion kidnapped her so many years before.

As Trentos peered closer he knew the girl was not she, but using his medical sensor device that blocked the necklace's aura, he knew without a doubt that this girl was his grandniece. Trentos also knew she was near a state of total collapse, there was severe trauma in her left ankle, evidence of exposure, and several nasty bruises. Catherine watched Trentos closely. He could almost feel her fear, which brought him to the conclusion that although Catherine wore that splendid necklace, she was innocent of her ancestry.

"You are to stay where you are for now young woman," he admonished her, "do not even sit-up." Then turning to At'r he drew him aside, out of her hearing range.

"How bad?" At'r asked.

"Exhaustion, exposure, bruises and a badly sprained ankle. In all, considering she was the prisoner of the Zerion, I would consider her in good condition. At'r," Trentos drew a deep breath, "that girl is Creasion, Royal Creasion, in fact I believe she is my grandniece. Where in the universe did you find her?"

"I didn't," At'r explained, "the Zerions did, and much to their chagrin, Commander Kron, as you know, found them." They turned toward Catherine as she struggled to sit. "She is from Earth." At'r concluded.

"Sire," Trentos cleared his throat awkwardly, "The prophecy, ah, I mean, will you take her as your wife?"

At'r's look was almost grim, "Yes!" he told his great-uncle. "She is from all indications the granddaughter of your brother. I can see by the readings on your scanner, the necklace she wears is authentic, it is likely the same necklace that your sister-in-law wore." At'r smiled slightly as Catherine managed to sit up holding his cape around her. "This should also quiet the Council about an heir."

"Later My Lord, when there is more time, I would like to hear the whole story." Trentos commented, "now," he indicated Catherine "she needs to rest."

"What do you prescribe for her?" At'r asked.

"I will tape the ankle." Trentos told him. "She hasn't eaten in approximately four Earth days. That can wait until she rests. Except for a period of time when she was unconscious, she has slept little. From the bruises I would guess she fought with someone." He paused, "Who won?"

"She did. It was the Zerion Captain." At'r answered.

"I would like to give her a sedative, she is very agitated and I doubt she would sleep without it, that is until she collapsed from exhaustion." He prescribed while still staring with wonder at his grandniece. Trentos turned to At'r inquiringly, "Have you told Betus, do you think he will accept her?"

"I have not yet told him, I intended to as soon as she is sleeping. Whether or not he accepted her could be critical but I think he will, after seeing her and your medical reports I doubt he could question her."

"You may be right, the sedative is ready, do you think you will have to hold her while I administer it?"

"Possibly, after the gash she left on the Zerion Captain's cheek when he tried to rape her." At'r looked toward Catherine, "But then, I do not fault her for that."

"I would say she is lucky to have escaped, her virginity intact." Trentos told At'r meaningfully.

"I had wondered…" they walked back to Catherine.

"Catherine," At'r addressed her, "you will do as Doctor Trentos requires." He did not miss the stubborn set of her jaw.

"Cat-r-ine," Trentos' pronunciation was rough, "your leg I will wrap with a clear bandage, please stay off it. Also I am going to give you a sedative, how you have stayed awake this long I do not know."

"Thank you Doctor, but I am fine, except my ankle, I do not need your sedative." Catherine protested, clutching the cape over her breasts.

"Catherine," At'r's voice was commanding, his cool green eyes holding hers, "Trentos has given his diagnosis and even I do not overrule him in these matters."

Catherine felt pressure on her arm as the drug was administered, "No!" she pulled away, but it was too late, already she could feel the alien substance working through her blood stream and taking effect. Not wanting to be any further under these alien's control she fought to stay awake. Wearily, Catherine knew she was losing the battle, At'r's face swam before her eyes and finally she succumbed to the potion. A look of peace spread over her tired features, making At'r feel strangely protective of her.

"Where are you going to quarter her, milord?" Trentos asked so he could run tests and check on her later.

At'r grew serious, not answering, leaving Trentos standing awkwardly in silence, finally after a long pause he replied. "She will sleep here with me. She is to be my bride." he reasoned, "I can not deny who I know she is and this way I can keep a close watch on her." He was quiet again for a moment, "She is beautiful and seemingly brave; however, I will wait for Betus' decision before I make my final decision."

Leaving Catherine laying on the sofa he walked over to his desk, pushing a button he awakened his secretary, "Kins," At'r was amused seeing his normally neat aid, disheveled, "wake-up." At'r realized he woke Kins two hours into his sleep cycle, "Sorry to wake you."

"What can I do for you, my Lord?" Kins yawned, "Sorry!" he was appalled.

"When you are awake, get High Priest Betus on my communication's screen, then contact our Chief Earth Agent. I will have a job for him. I will be waiting for your signal." Kins' face faded from the screen.

"Trentos, please accumulate a detailed report on Catherine, I am sure Betus will want your opinion." At'r walked back to the sofa. Seeing his uncle's concern for the girl he tried to reassure him. "Don't concern yourself." he said, gently picking her up from the couch. "If she develops a problem I will call you." Seeing something more in the old man's face, he added. "And I promise you, I will allow her to rest."

"I will get that report to you with-in a couple of hours. Knowing lord Betus, he will hop the fastest shuttle we have and be here as soon as the craft can reach us." Trentos laughed, "Goodnight sire." he left.

At'r carried Catherine to his bed. Laying her on the bed he drew his cape from her and removed her thin nylon panties, leaving her naked on the silken sheets. Covering her slowly, At'r admired her beautiful body as well as her face now framed by flowing auburn hair.

Although he did not want a wife, At'r was attracted to her. Catherine's long slender legs and rounded hips melted to a tiny waist, her breasts were full and inviting their nipples erect in the cool air. Her heart shaped face with sensuous pouting lips appeared tempting and soft. Behind her hazel green eyes, a feature uncommon on Creasion, At'r had seen fear, defiance, and a sharp mind. With a cool manner Catherine controlled the fire he saw in her eyes.

At'r speculated if she would accept her fate with him. Leaving Catherine to sleep, he went back to his desk to assimilate the information that was beginning to pour in from the captured Zerion disks, but found he had difficulty concentrating with Catherine sleeping in his bed.

CHAPTER 4

"Kins," At'r said into his visual intercom to Kins quarters, "are you there?"

"Yes, sire," Kins answered stepping before the viewer.

"What is holding up communications with High Priest Betus?" At'r asked, it had been well over an hour since he had requested the call.

"Lord Betus was called away on an emergency. He is due back soon. The channel has been held open and when Lord Betus returns, I will beep you." Kins explained.

"Very well. How long before we hear from our agents on Earth?"

"That could take a little time."

"Thank you Kins." At'r switched off the intercom. Only seconds passed when Kins beeped him to announce the call to lord Betus was waiting.

At'r switched the transmission screen on and Betus' image appeared. Betus bowed before At'r's image on his screen then straightened.

"Betus, what has happened? You look exhausted, please sit down." At'r ordered, amazed at Betus' fortitude. "Is your aid there?" he asked, a servant appeared on the screen and bowed, "Bring Betus' physician and summon his son Casso." At'r commanded the servant.

"I am here, sire." Casso said, stepping in view.

"Good! Let your father rest and tell me what has happened."

Casso briefly explained all they knew about the returned glow of the Diamerald Tower, which was little, adding to the growing mystery.

"At what time Casso, did the Tower begin to glow?"

"About two hours ago, planet time, sire." Casso replied, then asked, "Why?"

At'r related the details of the Zerion vessel's capture, and the prisoner they carried. "Her picture will come up on one of your smaller screens. As you see she wears a Royal necklace, from all indications both medical and physical she is the granddaughter of Empress Iza. It was two hours ago we brought her on board Tos-hawk One." At'r finished.

"I will be there as soon as I can get a fast shuttle, my Lord." Betus was on his feet, excited to hopeful to have found his grandniece.

"Only!" At'r voice was commanding, "If the doctors say you are fit for the journey."

"I will bring the physicians if necessary." Betus said. "But I will be there as soon as possible. How long do you intend to be in the sector you are currently in?"

"I will wait for you for two sun spans, then we move closer to planet Earth. There we may remain as long as twenty sun spans, the minimum will be five. While you are en-route I will send you information on her, as it is received."

"Thank you sire." Betus said smiling.

"Until you arrive." At'r bid him farewell, Betus and Casso bowed as their images faded.

At'r stood before the windows and gazed into deep space, he had much to think about. A girl lay in his bed sleeping, and as exhausted as he was, At'r knew he would not sleep there until he could have her. He must wait. Wait on the medical report and for Betus to claim Catherine as his niece.

If Catherine had just been an unlucky Earthgirl he could have slept with her without concern if he chose. At'r almost wished she were, then he would not have a wife. He did not want the emotional responsibility of a wife and family, his people had always been enough, but now they demanded an heir. 'Timely' At'r thought. 'Catherine appears wearing the gold version of my silver necklace.' At'r knew fate had declared they should be together. Still, he did not like being forced to do anything. Normally he did as he wished. Almost as if he were drawn, At'r walked to his bedroom and stared down at Catherine.

Gently At'r lifted the gold medallion from her chest, careful not to pull the chain. He examined the symbol closely. Indeed this was the gold Ankh set in the inverted Pyramid, an Ankh-Angle, which had been worn by each Empress until Iza had been taken by the Zerions. At'r turned it over in his palm, marveling at the craftsmanship and the clarity of the Diameralds. Three round cut Diameralds, one in each point of the inverted pyramid representing a homeworld moon, and a much larger teardrop Diamerald set in the center staff of the Ankh represented the planet Creasion. Never had At'r seen a gold original, Emperor Tor had worn his until his death and it remained in the Tower with him.

After he became Emperor, At'r's grandfather had commissioned the silver necklaces struck and consecrated, these versions the Royal family still wore.

After a time Catherine began to mummer softy in her sleep and At'r knew she was dreaming. A worried frown covered her brow. Seconds later she screamed sitting straight up in bed, instantly awake and confused.

Catherine looked around, her eyes wide and glassy. Seeing At'r, she remembered his bearded face from the vision that had appeared to her in the Zerion ship. She began to move slowly to the far side of the large bed. In Catherine's mind she moved quickly, but At'r still grabbed her arm and pulled her back toward him. Fear overcame her drugged mind, she struggled, becoming entangled in her loose hair. At'r, with little effort, wrestled her to the mattress.

"Easy Catherine, lie still." At'r commanded her sharply.

"Let me go!" Catherine demanded, still confused.

"Catherine! Lie still!" he commanded her again more sharply.

Finally, when Catherine had quieted he retrieved the fallen bed covers and covered her. Regarding her carefully At'r poured a glass of water from a crystal decanter next to the bed.

"Sip it slowly." At'r cautioned and gave her the glass. Catherine, clutching the sheet to her breast, drank slowly as instructed and returned an empty glass to At'r.

"May I have my clothes, please?" she asked unsteadily, trying to fight the effects of the sleeping potion, her eyes drooping.

"After you have slept longer we will discuss it." At'r told her, watching as her eyes became fixed on the silver necklace around At'r's neck, hesitantly Catherine's hand went to her own necklace. Once again the drug overpowered her will and Catherine's eyes closed. At'r eased her back among the pillows. He stood looking down at her innocent beauty, then slowly bent and kissed her lips. Catherine briefly opened her eyes and looked up at At'r.

"Sleep." he told her and she obeyed.

Returning to his desk in his private receiving room he found an incoming call on his screens, finally his chief Earth agent had check in.

"What news do you have for me, Qerns?" At'r asked him.

"Several interesting items, sire." He replied as he bowed, looking ridiculous in an Earth style business suit, "The details I have already programmed into your computer, I have a brief summary for you now."

"Good Qerns, please continue." At'r settled back, enjoying the feel of the comfortable desk chair.

"Catherine Izadra Kirk, age twenty, Earth years. Parents, Karl Kirk, diplomatic attaché' for the United States government, killed on

Earth one week ago under mysterious circumstances near the Zerion base where Catherine was taken captive. Her mother Ada Lyn Simpson Kirk was killed two years after Catherine's birth in an airplane crash caused by a terrorist's bomb. Her maternal grandmother, Iza Simpson, assumed almost full time care of her at this point as Karl Kirk traveled extensively in his occupation. At age six Ms. Kirk entered a private girl's school, which caused a breach between her grandmother and her father, the full nature of which is not known; however, when Ms. Kirk entered school she was three years ahead of her peers. After she started school Ms. Kirk only saw her father in the summer, and holidays were spent with her grandmother. When Ms. Kirk was fourteen, Iza Simpson died and two years later Catherine entered college, a private engineering school in Germany. She speaks four Earth languages and since her father's death has become a very wealthy woman by Earth standards." Qerns paused. "We have one other report sire, not directly connected, but dealing with her father. It is rumored he was doing private research on U.F.O. sightings."

"Thank you, Qerns, for your report." At'r said. "I will be in touch with you after your report and the Zerion tapes have been evaluated."

CHAPTER 5

*B*a-lyn stood behind the curtains of her dormitory windows peering out at the glowing Diamerald Tower. Her dormitory, shared with nine other girls, stood just across the courtyard from the Tower. Now Ba-lyn knew what had disturbed her sleep. The glow made her uneasy. Too well she knew the legend of the Tower and the return of the glow could only herald the arrival of the Empress Iza's descendent.

By birth Iza's heir would be given first chance at the very position Ba-lyn aspired to. This new comer, if that was what the Tower truly announced, would ruin her plans begun four years earlier, when the council had chosen ten girls with physic abilities from the few girls left in the Triangle.

These girls, though much younger than the Emperor, would be trained as priestess in hopes that one would catch the Emperor's eye and become his Empress.

Ba-lyn was fourteen when she had been chosen and only beginning to feel her powers, now she could control them. Ba-lyn's grades were the highest in the group and among the other girls her blond beauty set her apart. It was for her the council held the most hope of attracting At'r's eye.

Watching the excited coming and goings of lords Betus and Casso, Ba-lyn smiled smugly, secure in her mastery of what the priests had taught her and the forbidden knowledge of the Troscoss, taught to her since childhood by her mother. If Empress Iza's heir did return, Ba-lyn would eliminate her, 'after all' Ba-lyn thought, 'how knowledgeable could she be, coming from such a barbaric planet as Earth.'

Behind her the others began to wake. Their murmurs, softly at first became a torrent of confused conversations disrupting Ba-lyn's thoughts.

"Quiet!" she barked and everyone silenced.

Ba-lyn was not one to cross, every girl there knew it. She had far too much power. Unfortunately, neither the selective council nor Lota, their house-mother saw how nasty she could be. Ba-lyn was careful to cover her tracks.

Before Lota had come to be their housemother, there was another who saw more clearly through Ba-lyn. When she had confronted Ba-lyn with evidence of her forbidden rituals, the evidence had disappeared and the housemother with it.

"Ladies," a male voice called them away from the window. It was Casso, and as the girls turned, his gaze traveled over each one coming to rest on the more advanced in the group, Ba-lyn. Something about her distressed him, he did not trust her. When the Tower had started to glow he had been joyful for many reasons. One very good reason was, now that the heir had returned, Ba-lyn would not be allowed to become Empress. Jubilantly, Casso related as much as security would allow concerning the glow of the Diamerald Tower. His stay was short, leaving the housemother to calm her girls and get them back to bed.

An hour later most of the girls were sleeping, others dozed, only Ba-lyn remained awake and alert. All these events gave her a bad feeling. Her plan lay in jeopardy of completion. Finally she slept, a restless slumber full of dark and haunting dreams.

CHAPTER 6

$\mathcal{A}$ ccompanied by his aid, Kins, At'r walked through the busy corridors, passing a startled crewman in the security holding area. Entering the interrogation room At'r found the Zerion Captain sitting, restrained in a chair. Commander Kron saluted as At'r entered and introduced the Zerion as Captain Quar.

Unable to stare into the Emperor's blazing green eyes the Zerion averted his gaze only to have it drawn back by the low growl of the Emperor's voice.

"You had a very interesting captive passenger on-board your ship, be glad you did not harm her badly." At'r told him.

"Little Creasion slut," the Zerion spat, "I'll strangle her someday."

"You probably won't live long enough," At'r assured him. "We need little from you, we have extracted all the information from your data disks; but just to be sure, we have a way of," he paused "reading your mind." At'r smiled morbidity. "Do not worry Zerion, it is painless and generally does little damage, in your case we could make an exception." At'r looked at the Captain with disgust.

"Do as you will with me, but the Zerions will not be stopped and the loss of my ship, our base, or myself will not change that," he laughed feeling superior, "but I know very little of our Earth operations other than my own responsibilities."

"You have already told me what I needed to know, there are other Earth bases," At'r looked to Kron, "but use the decoder anyway, I am sure there are other pieces of information we can use." At'r turned and left, a worried frown covering his face after he left the Zerion.

Turning to Kron who had followed him, At'r gave instructions to hold Tos-hawk's orbit until Betus' arrival, then the ship would be moved to a lower orbit around the planet and moon instead of the system.

"Meanwhile, have a complete search of the planet Earth and the moon begun. I do not care about the Earthman's bases but if there are any more Zerion bases on Earth I want to know where and I want their bases destroyed, not one base is to be left standing." At'r commanded

Kins emerged from the interrogation room to join At'r and Kron, "Our technicians have taken over with the Zerion." Kins informed At'r. "I gave them a copy of your questions and they will have their report ready in about ten minutes."

"Good Kins."

"Sire," Kron bowed, "I am needed on the bridge, by your leave."

"Certainly Kron, give Kins the reports as they come in." At'r turned back to Kins, "When the search is complete I want to review the aerial photographs of the bases before any destruction plans are made." Kins recorded notes on his communications device. "Keep me informed on the arrival of High Priest Betus, and if Ms. Kirk wakes have me called, I will be on the bridge with Kron for a few moments." At'r walked onto an airlift and ascended.

As always, the bridge was hub of busy activity with Commander Kron sitting in the center ready to act on whatever problem came about. At'r's presence was noticed, one crewman on duty announcing his presence and drawing all on the deck to attention. Momentarily activity stopped as the crew saluted their leader.

"As you were," At'r said, watching as the group returned to their duties, At'r joined Kron in the center at the con, "How goes it, Kron?"

"Well, sire, the captured data has been entered in the ship's computers ready for your appraisal. Lord Betus' ship should arrive in twenty Earth hours, and I have just been signaled of the completion of the Zerion's interrogation, the report is being logged in the data system now."

"Good, can you be available to begin reviewing the alien information in about an hour?" At'r asked.

"At your command." Kron answered, "Your chamber's?"

"Yes, from all indications Catherine will sleep a while longer, I only hope she wakes before Betus arrives." At'r was quiet for a time, looking over the command center of his flagship. Finally with a nod to Kron he left the same way he had come, making his way back to his chambers.

First he checked to see if Catherine was still sleeping, she was, and soundly. Looking down at her peaceful but pale face, At'r wondered what she was like in a more normal situation. She handled the pressure well, with everything that had happened to her it had to be difficult. Catherine's home world knew very little of space and her grandmother, for whatever reasons had told her even less about her heritage. Yet aside from that, she had been kidnapped, nearly raped by the Zerion Captain, and now found herself the prisoner of the Emperor of Creasion. At'r mused at how she would accept the facts he must present her with when she woke. Turning, he went to his desk and began to weed through the many disks from the Zerion ship.

Time passed quickly and At'r became engrossed in the details of the Zerion's Earth operations. The captured Zerion Captain had only provided them with two other base's locations, but with the information obtained, the others would soon be located. Kron arrived, and since he was already familiar with the disks they were able to sort out the necessary facts relevant to the Zerion's weakness.

As Catherine slept and Betus journeyed toward Tos-hawk One, At'r, Kron, and a large staff aboard the ship deciphered not only the Zerion code but had located most of the bases and installations constructed by the Zerions. Five bases were complete and five were near completion, but were operational. Four others were only just begun. The Zerion's hold on the area was strong, yet only staffed by the slimmest contingents of construction crews and a few armed patrols. The main portion of their defenses for this faze of their plan had been devoted to deception of the local and national governments, not hiding from the Creasions. Working only at night, they used mirrored force fields to hide their bases during the day. This did not deceive the Creasions. As a matter of added security, the bases or installation Commander knew only a minimal amount of the other operations on the planet. He solely knew two other Commanders, generally on the same continent.

Drawing Commander Kron and several other officers together, At'r questioned them, and listening to their opinions began to form a plan to destroy the bases with minimal knowledge of the country's armed forces where the bases were located, but extensive recognizance would be necessary.

When Tos-hawk One had established their outer orbit in the Sol solar system, At'r had ordered Earth's communications and public broadcasts monitored. As of yet the Zerions were, as far as the public knew, undetected.

Public news sources only broadcast a few U.F.O. reports made by smugly amused reporters, and Catherine's disappearance had been hushed up, as had the strange events surrounding her father's death. The United States' military, however, had Red Star One in their possession and from de-coded messages At'r knew what they knew.

From the Zerion Captain's disks they learned the crew was ordered to take their own lives, only Red Star One's technology was lost and that would take the Earth people years to unravel. Few people on Earth would have known about the Zerion's presence, until it was too late.

At'r agreed with Kron, soon the Zerions would be sending full personnel and supplies for their new bases but there had been no indications of such movement in their communications to Zerion. A small substation on the Earth's only natural satellite relayed their messages home and had been quickly seized by the Creasion without opposition. The first steps had already been taken to stop the Zerion.

At'r turned to Kins, "Signal Commander Delia on Creasion, I wish to speak to her." At'r told him, "I want a progress report on Tos-hawk Two, among other things." A Yeoman entered and served refreshments. With-in a few moments Kins had Commander Delia on the communications screen.

Commander Delia had worked hard to achieve her rank. She posed in a formal salute ready to greet her sovereign. Delia smiled slightly thinking of the good news she would give her Emperor. His image appeared and her face was once again serious, admiration for him shining in her eyes.

At'r returned Delia's salute with respect. The beautiful Creasion woman before him was one of his best commanders. In numerous battles and confrontations with the Zerion and on several occasions with the privateers she had lead her command through and emerged victorious. In his chain of command she was second only to Commander Kron.

"Commander Delia," he addressed her, "do you have a progress report on your ship?"

"Yes, sire, I do, a very positive one. Tos-hawk Two is three weeks ahead of schedule, thanks to the persistence of our people, all tests have been positive. Tos-hawk Two should be operational within the week."

"Excellent, you are to leave to join us here as soon as the ship is ready, the sooner the better. Has there been any unusual activity by the Zerion?"

"They have just come from behind their back sun orbit and all seems normal; however, if they are up to anything here they will wait until we go behind the sun. We had hoped to have Tos-hawk Two ready to monitor them by then."

"Send out the usual monitor ships, but I need you here as soon as possible, I will relay the details on a more secure channel. Has High Priest Betus departed?"

"Yes, he left yesterday morning, I," she paused, "ordered a small escort force of five vessels to accompany him, I hope that was satisfactory?"

"Fine Delia, he may need the protection. Is the Tower still glowing?"

"Yes, still causing a great deal of excitement, rumors are running wild. None of them are accurate, but Lord Betus' departure fueled them."

"I will have an announcement to make sometime after Betus arrives. Until then Delia, keep me informed if there are problems. At'r out." her image faded as she once again saluted.

With tentative plans made to begin destroying the Zerion's bases and their moon base secured, At'r dismissed the meeting until all recognizance reports were in. Telling his aid, Kins, to summon him when lord Betus was six hours away At'r lay down on the sofa to try and rest. It had been many hours since he had slept.

CHAPTER 7

Catherine drifted upward through a thick mist to wake gazing into the cold, perfect beauty of space. She could neither think nor move hypnotized by the closeness and clarity of the stars. Time seemed non-existent as she floated on a cloud of midnight silk sheets and her only reality was space. Catherine lay still for long minutes, her drugged mind still unable to function.

'I must be dead.' was Catherine's first conscious thought. Nowhere else could she have found such a perfect peace, but rebellion came from deep within her spirit along with a stiffness in her body that caused far too much pain to allow her to believe she had died. She moaned, the sound jarring the silence, Catherine took a deep breath and scanned the dark room unable to distinguish anything or any-one. Memories flooded back to her, and she sat up.

Finding herself naked she clutched the sheet to her breast, her loose hair cascading down her back. Wildly she again looked around the dark room unable to see. She sat still, listening for any sound that might betray another person in the room. The room was silent.

Fear gripped her in the darkened room and tears trembled in the corners of her eyes, she forced them back.

"If only the lights were on." she mumbled, wishing aloud. Suddenly the lights came on, slowly growing to fill the sleep chamber with a soft glow.

Amazed, Catherine found herself in a bed that was the size of two king-size beds together and sat upon a pedestal two steps high. Midnight blue silk sheets covered the bed and curtains of the same hue hung from the window like skylight in the ceiling to encase the widow behind the bed. A day/bed of smoke with silver and midnight cushions dominated the remainder of the huge room, but she was drawn to the entranceway, wondering what lay beyond.

Pulling the sheet loose Catherine wrapped it around herself then tried gingerly to put her weight on her ankle. Although it still felt tired she could stand. Tossing the excess sheet over her shoulder Catherine walked to the entrance. Peering through a small hall she could see the living salon where she had met the Emperor. It did not surprise her to find she was still in the Emperor's suite, the sleeping room had a definite masculine tinge. Catherine walked carefully into the room, drawn by the view of space through the cathedral windows behind His Highness' desk. At'r was sleeping, well hidden by the tall back of the living room sofa, seeing no one, she stepped back into the hall bumping the wall, only to have it open, causing Catherine to almost fall on the bathroom floor.

Loosened by the sudden movement, the sheet fell from her body. In awe she stood mesmerized by the bright lights of the bath mirrors reflecting her naked beauty around the room. Out of shyness she quickly recovered the sheet and re-wrapped it around herself. Her courage and nerve regained Catherine explored the bath, finding not only the necessary but luxury as well.

To her amusement she found a small computer terminal in the toilet closet, just the proper height for the occupant to comfortably read the screen. Touching a small panel of lights on one wall, the wall opened to reveal the Emperor's clothes closet, the next set on the adjacent wall revealed a large tub, big enough to almost swim in, next to it was shower closet. This she contemplated for a few moments then stepped in and removed the sheet, hanging it over the glass splash door.

Looking around she saw no water controls, shrugging she said aloud. "Water please, but not too hot." The water sprayed from the shower nozzle a pleasant warm temperature. "A little warmer please." she asked again and the water grew warmer. Catherine stayed in the water for numerous minutes, letting the stuff rinse away many of her anxieties.

At'r woke after only three hours sleep, a low tone beep summoning him from a deep sleep to alert him to Catherine's awake condition. He rose slowly going immediately to his bed expecting to see a groggy Catherine, maybe sitting, instead he found an empty bed with the top sheet missing, his mind raced, 'Surely she would not try an escape dressed only in a silk bed sheet.'

Quickly At'r walked out of the room to alert security but he stopped, hearing water running in his bathroom. He waved his hand over the beam Catherine had fallen against, the door-slid open. Going directly to the shower At'r saw the sheet draped over the shower door and he knew he had found her. Without consideration of her state of undress At'r opened the door. A startled, wet girl drew back against the wall.

Suddenly the spacious shower room shrank and the water stopped. Catherine stared with large saucer shaped eyes as the water dripped from her wet body and hair.

At'r's burning eyes traveled slowly over Catherine, a red blush covering her. Catherine's eyes were drawn as if pulled by a magnet to his bare chest and the silver medallion that adorned his muscular neck. Awed, she remembered seeing the same medallion in a dream. Forgetting her lack of clothing, Catherine bravely reached out, laced her fingers in the chain and pulled with all her strength. The chain held. For some reason she could not fathom, it did not surprise her. Suddenly she dropped the medallion as if burned by the body warm metal, drawing back she was again aware of her position and her lack of clothing.

Trapped by the emerald eyes of the Creasion lord, Catherine lowered her eyes, unable to bear the fire she saw there.

"Please, Your Highness," she said barely above a whisper, "may I have a towel?"

Long moments passed, his eyes once again traveled slowly over her, heightening her hue. Reaching behind the door At'r retrieved a large bath towel and tossed it to Catherine, watching as she quickly wrapped it about her slender body. Looking up, her eyes again caught briefly on his necklace, she said nothing.

"Now," At'r said sternly, "what are you doing on that ankle? Dr. Trentos told you to stay off it."

Catherine had given little heed to the physician's prescription when she had gotten out of bed, the bandage was gone and it had not hurt, so she had walked on it. Now she stood before At'r and must account for her disobedience.

"Your Highness," she began, "the ankle seems fine, I am not in pain," she shrugged, "and it is my ankle." she stated defiantly.

She pressed herself against the wall as At'r entered the shower, fearful of the angry look in his eyes.

Before she could protest his action At'r had swept her into his arms, holding her close against the honey colored curls of hair on his bare chest.

"Until the doctor approves your use of that ankle, you will stay off it." He carried her from the shower through the bathroom and placed her among the misty cushions on the daybed/sofa in the bedroom. Pushing a button on the intercom he instructed Kins to bring in Lady Izadra's clothing and their breakfast.

"Your Highness, please, I prefer to be called Catherine, Izadra is my middle name, given to me to honor my grandmother Iza."

With a sly smile At'r answered her, "I am well aware of the origin of your middle name. We have many things to discuss after we eat, that is one of them." At'r told her leaving and going to the living area of his chambers. She heard the entrance door open and close and surmised At'r had again left, but a few moments passed and a small robot entered the room floating on a cushion of air from underneath the device.

At'r followed the robot, an amused expression on his usually serious face. "This will be your maid while you are on Tos-hawk One," he explained as the device stopped before Catherine and extended one of its mechanical arms bearing a length of fabric.

Hesitantly Catherine accepted the peach colored dress and held it at arms length. She knew the thin fabric would do little more than cover her, looking up, Catherine did not miss the gleam in At'r's eyes.

Turning her attention to the mechanical maid the Emperor had assigned her, Catherine marveled at the complex looking device. The robot had one huge eye that was set atop a long thin neck capable of extending the height of the four-foot high robot to a total height of ten feet. Two audio receivers were mounted above the eye on either side these served as the robot's ears. Below the extendible neck was a small body, consisting of flashing colored lights with two extending arms in front and one in back. Soundlessly it traveled on a cushion of air created by many air jets underneath the body and now sat on the deep carpet before her. Catherine looked to At'r.

"I had really hoped not to take advantage of your hospitality long enough to require a maid." Catherine said guardedly.

At'r's amusement faded, "As I said, we have much to talk about." His eyes taking on a strange glint, "You will change now, then we will have breakfast." Turning he strode to the bath, allowing Catherine time to change.

Simplicity was the style of the garment At'r had provided. It wrapped around her as the silk sheet had but the top was elastic and fastened with Velcro, leaving a long strip of the thin linen material, which Catherine tossed over her left shoulder. A pair of matching panties accompanied the dress and Catherine slid them on. Further contemplating the robot before her, she again sat on the daybed to await At'r's return.

"Can you speak?" she asked it.

"Yes." a slightly feminine, but still mechanical voice answered.

"Do you have a name?"

"I am T.A. three, model number eight, six..."

"Stop!" Catherine told it, "Will you answer to a given name?"

"Yes." the robot answered.

"From now on I will call you Roberta." Catherine said, hoping she could leave soon but unwilling to call the mechanical servant by the model number.

At'r came back from the bath and was joined by his aid, whom At'r introduced as Kins. Kins was pushing a cart covered with food and bowed to his Lord then to Catherine as he was introduced. Only moments passed until Kins left.

At'r turned to her, "I trust you are hungry?"

He stood before her offering his hand to help her the short distance from the sofa to the table. With some hesitation Catherine accepted. Her cold fingers were encased in his warm hand, his grip was both gentle and vice like, and Catherine had the strange feeling he would never let her go.

At'r seated Catherine and she looked into his dark emerald eyes wondering at their effect on her. He moved to the chair across the small table from her.

"You will please help yourself to the food, it is not the same as Earth food, but I feel you will find it appetizing." he explained.

"Thank you, Your Highness, it has been sometime since I have eaten." she said sampling some of the food on her plate, finding it delicious. Although her hunger had become a major concern, she burned with curiosity and foreboding at the same time about what they would discuss after eating.

"You are from a very interesting world, Creasion is in some ways similar in climate." At'r commented.

"We must seem primitive to you." Catherine stated, trying to appear composed.

"Primitive, no. Earth is only a couple of hundred years behind Creasion, in the span of the universe it is really not a long time. Once Earth's technology obtains light speed, they will be traveling to our world." he smiled. "Actually it will soon be time to send an ambassador to Earth."

For a while they ate in silence, Catherine's nerves ruining her appetite, At'r finishing his meal sat waiting patiently for Catherine to finish, she picked at her food aware of his eyes on her.

"If," At'r began, breaking the silence after a time and causing Catherine to startle, "you are finished, I will call the servant to clear the table, we have much to discuss and there is a time element."

Catherine looked up at him slowly, her eyes fixed on him. She feared this alien Lord, his presence making her knees weak and her nerves unsteady, but she refused to allow him to see her apprehension.

Her tone cutting to hide her fears she answered him, "I humbly beg your pardon, yes, thank you, I am finished." As if she were finished with him also, she stood and walked unassisted to the daybed, missing the fire in At'r's eyes. Her heart pounding in her ears, amazed by her own tenacity and fearful that in her bravado she may have gone too far. Intuition told Catherine, Emperor At'r was not going to return her to Earth and despair choked her as she sat waiting in deathly silence wondering how the Lord of Creasion would react to her behavior. Moments seemed liked eons. He called to have the table removed, then came to stand in front of her when they were once again alone.

"You seem to make a habit of incurring the wrath of the man who holds your life in his hands." He sat next to her on the daybed, very close, "I wonder if it is bravery, or stupidity?" His hand went behind her neck he leaned closer forcing her back among the cushions and beneath him. "Do you really have the courage to risk my anger?" his eyes stared into hers, questioning, probing, his lips just above hers.

Time stopped the moment he touched her, he was so close now Catherine held her breath. Her heart pounded and her world consisted only of At'r's presence and his power radiating through her body. She could not speak to answer him, nor did she have to. At'r's lips covered Catherine's as he pressed her deeper in the cushions. Weakly Catherine protested, trying to push him away but he held her arms forcing her to endure his embrace, leaving her breathless when he released her.

Catherine struggled to sit as soon as she could, At'r coming back to her after pouring two small snifters of clear liquid Catherine thought was water, but when she tossed it down she found it was strong liquor, distilled on the Creasion moon of Metem. Catherine coughed, the liquid numbing her throat after it traced a fiery path down to her stomach.

"By the Three Moons." At'r swore this time bringing Catherine a glass of water, now almost sorry he had so unnerved her.

Embarrassed, Catherine shyly looked up at At'r who stood waiting for her to catch her breath. "Thank you," she said demurely, At'r sat next to her again.

"Please Your Highness," she said softly, "will you send me home?"

At'r turned to face Catherine, reaching out he lifted the necklace from her throat. "No! I will not return you to Earth." he said firmly, watching her face grow even paler, almost tenderly At'r laid the pendant back against her chest, his touch causing Catherine to tremble.

"Why?" Catherine asked, her voice shaking, "And why do you wear a necklace like mine?"

"That is what we have to discuss." He took a deep breath, for the first time unsure of what to say. "You will listen, later I will answer your questions." He stood and paced a few steps, then turned and again sat beside her. "More than sixty Earth years ago, Creasion years are slightly longer, a marriage took place between Emperor Tor and

Lady Iza of the Royal House of Metem. At that time Creasion and Zerion were at peace, relations were strained but that was more normal than if they had been congenial. Several months passed and Lady Iza found herself pregnant, but on the day she was to have told Lord Tor the Zerions kidnapped her. On the journey back to Zerion they had to pass through a large asteroid belt separating their world from Creasion. This is similar to the meteor belt between Mars and Jupiter in this solar system. In those times navigation was not so advanced as it has become and in their haste the Zerion became lost. An ion charge between asteroids struck their craft, damaging the light drive device and causing it to stick in an open position. Off course, they traveled for days and hundreds of light years. Finally coming upon Earth and becoming caught in the gravitational pull, they crashed in one of the oceans. Few Zerions can swim, they just do not need to know how on their desert planet," At'r cleared his throat, "only Lady Iza survived the crash, afterwards we know nothing about her." He was quiet for a moment. "Emperor Tor was near heartbreak, there were no star range vessels in our fleet then, this made rescue impossible. He had to leave his wife and heir to his throne to live out the remainder of their lives on Earth. In his grief the night Iza was abducted, Tor stayed in the temple, there he was blessed with a vision. He saw the Zerion subdued but not conquered by his hand, he saw the construction of the Diamerald Tower and he saw the return of his granddaughter. After Tor had fulfilled the first part of the prophecy by subduing the Zerion and constructing the Diamerald Tower he abdicated his throne leaving it to a younger brother. Since Tor could not remove his necklace, his brother's was cast in silver. Tor lived the remainder of his life in the Tower, and as long as he lived the Tower glowed, now it is his tomb. No one has entered since."

Catherine sat in silence for several seconds, her voice broke the stillness, "You tell an interesting fairy tale, but I fail to see what it has to do with me?"

At'r had the feeling she was being deliberately vague, "When we first picked up the Zerion construction craft, your life readings read Earthling and Creasion. When you were brought on board Commander Kron's fighter, you were scanned by medical sensors, but they were unable to tell us anything more than our ships sensors had, half Earthling, half Creasion. Had they been able to give us your physical condition I would have known about your leg and exhaustion before your arrival. Only the special medical sensor that Doctor Trentos uses for me could determine your condition. This," he pickup her emblem, "blocks anything but a very special sensor, that is one way the necklace protects us."

Catherine was looking at him skeptically. "Subsequent medical test on you and metallurgical tests on your necklace while you slept confirm what we already knew," he paused looking directly in Catherine's eyes. "You're half Creasion, the granddaughter of our lost Empress Iza, there being your middle name Iza-dra, meaning Iza's heir, that is why you wear this necklace, I just do not know why Lady Iza did not explain this to you."

"Possibly," Catherine said coldly, "because my grandmother was not your Empress, I am sorry Your Highness, but I am not she whom you seek."

At'r considered her for some moments, "Yes, Lady Izadra, you are, there is no doubt in my mind, Doctor Trentos is also convinced as well as Commander Kron, but in less than an hour High Priest Betus is arriving, he is very anxious to meet you."

"It is a shame your High Priest has made such a long trip, I am sure," Catherine said firmly, almost defiantly, "that he will be disappointed, and regardless of the value you give my second name, I, prefer to be called Catherine."

"Accustom yourself to the name, I am sure your family on Creasion and Metem will expect you to use it." He leaned close to her, "and, so do I!" A buzzer alerted At'r to someone requesting admittance. Glancing at the miniature view screen mounted in the table, At'r saw it was Kron, "Enter." he said to the monitor.

"My Lord, my Lady, lord Betus' shuttle will be arriving anon, he has asked to see Lady Izadra as soon as Your Highness is ready to receive him."

"Thank you Kron, show lord Betus to our chambers when he arrives," At'r said warmly to Kron, "you may alter the course as we discussed earlier, after his shuttle is safely aboard." bowing again, Kron left them.

"Lord Betus' shuttle prepares to land." At'r told her and indicated the windows behind the bed. Through them Izadra could see a sleek shuttle maneuvering to land inside one of the great bays on either side of the ship beneath them.

Already shaken, refusing to believe what this alien Lord told her, Izadra's heart jumped most violently at the ship's presence, it did not go unnoticed.

"Do you fear lord Betus, or that he may agree with me?" At'r asked.

"And what if he agrees with me?" Izadra turned to stare hopefully into the alien's eyes.

Long moments passed, At'r's fingers wove through her long hair pulling Izadra closer, staring down into her defiant eyes. Izadra felt the strong compulsion of his will, and it took considerable concentration not to succumb. Breaking the spell, their lips met, Izadra's unyielding, At'r's demanding, forcing her to yield. At'r held her for a brief moment, suspended in time only to release Izadra, "Here you stay." At'r rose from the daybed, leaving Izadra and going to his desk in the other room.

Izadra had been close to tears before, but now it was nearly too much, silently several tears escaped. Drawing a ragged, choked gulp of air she made herself stop. Later, if she were ever alone again she would indulge herself, but now she must not. Soon this lord Betus would come, 'Maybe, just maybe he will be of some help.' Izadra reasoned. One thought was building in her mind, 'escape,' but how she did not know.

Forgetting everything except the sapping desperation she felt taking control of her, Izadra stood, going to stand at the foot of the bed to stare through the windows at the magnificence of space. It was entrancing and it gave her some solace. With her mind in turmoil she began to try to make some sense of her predicament.

It was evident what Lord At'r wanted. Why was he trying to trick her with this fairy tale? Izadra refused to believe it might be true. As she looked across the broad expanse of the massive bed she now knew was At'r's, she shivered.

Escaped seemed like an impossible quest, she had neither the skill nor the knowledge to pilot even one of the small Creasion vessels. If she could obtain a weapon of some sort she might be able to hi-jack a ship and pilot, but any plan of that nature would entail a better knowledge of the ship. Izadra doubted she could find her way to one of the hangers. Then there was the possibility of a foiled attempt, Izadra feared to contemplate the consequences. She was trapped, the unwitting prisoner of an alien Emperor.

The buzzer announcing another visitor interrupted Izadra's thoughts. Remembering she was told to stay off her ankle Izadra quickly walked back to the misty gray sofa and sat down in time to see an ornately dressed Creasion pass on the small view screen. Her intuition told her it was lord Betus. Izadra had expected an older man. Composing herself, knowing At'r would require her to meet lord Betus, Izadra would attempt to present a calm exterior. Voices began to filter through the hall between the living room and the bedroom, Izadra listened intently, not daring to enter the hall.

"Hail Emperor At'r, Lord of the Three Moons, peace be with you." Izadra heard a strange voice say.

"And to you, lord Betus, welcome and how was your journey?" At'r returned.

"Comfortable, and not too long, but I am anxious to meet your guest." Betus told him and Izadra heard At'r reply in a language that she could not understand, but seemed hauntingly familiar. For a long time they spoke in their language. It made her more apprehensive, Izadra knew they spoke of her. Their talk ceased, and she waited holding her breath for At'r to come for her, instead he entered the room followed by Betus.

Izadra stood in Betus' presence, astonished at his appearance. Almost as tall as At'r, his stature was that of a much younger man. Had it not been for his long graybeard and hair he would not have looked more than fifty years old, but his eyes reflected his longevity. Yet, they contained a warmth that was more than reassuring, as stressed as she was they were totally devastating. Izadra swayed slightly on her feet as she felt his mind touch hers and attempt to enter.

"No!" Izadra said and closed her enslaved eyes. She swayed again and At'r reached out a supportive hand, the contact felt like fire. Izadra pulled away glaring at At'r, then to Betus.

"The Zerions only tried to rape my body, you try to rape my mind?" her frigid stare turned toward At'r.

At'r regarded her, knowing now without hesitancy who she was, none other could have denied passage of Betus' mind into their own, At'r was not sure he could. He looked in Izadra's eyes and glimpsed an anger in her, suppressed and controlled only by her fear of him. Her spirit was strong.

Betus considered the strength Izadra had used to force him from her mind, though it was rough and unused she had mustered enough to push him out. He was sure now, she was his niece.

"Lady Izadra," Betus addressed her formally, "forgive me the intrusion, but it was the only way I could be sure that you are who we feel you are." those wise eyes were again fixed on her.

"And what is you conclusion?" Izadra asked defiantly.

Tension hung in the air awaiting his answer "You are she. You are my grandniece, my sister's granddaughter."

Izadra sat down rather abruptly, in shock, she had hoped he would dispute At'r's theory of her parentage. Slowly she looked up, each man surprised not to see tears in her hazel eyes.

"What," Izadra asked At'r with a shaky voice, "are you going to do with me?" she could not bear the suspense any longer.

At'r looked to Betus and back again, then said something in their language to Betus before addressing Izadra, "We will wed in twenty-two hours, for now I will leave you to become acquainted with your great-uncle." he turned and left them before Izadra could protest.

Betus studied Izadra sitting numbly on the couch, he sat in a chair next to her, "You do not believe we tell you the truth?" he asked.

"No, I believe it is all a trick or a hoax of some type, but I do not understand why."

"You do not want to believe Izadra, but you are she, if you had not been, I could have read every thought you had. I do not, on the other hand, understand why Iza did not tell you about your heritage. Do you remember her at all?"

Izadra contemplated Betus and his question, he did bear an uncanny resemblance to her grandmother. His eyes were the same green as her grandmother's, 'normal green' she thought, 'not that strange emerald color of At'r's eyes.' Betus' manner reminded Izadra of her grandmother. Finally she answered him. "I remember my grandmother, yes, but…"

Betus interrupted, "Tell me, when did she give you the necklace?"

"How would you know my grandmother gave me this?" Izadra touched the pendant.

"I would imagine she gave it to you just before her death, but tell me what my sister told you." he asked eager for information.

It was becoming more difficult not to believe what she had been told, Izadra wondered if they had, while she slept, read her mind and now schemed to use the information against her. Why, she could not understand.

"You are correct again, grand-mom gave the necklace to me less than an hour before her death. She told me it was the richest legacy she could leave me, then chanting a strange phrase the necklace fell from her neck and she placed it around my neck, there it has remained." Izadra drew a deep breath, "She told me it would protect me, I do not know how well it has done that, the necklace seems to be causing more trouble than avoiding it."

"And she never told you about the necklace or her origins and family?"

"My father explained to me, her family had been killed in World War II. He said she came from England."

"Why did she and your father argue when you were six?' Betus asked hoping to find the reason for Izadra's lack of information about her mother's family.

"How do you know these things, other than if you read my thoughts? But you say you have not." Izadra was suspicious.

"We do have a few recently placed agents on your birth planet, mostly historic and cultural observers, but they can obtain information on what ever item we wish, when it is warranted." Betus explained.

Drawing a deep breath, still leery of what she had been told Izadra answered, "I don't know why they argued. The only reason I was given was grand-mom wanted to educate me herself. She had been a fine teacher when she was younger and had taught gifted children, but my father felt I needed to be with other children."

"Did you visit her much after the argument?"

"Only on holidays, and a week during the summer, but after she became ill, the last two years before she died, I was allowed two weeks. I tried to stay longer on occasions. It was difficult because my father kept me enrolled in accelerated summer schools and advanced courses. His way of keeping me out of trouble." Izadra's tone was quiet and she sat for a few moments in silence, "Lord Betus," she started then paused, "Please sir, you really can not believe that I am who you look for, it is just a trick!"

Betus smiled kindly, understanding Izadra's shock and fear, "You are the image of your grandmother at your age, except those eyes. In them I see the spirits of your Scottish ancestors, on your father's side. The Celts were very sensitive to the super natural, as it is called on Earth. This may well be to your credit. During the next few days you may find an awakening of abilities you did not know you had. Be patient, you will learn to control them."

Smiling in a kindly manner Betus rose, "I must go now, I will see you again at the evening meal, we will discuss your wedding that will take place tomorrow," he looked out the windows, "I should say in twenty-one hours, time and space seem the same out here."

Izadra rose to stand beside him, "Stay here my dear," he admonished, "Lord At'r is concerned your ankle will interfere with tomorrow's ceremonies, they will be telecast to Creasion and the three moons live." She paled. "I see you did not know that, do not let it trouble you." At that he left her alone to ponder all he had said.

Izadra began to pace no longer caring if At'r objected. No matter how convincing the facts were becoming, she could not believe they were true. Idly she toyed with her necklace, her mind reviewing the things she had been told in the past few hours. It was just too unbelievable. Hearing the chamber doors open she turned toward the entrance expecting to see At'r but instead Roberta entered preceding a man Izadra remembered as Doctor Trentos. At their first meeting Izadra had not seen him as anyone but another alien. Now she saw a strong resemblance to At'r, but the doctor was older perhaps sixty earth years, his manner calm but commanding.

Bowing slightly Doctor Trentos addressed her "Lord At'r has told me you were up and on that ankle." he began sternly.

"The ankle is fine, thank you Doctor." Izadra returned.

"Please sit down and I will be the judge of that." Trentos told her, shrugging Izadra walked to sit on the daybed, followed by the physician.

The moment she sat Trentos began scrutinizing her with his special monitor, completing his monitoring with a "Hum" he knelt to gently take her left ankle in his hand. Finished he rose to look down at Izadra.

"You ankle is better; however, do not over exert it or you will limp during the ceremonies, that would displease Lord At'r." Trentos did not miss the defiant glint in her eyes, "And, you would not like to appear weak before you new people." he added.

"I will do my best Doctor," Izadra promised, "to not re-injure my ankle, you are correct I do not wish to appear weak." she conceded.

Trentos smiled and sat next to her, "You are much like your grandmother, I remember her well, she and my brother made a handsome ruling couple, that is until the Zerion stole her from us."

Izadra stared at him for a moment, "Then you also would be my great-uncle, if I were who you think I am?"

"I am your grand-uncle, there isn't a doubt of your parentage."

"You all seem so certain," Izadra let the sentence hang, "but I do not believe it, nor do I understand why someone as powerful as your Emperor would need to trick me." She sighed, "Perhaps a marriage to what your people thought was Iza's heir would be of some political advantage."

"Lady Izadra, please!" Trentos was amazed, "You are wrong, this is not a trick, if there was any doubt Lord At'r would not marry you, he does not trick his people and if you were but an Earthgirl there would be no reason to lie to you. Believe, Lady Izadra," he admonished her, "it is true." Gently he patted her trembling hand, "I know it is difficult. Now I must go." standing he bowed slightly and left her with Roberta.

Izadra turned her attention to the robot that moved to the daybed where she sat and extended a metallic arm holding a folded garment.

"What have you there?" Izadra questioned.

"Your evening gown." Roberta droned in its toneless voice.

"Thank you." Izadra accepted the sea green folded garment. "How do you know this will fit?" she indicated the dress.

"Lord At'r has programmed your dimensions in my memory."

"Does he choose my clothing?" Izadra asked.

"Yes." it confirmed.

Izadra stood momentarily contemplating the clothing she would need for her escape, but knowing At'r would return soon she went to the bath to change.

Consisting of two garments the outfit did little more to cover than the dress she was wearing. A floor length wrap-around skirt made from a light flowing material that tied in front with a long wide tie that hung almost to the hem, reminding Izadra of an ancient Egyptian skirt. A second long peace of the same fabric but double thickness was all that remained for a top, this she wrapped around her torsos and crossed her breasts tying it behind her neck and leaving two long streamers flowing behind her.

After brushing her longhair with the brush Roberta had furnished, Izadra pondered her reflection in the mirror. Sighing, she returned to the sleeping room.

At'r waited for her, closely appraising her appearance. She looked beautiful. Sleep had wiped away the dark shadows from beneath her hazel eyes and replaced them with a slight glow in her cheeks.

"You are lovely, Lady Izadra." At'r said extending his hand to her.

For a brief moment she waited, apprehensive as always about taking his offered hand, still half fearing he would change from the viral man he was and become the monster of so many science fiction novels.

For dinner he had dressed in his military uniform, a high collared tight fitting tunic and equally tight pants of dark forest green that tucked in his highly polished black boots. He wore his Royal necklace outside the tunic and as always when he was in public, the gold band of authority sat upon his head. With his collar length hair and well manicured beard, his green eyes firmly fixed on her face Izadra wanted to run more than accept his hand, but compelled by a greater urging than she could deny she placed her hand in his, in silence At'r escorted Izadra to dinner.

Lord Betus and Kron waited patiently for them in the dinning room, both bowed slightly when At'r and Izadra entered.

At'r seated Izadra on his right with Betus and Kron occupying the other two places at the table. The servants placed their meals before them and left as they had been instructed.

At'r turned to Betus "I hope your chambers are comfortable and that you had a pleasant rest before dinner lord Betus?"

"Thank you, yes my Lord, Tos-hawk One is very impressive and very comfortable. Kron gave me a small tour and I must compliment you for considering your crews comfort as well as that of your guests."

"The crew's security both physically and mentally are a premium concern. Sometimes they must live on board for long periods of time."

"This has certainly become an interesting maiden voyage." Kron commented.

"One of your more unusual treks." At'r agreed.

"If you had not been on test maneuvers, the Zerion ship Lady Izadra was on would never have been detected."

"Very true lord Betus, but had it not been for your son I don't think the capture would have been as simple." Seeing Izadra's confused expression At'r explained, "Lord Betus is Kron's father."

"One can not help but wonder," Kron projected, "if it were luck, or if it was fate."

"It was luck." Izadra said dryly, "My bad luck." she placed what looked like a large Concord grape in her mouth.

At'r scowled at her. She placed another grape in her mouth, undaunted in Betus' and Kron's presence.

Dinner finished, Kron excused himself to attend his command, "I must go sire," he said to At'r, "I will have an up-dated report on the Zerion's Earth activity and our plans to neutralize them when you are ready."

"Thank you Kron, I will call shortly."

"By your leave," Kron said bowing, then turned on his heel and left.

Clearing his throat, "We have much to plan for and discuss," Betus began, "with the ceremonies only a few hours away."

At'r rose and offered Izadra his hand, escorting her toward the couch in the living room, but before she sat their eyes met.

"I must tell you," Izadra's voice was low and unsteady, "before you make your plans, I will not marry you, I do not love you."

At'r held her eyes with ease and although she wanted to draw away from the fire she saw there, she could not.

Izadra wished she was the fainting type, but that avenue of escaping his wrath was firmly closed every fiber of her body was alert.

"Because you are the daughter of a Royal house, because you are the one foretold, because you are ignorant of our laws and customs I tell you this." his voice was also low but the words were clear and measured. "You will marry me, and tomorrow evening, if you refuse or show any signs of rebellion I will have you given a drug that will insure your cooperation." he touched her cheek with a gentleness that was contrary to the tone of his voice. "If I choose, a proxy could even take your place, but your presence before our people is a paramount concern. They must see a happy, united bride and groom." he smiled cruelly, "Love has no place in this or my life, only duty to my people. You are part of that duty. Do you understand?"

Surprised by the rigor of his threat, Izadra could only nod her understanding. She looked to Betus. "You say you are my great-uncle. You would allow him to do this?"

"My dear, I have no authority over Lord At'r, and as in all things he places his people's interest before his own. I would not stand in the way of that." he smiled, kindly, aware of her trauma, "You are still tired and I doubt anyone could fully comprehend everything that has happened to you the last few days. Do not fight your destiny."

Sedately she sat down. Izadra's troubled mind wandered to center around her grandmother, they had done many things together until Izadra's father and she had argued. Izadra's father had restricted their time together and Izadra had found herself in an excessively rigid girls school in Switzerland with only a few holidays and a week or two in the summer to spend with her grandmother.

A mind jarring thought came to her. In the will her grandmother had left was a packet sealed with her old wax seal and specified to be given to Izadra after her father's death. But Kevin, the family attorney, had not had time to send for the documents from his Washington D.C. office after her father had been killed. Izadra wondered what was in it and she wondered how Kevin was taking the news of her disappearance. It was possible he did not know she was missing. For some reason she could not fathom, the thought depressed her, suddenly Izadra felt terribly alone and aware for the first time she was the alien here.

"Izadra!" At'r was calling her, dazed from her deep reverie she forced herself back to the present. "Madam, would you give us the courtesy of answering lord Betus' question?"

"I beg your indulgence." Izadra snapped, wondering what question would need an answer from her. "Since you seemed to have matters well planned already, my thoughts were with those on Earth who are undoubtedly trying to find out what has become of me. I did not hear lord Betus' question. If you care to repeat the question, I will answer." Izadra raised her chin a notch in defiance.

At'r's stare threatened to melt Izadra's composure, but she held her head proudly and did not allow him to see her trepidation. "Lord Betus asked if you knew anyone on board Tos-hawk One who you would care to honor by serving as your maid for the ceremonies?" At'r was amazed at her tenacity, none dared to speak to him in such a manner, but he recalled her grandmother had been noted for her spirit, Izadra seemed to inherit that also.

"I know no one here." Izadra said quietly looking down at the table in front of the couch. On it lay the pin Lieutenant Kara had given her to pin her torn shirt, "Yes," Izadra said a bit louder, "there is," she picked up the pin and gave it to At'r, "The young officer who gave me this."

"I will see she is notified." At'r assured her, "Expect her two hours before the ceremonies begin. Her name is Lieutenant Tari Kara, she is from the moon Tross, and has earned several honors for valor and bravery for one so young."

"That concludes what I needed," Betus said rising from his chair and stretching.

"Do not over work yourself Betus." At'r said fondly, "If you need help of any kind, summon whomever you need, I will be remaining up for sometime yet, so feel free to call if you have questions."

"Thank you sire, and goodnight." he bowed and left.

Izadra had stood when her granduncle had left, bidding him a goodnight shortly afterward she nervously sat back down. At'r joined her, sitting close and making her more ill at ease. She started to rise, but At'r restrained her.

"We are not finished." At'r told her and encased her in his arms. "So, you do not want to marry me?"

"No." Izadra answered in a breathless whisper.

"If you had just been an Earthgirl I would already have made you my mistress, but you are not. For that reason we must marry and have," he pulled her closer, "many children, I do not have to love you to want you." At'r seemed to relish the obvious discomfort he caused her. He released her suddenly to push a button on the small control panel in the couch arm. This activated a wall screen hidden behind in invisible panel. "This is a composite disk of the information dealing with you that was taken from the Zerion ship you were on." At'r explained.

Izadra watched as the drama played out on the screen staring in amazed silence she noticed things she had not before. The Zerion that had chased and caught her was Sub-captain Stx. He as well as two other Zerion officers stayed behind to supervise the execution of the two Zerion searchers who had not found her during the daylight search. With renewed horror Izadra watched again as the two died beneath the exhausts of the Zerion construction craft. It was one of worst things she had ever seen. Izadra turned her head away, nauseated. Slowly she looked back fearful of seeing the Zerion Captain's rape attempt, but it was not included and the disk ended with the Zerion ship's capture.

"Now," At'r said, "the next disk is of newscasts since your departure from Earth."

Most reports told the same story. "Ms. Catherine Kirk, ambassador's daughter. Distraught over her father's recent death is missing after what was left of her car was found over the side of a cliff in an accident similar to that of her father's and in approximately the same area. No body was found and authorities hope Ms. Kirk is still alive but fear she is possibly lost in the mountains or has amnesia." The last report was two hours old, and it said the search for had been abandoned, authorities now felt she had died in the crash, the disk concluded but the lights stayed down.

"Why did you show me this?" Izadra questioned him.

"I want you to see there is nothing for you to go back too on Earth, your future is with me now." he paused, "I have one more disk to show you."

Again the screen brightened, Izadra watched, her face pale, hardly breathing as a tan Mercedes dodged lazzer beams, finally being hit by one and forced over the side in flames. Izadra saw the Sheriff's car stop and then from the Zerion craft's point of view, saw them close in on him, only to back off as other emergency vehicles came into view.

"Do you know that auto?" At'r asked in the darkness after the disk had ended.

"Yes," Izadra said slowly, "it was my father's."

"I suspected as much. It was Captain Quar who killed your father." he turned the screen off and the lights brightened.

With eyes glistening from withheld tears, reflecting the pain and loneliness she could not hide, Izadra turned her face to him. "You are a cruel man, Your Highness."

"I do what I must." He replied grimly, "Now I want your word on your good behavior tomorrow, hopefully, I can trust your word?"

Izadra was quiet for a time, causing At'r to wonder if she would guarantee her behavior.

"You have my word, I will do as you say." Izadra promised wearily.

"I am gratified to see your judgment is not hampered by the strain of the situation." He stood pulling her up with him, "Now you should go and prepare for sleep, I will check on you a little later."

"Do not trouble yourself, I have not been tucked in since I was six, I am sure I can manage." Izadra turned and walked back to the sleeping room alone.

At'r watched her leave, enjoying the sway of her shapely hips, the elegant way she held her head and that beautiful mass of red hair, with a spirit that matched. Since Izadra's arrival he had slept little, when he found time for a few hours rest she invaded his thoughts. He wanted her, but that was all, he told himself, he would not allow himself to fall in love with her. Tomorrow night he would satisfy his hunger, until then his self-discipline would suffice. Dismissing Izadra from his mind At'r turned to the other pressing matters and signaled Kron for the report on the Zerions operations and their plans to stop them. It would be a few minutes before Kron would arrive with his report, absently At'r wandered into the sleeping room. Izadra had retired, seemingly sleeping. She had loosely braided her hair and it lay over her right shoulder in one long thick rope. At'r pulled the restraining ribbon and the braid fell free, Izadra opened her eyes to look up into his.

"Sleep well tonight with your ethereal dreams, tomorrow you will have more substantial company." Turning At'r left Izadra, but she could not sleep.

Lying awake, gazing almost lost in the celestial view through the window over the bed, her mind began to clear from the fit of crying that had over taken her in the bath. It had all caught up to her, with the shower running to mask the sound, fearful At'r might hear, Izadra had wept. Feeling drained and exhausted she had gotten in bed only moments before At'r had come to check on her. After he had gone she drew a deep breath of relief but still could not sleep.

Reason returned, and Izadra again began to think about the package her grandmother had bequeathed to her and what it contained. Somehow she must get that packet, maybe it could explain, she stopped, suddenly fearful. If the packet explained what was happening, it would prove true what the Creasions had told her. Yet, she hoped, it also might give her a way out, another choice.

Izadra's thoughts were interrupted by voices coming from At'r's living room area, Kron had come for the briefing on the Zerions. As she rose from the bed to venture closer to the hall Izadra listened intently hoping to hear something that would aid her in a desperate escape attempt, not only from At'r, but to retrieve the packet her grandmother had left for her.

They had finished the amenities by the time Izadra was in position to listen comfortably and un-seen. She waited sometimes forgetting to breathe as their conversation began to discuss the extent of the Zerion's hold on the Earth.

"Had we not intercepted the Zerion construction craft where we found Lady Izadra, the Zerion would have gone un-detected until much too late for us to have been of any deterrent in the take-over of the planet." Kron began explaining. "As it stands now our intelligence and reconnaissance tell us our elimination of their bases can go as originally planned. The smallest, most isolated first, that is the one in Brazil, and the largest last, this will be a joint effort, several bases must be taken out, the bases in Russia and the United States at the same time, they will be last. They will also be the trickiest, we must avoid detection by these two, least they think the other is attacking and possibly cause a major nuclear confrontation needlessly."

"What reaction will my wedding cause with the Zerion? You know they monitor our public broadcasts on Creasion, we know they have missed the arrival of the ship we took. Of course, I know the Zerion's Earth bases will not be aware, as we control their communications from the Earth's moon. But the main planet Zerion will know, and the story is set to be told just as it happened, I will not lie to our people, they deserve the truth."

"Before the Zerion can speed up their fleet's arrival to activate their bases, we will have already destroyed all but the largest bases. The last bases will be gone before they get here, it would be best if Tos-hawk Two were coming in to back us up, but we should have a good margin of safety with the sensor invisibility shield should we encounter the Zerion fleet." Kron explained, "Also we will block any incoming ships from the broadcast, so if the fleet were already in route they would not receive the transmission."

"When will the first bases go?"

"Tomorrow night, six hours after the ceremonies. The last will be five days from now. I will lead the raid on the largest in the United States, the base near Washington D.C., two days before I will go on a final reconnaissance check." Kron continued to explain the details of each base's destruction but Izadra had heard what she wanted. Somehow, she would be on the reconnaissance flight Kron was taking near Washington then she hoped she could fade into the brush. It was a long shot and risky, if she were caught Izadra could not begin to imagine the depth of At'r's anger but neither could she stay. Izadra wished it could be sooner, but it wasn't. Now she must prepare to calmly survive the next three days. With that thought in mind she stole back to bed and fell into a restless sleep.

CHAPTER 8

Izadra felt as though she had just fallen asleep, now someone was calling her, a young feminine voice, Izadra forced herself to wake, focusing slowly on the face above her.

"I am yeoman Loka, I was asked to assist you until Lieutenant Kara could be here. She will bring your gown and cloak about two hours before the ceremony."

"And when is the ceremony?" Izadra asked, yawning, "And how are you to assist me?"

"The ceremony is in eight hours, Your Highness, and I am to do anything I can to help you feel at ease. His Highness asked me to style your hair and prepare your face, Lieutenant Kara will see to your dressing." the girl replied.

"I am not accustomed to help in dressing." Izadra protested.

"Highness, Lord At'r has instructed me to tell you." She paused, "Please Lady Izadra, I only wish to make this day easier for you and His Highness will be angry if you do something out of custom because I did not explain it to you. She smiled in a friendly manner.

"Very well Loka, I will heed your instructions as best I can. Where do we start?"

"With breakfast." Loka said and Roberta came in caring a tray full of food.

"My Lady will have a long day and your bridal dinner this evening is many hours away." Loka told her.

Izadra began eating from the tray while Loka tried to explain the intricate ceremonies Izadra would participate in.

When Izadra finished eating, Loka brushed her Lady's long hair while Roberta cleared away the dishes. Loka then hustled Izadra to the bath to wash her hair and apply a conditioner, explaining to her mistress that her hair did not have the shine it should after her recent adventures.

Rinsing the cream from her hair Loka gently blotted the water out of the clean mass. Next she allowed Izadra to soak in the swirling waters of the hot tub for ten minutes while she brushed the tiny tangles from her hair. These simple and time consuming activities would have driven Izadra crazy but she kept her thoughts on her escape and planning over and over the details and possible problems.

Wrapping Izadra in a large warm bath sheet, Loka sat Izadra on a comfortable chair before the bathroom's space viewing window. Here Loka brushed her mistress' hair until it seemed to reflect the starlight from the windows in her long auburn tresses. Coiling the glistening hair in a heavy bun at the nape of Izadra's neck, Loka covered it with silver cloth securing it with crystal clips.

"Come with me." Loka told Izadra and led her to a Plexiglas table that Roberta had pushed in earlier, "Please my Lady," she indicated the table and reluctantly Izadra stretched out on the hard surface.

With skilled hands Loka massaged Izadra's tense muscles quickly finding out the hot tub had done little to relax her.

After twenty minutes of Loka's attention Izadra lay half-asleep on the table, unmindful of Loka's actions when she lowered a clear, half dome cover over her. Loka had left her neck and head outside the dome and Izadra felt a light, pleasant tingling over the remainder of her naked body as the chamber filled with lavender mist. Clearing as fast as it had filled, the mist in the chamber dissipated and the cover lifted automatically. Izadra sat up to find all body hair gone except what had not been in the chamber, her neck and head. Embarrassed, she looked to Loka.

"You can not expect me to," she stopped, her face red, "Oh Loka how could you, I…can not appear before His Highness like, this!"

"Milady," Loka's voice was apologetic, "His Highness ordered it. Most Creasion women prefer this as do our men."

Izadra reached for her robe, "How long until it grows back?"

"Never my Lady, it is gone permanently." Seeing how frantic Izadra had become Loka assisted her back to into the whirlpool for ten more minutes. In the few hours that followed Loka finished telling Izadra what would be expected of her before the ceremonies through her bridal dinner, as she did, she completed Izadra's make-up and styled her hair. Just as Loka finished, Lieutenant Kara joined them.

Izadra was sitting in the center of the spacious bath chamber when Tari entered, seeing Izadra she bowed.

"Please Lieutenant Kara be at ease." Izadra told the young woman before her.

"Thank you, my Lady." Tari said.

"How old are you?" Izadra asked, marveling at the girl.

"Twenty-one, your Earth years, Twenty by Creasion years."

Izadra considered her, they were the same age. But Tari seemed in control of herself and her future Izadra wondered how Tari would handle her situation, if the situation were reversed.

Loka, who had laid out the gown and undergarments of Izadra's trousseau now bowed before Izadra and excused herself, leaving Izadra and Tari alone.

"This is your dress uniform?" Izadra questioned admiring Tari's apparel.

"Yes, my Lady," Tari turned slowly modeling her uniform proudly. Beneath a dark blue cape she wore a lighter blue shirt of glossy fabric that also lined the inside of her cape. On each collar was a silver pyramid pin that identified her rank, at each shoulder Tari's cape was held folded back by a row of jeweled pins symbolizing honors earned. Tari's pants were of the same dark blue fabric as her cape and fitted tightly accenting her slim figure, Tari wore the pants legs tucked inside highly polished black boots that shaped her calf and ended just below her knee. A carved silver buckle held together the belt her sword and holstered lazzer pistol were on. Matching her uniform a barite covered her blue black hair and Izadra didn't miss the pride in her sapphire blue eyes.

"I want to thank you, Tari," Izadra paused unsure, "I may call you Tari?"

"My Lady I would be honored if you would." Tari replied.

"Is it permissible for you to do the same?"

"Only in private my Lady." Tari told her following Izadra to the bedroom.

"Please do so. Now, as I said, I want to thank you for your thoughtfulness on-board the Zerion ship, you saved me considerable embarrassment. And it was so good to see another woman."

"It was my pleasure and I must tell you, what you did to the Zerion Captain's cheek has become legend." a slight smile played upon her lips.

Izadra smiled a little too, glad for the company the day brought, if not for the event. "I was scared and acted in desperation."

"Let us hope," a masculine voice joined, "you do not have to go through such an experience again."

Both turned to face At'r, Tari immediately bowing, Izadra's smile faded and she looked coldly at At'r.

"Your Highness," Izadra said and slightly inclined her head.

"Lieutenant Kara, please, a few moments alone with my bride." At'r requested of the young woman, she bowed again, leaving them alone. Izadra's yeoman had done an exquisite job on her make-up and hair and At'r briefly pondered if the yeoman had succeeded in his other orders, remembering Izadra's lovely body.

"How are you?" At'r asked touching her gently beneath the chin.

Izadra considered him for a moment, "Do not concern yourself Your Highness, I will keep my word."

"I do not doubt you," he replied and handed her a small thin rectangular Black Crystal box, "I wish you to wear these, they have been passed down for many generations and survived several wars."

Hesitantly Izadra accepted the exotic box and lifted the lid to stare at the most beautiful jewelry she had ever seen, "They are exquisite, I have never seen Emeralds like them."

"They are not Emeralds, but Diameralds, they have both properties of your Earth Diamonds and Emeralds, plus something more. In our ancient legends they were known to be conductors of mind-powers, but it has been eons since anyone could use their powers, if they ever could."

Curious, Izadra lifted the necklace from the box, the gold chain was long enough that it would hang just below her permanent necklace, the Diamerald was the shape of a teardrop and the size of a silver dollar.

Izadra turned her questioning eyes to At'r, "Once on, will it come off?" she asked.

"Of course," he smirked, and taking the necklace from her placed it around her neck, his hands brushing her bare shoulders and lingering briefly when he finished, At'r kissed the faded bruise on her shoulder. "I will leave you now to finish dressing." moments after his exit, Tari returned.

Tari marveled at the gems, "Those are the Royal Diameralds, there are no larger or purer, lord Betus was rumored to have brought everything needed for a proper wedding. It seems he has." Gently Tari raised an earring to closely examine it, then laid it back in the box, "but time grows short." Going to the bed Tari smoothed her hand over the silver white gown and matching train."

Rising with leaden feet, her soul filled with dread, Izadra went to stand before a large mirror where Tari could assist her in dressing. Numbly she allowed Tari to dress her, making the necessary movements in a deepening daze. Izadra stared into the mirror not recognizing the alien she saw standing in her reflection as herself.

"Your wedding gown was made of fine Tross silver, so pure it seems white. Each silken like thread was woven into fabric and then sewn into a gown." Tari explained, "It was designed for your grandmother," Tari smiled at Izadra, "another thing your great-uncle, lord Betus, brought with him."

Tari carefully picked-up the lace-train and began attaching it to the gown. "The train is made from a similar method." Tari concluded placing the Diamerald earrings in her ears.

Izadra was surprised by the perfect fit of the gown. Cut low in the front the Diamerald pendant accented the severity by hanging just above her cleavage, the back, cut even lower to her waist made her thankful for the train. Attaching at the shoulders it helped hold up the front, until the train was added the top was supported only by thin straps crossed in the back. A simple gold band had been placed among the artfully styled tresses of her hair and Tari gently lifted the auburn mass and placed it inside the large hood that was part of the train, Tari then drew the hood over Izadra's head.

"We are ready Your Highness." Tari said softly.

"How much time do we have before we must go?" Izadra inquired, still astonished at the stranger staring back from the reflection.

"We should go now." Tari answered, thankful Izadra's toilet had taken just enough time not to allow any pensive moments before the ceremony.

Unsure, Izadra turned from the mirror to glance at Tari, "Very well, I am as ready as I will ever be." she walked with Tari from the room through the living room, the formal receiving room she had come through when she had arrived and passed the large guarded doors.

Stopping, Tari painstakingly folded the train of Izadra's gown over her arm, then turned to one guard, "Have the halls cleared between here and the hangar where the ceremonies will take place."

"Lieutenant Kara," Izadra questioned, "if that is for my benefit, please don't. Their curiosity does not bother me."

"Very well, Your Highness." Tari conceded and they began the walk to the larger hanger that had been renovated temporarily to serve as an enormous chapel.

They received few curious stares. Upon Izadra's appearance the crew either saluted or bowed leaving an un-obstructed isle down the spacious corridors.

"First," Tari told her as they neared the place, "We will go inside a smaller room where only lord Betus, lord Kron and His Highness are waiting. Here lord Betus will accept you as a member of your grandmother's family officially then the wedding will take place. Most of the crew will be in attendance, only a skeleton crew and two patrol squads will be on duty."

Ahead Izadra saw the entrance to the room it was unmistakable with the two Royal bodyguards at the door. Stopping several feet from the door, Izadra's feet felt glued to the floor.

"My Lady," Tari said gently, "they wait." still Izadra did not move, "Your Highness," Tari said a little more firmly, "His Highness expects you to be prompt."

Slowly Izadra turned to look sadly at Tari, "I know." she said slightly above a whisper. With sheer strength of will Izadra walked toward the doors, her face pale despite the cosmetics she wore.

At their approach the two guards drew to attention and opened the doors. Izadra drew a deep breath and bravely walked through, stopping just inside as Tari closed the doors behind them.

It was as Tari had said it would be, a small room where Betus, Kron and At'r waited. Remembering her promise, Izadra walked calmly the short distance to where At'r sat and sank before him in a deep curtsey as Loka had instructed her. Turning to Betus, Izadra knelt on the white satin cushion placed on the step below where Betus stood.

In a low chanting voice lord Betus prayed over Izadra's head. He bent and taking her Royal necklace in one hand touched the Diameriald on the medallion with a larger one that seemed to glow.

Izadra felt strange, she swayed slightly as she became a prisoner of lord Betus' chant. Again he touched the Diamerald this time even the jeweled necklace and earrings At'r had given her began to glow. Izadra ceased to sway her head down resting on her chest, her breathing shallow and slow.

At'r stared, amazed at the reaction Izadra was having, the glow from the energized Diamerald giving her a spiritual appearance. Again Betus began to chant and Izadra joined the chant saying words in a language she had been taught as a child and did not recall until she was entranced, then in the language of her ancestors she declared.

"I am she, the heir," Izadra was silent again, as if she were asleep.

At'r rose from where he sat to go to Izadra, gently he cradled her head against his arm, "Izadra," he called her softly, "wake up."

Izadra's eyes opened slowly at his command, she looked around at the faces looking down at her, "Did I faint?" she asked, confused.

"No, my Lady." Betus answered, "Do you remember nothing?"

Izadra thought for a moment, "Only the Diameralds glowing," she paused, then whispered, "I was lost in their glow…words, words I could not understand."

"Do you think you can stand?" At'r asked.

"Yes." Izadra replied and At'r helped her to her feet.

"Can you continue with the ceremonies?" he questioned further.

Izadra turned to face At'r, "Yes, Your Highness, if I must." she answered him defiantly.

At'r turned to Tari, "Please assist Lady Izadra, I will have you signaled when to enter the hangar." At'r left followed by Betus and Kron.

As soon as the door had closed Izadra turned to Tari, "What happened to me?" she asked wishing she could sit down, but the elaborate gown and train would not allow it.

"My Lady, you chanted with lord Betus, in the old language, then you said, 'I am she, the heir.'"

"How long do you think before I am called?" she asked absently. 'Could it be true?' she asked herself, 'No, it was impossible.' she refused to contemplate the possibility.

"Only moments my Lady," Tari answered straightening Izadra's dress as she stood and replacing the lace hood that had fallen from her head.

Izadra jumped when the door opened, through it came one of At'r's personal bodyguards. His face impassive, his manner formal, he bowed before Izadra informing her "His Highness awaits."

"Thank you." Izadra managed to say and smile at the messenger, dismissing him.

After the guard had gone, Izadra and Tari walked from the room stopping in the hall before entering the renovated hangar allowing Tari to arrange the long tail of Izadra's train to flow behind her. Checking Izadra's appearance before she entered the hangar, Tari noted her solemn expression.

"Remember Izadra," she whispered, "brides are 'happy.'"

"Thank you Tari." Izadra drew a deep nervous breath, a serenely happy expression spreading over her face.

Before them the huge hangar doors swung open. Lieutenant Kara stepped through them before Izadra, and accepted a large bouquet of cascading red roses handed to her by one of Commander Kron's aids. Tari presented them to an amazed Izadra who looked questioningly to Tari.

"Commander Kron's compliments, milady." the aid explained. "He acquired those on his latest reconnaissance trip to Earth."

Pleasantly surprised by the gift, Izadra smiled and smelling the vibrant buds felt strengthened by their fragrance.

Izadra turned, scanning the crowded hangar. Someone had gone to a great deal of effort decorating the hangar. Exotic multi-colored flowers graced the white, and emerald green hangings that hid the girders of the ship, curtains of the same colors lined the walls.

Each side of the wide center isle was lined with the ship's crew not on duty, from the lowest ranks to the highest toward the front. The center isle was carpeted in white and at the end, with the grandeur of space behind him waited Emperor At'r.

Unseen trumpets blared, followed by Tari's clear, steady voice ringing out over the hushed assembly announcing Izadra's arrival.

"Behold, the Royal Heir of the House of Metem and of Empress Iza. Her Royal Highness, Catherine Izadra Kirk Metem."

Careful to maintain her composure, Izadra's heart pounded as she forced herself to take the first step, proceeding as she had been instructed at a slow pace, doubting she could have moved faster toward her decreed fate had it been required. Inwardly she was in turmoil, every instinct screaming for her to turn and run. She felt like the virgin sacrifice at a pagan mass. With dread in her soul, but a blithe smile on her lips to mask all else, Izadra covered the distance too quickly. At the foot of the raised dais where At'r stood, Izadra stopped and for the second time in her life knelt before the Emperor of Creasion. A moment passed and At'r offered her his hand for support as she rose. Looking up, Izadra accepted his hand without apparent reluctance.

At'r also had dressed in silver and white. Fitting his powerful body closely the tailored jacket and tight pants only hinted at the virile form beneath them. A kingly cape of heavy rich emerald fabric draped his shoulders and had been folded back held at each shoulder with Diamerald Ankh-Angles. He was omnipotent over his willing subjects and over a much less willing Izadra, radiantly she could feel his will draining her own.

Betus, Tari and Kron joined them taking their places around the couple. Betus before them, Kron beside At'r and Tari next to Izadra. Betus motioned them to kneel. He began to pray.

The prayer finished all rose, At'r still holding Izadra's hand. Izadra looked up and as she did the ship's course turned so Earth was visible behind Betus in the open end of the hangar. Izadra froze, captivated, At'r supporting her. At'r swore almost silently, then turned to Commander Kron.

"I gave very explicate orders that this was to be avoided, I do not wish to up-set Her Highness any further."

"You did sire, shall I check it out?"

"Later!" At'r turned to Betus, "Continue!" then to Izadra he leaned close, amazed to see a tear slip from the corner of her eye. "Izadra, remember your promise."

She turned solemnly to At'r, the hood covering her face so the audience and the cameras did not see, "As long as I live, I will not forget it!" then the slight smile returned, her face a mask of serenity, only her trembling hands betrayed her.

Izadra completed the ceremonies in like manner, blushing before the assembled company when At'r kissed her at the end of the ritual. It amused Izadra that the marriage ceremony here was sealed by the same symbol as on Earth.

Turning with At'r to face the company, Izadra's smile rivaled his. Looking down at her, At'r decided she was a convincing actress. Pleased with Izadra's performance, At'r led her from the room as the gathered party bowed at their passage. Once outside her smile faded and she turned to At'r.

Bowing slightly, Izadra asked, "Was I a convincing 'happy' bride?" She could restrain herself no longer, even her fear of At'r did not equal the frustration she was feeling.

Seeing the coming storm, At'r drew her alone inside the small room where they had met before the wedding ceremony.

"You ask far too much, Your Highness." she said raising her chin a notch.

"I will yet ask, and get more from you, the evening is not over and your promise not yet filled." he had moved closer to her.

"You refer to our wedding night, do you also threaten to drug me if I do not submit to you then?" her temper flared hotter.

Now he stared down into her flushed face, "I refer to the coming banquet we will attend, as for our wedding night," he pulled her to him suddenly, the flames in his green eyes scorching her determination not to allow him passage into her soul. Confirming his control over her, At'r kissed her fiercely commanding her breathing and her body if not her mind. Releasing her suddenly, he laughed cruelly "I do not think drugs will be necessary." At'r watched her for a moment, "Now if you are ready, we will go to dinner and you will eat." He saw the defiance in Izadra's eyes, "In fact you will have a hearty appetite, I do not want you fainting in bed this evening." Opening the door he motioned her to precede him from the room. Dutifully, Izadra obeyed.

Attended by only a small group of officers the banquet was lush; and though the remainder of the ship's crew did not attend the Emperor's table, there was wide celebrating through out the ship. Izadra managed only a few mouth fulls, constantly aware of At'r's eyes on her diminished her appetite. As Izadra had done several times in the past few days, she ate in a daze, a pleasant smile on her composed features and an occasional polite comment to a friendly neighbor. Tari, who had been seated next to Izadra touched her hand slightly and leaned to whisper in her ear.

"My Lady, it is time for us to retire." Tari informed Izadra after a pre-decided signal from At'r.

Izadra looked back to At'r on her left and he stood drawing everyone's attention. "Lady Izadra is retiring for the evening." a muffled chuckle passed through the dinner guests, "anyone wishing to do the same is excused."

Commander Kron rose and raising his glass of green wine declared, "A salute," and waited while the others raised their glasses, "To Emperor At'r and Lady Izadra," he smiled, "and to their children." While all others drank, Izadra's glass remained filled and went unnoticed by all but At'r. Curtseying slightly before At'r, Izadra left with Tari in close attendance.

CHAPTER 9

*I*zadra's and Tari's trek back to the Royal Chambers was tedious and Izadra was forced to re-adopt her smile for the crewmembers she passed. They were happy, joyous to see their beloved sovereign married, and in Izadra they saw a prophecy fulfilled. With the promise of a victorious peace and safety from their old enemy the Zerion, the crew was jubilant. Most, having heard the story of how Izadra wounded the Zerion Captain had accepted her with respect immediately and were even more won with her smile which, quickly became more genuine with each person she met. Had it not been for Izadra's destination she could have been more taken with their enthusiasm. Izadra had the impression they were openhearted people until crossed, as the Zerion had done so many times, then they became fierce warriors. All too soon her guarded chamber doors appeared draining the good feeling the celebrating crew had given her. Going through the double doors her smile faded with her enthusiasm.

After bathing, Tari assisted Izadra in dressing. Like a cloud, the sheer white nightgown drifted down covering Izadra but hiding nothing. Tari tied the two ribbons on each shoulder and held the matching silken robe for Izadra to slip on. Aside from the heavy gold embroidering across the shoulders the robe was as sheer as the gown. Together they did little more than tease the imagination about the body of the wearer. Izadra found the peignoir far too gauzy but knew it was better than nothing. Tari brought a small stool for Izadra to sit on before the full length mirror while she undressed her long auburn hair, then brushing it until her tresses flowed in one shinning body down her back.

Finally Tari set about placing away Izadra's gown while Izadra paced nervously around the spacious bedroom. Absently she picked up the still open jewel box lying on the bed.

Captivated by the luminous intensity of the Diameralds she was absorbed, staring deep inside the green infinity of the tear drop pendant. It seemed to draw her inside, beckoning her to venture further, but the intensity was too great, shaking herself mentally she laid the necklace back in the box, careful to close the lid.

"I must leave you now," Tari told Izadra breaking the silence, "His Highness will be here anon."

"Thank you Tari, with out you I would not have gotten through it."

"It was my honor and my pleasure Izadra, if you need me call Roberta, she will know where to find me." Tari referred to the mechanical servant always present.

"Thank you again Tari." Izadra smiled slightly as Tari went back to her military duties.

Izadra stood alone in the bedroom, turning she caught sight of her reflection in the mirror, embarrassed, she wished she dared change. Unable to bare her reflection any longer Izadra helped herself to a glass of At'r's favorite brandy, coughing after she sipped it. The mystery of space drew her to the windows she wanted to loose herself in the vastness. Contemplating At'r's arrival Izadra remembered the Zerion Captain's arrival in the dingy, dimly lit cabin and she remembered the knife she had slipped up her sleeve to defend herself. The weapon would have been useless to her now. At'r was far more threatening and would not be so easily deceived. Numbly Izadra leaned her head against the glass letting the coolness soothe her flushed face and sipped the brandy, allowing the liquor to soothe her nerves somewhat.

Izadra's wait was not a long one, draining her glass she sat the short stemmed crystal snifter on the desk as the door hissed open. At'r strode in, his presence filling every corner of the room, his eyes held Izadra's for a brief moment then swept over her leaving her feeling even more naked despite the negligee'. Izadra's heart pounded in her throat as he covered the distance between them, she stood frozen, rooted to the spot, his unwilling captive. At'r placed his hands on her shoulders, again taking possession of her eyes. A gentle push and the silk robe slid away causing a chill to run through her as the garment fell to the floor.

"You are beautiful." At'r informed Izadra drawing her into his embrace, his touch on her bare flesh causing her knees to almost buckle as his lips covered hers. At'r's passion seemed to consume her, stealing all rebellion, his hands molding her body to his. But when he released her, Izadra drew away fearful of the fire in his eyes. Tonight she knew she would not escape him, or his desires.

At'r drew Izadra back encircling her in his arms, but Izadra could no longer control her fear. Panicked, she struggled against his powerful hold. "No!" she said several times and managed to wrestle herself free of his grasp. Running to the automatic door, that did not open, Izadra bumped the closed portal abruptly. A little dazed she did not resist when At'r swept her up in his arms. With an amused smile tugging at the corners of his usually serious eyes he lifted Izadra from her feet and carried her to his bed.

Laying her gently on the bed he considered Izadra for a moment before slipping out of the heavy green robe he wore. A red blush covered Izadra's face, never had she seen a man aroused before. At'r sat on the bed.

"Where would you run?" he asked, amusement in his voice.

Izadra did not answer, she had not contemplated where she was going, she had only run, unable to fight her primal reaction to fear any longer.

Leaning forward At'r kissed her shoulder, Izadra was certain from the heat he had branded her. At'r stretched his muscular body out, lying next to his tense bride. Resting his head on his hand, propped up by his elbow, he studied her face, watching her eyes while his free hand smoothed over her breast, feeling their heat through the thin gown. At'r pulled the ties on the gown and pushed the silk out of his way. Izadra closed her eyes, her hands clutching the bed covers tightly. Slowly At'r kissed her, gently touching Izadra's face, running his fingers through her luscious long hair.

Izadra placed her hands against his shoulders and pushed, managing to end his amorous embrace. Gasping for air she tried to roll away from him but At'r stopped her. Izadra lay beneath him on her stomach.

With one sweep of his strong hand he gently pulled her long hair away from Izadra's slender neck. Where, much to Izadra's dismay, At'r placed several heated kisses and nibbling lightly on her ear lobes sent her blood racing through her veins at a dangerous rate. At'r's weight successfully held Izadra to the mattress leaving his hand free to explore her supple body. Quickly At'r discovered the back of her neck was vulnerable to his kisses, as well as her back and the backside of her knees. With a gentle hand he caressed her firm buttocks and her long shapely legs, though Izadra kept them tightly together.

Sorry now she had rolled onto her stomach, confused and bewildered at her body's response to At'r's touch, Izadra felt tears sting her eyes as she fought to control the wild frustration she felt.

Something was happening to her, the nature of the sensations overwhelming. At'r sensing her heightening ardor rolled her onto her back, amazed at the flames of passion he saw growing in hazel eyes. His desire for her quickly becoming more than he could control.

"I have wanted you since Kron brought you to me." At'r whispered to Izadra, his voice husky. "Now you are mine." his lips took hers possessively, stilling the meager protests Izadra made by drawing both her arms above her head, holding them there with one of his huge hands, leaving her defenseless beneath him.

Trembling, not from cold, but from the emotions assailing her, she kept her legs together yielding only when At'r wedged his knee between them. Once parted, he rested one leg between Izadra's legs. With one slow caress At'r ran his hand along the inside of her thighs and up over her body to cup a full breast gently in his hand, kissing and sucking the nipple until it hardened, releasing her hands he cupped the other breast giving it like attention. With his weight full on her, Izadra could feel his manhood pressing against her. She could not doubt his passion for her. In At'r's power completely now Izadra was unable to resist his burning kisses on body.

At'r's hands now freely explored her tortured body and through a mist of rapture Izadra remembered her lack of body hair as he smoothed a hand between her legs. A moan escaped her lips and Izadra covered herself with her now free hands. Tenderly At'r removed her hands and held them at her sides while placing several light kisses on the sensitive area. At'r lingered, exploring her lovingly, his tongue sending waves of ecstasy pouring through her throbbing body.

"Ah, my beautiful captive." At'r said moving to look at her face, "I have kindled the smoldering fire you've kept locked away and hidden." he smiled possessively, noting her quickened breathing, he covered her trembling lips with his.

Izadra reeled, consumed in the heat of their lovemaking. At'r released her hands again, his lips drugging any resistance from her, Izadra knew she was defeated, she could not fight the power of the passion he mercilessly aroused in her. Knowing she had surrendered to him, At'r drew back to gaze down into Izadra's passionate eyes. Izadra felt his hardness between her legs followed by sudden pressure, then pain. Fearfully she pulled away, but At'r drew her gently back under him. Hugging her close he kissed her, swiftly pushing through the barrier of her virginity, lying still for a moment to whisper softly to Izadra. Her hesitance At'r soothed away by his kisses and caresses, and soon Izadra once again found herself in a whirling mist of pleasure that mounted to become a tempest of sweet ecstasy leaving them both drained.

But as the euphoric mist faded, Izadra drew away to the far side of the their massive bed pulling the satin white sheet over her naked body. She was appalled with herself, hating At'r for his control over her body. Izadra swore to herself, she would never allow him to control her mind and if it were possible, she would not succumb to him carnally again.

After several minutes Izadra heard the sound of At'r's even breathing as he slept. Quietly she stole from the bed and going through the bath entered the whirlpool. Izadra sank gingerly down in the hot swirling water allowing it to soothe away the strange turmoil she was feeling. Rolling over she flipped her hair over her head to land on a towel she had placed on the tile, then laying her head on her folded arms she let the rest of her body float in the now comfortably warm water. How long she lounged there she did not know, but after a time Izadra began to feel eyes on her, the feeling persisted and she looked up parting her hair to see. At'r stood watching her, a strange expression on his face.

"How is the water?" At'r asked casually stepping down in the bubbling water with her.

Izadra did not move other than to place her head down again resting on her folded arms, hoping At'r would not disturb her, his presence was disturbing enough.

Turning slightly she saw At'r relaxing in the water, his eyes closed and a peaceful expression covering his handsome face. Seizing the opportunity Izadra quickly got out of the bath, and wrapping herself in a towel started for the bedroom, but was halted by At'r's voice.

"Pour me a glass of brandy, will you Izadra, and help yourself if you wish." although he asked, it was a command and mechanically she complied, stopping only to slip on a heavy bathrobe. Returning to the whirlpool her hands full he again stopped her, "Bring my robe Iza." he abbreviated her name.

Setting the two glasses on a small table next to the pool, Izadra gave At'r his robe as he emerged from the water naked, she quickly turned back to the two drinks, handing At'r to him only after he finished tying the belt to his robe. Leaving him, Izadra went back to the living room.

At'r followed her, "Izadra we are going back to bed as soon as we finish our drinks, you are accompanying me on a flight in a few hours and we both need to be well rested." He saluted her stiffly with the remainder of his brandy and downed it.

Izadra watched him as coolly as she could under his warm appraisal, the evening's earlier events having only served to whet his appetite. She was in no hurry to gulp the warm liquid and she was in even less of a hurry to return to his bed. Izadra sipped her small amount of brandy.

With the flames in his green eyes burning brighter he approached Izadra, she took another slow sip. Delicately she tipped the glass and At'r placed a commanding finger on the bottom forcing the glass back further, either Izadra drank all the liqueur or it would run down her chin. Caught off guard she still managed to drink most of it, leaving only a small amount to trickle down her chin.

Looking up at At'r with tearing eyes from the heat of the liqueur she coughed and wiped her chin with the back of her hand, giving him a murderous glare.

Taking her other hand he drew her toward him laughing at her outrage, and holding her close kissed her intoxicating lips.

"Come to bed, wife." At'r said huskily, pulling her toward the bedroom. Izadra knew his iron grasp on her wrist was unbreakable, dreadfully she followed him to bed.

With her back to him Izadra dropped her robe and quickly slid under the covers on the far side of the enormous bed they now shared. Lying on her side with her back to him Izadra felt her heart stop, if only for a moment when At'r smoothed his hand over her hip.

"Come to me, Izadra." he commanded softly, but she could not move, "Izadra!" his voice was compelling, slowly she turned toward him. Drawing her closer until her head rested on his shoulder, At'r looked down into her eyes.

From his body heat and the way he looked at her, Izadra knew he wanted her again. She shuddered, wishing her pride would allow her to plead with him, but she knew he would not spare her. His lips covered Izadra's smothering her "No!" protest, his kiss more urgent, different from before, more compelling.

Astounded, Izadra felt her own body heat rise to his and though she hated herself for it, and At'r for making her feel so, Izadra could not fight the growing passion that guided her arms around his neck, hugging him nearer. Fire traced his lips in an exquisite trail down her throat to her breasts his hands caressed her legs, still hesitant to open, fearful of the previous pain. At'r's lips moved still lower over her slender waist and belly, his hands putting persuading pressure on tight muscles until her legs were open to his access and pleasure. Loving her, his kisses answering her moans, encouraging her pleasure taking them both to a dimension of contentment neither had known before. Izadra fell asleep in At'r's arms, kissing her forehead he slept too.

CHAPTER 10

$\mathcal{E}$ ight hours later a low toned beep woke At'r, Izadra stirred next to him, but did not wake. At'r quieted the alarm. Sliding out of bed he stared down at his sleeping wife, remembering the feel of her body beneath his. He lightly ran his hand over her curves and considered waking her with his kisses. But even in the low light of the sleep chamber he could see the stains of her lost virginity on the sheets, reminding him how new and tender she was to lovemaking. Turning away he went to the shower to clear his head, then dressed and made his way to the bridge where Kron awaited him.

So busy was the crew personnel only Kron noticed the Emperor's entrance. Saluting At'r he started to alert his crew but At'r stopped him.

"They are all engrossed in their task, leave them. Is my ship ready?"

"Yes my Lord, as you have ordered, still, sire, I'd rather you would not go we have not thoroughly checked all the planets in this system, the Zerion may yet have a small base among them."

"Rest easy Kron, I will not take chances where Izadra is concerned, you know my trek plan, send a patrol out before we leave and have them scan the area, but I want no other ships around, I'd like a little time alone with Izadra."

"Very well sire, as you wish it." Kron conceded.

"Have you learned anything new from any of the recent recon reports?"

"No, it is as expected, but I am sure they will be sending the military staff soon, after my mission to their largest base I will have a better idea of their time table, we may need to push forward a day."

"If we must, then we will do so, I do not want the Zerion controlling this system." At'r stayed a while longer discussing the Zerion.

Still sleeping Izadra stretched, enjoying the feel of the silk sheets and resisting waking, but her mind would not let her sleep, the events of the hours past brought her fully awake. She cautiously opened her eyes and seeing the room vacant sat up pushing the covers back, stopping to stare at the small amount of blood spotted on the white silk. Tangible proof of At'r's desire for her and of the passion they had shared. A paradoxical bolt of electricity flashed through her at the vivid memory. Izadra's face burned in shame remembering how he had made her feel and the power he had to control her.

'Somehow,' Izadra vowed to herself, 'that must not happen again.' At'r's power over her seemed insurmountable. Only her ability to keep him from entering her mind kept At'r from having full control. Izadra knew she could not withstand him much longer. Escape from this alien Lord seemed her only chance. First Izadra had to find out where Kron's ship was hangered, and what time he would be leaving. But the difficult part would be to contrive a means to get on the craft without detection and without her absence being discovered until she was on Earth, hopefully safe and away from the Creasions. Roberta joined Izadra as she sat pondering her seemingly unsolvable problems.

"Good morning my Lady." it droned, "I have your clothing and His Highness asks me to inform you to dress quickly, he will breakfast with you in a forty-five minutes, then you will accompany him on an excursion of several planets in this system."

Taking the offered azure garment Izadra held it up at arm's length to examine it then laid it on the bed. "Roberta, I wish to order a few clothes of my own design, could I do that now?"

Roberta was silent for only a moment, "Yes."

"Do you report to His Highness what I order?"

"No."

"Good." Izadra thought, considering what she would need, and asked, "How long after I order will you be able to deliver?"

"Twenty-two minutes my Lady."

Izadra was pleased, "I need a pair of blue jeans, do you know what I am taking about?"

"Yes, the garments you were wearing upon your arrival."

"Can you reproduce them, and a shirt and denim jacket?"

"Yes, when do you wish them?"

"Later tonight, ah, when His Highness is not here, they are a, ah, surprise for him."

"As you wish it my Lady."

Going to the shower Izadra's mood was lighter, plans for her escape running through her imagination. Returning a few minutes later to step through the legs of the tight fitting uniform jumpsuit. It fit as if it were made for her, Izadra zipped it up and accepted the dark blue flight suite that she would wear later. Standing before the full-length mirror, Izadra had to admit the uniform looked good on, At'r had chosen well for her. She pressed the Velcro comfortably tight around the neck and paused to look at the Ankh-Angle on each shoulder. They did not signify rank, but Royalty. Sighing Izadra turned away from the mirror, going in search of the hairbrush she had used the night before, finding it where it had fallen under a chair near the bed. Brushing her hair as she went through the bathroom door, Izadra stopped before the vanity mirror and twisting her long hair pinned the coil underneath the hair at the nap of her neck. Laying the brush on the vanity, Izadra went back to the bedroom and sat on the sofa to pull on the matching uniform boots.

Roberta waited, standing silently as Izadra paced, nervous about seeing At'r after last evening's events and about where he was taking her. Izadra dared not hope it would be to Earth. Their breakfast appeared before At'r did but she knew he was close behind, hearing his voice in the living room she held her breath as he came in.

At'r strode in the room and across the expanse between them taking Izadra briskly in his arms, kissing her thoroughly.

"Come, let us eat, then we are off to tour a few of the planets in this system."

Izadra pushed herself away from him, glaring coldly back, determined not to allow him to gain more control of her. "Earth would not be one of the few, would it?" she questioned bravely.

"No. We need information on the unpopulated planets, we already have more information on Earth than most of the planet's scientists. Come," he said taking her hand, "let us eat so we can get started." He ushered Izadra to the table.

Izadra was becoming more accustomed to the alien food and ate most of the generous portions she was given.

"I am happy to see your appetite has improved." At'r remarked casually, "It will be sometime before we return to have the evening meal. We are taking my private fighter. It is a newer design than the one you arrived in." he explained incidentally and Izadra could hear the pride in his voice. "You will need," he continued, "a better knowledge of space, and your first trip was not a good experience."

"No, I can not say it has been a good experience," Izadra agreed rather icily, "in truth, I could be satisfied with one more trip, to Earth and content to take no others."

"That is one trip you will never take, my dear." At'r told her firmly. Izadra smiled to herself thinking of her escape.

They finished their breakfast and At'r waited impassively as Izadra donned the fight suit. Zipping it up she found it to be a looser duplicate of her uniform. "I am ready," Izadra said finally.

"No, you are not." At'r told her, handing her the gold band she had worn in the ceremonies, "From now on, when you leave our chambers you will wear this." he watched Izadra in the mirror as she placed the band on her head. "Now you are ready, Lady Izadra." he took her hand and they left their chambers.

Izadra spoke little, trying hard to memorize every detail of the passage and each turn of the corridors, hoping it would assist in her escape.

It was an intricate path, unlike the trip she had taken with Tari to her wedding. Twice they were in elevators.

Finally coming to a set of double doors, Izadra knew they were entering the upper level of the hangar area. The doors slid open to an area larger than two football fields, so much open area within a ship amazed her. When Izadra had arrived on Tos-hawk One the hanger had been empty, but now was filled with various types of crafts and still was not crowded. Some of them smaller than the fighter Kron had rescued her in, some five times that size. Izadra was impressed. As they entered the noisy hanger a hush fell on the scope of people about their important tasks, and in one voice of both male and female, cried, "Salute!" then waited for their monarchs to release them.

"Be at ease." At'r said in a loud voice that carried the length of the great hanger, again the hanger turned into a noisy mass of crew persons working toward one goal, destruction of Zerion's on Earth. Still suspicious of these aliens, Izadra was not totally convinced they did not want to stop the Zerions just so they could control the Earth. The thought had nagged her since her rescue from the Zerions. Now seeing the force the Creasions could muster she knew if they wanted the Earth they could take it with one ship like this one, and Izadra knew At'r had commissioned three others with the next one almost complete and battle worthy.

Mechanically Izadra had followed At'r while taking in the magnitude of this hanger and when he stopped before his ship to speak with Commander Kron, who awaited them, she came close to bumping into At'r. Fortunately Kron had bowed, not seeing her near collision or the scowl At'r flung her way. Blushing slightly Izadra murmured her apology as Kron rose.

"Your ship is ready and waiting sire." Kron informed his Lord, "I have sent a patrol out. They will sweep the area approximately thirty minutes prior to your ship entering the area you have scheduled, I doubt you will see them."

Izadra listened closely, getting the impression Kron would rather they did not go alone. Wondering at At'r's desire for privacy, she kept silent as they discussed flight plans. While Izadra and At'r were exploring the near-by planets, Commander Kron accompanied by a small contingent would case the last Zerion base in Russia. Tomorrow they would do the same at the last and largest base outside Washington D.C. It was on that reconnaissance mission that Izadra would attempt to stow-away and escape from At'r.

"We should return before you do Commander," At'r was saying, "If you run into trouble you can signal us on my private channel. Until later," At'r returned Kron's parting salute. Turning to Izadra he bade her go up the ladder to the ship's cockpit.

Without reluctance Izadra entered the ship, followed closely by At'r. She was amazed at the comfort in the cabin cockpit of the small ship. Two large couch chairs sat slightly back from the controls. Behind them was a small bench underneath it was storage compartments. The whole area was upholstered in dark blue and slightly padded. Smaller than Commander Kron's fighter but shaped much the same, At'r explained it was the fastest in his fleet and carried the firepower of a full sized fighter. At'r directed Izadra to the couch on his right, taking the pilot's position himself.

Handing Izadra a helmet, At'r placed his on his head. Following his example Izadra did the same, finding the light helmet comfortable and well fitting. Through small speakers inside the helmet Izadra could hear the traffic controllers monitoring and directing the many flights, not only from this hanger, but also from the other three as well. Izadra watched as At'r began to activate the many systems of the craft in order to depart.

"Is there a certain sequence that you energize the ship's system?" Izadra asked, drawing At'r's attention away slightly.

"Yes," he answered, but did not offer any other information. "Have you flown," he pause, "you call them planes?"

"Yes, planes, and yes, I have piloted a few of the smaller types." Izadra told him.

"Good." At'r responded before addressing the traffic controllers for flight clearance, the voice answered immediately.

"Royal Star One are you able to await departure until present traffic cycle is complete, or do you require immediate launch?" the young female voice asked.

"Control, we can wait for the next cycle, clear all military missions through first. Royal Star One standing by." At'r responded turning to Izadra, "Since we have a little time, and since you are curious, I will explain how the ship functions." As he explained the ship's workings to Izadra, Commander Kron was instructing the traffic controller who would direct the launch of the Emperor's ship.

"How long will His Highness' ship be on hold?" Kron asked her."About eight minutes, sir." she explained.

"Delay it to ten minutes, and alert Lieutenant Kara's squad, have her report to me directly, in two minutes." While the communication was sent to Lieutenant Kara, Commander Kron went over his pending mission for the third time. By far this recon mission deep inside of Russia was trickier than the one inside the United States, even so close to the nation's capital city.

Momentarily Lieutenant Kara joined him, she had been close by when the summons came. Commander Kron had called her away from a pre-lift-off checklist of her ship with the other two in the squad she commanded. Tari now stood before Kron and saluted him.

"Lieutenant Kara, reporting sir."

"Lieutenant, have your patrol ready in ten minutes. I want you to fly a security patrol for His Highness. He will not know you are behind him, so stay just outside his scanner range, if you should slip inside his range, you will explain you were slightly off course. Lord At'r is taking Lady Izadra on a fact gathering mission and orientating her to space a little more. He wants privacy, but I do not feel it is safe. I have sent a patrol ahead, but I want you as back up. Use your new long-range detector and the masking device to keep your presence as low keyed as possible. Questions?"

"One sir. If we encounter Zerions, what course of action should we take?"

"If His Highness can safely hand them, keep your distance. If you see them first, shoot to kill. If Lord At'r needs any kind of assistance, do so at once."

"Very well, sir, we leave in less than ten minutes." Saluting once again, she left. Kron admired the way Tari's uniform contoured her figure.

Reaching her ship Tari looked at the other two pilots in her command, "Is the check list complete?"

"Yes." they answered together. Tari watched Lord At'r's ship beginning to move, and turning back to her subordinates, explained their new mission.

Interrupting At'r's explanation of the deflector device the female controller's voice told them they were now cleared to leave. Buckling their seat belts with auto-locks, At'r turned to Izadra. Seeing she was ready, he turned back to the communication console and acknowledged their readiness.

"Be prepared for acceleration when we clear the hanger." At'r informed her, "We must clear the ship as quickly as possible."

Izadra waited breathlessly, and as the engines hummed louder a light floating sensation assaulted her, the craft hovering just inches above the hanger floor. She watched At'r push the control ball gently forward easing the ship in the same direction following the red stripe beneath them. At'r guided the ship expertly turning the ship as the red stripe turned. Beneath his left hand was a similar ball, once activated this controlled the ship's defenses.

Ahead, Izadra saw the red line stopped at a track which At'r locked the ship in. The female voice announced "Launch in ten seconds." she counted down the launch to "one!" Despite its small size the ship reached sub-light velocity in seconds after launching from the mother ship.

At'r turned the ship over to the navigational computer and directed his attention to Izadra. She had been quiet all through the launch and acceleration procedures, not from fear, but from curiosity.

"How fare you?" At'r questioned her, concerned.

"Well, thank you." Izadra answered, trying hard to hide her enthusiasm.

"Our first destination is the planet Mars." At'r told her, "We will make two passes on each of the planet's moons, four on the planet itself." With a light beep the computer signaled a course change putting the craft on course for Mars.

On board Tos-hawk One, Lieutenant Kara and her patrol launched, careful to stay well behind her Emperor and his new wife.

CHAPTER 11

Stx sat in his office deep inside the largest Zerion base on Earth. Construction was now complete and his labor almost finished. Concealed in a drained mountain lake construction of this base had been much easier than the constantly interrupted Rocky Mountain base. In one night they had pumped the water from the lake into a taker ship. Construction of the hull had been completed the following night, the last two nights had seen the inside work completed and water drained back to fill the lake to a depth of ten feet providing a false cover.

With all systems checked out, Stx's remaining task was to wait for the military contingent to arrive. As of this morning, moon communications still did not know when that would be. With all bases in readiness the hierarchy had become very secretive about when the fleet would arrive.

Another matter came to mind, since Captain Quar had left, Stx had not heard from him, normally Quar would notify Stx of his safe arrival. Stx had questioned the moon base communications crew and they had not been notified of his arrival either. Stx was uneasy, and had been since Quar had left the night that they took the Earth girl captive. Something about her worried Stx, but he could not determine just what it was.

Stx switched on the desk computer and began feeding it seemingly unrelated facts.

First, Quar's failure to report his safe arrival; second, the sudden drop in communications with the central communications base on Earth's moon; third, the two incidents at Flaming Gorge base in the Rockies. He waited for the mechanical brain to reach a conclusion, which it did not do.

Still his intuition told him something was not right. He called his secretary.

"Isn't there a small shuttle going to Zerion tonight?" Stx asked the man.

"Yes sir."

"Have the pilot brought to me at once." Stx ordered and several minutes later the pilot appeared before him and saluted. "You will pilot the last of the construction shuttles home tonight?"

"Yes sir." the young Zerion pilot answered.

"I wish you take a different route, and when you reach Zerion I want a message from you. I want to know if Captain Quar arrived."

"As you wish sir. What is the new course?" he asked and Stx explained, instead of going by the moon then through the asteroid belt, Stx told him to cross the belt without going directly by the moon then to cut back to the normal course. He could not explain why, but Stx felt the moon base had somehow been compromised. If he was wrong there would be little time lost by having his man going a different way. If Stx was right in his fears and this man got through to Zerion to find Captain Quar had not arrived then the base was suspect. Dismissing the pilot he sighed, at best it was a long shot, but Stx would still send a four—fighter escort with them.

As Izadra and At'r neared Mars it grew from the tiny speck Izadra had watched as a child on Earth to become the luminous red-orange globe dominating the front windows of the fighter. Unlike Earth, no clouds shielded the planet from the intense white light of the sun. At'r established their first orbital pass high above the planet with the next two gradually lower, the third only two hundred feet off the planet's dry, lifeless surface. Passing over the surface at this low altitude, At'r slowed their air speed. Below them Izadra spotted an old explorer craft marooned forever, spent and dead. A massive pile of expensive camera and automated soil sampling equipment now standing only as a reminder of man's intrusion.

At'r noticing her interest turned and flew back to the spot where the probe had landed, assuming a lower altitude hovering over it, allowing Izadra a closer look.

"One of Earth's earlier probes?" At'r asked.

"Yes," was all Izadra said, her eyes becoming transfixed on the small flag on the probes side, "The United States, to be exact." she looked to At'r, "my country's probe."

"I grow weary reminding you—you are Creasion!"

"I was born there, I will always be an American!" Izadra said with pride and turned away once again watching the Martian landscape. Within moments At'r rocketed away from the planet to orbit the moons.

"There seems to be the beginnings of one cell life on Mars, did your scientists know?" At'r asked.

"They are just beginning to find out." Izadra answered.

Leaving Mars rapidly behind they neared the asteroid belt between Mars and Jupiter.

"This asteroid belt is calm compared to the one separating Creasion from Zerion." At'r explained, "A phenomenon, similar to lightning on Earth, occurs, but it is an electrical charge between huge boulders with positive and negative charges tumbling through limited space together. It can happen at any time and makes for a most interesting journey through that section. It was one such charge that caused the Zerion ship your grandmother was abducted on to become damaged and speed out of control to Earth." At'r slowed their ship to enter the belt.

At'r's skill as pilot was impressive. He flew between the hunks of rock and ice maneuvering with delicate care. Minutes sped by as Izadra watched him concentrate on their trajectory. Clearing the rocky belt was abrupt, the ship flew through one massive but porous asteroid and they found themselves in open space. Ahead Jupiter loomed like a glowing basketball and At'r altered course to orbit the planet.

Izadra jumped as a loud buzzer broke the silence, followed instantly by the normal green glow from the instrument panel being replaced by red. Inside her helmet a scrappy mechanical voice came through the tiny speakers.

"Alert!—Alert!—Zerion ship thirty dicons ahead." it droned through not only At'r's helmet, but also in Izadra's.

Busily pushing buttons, At'r prepared his fighter to do battle with the now visible Zerion ships. Seeing At'r's busy activity Izadra said nothing but watched hoping to learn and remember all she could.

Finally At'r spoke, "We should be safe." he assured Izadra, hoping she would not panic, "The blocking device is functioning and all our lazzers are fully charged." He turned to look at her, expecting to see some hint of alarm, but saw none.

"We must not allow them to get away, they could ruin our plans." his face was grim, he disliked killing, even Zerions, "Do you understand?"

"Yes," Izadra answered coolly "you are going to destroy them."

At'r turned back to the controls, thankful Izadra was of a stable nature. Taking aim on the center craft, At'r fired on the Zerion fighter but only produced light damage.

"At'r!" Izadra said sharply, and as he turned to look he saw why she had called him. Two more Zerion fighters were closing on them, having spotted the Creasion ship when she fired.

"By the Third Moon, they've trapped us!" At'r swore, firing directly at a closing Zerion fighter and exploding it as it fired. The

Zerion's salvo still found them and damaged their blocking system, now they were totally visible. At'r fired at the second fighter as it flashed by, allowing the shuttle and the damaged fighter to speed further away while At'r fought off the last two fighters.

"Do my controls work?" Izadra asked, pointing at the lit lazzer panel before her.

At'r considered her for a moment "Yes." and he quickly explained their workings. "Can you do it?" he asked firing and missing a closing fighter.

Izadra answered by firing at the second attacking escort fighter, she hit the craft in the tail section disabling his ship seconds later the craft exploded. At'r turned back to the three remaining vehicles to find three Creasion patrol fighters had appeared and were engaging the remainder of the Zerion excursion.

Moments later, the debris cleared, At'r was summoning the three Creasion ships, "Royal Star One to Creasion fighters. Identify yourselves."

"Sire, this is Lieutenant Kara and pilots Koes Tar, and Cz'r Tr-iy."

"Thank you for the assist, how did you happen to be in this sector?"

"We were off course, slightly, and picked up the explosions of the fighters on our outer range sensors." Tari explained, "we came as fast as we could."

"I commend you for your quick response, you may continue your patrol, Lady Izadra and I are returning to Tos-hawk One." With one fluid motion At'r turned the fighter and activated the light speed mode flashing into space, leaving the patrol behind and turning the stars to white blurs.

Grimly Stx received the report on the destruction of the shuttle and escort. It distressed him further to hear the final transmission from the doomed expedition confirming their attackers as Creasion, but even more astounding, a Royal Creasion fighter. Dutifully, Stx notified his Zerion superiors going through the Moon base communications center, his only link with home. As he had expected, the dispatch fell on disinterested ears, the Moon base informing him they would relay the message when possible, not telling him when that would be. They had not been impressed by his urgency. Stx was now convinced the Moon base was no longer under Zerion control.

CHAPTER 12

Nearing Tos-hawk One At'r began the braking procedure to sub-light speed before turning to Izadra. "We will land in five min-utes." he paused, turning back to the controls, "You handled yourself well back there." Again he was silent until the traffic controller sum-moned him.

"Welcome home Royal Star One, proceed to Alpha landing hanger and follow the green lighted track in, we have a team of technicians ready to repair your damage. They will take your craft from the dis-embarking bay, Controller Sena, out."

"Thank you Sena," At'r replied, "we will follow the green tract into hanger Alpha to the disembarking bay. At'r out."

Expertly hooking the damaged fighter in the track's locking sys-tem At'r engaged the computer controlled braking all Creasion ships were equipped with. Automatically the computer brought the ship to a safe stop before the landing bay disembarking ramp.

Here a white coverall clad technician waited, bowing low as the Royal couple descended from the ship he then took over the respon-sibility of the fighter and the necessary repairs. Moments later the fighter moved away from the bay and Kins hurried to his Lord. Stop-ping, he bowed and informed them of Commander Kron's eminent arrival.

"Good Kins, how successful was his mission?"

"All went as planned, sire."

"I am pleased to hear that, Kins. When Lieutenant Kara and her patrol return, inform them they are relieved of their duties for the evening and invite them to dine with Lady Izadra and myself, about two and half hours from now, also I wish Commander Kron and lord Betus to attend."

A loud buzzer interrupted their conversation followed by Commander Kron's arrival being announced, At'r turned to Izadra, "Do you wish to stay and welcome Kron? If not you may return to our chambers to prepare for dinner."

"I will stay Your Highness." She replied simply, watching a shuttle several time larger than a fighter enter the hanger. Ten crew persons left the ship before Commander Kron appeared at the door, the last out. Seeing At'r and Izadra waiting for him, he smiled broadly and saluted, then descended the stairs to stand before them.

"All has gone well and proceeds normally as planned, sire." Kron reported, "though the absence of military personnel worries me, they must be sending them soon, the construction Commanders are beginning to suspect their Moon base is not under their control, for all the good it will do them."

"I tend to agree with you Kron, we had a little encounter with a Zerion construction craft and a fighter escort of four. It seems they were sending their return craft another way." At'r said watching the incredulous look on Kron's face. "Do not concern yourself Kron, what Lady Izadra and I could not handle, three of your officers, slightly 'off course', did." At'r raised his voice, he knew Kron had assigned the three to follow them and he was thankful for such a close friend.

"Tell me, sire, what happened."

"I will tell you at dinner. I will also want an updated report on Zerion's Earth activities and finalized plans for the bases destruction day after tomorrow."

"I will have all ready when I come to dinner." Kron told him.

"Excuse me Your Highness." Izadra interrupted, "I would go to our chambers, if you will be much longer."

"Not much longer, milady, but go if you wish." At'r told her, "Can you find your way back?"

"Thank you, yes milord." She turned to Kron, "And thank you Commander for the roses you acquired for me yesterday." Izadra smiled at him and Kron bowed slightly, pleased she had remembered.

Izadra followed a group of crew persons through the hanger door, watching them as closely as she dared. She had hoped to remain inconspicuous but almost immediately her presence was noticed. Their jovial banter stopped and the group respectfully bowed.

Disturbed by their display Izadra hurriedly released them, "Please, be at ease." she said simply.

"Thank you." said the highest-ranking crewmember present. "We are honored Your Highness. Is there any way we can be of service?" The young Lieutenant was struck by her beauty, and captivated by the legend in progress that was swirling about her, drawing all on board along for the adventure.

"Please, I am a little lost," she admitted.

"May I escort you, Your Highness?" the young Lieutenant asked, smiling in a friendly manner.

"Just directions, if you please." And while the young man gave her careful directions, which Izadra repeated back to him, she also noted they all hung up their flight suites in a series of unlocked lockers along the wall. Thanking him again for directions, Izadra left the locker room and secluded herself just outside until they had left. Holding her breath, fearful someone would come and her entire plan would be ruined, Izadra quickly took one of the women's flight suites. Folding the suit a small as possible, Izadra contemplated telling At'r she had become lost if he arrived at their chambers before she did.

Following corridors and trying hard to remember them, Izadra contemplated her escape. Tomorrow she would blend in with the other crew and board the Earth bound shuttle, hopefully un-noticed. Izadra's stomach knotted at the thought of discovery and nothing she could think of would quell her fear, if At'r caught her, his wrath would be awful. Before Izadra loomed the doors to the quarters she was forced to share with At'r. Silently she passed through them and past the saluting guards, hoping they did not notice what she carried.

Alone in the bedroom she looked around in dismay. Knowing At'r would soon come, Izadra immediately looked for a hiding place for her stolen jumpsuit. The closet was out of the question, her things, what few she had, shared the space with At'r's. In desperation, Izadra threw back the bed covers and the cover on the mattress she then laid the flight suit out flat, remaking the bed. Izadra had been careful to put the garment on her side of the bed. Moments after she smoothed the top coverlet At'r joined her.

"I expected to find you in the bath." he said lightly, walking toward her to pull her close in an amorous embrace.

She pushed away, "Why? I would only need another after you finished slobbering all over me."

At'r released her causing her to land on her behind as she had been pushing against him with all her strength and her balance depended on him restraining her. A growing smile tugged at the corner of At'r's mouth, and a mischievous gleam glinted in his green eyes, unable to control his amusement any longer he laughed not seeing the growing look of indignation in Izadra's eyes. Suddenly he felt his legs swept from beneath him only to land abruptly on the carpeted floor. On instinct taught from many years of fighting both in practice and reality he reached out and grabbed Izadra's leg pulling her back to him as she scrambled to escape. Now panic stricken, Izadra realized her folly, she fought him until he wrestled her into submission, pinning her arms and straddling her legs. With eyes wide from fear and her chest heaving with the exertion, she saw his amusement had gone only to be replaced by desire. Closing her eyes as he bent forward and kissed her deeply, his mouth moving from her mouth to nibble on her ear, his voice came in a hoarse whisper as Izadra struggled for her freedom.

"Ah, last night milady, you did not mind my kisses." he felt her shudder, followed by another as he un-zipped her flight suit, then the uniform underneath to caress her warm breasts.

"Please Your Highness," Izadra pleaded weakly.

"Say my name Izadra, we are a little past titles." he told her, once again possessing her lips then releasing them to demand, "Say my name."

Opening her eyes to stare into his, Izadra obeyed, "At'r," she said breathlessly, "please!" but again he kissed her.

Ending his embrace At'r pulled Izadra roughly to her feet, almost causing her to faint he pulled her up so quickly. At'r pushed both garments off her shoulders at once, getting little resistance, but no assistance from her, the garments fell to the floor. Izadra now stood before him, her head bowed, her hair covering her face and her breasts.

"You are exquisite," he told her lifting her up in his arms and placing her in the center of the bed. After pulling off his boots he quickly shed his clothing.

Joining Izadra on the bed At'r pulled her tense body close in his arms, his hand exploring her smooth skin causing her to tremble. Gently he rolled her on her stomach and pulling her hair aside kissed her neck. Izadra moved away unwilling to respond to him again, knowing if he continued she would succumb. Again he rolled her over, but before he could kiss her, Izadra turned her head only to find it drawn back by At'r's hand cupping her jaw and his lips touching hers'. Izadra felt his knee spread her legs, now he knelt between them.

"Look at me!" he demanded. Hesitantly she looked at him in the dim light, the stars visible behind him through the windows. Slowly he merged with her body, his eyes darkening as he took her.

Izadra closed her eyes, the battle lost, again. Now if she could only force her body not to respond to his so easily, but try as she might At'r would not allow her any control. As the intensity of his thrusts increased, her will fled, to her shame Izadra hugged him closer, fearful he would leave her.

"Feel the heat Izadra?" At'r asked her, his voice ragged.

"Yes!" came Izadra's breathless answer.

"Shall I let it consume you?" he demanded, stopping his rhythm.

"No!" was her desperate reply, "Please, Your...At'r." Izadra became lost in a dream world of pleasure and warmth. She looked into At'r's eyes becoming entranced, controlled by At'r as if she were one of his robots. His touch was fire but suddenly Izadra thirsted for it. His piercing thrusts within her became more urgent and with a moan of submission, Izadra closed her eyes. At'r felt her tense and knew soon she would climax, allowing his body to respond to the waves of pleasure that spread through it, he too felt as if he were burning, the fire becoming so hot he could not contain the cry that burst from him. Finally quenched, both lay exhausted next to each other.

Tears, unseen by At'r streamed down Izadra's face, never had she been so confused and frightened, gathering her courage she rose from the bed and made her way to the shower, standing under the hot water until her skin turned pink. Only one thought gave her comfort, tomorrow she was going home, At'r's anger no longer haunted her.

With new resolve she completed her shower and toiletry, only to almost collide with At'r as she left the dressing area. Moving to step aside he stopped her.

"Stand still!" he said sharply, "Let me look at you."

Izadra had dressed in the peach gown, her hair was combed and the gold band adorned the shining mane. She wore a small amount of cosmetics knowing At'r wished her to look good and not wanting to incur his anger, normally she wore none. Under his close scrutiny she fiddled nervously with the crystal wedding band on her finger.

"Do I meet your approval?" she asked capriciously, squelching the lusty craving his touch invoked deep inside.

"As I said earlier, you are exquisite." he left her with a slight blush at his reference to their lovemaking brushing past on his way to the bath.

Shortly At'r returned dressed in his daily uniform to find Izadra standing before the windows behind his desk staring out into space. She jumped, startled when he addressed her.

"You seem to enjoy space." At'r commented casually.

"I can not deny the beauty and beckon of it." Izadra told him.

At'r came to stand behind Izadra, hugging her from behind, pulling her closer. "You?" he asked, slightly surprised, "Hear the call?"

Unwilling to share anymore of herself than she already was forced too, she answered only, "Yes." then added, "Given time I would explore it all, but I miss the sunshine and blue waters of home."

"You will be pleased with Creasion, there too is sunshine and blue waters." he assured her.

Relieved to hear the tone announcing dinner, she reminded him, "Your guests will be waiting."

"That is one advantage of my position," he turned her to face him, "they will not start without me. But come," he took her by the hand, "your temper grows short, you must be hungry." he kissed the back of her fingers.

Upon entering the dinning hall, adjacent to At'r's chambers, all present rose and bowed then waited until At'r and Izadra were seated before they resumed their places. Their show of respect made Izadra uneasy.

"Welcome," At'r said warmly to them, then turning to the servants, "Please begin."

Throughout the meal Izadra listened intently, saying little. First At'r recalled the days events, drawing attention to Izadra's destruction of the Zerion craft, next he began a discussion on the up-coming reconnaissance mission, the last one. To this Izadra was most attentive, memorizing each detail that would aid her in escaping and trying to devise a more complete plan. Tomorrow she would escape, then two days later she would no longer have to concern herself with the Zerion, knowing At'r would destroy them.

Izadra's mood changed and she became almost jovial as the business was concluded and the group's discussion turned to more pleasant things.

Finally the evening drew to a close, At'r opened and bottle of brandy that Kron had retrieved on the recon mission he had completed earlier.

As their guests left, At'r bid them a goodnight, his hand possessively resting on Izadra's shoulder.

Lord Betus was last to leave and soon as the door closed behind him, Izadra stepped away from At'r, once again on the defensive now that they were alone.

"Prepare for bed, I have a busy day ahead and need to sleep." At'r told Izadra as they entered their sleeping quarters.

Izadra eyed him suspiciously and went to change. She returned a few moments later and cautiously slid beneath the bedcovers, watching every move At'r made, hoping she would escape his amorous intentions tonight. Seemingly, he did not notice her close scrutiny and went to the bath, returning several moments later to join Izadra beneath the covers.

Izadra lay with her back to him at the far end of the bed, she held her breath, hoping against hope he would leave her alone. His light kiss on her neck told Izadra it was not to be. She did not move and he placed another kiss on her bare shoulder. At'r seemed to know what place on her body to assault, so when he rolled her over in his arms to take her trembling lips she did not resist him, gently his lips parted hers. At'r's hands molded her closer and Izadra had no doubt of his passion for her. His lips left hers and traveled to her breasts. Nuzzling and kissing each one until they stood erect the nipples hard and sensitive. Slowly he took her, building their ardor into a crescendo of pleasure, both falling asleep entwined in each other's arms.

Izadra woke first, still held tightly in At'r's arms. Gingerly she looked over his shoulder at the alien clock she had learned to decipher. They had only slept two hours. It would be another five hours before it was time to rise and put her escape plan into action. Izadra lay back, sleep overtaking her again. But instead of peaceful slumber, her sleep was invaded by vivid dreams of crystal blue waters and green forests. Waking with At'r at the sound of the wake-up tone, Izadra thought she had dreamed of Earth and pushed the visions from her mind as she tired to clear her tired and blurry head, she stretched, her body stiff.

Before she could escape him, At'r pulled her closer and thoroughly kissed her good morning, "You may go back to sleep Izadra." At'r said when released her, there isn't any reason for you to rise until later." He went to dress. After dressing At'r checked on Izadra to find her sleeping, or so he thought, before going to meet with Kron at the ship's command center.

CHAPTER 13

When Izadra was sure At'r had left she rose from the bed and removed the flight suit she had so carefully concealed, then replaced the bottom covers so her tampering would go undetected.

Roberta had manufactured the clothing she would wear on Earth until she could reach Kevin. Quickly Izadra dressed, knowing time was not on her side, At'r could return at any moment for any reason, a servant would not enter until summoned, unless At'r had ordered her breakfast. Izadra was also unsure of Kron's departure time and she wanted to be well secured in a safe part of the shuttle before it lifted off. Dressed, she braided her hair and coiled it into a bun at the nape of her neck, Izadra's nervous fingers taking longer than they normally would to perform the simple task. Finished, she laid the brush down, her fingers moving to the gold band. For a moment she contemplated the article, and all it implied, then turned and walked away leaving their chambers through a door that At'r did not know she had found. It exited just around the hall from the two guards at the main entrance.

Carefully Izadra opened the door and seeing the hallway empty entered it, closing the door behind her, checking the flight suit collar to be sure it was fastened and concealed her necklace. Taking a deep breath she moved to the quick gate of the other crewmembers and managed to blend in with the bustling throng of activity. Nearing the hanger she was assaulted by doubts and suspiciously glanced back several times in fear she was being followed.

All the halls were monitored by cameras at sometime and Izadra wondered if At'r and Kron were secretly watching her from a private vantagepoint, laughing at her doomed attempt. She forced the thought from her mind, 'I must concentrate on only the escape.' she told herself.

Another thought came to Izadra. What would she do if Kron spotted her before she could slip from the ship to the safety of the woods on Earth, again she forced the ill vision from her.

The hanger doors were before her, and Izadra entered with two others dressed as she was. Across the expanse of the hanger was the shuttle, to her dismay Commander Kron and At'r stood before the entrance. Two other crew members joined the two she was walking with, one of them a woman, bravely Izadra stayed with the group as it neared the shuttle, staying on the far side and away from Kron and At'r. To her relief the group moved around toward the rear of the craft and another entrance for the crew or passengers, she entered the passenger part of the ship without difficulty.

Inside there were nine others and seats for twelve. Izadra knew all would be taken, so she made her way forward while the crew was occupied with their own jobs. Finding a small closet she settled herself in. Without intending too, Izadra had inhabited a storage space next to the control cabin, and when At'r and Kron entered their voices were so close she dared not breath for fear of exposure. They were well along with their conversation when they entered and At'r continued as Kron began checking his on board systems.

"From what Doctor Trentos has told me, she should bare many fine children, and although I would have rather avoided marriage, she is beautiful and seems intelligent, if a bit on the stubborn side, she still refuses to mentally bond." At'r told his friend.

"It is new to her, patience." Kron counseled, "Flip that switch please." she heard Kron ask At'r and a slight snap "thank you At'r."

"At'r, you knew marriage was unavoidable, and you gain many more advantages with this marriage than you might have on Creasion."

"Yes, you are correct." At'r agreed as they left the cockpit and Izadra heard no more of their conversation.

After what she had heard, Izadra was glad to be leaving, 'many fine children', she swore under her breath, 'patience—huh!' but quieted when she heard Kron returning, alone.

He closed the door and secured it, his co-pilot entered from the crew's cabin and they buckled their security belts for the flight to Earth. After obtaining clearance for lift off from central control, they departed for their last reconnaissance mission.

It would have been a pleasant flight but half way there Izadra began to feel strangely tired, exhausted in fact and she struggled to stay awake fearing if she fell asleep she would be discovered. Time stood still, what seemed like hours was only minutes, Izadra's head dropped and she succumbed to the lure of sleep.

Voices startled her awake, Kron was remarking to his co-pilot that Earth was an exceptionally beautiful planet, to which the co-pilot agreed. Still secure in her hideout, new hope of success sprung up in Izadra and the strange symptoms passed. Soon she could feel the gravitational pull of the planet on the small craft as the engines reversed to provide them a safe, soft and undetected landing with in only five miles of the Zerion's largest base. Using the blocking device they went undetected by not only the Zerion but the local authorities as well. A jolt alerted Izadra she had returned to Earth, she remembered at one point she did not think she would ever return.

Still she must be patient a little longer. Izadra waited for several minutes after the others had left the ship to slip out of the cramped closet.

Smelling the clean air of the wooded area where they had landed drew Izadra out, and reaching the back entrance she cautiously surveyed the area. Bright sun light bathed Izadra almost blinding her, shading her eyes with her hand Izadra squinted at the brown land-scape of late fall in the Blue Ridge mountains. Descending the steps Izadra stepped on the soil of home, but hearing voices she scrambled to hide in the underbrush of the area. For a brief time she listened as Kron briefed his people on their mission.

Satisfied her presence was not noticed Izadra slipped away from the landing area. From listening to the plans made for this mission she knew the Zerion base lay west of their landing sight and Izadra knew a small town lay ten miles east of the sight with a paved road four miles away. That was her first destination, from there she would hopefully catch a ride. Walking would leave her vulnerable for a longer period of time, but she was capable of the trek.

Traveling quickly was important but for a half mile she tempered her enthusiasm and her pace, determined to be as quiet as possible. Izadra enjoyed the smell of pine that hung heavy in the air, and the cool crispness stung her lungs as she ran.

At this distance she felt more confident and stopped to catch her breath. Around her Izadra could hear the wind in the bare trees and the cheerful babbling of a nearby creek.

Following the enticing sound, Izadra found a waterfall splashing down water smooth stones to form a trout stream. Leaves of red and gold cluttered the banks and gave the ground the appearance of sculptured carpet. Careful not to slip, she drank from the cascading waterfall enjoying the clean taste of the sparkling water. Her thirst quenched, Izadra again set out for the paved road. Only yards from the waterfall she heard voices. Unable to determine their origin or direction she hid behind a rock out-cropping.

Fear Izadra thought she had left behind on the shuttle returned to remind her, she was a fugitive. Close on the other side of her hiding place was a Zerion patrol, lead by a face she remembered well. It was Stx, the Zerion who had captured her in the Rockies. 'These Zerions get around.' she thought briefly and knew by their direction that they would soon discover Commander Kron and his reconnaissance team.

Indecision became her dilemma as the patrol passed. If she went back and warned Kron, Izadra knew he would try to detain her and force her to return to Tos-hawk One. If she did not go back, Kron and his patrol would be totally surprised and probably killed. No matter how much she wanted her freedom, Izadra did not want it at the price of so many lives. Kron had saved her from the Zerion, and she would return the favor.

Izadra ran through the woods, her feet carrying her faster than before. As she ran she felt something in one of the many pockets in the fight suit, opening it while she ran Izadra found one of the small lazzer discs weapons used by the Creasion. Izadra could not believe her luck the device was fully operational and loaded.

Without having time to stop she burst from the bushes and drew the immediate attention of Kron and everyone else in the clearing. Managing to stop just before she crashed into him, Izadra stood gasping for breath.

"Lady Izadra? What? How did you get here?" Kron demanded.

Ignoring his questions Izadra told him, "There is a Zerion patrol close behind me, I came back to warn you." She saw the disbelief in his eyes. "Please Kron, there is not time."

Seeing her urgency Kron alerted his crew and turned back to find Izadra several yards away from him. "Lady Izadra, His Highness will be angry, he will come after you."

"I am sure Kron, that he will be angry, but I doubt after what I heard in the shuttle that he will come after me." Izadra said edging a little further away, their awkward conversation coming to an abrupt halt as the Zerion patrol burst out into the clearing. Izadra's, and Kron's attention was diverted to the invasion, Stx's eyes and Izadra's met, his surprised; hers cool and unwavering. She had faced worse at the hands of his superior.

In what seemed like a slow motion scenario Izadra watched Stx take aim at Kron, but her reactions were not slow and remembering the disc-weapon in her hand, pointed it at Stx and fired before he did, the alien Commander fell to the ground.

Distracted by the fighting around him and Izadra's shooting of the Zerion, Kron did not notice she was slipping away until he saw her disappear through the brush. Kron could not give chase after Izadra as the Zerions had him and his crew fully involved in the skirmish. In his anger and frustration Kron smashed his fist into the jaw of a Zerion who attacked him. Tossing the smaller framed Zerion aside, Kron tried to make his way across to the area he had seen Stx fall, hoping to take him prisoner. He knew Izadra had only wounded him. When Kron fought his way to the site he found no trace of Stx he too had escaped. With what sounded like the roar of an enraged lion, Kron's war cry echoed through the woods.

In all, his crew took two prisoners, the other had either escaped or lay dead on the Earth's soil, their bodies disintegrating in a blaze of phosphorescence fire as Zerions did when life left them in the higher oxygen content of Earth's atmosphere. Two of Kron's crew were severely injured and needed medical attention, Kron realized had Izadra not shot the Zerion Commander he would either be dead or one of the seriously wounded. She had saved his life and possibly his entire crew. Barking orders Kron vacated the area and headed the shuttle back to Tos-hawk One to tell At'r what had happened, a task he did not look forward too.

CHAPTER 14

*I*zadra had pushed herself almost past her point of endurance, jumping a rotted log only to find her legs would not support her landing and she fell to the thick carpet of colorful leaves. For long moments she lay gasping for air, her chest aching from the exertion, her ears straining for a sound that might betray a pursuer, but she heard none. At last able to role over onto her back, Izadra managed to stop the spinning of the world.

Sitting up she scanned the area, but it was not until Izadra turned all the way around that she saw the paved road. In amazement, Izadra stared at the asphalt, and standing too quickly, she had to steady herself against a tree. At a slower pace she took off the flight suit, carefully folding the garment to form a small square that resembled a purse. Inside were only two things, her wallet, which she had succeeded in hanging on to through her adventures and the little compact lazzer devise.

Smoothing back the stray hairs that had slipped from the tightly braided bun at the nape of her neck, she set out walking down the country road. With each footstep further from the landing site and the battle going on there, the more confident Izadra felt. A loud shrieking broke the stillness fearfully Izadra looked skyward to see the shuttlecraft streak overhead and she quickly lost sight of it. Izadra sighed, it was over and they were gone. Now she only had to call her lawyer and friend, Kevin, and he would come and get her. Maybe then life would again take on some form of normalcy.

A car passed her traveling toward town and it was only when it stopped that Izadra realized it was a Highway Patrol car. To her dismay, the auto's back-up lights came on and it backed to where she stood. Stepping out and resting his arm on the roof of the patrol car, the officer obviously contemplated her.

"You know Miss? This stretch of road is dangerous to travel, especially on foot. Where are you going?"

"Into town, officer." Izadra replied simply, wondering what he would say to the truth.

"Get in and I will give you a lift." he told her, and seeing the hesitancy in her face, further assured her by tossing his identification to her.

Reading the officer's card, she looked up. "Thank you Officer Towers, my feet are aching." Opening the front door, Izadra slid in, thankful for the rest.

Settling himself in the driver's seat, Officer Towers accepted his credentials back and started the engine. "We've had some pretty strange things happening around here lately." He told her as he drove. "U.F.O.'s the press keeps calling them. Been reporters in and out of the area for about a week now. I've seen three U.F.O.'s myself, about a week ago, and one, very different from the first three only a few minutes ago. You really should not be this far out alone and on foot. Why are you out this far?"

Izadra had not thought about an explanation but she quickly made one up. "My boyfriend and I had a fight, he left me out here, the bastard." she swore under her breath convincingly.

"Nice boyfriend," Towers commented. "You from around here, Miss?" he accented the 'Miss'. He wanted her name.

"Ah, Catherine Kirk," she told him truthfully, hoping the name would not mean anything to him, "and no, I am from Washington

D.C. When I get to town I will call my brother to come and get me; he's a lawyer there."

"Good!" the Officer said and they entered the town limits.

He pulled up next to a small cafe, and thanking him for his kindness, Catherine got out and walked through the restaurant door, waving good-by as he drove away.

Inside Catherine sat in a booth that was placed slightly back from the window but gave her a good view. Picking up the menu, she decided she would order breakfast then call Kevin. In a few moments a waitress wearing tight stretch latex pants and an oversized, low cut sweater came to take her order, chewing her gum as she wrote.

"Won't take long," she drawled as she walked away.

Amused by the stereotype waitress, Izadra smiled and made her way across the small diner to the pay phone and called Kevin, collect. It rang three times before Kevin answered and she listened as he accepted the charges on the call, his voice incredulous.

"Cathy? Cathy? Is that really you?" he asked, excited.

Catherine hated the shortened version of her first name and a peculiar feeling came over her as somewhere in her memory the sound of At'r's voice saying her name instantly came back to haunt her. "Yes, Kevin," Catherine managed to say, "It is me, Catherine, can you come and get me?"

"For heaven sake, where are you?"

"A little town called Haymar, do you know where it is?"

"Yes!"

"How did you get there? Where have you been?" he demanded all at once.

"I will explain when you get here. And Kevin, please bring that package my grandmother left for me, it is very important."

"Important, that's only the half of it, you would not believe how many people are trying to locate that document. I'll be there in an hour, if the traffic isn't bad, where will you be?"

"I'll stay in this little diner, ah," she looked for the restaurant's name, "Rose's Cafe', it's the only one in town. Please hurry, Kevin."

"I will." Kevin hung up.

A hollow feeling possessed Catherine as she made her way back to the booth. She sat down as the waitress poured a cup of black coffee. Sipping the hot brew, Catherine was thankful it was strong. She had missed coffee on board Tos-hawk One. Her breakfast came and she found her appetite had waned. Catherine ate slowly, her nerves becoming more on edge. After half and hour the waitress removed the plate and poured Catherine another cup of coffee. Catherine then settled back with a copy of a Washington newspaper. Midway through a sip of coffee she saw Kevin's car pull up on the other side of the street. She watched, as in his excitement, he did not lock his car. He seldom left the expensive Mercedes un-locked. Kevin hurried through the door, and seeing Catherine sitting in the back crossed the small area as she stood. Suddenly Catherine found herself crushed in his arms.

"Catherine, I have been so worried, what happened?"

"Did you bring the packet?" Catherine asked, not seeing it.

"Yes, it is well hidden in the car, that packet has been subpoenaed and is only here because the authorities are looking for it in Denver." Kevin signaled the waitress and paid the bill giving her a generous tip.

Since Kevin had told her the packet was in his Mercedes, Catherine had not taken her eyes off the car, now she watched as a plain tan Chevy pulled up and parked behind it. Two men got out and looked briefly inside the two-door sports car, then looked toward the diner. Kevin was receiving his change as Catherine backed away. Before he noticed her disappearance, the two men were addressing him.

"You are Kevin Bonnett?" Agent Brooks questioned.

"Yes." Kevin answered.

"I am Agent Brooks, and this is Agent Lutz, we are investigating the disappearance of Catherine Izadra Kirk, and we have reason to believe you have seen her, possibly with in the last hour?" He explained, flipping his credentials out for Kevin to read.

"As you gentlemen probably know, I am Ms. Kirk's attorney. Anything I may know is under the strictest confidence." He smiled confidently at them, "Believe me, I have no idea where she is now, or where she has been." His face grew serious, "By the way, how did you know where I was? Are you following me?"

"Ah, thank you for you cooperation, sir." Agent Lutz said, leaving Kevin's question unanswered, the two walked away each going separate ways upon leaving the diner. Kevin decided they were not only following him but most likely his phone was tapped. Kevin swore. Now Catherine was gone again, he wondered what she had gotten involved in. Not having the slightest idea of what to do next, he considered waiting to see if she re-appeared or if the agents found her, finally he walked to his car and got in.

"Kevin!" a whispered voice said, "Get me out of here!"

"Catherine, how?" He started the car and slowly drove out of town hoping to attract as little attention as possible.

On the sidewalk he saw Agent Lutz and waved briefly, turning to take the road back toward Washington. When they were well out of town, Kevin told Catherine to sit up. Guiding the auto onto the interstate, Kevin turned away from Washington to hopefully confuse anyone following them.

"Now," he said to Catherine, "I want to know everything, where you have been and why those government agents are looking for you."

So as they drove Catherine explained what had happened, her voice trembling as she only skimmed over her forced marriage to At'r.

"But how could you marry him?" Kevin demanded.

"I had no other choice, you do not understand," Catherine explained, absently turning the crystal wedding ring on her finger. She had neglected to remove the symbol of their union upon her departure from Tos-hawk One. Catherine pushed the strange feeling that it gave her to the back of her mind. Later she would examine her reasons for not removing the ring. "He has complete power onboard that ship." she further explained, feeling underneath the seat for the packet Kevin had hidden there.

Catherine pulled out the packet, marveling at the wax seal, it resembled the Royal Seal of Creasion. Drawing a deep breath to still her nerves she briefly pondered the package, what would she do if the contents confirmed what At'r had told her.

"Catherine," Kevin's voice was distracting her.

"Yes."

"You know if those agents catch you, I haven't any power to intercede for you. This is considered a matter of national security."

"Why would my disappearance and reappearance be of any importance to our government?"

"It's the way you disappeared and reappeared," Kevin paused, "and the strange way your father died. Did you know he was gathering information on the aliens for the government? Then there are the multiple sighting of the strange craft that seemed to be occupying our night skies."

"They may become a bit more frequent before they leave." Catherine said softly, but Kevin heard her anyway.

"What do you mean by that? Is there reason for concern?"

"No, At'r will be very thorough when he destroys the Zerions." Catherine fell silent for a moment, "Kevin, I must have a car and not this one, it is too well known. I would prefer to fly but all the airports will be watched. Perhaps in Canada I will be safe, maybe Mexico." she told Kevin sadly.

"Stick with Canada," Kevin warned her. "I have had all your assets transferred to Switzerland, most had been moved before your father's death on his request, the other I moved when you disappeared, and it is a good thing I did or you'd be broke. All of your, and your father's accounts in this country would now be on hold." Now Kevin fell silent, thinking. "Catherine, will that package tell you if you are, ah?" he paused. Afraid he had asked too much, hoping she wasn't, suspecting she was. Catherine had always had an air of mystery around her, "The woman they think you are?"

"I think so Kevin." she answered.

"It is not safe for either of us to go back into Washington together. We would be arrested possibly before we arrived there. I will arrange a car for you in this city. One of the car dealers in town is an old friend." Kevin turned his car onto an off ramp going east and toward his friend's business.

"It had better be fast." was Catherine's only comment.Kevin was still unsure if this was the proper way to handle the matter but he could not think of any other way. Signaling, he turned his Mercedes into the driveway of a car dealership, one that specialized in unusual cars. They both got out of the sports car and walked together toward the small red brick structure that served as the office for the business and entered through glass doors etched with racecars.

"Don!" Kevin called, "Don!"

"Just a minute, Kevin." a voice called from behind the only other door in the small building, the door opened to reveal a closet and a middle aged man who's open manner was easily read on his friendly face. His smile faded upon seeing Catherine, he looked to his friend and the smile returned a more mischievous gleam in his eyes.

"This the one you told me about?"

"Yes, Don this is Catherine," Kevin turned, "Catherine, this is Don."

"Nice to meet you Catherine." Don said extending his hand to Catherine, "So you finally showed up, I told Kevin you would, and from the look on your faces I can tell you've got trouble."

"That is an understatement, if I ever heard one," Kevin complained, "and we've little time to explain now, but we need a fast car, I should say, Catherine needs a fast car."

Don grinned at Catherine, "Who's chasen'ya honey, a jealous lover?"

"Not exactly." Catherine said blushing, thinking of At'r, wondering if he would come after her, and a little amazed at Don's intuition.

"Oh, so the laws after you." he looked surprised, "What did you get yourself into?"

"Do you have a car, Don?" Kevin asked, urgency in his voice.

Don scrutinized both before answering, "Of course, the question is," he paused, smiling wider still, "can you drive it." he asked Catherine pointedly.

"I can drive it." Catherine returned with more confidence than she felt.

"Follow me." Don said beckoning them to follow. Going out the front door they followed him to a large garage building with three double garage doors. Opening the last door on the right, Don revealed a Silver and Black Lamborghini that gleamed even in the shadows of the unlit shop. Don walked inside the building and opening the car door got in and started the powerful twelve-cylinder engine. The building shook and the closed space of the shop reverberated with the sound. Lovingly Don eased the clutch in, and putting the car in first gear moved the Lambo out to be bathed in the sunlight. Leaving the engine running and the transmission in neutral to bring all the systems up to operating temperature, Don emerged with a broad smile on his amiable face.

"Beautiful, isn't she." Don stated, beaming with pride.

"She is." Catherine agreed, lightly running her hand over the flawless paint of the fender.

"I think this will be fast enough for you." His smile faded. "Try not to wreck her, Kevin told me what happened to your Cobra Stang."

"Believe me Don, it wasn't my idea." Catherine turned to Kevin, "Pay the man." then she thought a minute, "In cash Kevin, no receipt, Don, in forty-eight hours call and report the car stolen." Seeing their puzzled looks she explained. "That way the authorities can not prove you helped me."

"Are you that hot?" Don asked.

"If Kevin is correct, it would seem so." Catherine answered sadly.

"Kevin, I'll need some cash myself."

"I have five hundred on me," he said, "anymore and I will have to go to the bank."

"I can loan you two thousand." Don said quietly, "but one condition."

"What's that?" Kevin asked.

"I want the whole story, nothing omitted."

"Done," Catherine agreed, "but after I've gone. Kevin can tell you all he knows."

"Is that the entire story?" Don persisted.

"He knows it all." Catherine assured him.

"Are my charge cards still active?"

"Yes, but don't use them, the agents can track you that way." Kevin warned.

"I know, but in the next town I come to, I've got to buy a few new clothes, that I do not care if they know." Catherine smiled at Kevin, knowing it was time to leave, knowing she might not see him again, "I have to go…" she said quietly.

"I wish I could think of a better way. Call me when you can." Kevin requested.

Catherine touched his cheek. Don cleared his throat uncomfortably and walked back to the shop leaving them alone. "You've always been like my brother, and I know you wanted it otherwise, but it just can not be."

Kevin kissed the palm of her hand. "Take care of yourself, when you feel safe call me and I will join you." he smiled.

Don returned to explain the car's functions and to give Catherine the cash he said he would. "Good luck, Catherine. If you have to leave her somewhere," he referred to the Lamborghini, "tell Kevin and he will call me, I will come and get her."

"Thanks Don, you've been a godsend and are obviously a good friend to Kevin, keep an eye on him for me." She smiled sadly, "Good bye."

Pulling the door closed Catherine amazed Don by pulling out of the parking lot without stalling or overpowering the engine. Once out in traffic she was out of sight in a moment, leaving Kevin behind to explain the fantastic story to Don. Catherine doubted he would believe it.

Going back out of town the way she had come in, Catherine sped onto the interstate and accelerated the powerful auto, stifling the urge to go much faster than the posted speed rate. Shortly Catherine stopped at a large shopping mall next to the interstate to purchase the items she would need for several days. Contemplating the crowd of shoppers, watching each face, all the while fearing one would be an agent looking for her, or a Zerion who might recognize her. Once back inside her car Catherine felt safer but caught sight of the two agents entering town. They did not see her thanks to the dark film on the windows, though both looked directly at the car. Catherine knew the car was unusual. That was the biggest drawback, it was very visible, after the description was made public it would be an easy target, but until then the speed was worth the risk. Once out of town Catherine turned in a northwesterly direction going around the area she knew was occupied by the Zerion, planning to be well away from the area before dark.

Keeping mostly to back roads Catherine made her way into West Virginia as the sun slipped behind the western mountains. She dreaded the night, that was when the Zerion would be out, and she knew Stx had only been wounded. He would be looking for her if he was able, and the Zerion's technology was good enough for him to find her. For this reason Catherine planned to drive through the night in hope of out distancing any possible pursuer. By going west instead of directly north, she hoped to confuse any trackers. Rural roads in Appalachia differed greatly from those in the Rocky Mountains, and the back roads of West Virginia were classic examples. Sometimes the small towns were not named on the most comprehensive of maps and little country post offices that also served as grocery/hardware stores dotted the back roads as did a plentiful supply of sawdust floor bars. Twice Catherine had taken wrong turns, the second time she had stopped for directions at such a bar. It had been a strange experience, but she had gotten good directions, better than the maps, and a stiff drink of moonshine that still burned in her belly from the kind-hearted people who owned the tavern.

Before sun down smoky mists had began to settle on the tops of the mountains, covering the still green spruce and barren maples and oaks in their winter array. Catherine knew in the spring, summer and fall this area was breath takingly beautiful, but in winter in was drab and threatening. After dark the mists thickened and settled over the small creeks that ran along the valley floors and spilled over the roadways that paralleled them. As the pavement climbed higher, the narrow roadway combined with tight twists and off kilter turns and became non-maneuverable when another vehicle was going the opposite direction. By midnight Catherine was so tired she had to stop. Ahead she saw a small grouping of cottages and the vacancy light burning bright on the sign out front. Wearily she turned her car and pulled up the driveway. Stretching after she got out, Catherine felt more alert and walked inside the dimly lit office. A toothless, ancient face greeted her with a worn smile.

"Howd'y," he drawled.

"Hello, I would like a cottage for the night, please." Catherine requested.

"Ok, last one the left, and that'll be thirty-nine dollars."

Without question Catherine paid the man and turned to leave taking the key with her. Driving down to the last cottage she parked, setting the emergency brake because of the incline.

Tiredly gathering the packet and her flight suit/purse Catherine walked the few steps to the door. Turning the key and switching on the lights, Catherine was pleasantly surprised to find a clean, neat room decorated in a country motif. She went back, locked the car and returned to the cottage securing that door behind her.

Catherine sat down on the bed and studied the wax seal, a few weeks ago she would have broken the seal without looking at it. Now it seemed all too familiar. Suddenly afraid the contents would confirm what she had been told on board Tos-hawk, Catherine laid the package down and went to shower. Only to be faced with the same dilemma a few moments later, when wrapped in a towel she exited the bath and again began to ponder her inheritance. Catherine's natural curiosity would not allow her to leave the package alone. Her fear of what it might tell her kept her from opening it.

Absently Catherine had turned on the television, not paying much attention to the program. She glanced at the screen blankly, her attention immediately focusing on the special news bulletin. A man and his family had been hiking in the woods where the Creasion shuttle had landed. Here on the screen was the home video he had taken of the shuttle's ascent from Earth.

Next, at about dusk, the same man had captured the departure of three Zerion vehicles. If Stx had known these pictures were being taken—he would have killed the entire family. They had been very lucky, and Catherine was sure they did know how lucky. Promising more details at the next scheduled news program, the network returned to the original program. Absently, Catherine wondered how Kron had fared in the battle with the Zerion after she had gone.

With an ominous feeling haunting her, she opened the desk drawer and finding a letter opener, gently pried the wax seal free of the large paper envelope without damaging the seal. With shaking hands Catherine pulled the hand written letter out of the envelope and began to read

CHAPTER 15

My Dearest Granddaughter:

It has become clear that while I live I will not be able to explain to you, your family history or what I see for your future. Realizing this, I have composed this letter to be given to you after my death, on your twenty-first birthday, or after your father's death. I ask you in advance to retain an open mind and try to understand though the truth may seem strange. My past, the argument with your father, the necklace you now wear and your future I will explain.

Contrary to what you have been told, my family did not come from Europe, nor did I. I was born on a moon called Metem. This moon orbits the planet Creasion many light years from Earth. Earth's telescopes have not yet discovered our system, as we did not wish it be discovered.

Planet Creasion is larger than Earth but similar in many respects. Most of Creasion is under deep fresh water oceans, only a scarce handful of eight lakes on the planet are salt. During all months except the three winter months tides run drastically high and low, changing in a matter of a few minutes, this is caused by the pull from three moons. For many centuries the tidal return prohibited all but minimal use of our seashores, but once the tidal exchange was harnessed it provided endless power for our people. During the three winter months when the pull from the moons is at the weakest point, the tidal exchange stops and the water freezes to a depth of ten feet. This melts slowly during spring and by mid-summer the water is comfortable for swimming.

Summer brings storms that can turn into hurricanes in a matter of hours. These storms generally stay well out to sea and seldom do damage. Fall is short and almost seems non-existent some years.

This is the planet, but the moons each are different. Metem being rich in natural gems and natural crystal, the climate is mild and the people friendly and trusting. On this moon I grew up in the house of Metem, an old and honored family. My father was the family leader he ruled our moon and sat in council with the Emperor of Creasion. From our house came many priests and what is called psychics; however, I was unaware of my abilities until after my marriage.

When I was nineteen my father, after much convincing and coaxing, took me with him to the planet Creasion when he was called to attend a council meeting. His busy schedule allowed me time to explore the Emperor's private gardens and I believed my passage had gone un-noticed. I was mistaken. That evening my father returned with an invitation to dine later at the Emperor's table. Neither my father nor I knew why we were so honored. Nervous, I chose my wardrobe for the dinner carefully and at the appointed time accompanied my father to the dinning room.

We were both surprised to find the table set for three, we had expected a large gathering. That night we dined alone with the Emperor, who was a most charming host, but as the evening wore on my father and the Emperor's conversation moved to government business and, although bored, I listened attentively. It was not until the next evening that I found the Emperor had watched me in his garden and from that came the dinner invitation. Later he asked my father for my hand, which my father gave without consulting me. But the Emperor, as I said, could be most charming and totally persuasive. We were married a few months later, and he was to have crowned me his Empress soon afterward.

In time I found I was expecting his child, and on the day I would have told him I sat contemplating my coming motherhood in the garden where he had first seen me. Hearing a rustling in the bushes I stepped closer hoping to see one of the colorful creatures that inhabit such areas but instead bumped directly into a Zerion Commander. Zerions are our worst enemies, they are treacherous, cruel creatures and unfortunately, humanoid.

To this day I only remember screaming, then blackness, how they got me off the planet I will never know. I woke in space just as we entered the asteroid belt between our worlds. In their haste, their navigation was not accurate and soon we found ourselves in the part of the asteroid belt known to be particularly bad for ion storms. One such storm hit. Electrical charges, similar to lightning on Earth, danced over the ship damaging the light-speed control and causing it to stick open, soon we were in uncharted space.

Day's later Earth's gravitational pull caught the helpless vehicle and pulled it through the atmosphere, where we crashed in the Mediterranean sea.

Zerions can not swim. Their planet is dry and desert like, except a small portion at each pole, so there isn't any need to learn to swim. They all drowned, and although I could swim, I too would have drowned had not a man seen the crash and pulled me from the water, this man was your step-grandfather. The child I carried from Creasion was your mother.

At first, heartbroken over finding myself on this planet I feared the worst, but Bradford fell in love with me. Knowing already that he could not sire children Brad begged me to marry him.

Knowing hope of rescue from Creasion was not possible and knowing I must provide for the child I carried, I agreed. At first only out of necessity; however, in a short time I found Brad a very easy person to love.

Your mother was born, and from the first I knew she would not be the one who would return to Creasion. She grew up as a normal Earth child and married what was considered 'well'. You came shortly afterward. Just as I had known your mother was not, I knew you were the one. Your bright mind and quick wit foretold a promising future, and my future sight told me you would return home, even though I know I never will.

Seeing the future does not always prepare one for it, and when your mother was killed it affected us all. Shortly afterward your father turned your care over to me.

Remember back when you were a small child, I called you Izadra. Remember the things I taught you then, they will come back naturally if you allow them.

When your father visited, he found you far ahead of other children your age. Because he felt you needed to be with other children your own age, he placed you in a European girl's school. From his decision came the revival of the old disagreement about your middle name.

Never had he forgotten your middle name was given to you by me while he was away. From then on our time together was limited and precious, small amounts of time stolen on holidays and vacation.

Now my time draws nearer and I am faced with the responsibility of passing your heritage to you the only way I can. When my time comes I will give you the one thing I have of Creasion, my necklace. Only prior to my death can I remove it and pass it on to you. This necklace will protect you and guide you to your destiny. Do not fight against it.

Your future holds many wondrous things for you. You will return to Creasion, this I have seen, do not lose hope.

My story is finished now, and I must tell you good-by. Once again, do not fight your fate, you may find it well to your liking.

❈   ❈   ❈

With tears in her eyes Catherine gently laid down the last page, the document was signed Empress Iza, House of Metem, and a seal identical to the one on the envelope was affixed. Closing her tired eyes Catherine was assaulted by a vision so real she could hear her grandmother's voice and see her smile.

"What have I done?" she cried aloud to the still room. Catherine remembered At'r's kisses, hot on her mouth and how he made her blood race, but Catherine also remembered how frightening he was to her and how awesome his powers seemed. Had she stayed he soon would have been able to see into her mind. Confusion became her worst enemy, and Catherine allowed herself the luxury of crying herself to sleep.

CHAPTER 16

❁

*K*ron guided the ship alone. His Co-pilot was badly injured and unconscious in one of the makeshift cots in the back of the shuttle. Tos-hawk One was visible now, and Kron once again tried the low frequency ban on his communication's panel. One lucky shot from a Zerion lazzer had rendered all communications but this inoperable.

"This is Commander Kron. Emergency landing procedures alert, clear this shuttle at once, all else can wait." he instructed the space controllers.

"You are cleared to land on Alpha deck." the voice answered him.

"Have security and medical teams waiting, and where is His Highness?"

"The teams are waiting, His Highness is on his way to his quarters, I have dispatched a messenger to inform him of your arrival." the voice paused, "Sir, we were becoming concerned: we lost contact with you after your landing."

"There were," he halted, "complications." Kron informed the controller as they landed.

Seconds later Kron brought the damaged shuttle to an abrupt halt inside the hangar and was the first one off as the security and medical teams poured on-board to attend the captured Zerions and wounded Creasions. Adrenaline pulsing through his blood, Kron ran to his Lord's chambers arriving there just as he entered the small formal receiving hall. At'r's concerned welcome died in mid-sentence as his Chief Commander forwent his usual salute and stumbled to his knees.

"What has happened Kron?" At'r asked surprised, "Get up you know that is unnecessary."

"My Lord," Kron said trying to rise and suddenly the exhaustion and injuries denied him.

At'r clasped arms with his friend and pulled him to his feet, "Tell me." he said.

"I have the unpleasant task of tell you." he stopped and started again, "Sire, your Lady." he stopped again, "At'r she stowed away on the shuttle and escaped."

At'r's face went white, his lips clenched together in a tight scowling line, and with cold emerald eyes he looked at Kron, "I want to know what happened and in detail." At'r said. Observing Kron's ragged and bruised appearance, he beckoned Kron to follow. Once in his chambers At'r poured them each a drink and another after that was downed before he told Kron to begin his story.

Kron left nothing out. He explained the mission and what went wrong and what could have happened if the Zerion patrol had ambushed them. After Kron finished At'r rose, standing with his back to Kron. Long minutes passed for Kron as At'r considered what he had been told. Kron had never seen At'r so cool. It was eerie, and he wondered if At'r would hold him responsible for not bring Izadra back.

At'r stared out at the Sol solar system laid before him and the stars beyond. Earth floated to his right, only partially illuminated from their present orbital station. It was strange, the first memory he had of Izadra when Kron told him she was gone, was of her standing before him in ripped clothes and bruises. At'r knew he should have watched her more closely. Izadra was not, after all, one of his proper subjects who would do his bidding on command.

"So," At'r said turning and finishing his liquor, "Izadra does not think I will come after her." He pushed a button on the panel, "Kins!" he said after switching on the small intercom and his aid entered the room seconds later.

"Sire?"

"Have my fighter readied, get my Chief Earth agent on the communications screen. Call a conference with the strike force leaders as soon as they can get here." He turned to Kron. "Do not fear old friend, I do not hold you responsible, but when I get her back..." he shook his head, at a loss for the first time in his life. "This will change things, the Zerions will know we are coming, so we will strike earlier. I want the strike force ready by tomorrow, noon, New York time. By the time positions are manned and ready, we should hit the United States just after dark and Russia just before dawn."

"My Lord, are you contemplating going after Lady Izadra yourself?" Kron asked haltingly.

"Who else Kron? You have other duties." At'r told him firmly.

"Do you want to inform the attack group of Lady Izadra's disappearance?" Kron asked, "I can not see where they need to know."

"I agree, but our Earth agents will have to know. Choose two trust worthy pilots to assist me. You will, of course, lead the strike force as planned. Explain to the others we have moved up the time and get a revised plan workable. I am going to change." At'r left the living area and went to his bedroom.

Looking around he could feel Izadra's presence around him. At'r picked up the gold band of royalty she had left behind. "Damn!" he swore aloud and tossed the band across the room, then stalked to the bathroom where he was assaulted by the vivid memory of her in the shower when he had surprised her. "It would serve you right if I left you on that backward planet." He mumbled to himself, jamming his legs down the legs of the flight suit. Zipping it up he joined the growing meeting in his living room.

At'r was not able to concentrate on what his advisors and ships officers were discussing. He found his mind dwelling on the dangers he knew Izadra was facing. Although he had shown her the reports of her government's attempts to find and apprehend her, Izadra had not believed him. She could not know how desperate the Earth's governments were for information on the strange alien events that had been taking place on and around their planet. At'r wished his Earth agent Qerns would check in, hopefully with encouraging news.

For now At'r forced the vivid image of his wife from his mind and brought his thoughts back to the pressing details of an advanced schedule attack plan. At'r looked to each person present and found only Kron had noticed his wavering attention, Kron nodded in understanding. Finally concluding the meeting, At'r confidently sent his people to their tasks, leaving only Kron.

"Now, Kron," At'r began, "we must make plans to find Izadra, she does not know the danger she has put herself in."

"Milady seems to be good at that, I could not believe my eyes when she burst out of the woods at the landing site on Earth, closely followed by the Zerion patrol."

"Would your casualties have been higher had she not warned you?" At'r asked.

"I think we would not have made it back, I know I wouldn't have, had she not shot the Zerion patrol leader. She jeopardized her chances at escape and risked the Zerion killing or capturing her by coming back." Kron said, then added, "She is brave." admiration in his voice.

At'r grew quiet for a moment, "She did not think I would come after her." he stated once more, Kron nodded, "Well, she is wrong." he said with some force.

"Has the Earth agent reported in yet?" Kron asked.

"No, I expect him to anytime now." At'r said even as a signal on his desk alerted him to an incoming message, "Yes, Qerns, what have you to tell me?"

"My Lord, I have an updated report for you. From all indications Lady Izadra called her attorney-friend Kevin Bonnett. He picked her up in a small town, known as Haymar, not far from the shuttle's landing site. Earth's government authorities know she has returned and they have been following her lawyer. The agents came very near to apprehending her, but she cleverly escaped. An interesting point sire," he paused catching his breath, "One of the Earth agents, Agent Lutz, is a Zerion, the Earth man working with him, Agent Brooks, does not know his partner is an alien. The existence of a package left to Lady Izadra by her grandmother, Lady Iza, has been discovered. The lawyer is holding the package, but may have turned it over to Lady Izadra by now the agents have a subpoena to take the package, if they can locate it. So far, the lawyer has avoided turning it over to them.

"Good Qerns, now I want to know where the lawyer can be found, I wish to talk to him, so you will provide landing coordinates some-where safely outside the city and meet me there with transportation."

"Sire?" Qerns questioned, his concern echoed by Kron. "Sire, please it is too risky." Kron beseeched his monarch.

At'r affixed his Commander with a cold stare, Kron sat down and At'r turned back to Qerns. "Where can I land?"

"Sire, I could not suggest a location with in fifty miles of the city. Even using the filtering devise, your ship might be seen."

"So, with all the current alien activity I do not see how one more such sighting would harm our cause." At'r said patiently, "and at this point I do not care. You will furnish landing coordinates promptly; I am leaving with in the hour and should meet you two hours after our departure, call me back when you have the position."

Turning the screen off, At'r turned to Kron, "Commander, I know the danger of going to Earth, but she is my wife, I would not allow anyone else to go, and her lawyer seems the logical place to begin. Also, if he has not given Izadra that package, I want it before those government agents get it."

"Sire, could I not go and talk to this Earth man before the attack, or bring him back here for you to question?" Kron offered fearing for his friend's safety.

"No, Kron, according to our plans you should be leaving Toshawk One about the time I leave Earth, we should pass."

"Very well," Kron conceded, "I will go see to your fighter and the two who will escort you." Kron paused, "But know this, as head of your bodyguard, I am against your going."

"Your objections are noted." At'r responded formally.

Kron drew a deep breath, "Please At'r, be careful."

"Thank you, Kron, for your concern." At'r clasped Kron's arm in friendship, Kron bowed briefly and left At'r alone in his silent quarter.

At'r looked at his spacious chambers, he had spent two months in these rooms alone before Izadra had been found, and they had not seemed lonely, until now. Several unfamiliar emotions assailed him, he was worried about Izadra's safety and he was angry with her. He would not allow himself to believe he missed her or had any affection for her. Izadra was his duty, to fulfill the prophecy and to produce an heir to succeed him. With a last look at his empty chambers he left to check on the readiness of his ship and to brief Betus on current events.

At'r found Kron on the flight deck. Always a place of immoderate activity, At'r's presence did not interrupt their work since the technicians had been excused from formalities until the Zerion's destruction was accomplished. Kron looked up and quickly saluted.

"Your ship should be ready shortly, perhaps thirty spans."

"Good, call me when it is, I will be briefing your father on Izadra's escape." At'r left as he had come.

Kron turned to his aid, "Have His Highness' fighter pre-flighted. And get Agent Qerns on the communications viewer." Kron instructed hoping Qerns would have new information. Moment's later Qerns' image appeared on the screen.

"Yes Commander?"

"Were you able to locate Lady Izadra from the location of her last phone call?" Kron asked hoping Qerns would have a positive reply.

"We have a general location and direction of movement. this information came in just moments ago."

"His Highness will be pleased and he will be journeying to that area soon. Can you have a security team ready if we need them?"

"Consider them ready, I will have them flown to the area to secure the landing site."

"Thank you, Qerns. Commander Kron out." Qerns' image faded.

With a light step Kron headed for his father's quarters to tell him and At'r the good news. Kron had not told At'r they had gotten a limited fix on Lady Izadra's location just before they had lifted off to return to Tos-hawk One after the encounter with the Zerion. Qerns had monitored the trace on the phone to call her lawyer. Now between the two sources Kron had a positive report to give to his Emperor and friend.

Passing Captain Kara in the corridor he stopped her. "Tari," he said, addressing her personally, "how soon can you be ready to go on another mission?" he asked realizing she had just returned from patrol.

"As soon as the ship can be refueled. What's up?"

"Lady Izadra escaped on my earlier recon mission, His Highness is going after her, I need you to accompany him."

"No problem. I'll see to my ship." turning she hurried back to the hanger, Kron proceeded to Betus' chambers.

Entering his father's chambers he greeted both At'r and his father. "Good news, sire." he said with a smile.

"You have found her?" At'r's attention was immediately on Kron.

"A good lead. Before we lifted off a limited fix was acquired on Lady Izadra, and Agent Qerns traced her last phone call to the same general area and we now suspect that Lady Izadra is indirectly headed for Canada."

"At last!" At'r said, "You will please have the location and direction fed into my fighter's computer."

"It is being taken care of at his moment, I have asked Captain Kara to fly back-up, on your approval, of course."

"Thank you Kron, an excellent choice. I will be glad to have her along." seeing Kron's concern he added, "I know you are anxious for my safety, but I must go." Excusing themselves, At'r and Kron covered the distance to the hangers quickly.

At'r and Kron found Captain Kara and Captain Larn checking their fighters, both coming to attention at the approach of their Emperor and Commander.

"Captain Larn," At'r acknowledged him courteously. Then turned to recently promoted Captain Kara, "Congratulations on your promotion Captain." he grew serious, "We will be flying to Earth on the dark side, the landing coordinates have been programmed directly into your ship's computer. Captain Larn you will fly cover in space, keep a sharp eye open for any Zerion ships. These you will destroy. Any Earth ships are to be disarmed." he turned back to Captain Kara, "You will accompany me to Earth, we will be paying a visit on Lady Izadra's Earth lawyer and friend."

"Sire," Commander Kron stepped forward.

"Yes, Commander?"

"I have briefed Captain Kara on the purpose of this mission, considering her knowledge of past events."

"Thank you Commander," At'r turned back to the two pilots, "to your ships." They followed, allowing At'r to enter his ship first. Moments later the three blasted out of the hanger on course for a two hour journey to Earth.

Early morning stars shone on At'r and Captain Kara, illuminating their landing in the isolated pasture approved by Kron and Qerns. They had to be back to their ships and out of Earth's atmosphere before dawn, and dawn was five hours away. Using his ships sensors At'r checked the area as did Captain Kara and found six other humanoids in the area, all registered Creasion. Carefully both descended from their ships to find Agent Qerns and sub-agent Devus at attention and saluting, both looking absurd in their three-piece business suites.

"Be at ease gentlemen." At'r said to them quietly, "and please no more saluting, you are excused until this visit is over, it would be difficult to explain such a gesture to an Earthman." Both men stood less tensely.

"I have brought agent Devus with me to guard your ships, as will the four agents hidden in the woods around us." Qerns explained, "I hope this meets with your approval?"

"It does Qerns, how long will it take to reach the lawyer's residence?"

"About two hours, I have brought clothing that more closely resembles the earth styles, if you wish to change."

"Thank you Qerns, we will in the van you have brought." At'r moved toward the earth vehicle, "Let's go."

Qerns started the customized van he had rented as Captain Kara closed the sliding side door. He turned the vehicle around and slowly made his way down the dirt road he had driven in on. Maneuvering the van through the narrow tree lined and pothole filled road took most of his skill and attention while Captain Kara changed from her uniform to the silk dress he had purchased for her. When finished, Tari took the front passenger seat from At'r and he went to the back and donned the expensive suit provided. He felt restricted and uncomfortable in the garments.

"How do you manage to work in such clothes?" At'r asked after several failed attempts at tying the matching tie.

"It was not easy, at first, but it was necessary to hold my cover." Qerns explained.

"I must say," Tari Kara said, "the dress is not uncomfortable, but these shoes, you called them high heels? I think they are a form of Zerion torture." she giggled, wiggling her toes outside the shoes.

With a jolt they drove onto the paved highway and At'r tossed the tie aside in disgust, he just would not wear it. Qerns urged the van forward, setting the cruise control on ninety-five miles an hour and engaged a little radar altering devise he had invented. It was an ingenious invention and would make him a fortune here on Earth. The gadget had a practical use now, and for that reason he valued it. True to his word they arrived at the lawyer's door at three in the morning, and were surprised to see the lights on. Their hand held detection sensor device registered an awake person inside, an Earthman. There was no sign of Izadra. Qerns rang the doorbell and moments later the porch light came one.

"Who is it?" a male voice asked.

"We wish to speak to you about a mutual friend, Catherine." At'r said pronouncing Catherine's Earth name with an accent.

"Who are you?"

"It is a little difficult to explain from out here." At'r returned, growing impatient, he could use his lazzer on the door lock and open it.

Kevin had become cautious since Catherine's disappearance the first time, but since her re-appearance and the appearance of the government agents he had become leery. Now three strangers appear at his door at three in the morning asking to talk with him about Catherine. They were not from the government, but they might be foreign agents, or they might be aliens, he wondered which.

As if to confirm the latter suspicion the door lock and handle began to glow red, opening with a slight click. Kevin backed up, bumping the antique table in his foyer and stood frozen, waiting breathlessly for the door to open.

Kevin was immediately drawn to At'r, knowing without introduction that Catherine had been wrong, the alien Lord had come after her. At'r's presence, even dressed in earth clothes was disarming. At'r wore a silk business suit without a tie and Kevin noted the necklace around his throat, it was the silver version of Catherine's gold.

Finding his voice again, Kevin told At'r, "She is not here."

"That much we know Earthman, but there are other things I wish to know." the alien paused, "Do you know who I am?"

"I think so."

"I am At'r, her husband, and you will answer my questions."

Kevin stood straight, "That sir, depends on the questions." Inwardly he flinched at the fire in the alien Lord's eyes. He now understood why Catherine had run from him. With a regal sweep of his arm, At'r motioned Kevin to lead them into his home. Feeling compelled by their presence he did.

"Please, Mr. Bonnett, sit down, you look pale." At'r said in a bored tone, and after Kevin had complied he asked, "Do you know where she is?"

"No!"

"Do you have the package her grandmother left for her?"

"Yes, it is now in her possession where it belongs." Kevin looked at the other two. The girl he guessed was the one Catherine had described to him, the other alien seemed more at home in the Earth clothes. 'An agent,' Kevin thought. Again he spoke directly to At'r, "There is very little I can do for you."

At'r looked at him for a long time causing Kevin to become more nervous than he was already. Breaking the silence that had fallen in the room, the phone rang and Kevin jumped slightly, startled.

"What is that?" At'r questioned.

"It is a telephone, sire," the agent Qerns answered, it rang again, "it has a listening device attached."

"I had suspected as much." Kevin said with disgust.

From his pocket Qerns withdrew a miniature calculator, or so it seemed, but the device emitted a high pitched whine for about two seconds, the phone rang again.

"Now you may answer it, the tap has been neutralized." At'r assured Kevin.

CHAPTER 17

Stx had managed to escape the fighting between his men and a small Creasion reconnaissance patrol. He held his injured shoulder with his right hand and although he was assaulted by waves of nausea he continued on to a hidden entrance leading to his base. Looking around cautiously to be sure he was not followed, Stx slipped through the brush that concealed the passage. Once inside he heard the Creasion shuttle take off and knew the battle was over, his team had lost. Wearily Stx leaned against the cold metal on the outside of the security doors. Seconds later all went black, the door opened, and he fell unconscious before two of his security personnel. They rushed him to their small medical facility and the doctor brought him back to consciousness then bandaged his wounds. Before he had finished the examination, Stx was issuing orders.

Many interesting things were going through his mind. The Creasion girl who had shot him was protecting none other than Commander Kron, the Creasion Emperor's Chief Commander, and she was Creasion also, Royal Creasion. The necklace she wore blazoned her Royalty. Something so familiar struck him about her. She was the same Earthgirl he had captured in the Rockies and the same girl Captain Quar had taken captive to Zerion, obviously Quar did not make it to Zerion. Now the events of the past days were less mysterious. The Creasions were closing in, now he was sure, but Stx had no idea of how much time he had before the Creasion began their strikes. Of one thing he was sure, Stx wanted that girl dead. She had caused nothing but trouble, he would have killed her the first night had his superior, at the time, not desired her.

"Get my fighter ready for tonight, and get agent Lutz on the communications console."

Moments later the agent's face appeared on the console, "What have you to report?" Stx demanded.

"Little, sir." Lutz said nervously, "We are still observing the Earth-girl's lawyer, he does not know where she is either." he explained.

"That isn't an Earthgirl, she is Royal Creasion." Stx told the agent.

"If I find out anything I will contact you."

"You will do better than that." Stx said sternly, "She is Creasion, I want to know where she is."

"Shall I attempt to capture her?" Lutz asked.

"No, I want the location, even if you only get an approximate area. I will take care of her after that."

"Very well sir."

A blank screen replaced the agent's face and Stx tried to get a little rest before nightfall, then he would begin a computer scan search of the area he hoped Lutz would provide. He still remembered the strange readings they had tracked her on before.

Just before dark the agent called back, telling Stx all he knew, giving him only a general idea of where she might be. One hour after sundown Stx burst from his hidden hanger to streak up into the starry night sky over the earth and flying low followed a tracking grid until he picked up her readings three hours before dawn. Stx had almost given up. Hovering over the small cottages he scanned each until he came to the last one where the readings seemed the strongest, but still fluctuated. Stx knew the gold necklace the Creasion woman wore was preventing him from obtaining a pin point fix.

Something woke Catherine. An unearthly silence filled the cottage like a cold draft. She sat up, sweating in the chilly dark room. Gathering the letter together and roughly shoving it back in the envelope Catherine picked up her keys and gingerly opened the cottage door. Walking across the porch she went directly to her car and quietly opening the door got in.

Flashing lights caused her to freeze and she looked up at the night sky, fearful. An ambulance sped by and Catherine realized this was the source of the flashing lights. Suddenly she felt very foolish.

Catherine yawned and stretched, then rubbed the sleep from her tired eyes only to find a brightening bluish white glow lighting the area when she opened them again. Fear saturated her being making her arms and legs too heavy to lift. Managing to push the car's clutch in, Catherine was thankful for the incline of the parking lot that allowed her car to roll down the hill. Seconds later a white beam touched the building she had just vacated, imploding the wooden structure and setting it ablaze.

From Catherine's position she saw the cottage's owners run from their home, the man struggling to get his pants on and his wife, curlers in her hair, clutching her bathrobe closed against the cold night air. Their first startled stares at the burning cottage gave way to shrieks of terror when they saw the hovering alien craft. Turning, the Zerion craft disappeared into the darkness of the night sky.

When the man and his wife ran back inside their house that also served as an office, Catherine started her car and sped away, shaking from what she had seen. Clearly the Zerion were after her as were the government agents. How the Zerions had found her and what had alerted her to the danger was a mystery. She glanced at her watch, three fifteen in the morning. Nearing a town she found a phone and called Kevin.

"Hello!" Kevin's voice sounded tired through the receiver.

"Kevin, it's me." Catherine said hesitantly.

"I thought it might be you, are you all right?"

"For now, but," she fell silent, "Kevin I think your phone is tapped, I just wanted you to know I am alive. When you read about the cottage…" silence again, "I've got to go, if they trace this call they will know where I am."

"Catherine!" Kevin's voice broke in, "I can confidentially tell you the phone is not tapped, tell me where you are?"

"No Kevin. I have put you in enough danger." Her voice broke, "God, those damn Zerions know I am on Earth, they just tried to kill me. I have to go…I'll call when I can." the phone went dead.

Did you pin-point her location?" At'r asked turning to Qerns.

"General area only sire," Qerns' replay was interrupted by a loud pounding on the door.

"Open up or we will force the door." they threatened. "This is the Secret Service."

"What now?" Kevin asked again.

At'r turned to Kevin, "What do they want?"

"The document I gave Catherine, and possibly to arrest me."

"What will happen if they, ah, arrest you?"

Kevin shrugged, "They will want to know all I know about Catherine, and you. I won't willingly tell them." he stated flatly.

"Earthman, you know far too much to allow them to arrest you." At'r paused as the pounding returned, "You will come with us." he decided.

"And if I do not want to come with you?"

"Would you rather stay here?"

For a moment the two men's eyes met. At'r's powerful will looking inside the human's mind with ease. There he saw Kevin's concern for Izadra, but At'r refrained from invading the privacy of his mind, it was against their basic moral laws to use force. A vague thought came to At'r, could it be that Izadra preferred this human? His eyes narrowed slightly.

Kevin studied At'r, he felt At'r's mind touch his. So, Catherine had been correct. These people, the Creasions were telepathic. Kevin concentrated his thoughts on Catherine and his concern for her safety, this was all he wanted the alien to know, but from the strength

At'r's mind projected Kevin knew At'r could look as deeply as he wished. Kevin found the experience disquieting.

"Very well, I guess I have no real choice." Kevin stood as the agents began an attempt to break in the door.

Qerns had left the room and now returned, "I have activated an electronic barrier, but it will not hold for long. Is there another way out?"

"This is an old house, luckily a basement door opens out into the alley, I doubt they know about it. Follow me."

With the sound of the door beginning to splinter the group hurriedly followed Kevin down a flight of stairs after going through a concealed hatch in the kitchen floor. "This was a wine cellar once," Kevin informed them as he pushed away some debris that covered the outer door.

It took Qerns, Kevin, and At'r to force the door. Above them came the clamor of footsteps on the kitchen floor but the hatch went undetected and with a second hearty push the cellar door opened and they rapidly climbed the steps up to the alley.

While the agents searched his home, Kevin and the three aliens sped away. Sitting quietly in the back of the van, Kevin studied the three. Qerns was an agent who seemed to have a variety of skills, and Kevin wondered what his cover was during normal operations, perhaps just an observer.

At'r was much like Catherine had described him, formidable. His presence filling the room, his questions Kevin felt compelled to answer. Kevin smiled sadly, he knew Catherine's temperament too, and he knew he had lost her.

Captain Kara, Tari, Catherine had called her. What an exotic beauty! Sapphire blue eyes and long black hair that Tari wore back restrained by two large barrettes behind her head. In the earth style, blue silk dress that matched her eyes she was gorgeous and Kevin found himself admiring her long legs encased in black silk stockings.

As if feeling his eyes on her Tari turned toward him, Kevin smiled, she returned his smile.

"Your Highness?" Kevin addressed At'r.

"Yes Mr. Bonnett?"

"You could drop me off in this next town…" Kevin suggested, not sure what the aliens had planned for him. "Please do not think me ungrateful," Kevin paused, "but it isn't necessary that I go with you."

"On the contrary, Mr. Bonnett, I would not hear of it." At'r stressed, wanting to keep close watch on the Earthman who had such a prominent role in his wife's life.

"Captain Kara," At'r turned to Tari. "Take Mr. Bonnett back to Tos-hawk One in your fighter, see to it that communications on board Tos-hawk One ties in a line to the lawyer's phone. We don't want to loose track of Izadra should she call again." He turned back to Kevin; "I want you to be able to talk with her in security." Then back to Kara, "Mr. Bonnett is our guest for the time being, see that he is properly treated, I will refuel from one of the outer docks and return with Commander Kron for the strike."

"What strike?" Kevin had been listening intensely.

"Captain Kara can explain during your flight."

Bumping onto the dirt road brought their conversation to an end, another half a mile and Kevin saw the two alien fighters sitting in the clearing ahead. When the van stopped Kevin slowly got out, still staring at the fighters. Mingled with the fear Kevin felt was a sense of enthusiasm. He would get to see space, the stars unobstructed by the Earth's atmosphere. Feeling Captain Kara's hand on his shoulder, Kevin courageously followed her silk clad figure up the ladder and boarded her fighter. Inside he gazed in amazement at the advanced interior of the space fighter. While he was absorbed in the intricacies of the ship, Kara quickly slipped out of the dress and donned her uniform flightsuit. Kevin watching discreetly and admiring her beautiful figure as she finished by pressing the Velcro around the wrists. Tari instructed Kevin to settle himself in the co-pilots couch and prepare for lift-off as she began the sequence to start the engines.

Moments later, just after the smaller Royal fighter ascended, Kevin felt the ship begin to float, then with a burst of amazing thrust they followed the Emperor's ship. Kevin watched the ground disappear under the darkness of night and soon the clouds were left behind, ahead the clear stars of space beckoned.

CHAPTER 18

To Catherine's relief the first ray of the sun began to filter through the high light clouds of a winter sky and it felt reassuring. In total, Catherine had gotten two and a half hours sleep, her eyes burned and she was thirsty but had not passed an open store to stop at. In was fully daylight when she found a traveler's inn. Buying a thermos of hot black coffee and a couple of stale doughnuts, she also filled the car with gas, checked the oil and was on the highway again.

Catherine stayed in the mountains and kept to the secondary roads, heading in a southwesterly direction she entered Kentucky early in the afternoon. In a small coal town she stopped and called Kevin. Her eyes traveled over the dormant town, peaceful on a winter's Sunday afternoon, the phone rang in her ear.

Railroad tracks ran through the center of the town and by the weather seasoned train station. Gathered around the train station all the other structures were of a similar timber and built around the turn of the nineteenth century, except the bank, it stood as a stone pillar of the town, alone and aloof. Homes dotted both sides of the mountainside almost to the top, and halfway up on the western side stood a time and weatherworn church next to an old cemetery. Paralleling the railroad tracks through the valley flowed a quick moving stream disappearing beneath a rusty suspension bridge where the train tracks crossed the valley just outside town. Loitering on the steps of the general store/post office a group of four young men openly stared at the sleek black car Catherine had gotten out of, their interest soon turning to the car's occupant. They eyed her appraisingly, but none were bold enough to approach her. In the near distance she heard the lonely whistle of an approaching coal train, and shivered in the freezing wind moments later as the train roared by. After twenty rings, Catherine hung the phone up and wearily got back in her car, taking a moment to check her map she changed her course to a more northerly route.

At sundown on the second day Catherine's progress found her nearing the state line between Kentucky and Indiana. Thanking whatever forces seemed to be influencing her fate as of late, Catherine was grateful she had not seen many police officers. She had been careful to obey posted speed laws, and keep as low a profile as the exotic auto would permit. But it had to happen, Catherine knew, by now her description had been circulated to the authorities in most of the regional states or possibly further. So she wasn't surprised when a police car sped up threateningly behind her and flashed his lights at her. Calmly she glanced back.

Behind the wheel of the white and green Sheriff's car sat a formidable looking officer. His round green hat was pulled down on his forehead and his sunglasses beneath it obscured all but the nose, mouth and lower jaw. His lips were drawn in a tight line and his determination was obvious even in his reflection in her rearview mirror. Catherine thought he looked like a bulldog.

Catherine could not decide what she wanted to do. Should she stop and see what he wanted, perhaps a minor traffic offense, no, she knew she had been careful. Still she had always been taught to stop. She remembered the Sheriff's chase in Utah, had she stopped then this might have all been avoided. Hesitantly she slowed and pulled over to the curb, the Sheriff's car followed her to a stop.

"Step out of the car!" came a sharp command from the Officer. Looking back Catherine saw he was drawing his pistol as he exited his car.

Panic flooded her blood stream and she mashed the execrator, her tires gaining traction in the small gravel on the curb to through a shower of the small stones and dirt on the Sheriff and his patrol car. Catherine had disappeared by the time the Sheriff had recovered, and much to the Officer's dismay found his radio antenna badly damaged from the rock shower. With lights flashing and his siren blaring he sped down the road hoping for a clue to her direction, but reaching the state line without seeing her, he gave up to return to base for repairs.

CHAPTER 19

*K*evin did not bother to think about how many hours it had been since he left Earth. He was much to busy and distracted. Space had been all he had imagined and much more. As Captain Kara, Tari, had rounded the moon to the dark side they had encountered a fleet of Creasion fighters and troop carriers en-route to destroy the Zerion's bases. Here At'r signaled he would join Commander Kron's forces. Tari and Kevin journeyed on to Tos-hawk One, Kevin could tell she was disappointed at missing the coming battle, but he wasn't. Only after he had a close up view of the moon and Mars did Tos-hawk One loomed ahead of the small ship.

Tos-hawk One was unlike anything Kevin had ever experienced even in the most elaborate science fiction novels he loved to loose himself in. From a distance she looked like a black hole in the star field, as they closed the space between them, he could appreciate her size. Tos-hawk One would dwarf an Aircraft Carrier. On either end were lighted landing bays; outside the ship were two free floating refueling docks capable of refueling fifty ships each. A fighter escort of four, two on each side took up position, and the traffic controller's voice broke the silence.

"Royal escort fighter, please proceed to landing bay one and follow battle security procedure Alpha. We are on alert condition until the completion of the Earth strike."

"Affirmative Controller." Tari responded, then turned to Kevin, "We will be braking suddenly, just wanted you to be aware."

Seconds later he stepped out of the fighter to stand shaken on the hanger deck. "What a ride!"

"You should try piloting one." Tari told him with a smile.

"I'd like that. I flew fighter jets in the Navy."

"His Highness might be persuaded to allow it. You could always ask."

Tari escorted him to his quarters, arranged the phone link and in general helped him to feel comfortable in the alien atmosphere. Then left him to rest, assuring him At'r would notify him if they found Lady Izadra and explaining he could watch the fleet's progress on the ship's viewer. Tari then went directly to refuel her ship and fly patrol around Tos-hawk One just in case the Zerion fleet showed up.

From a high position, far above Earth's atmosphere At'r sat in orbit watching the Zerion bases destruction and hoping for more information on Izadra, none had come in recently. As the hours passed he grew restless and flew down to monitor an area Izadra had been going toward, she wasn't there.

Finally with the last Zerion base a smoldering ruin, the Creasion force turned toward their Battle-station and a well-earned rest. At'r too had to return with them, his ship was low on fuel and he was frustrated and near exhaustion. Reluctantly he turned his fighter toward Tos-hawk One, concern for Izadra weighing heavily on his mind.

CHAPTER 20

Catherine had managed with the help of a lot of black coffee to drive through another night, stopping about every hour to stretch her legs and walk around to wake up. She had not been spotted again by the authorities and she felt lucky not to have seen the agents she suspected were looking for her. Perhaps she had evaded them. Hunger gnawed at her stomach reminding her the last meal she had eaten was twelve hours ago, the last time she had tried to call Kevin. He had not been home.

Spotting a truck stop ahead Catherine tiredly pulled into their parking lot and locking the Lamborgini went inside to have breakfast. She sat, as she always did now, near a window, just so she could see the car and who was entering the parking lot. Several of the truck drivers looked admiringly at the black beauty of a car she drove but otherwise she had a peaceful meal.

Paying her check, she bought two newspapers and was back on the road in under an hour. Feeling more awake she drove on for several more hours until finally exhaustion forced her to find a place to rest.

Intending to call Kevin, then obtain a room for the night at a hotel, Catherine pulled off the interstate she had been on to enter the parking lot of a large hotel. After what seemed like an enormous amount of time, the phone began to ring. After two rings the phone was picked up.

"Hello!" Kevin's voice sounded close.

"Kevin."

"Catherine?" Kevin's voice was flooded with relief. At'r who had been talking with Kevin when the phone rang listened intently. "You've been out of touch for a long time."

"I called, you were not home."

"I had to be out for a time." was all the excuse he gave.

Strange, Catherine thought, what if the government has arrested him. "Kevin, can you talk freely?"

"Yes, Catherine."

"You sound strange, is there anything wrong?"

"Just not knowing where you are."

"You saw the papers, and I am sure the news?"

"Yes, I saw!" Kevin told her, "Catherine, tell me where you are. I…Hold on."

Kevin turned to At'r, "Please, let me tell her, give her the chance to…" Kevin held up his hand.

"Catherine," he paused, "Catherine!" he said again.

"Kevin!" her frantic voice came over the receiver,

"Those agents just pulled off the interstate, I've got to go."

"What interstate, Catherine?" Kevin yelled through the phone, but she had hung up. "She's gone again." Kevin said sadly. He looked at At'r, his face a grim mask.

Catherine casually got back inside her car. She had parked next to another black car and the agents drove past without seeing her, she sighed. Catherine wasn't sure they knew what kind of car she was driving, but somehow she knew they did. She waited until her pursuers were well out of sight to pull out of the parking lot, then going back the way she had come raced away from the traveler's haven.

Catherine set the cruise control just a little over the sixty-five miles per hour speed limit and kept a close watch on her rearview mirrors. After an hour she eased up and began to look for a place to rest. Too well she remembered traveling this way only hours ago, and there wasn't a hotel with in another hundred miles, only a state park.

Catherine knew this was her only option, she would park for a while, then before dark return to the area she had fled, and there she could get a room for the night.

Careful to pull well inside a heavily wooded glen where her car was completely hidden from the road she sat and read the newspapers, the headlines bold and frightening;

SPACE WARRIORS ATTACK; ALIEN BASES BLOWN UP BY OTHER ALIEN WARCRAFT—MILITARY ON FULL ALERT!

Catherine was astounded at the depth of destruction to the Zerion's bases. At'r had succeeded in a complete surprise attack on the larger bases, but the aftermath could not be camouflaged from the people on Earth. And whether or not At'r intended it, the ruins provided a warning to the residence of the planet.

On the third page from the cover story Catherine stopped, her picture, along with one of her father headed one of the articles. The article questioned her father's strange death and her strange disappearance, and proposed the aliens were to blame. Catherine laughed, then began to cry, if only they knew. Leaning her head back and easing the driver seat back in a reclining position she closed her eyes for a short nap. Confident of At'r's thoroughness in dealing with the Zerion, now only the agents would be searching for her.

Catherine discounted At'r, she didn't think he really would come after her. The thought left her with a strange feeling of emptiness she could not understand. At'r triggered so many foreign feelings inside her and if she had not left he would have soon been able to see into her mind. Then he would have controlled her, this she would never allow. But the other feelings, her blood raced remembering his kisses and touch that frightened her too. Still thinking of At'r she drifted off to sleep.

What was intended to be a short nap became a long night's sleep that extended into the next day. Catherine woke around noon when the sun slanted through the windshield of her car. Disorientated she stared at her watch, her eyes so blurry she could barely read the time, twelve-O-two, Catherine tried to focus on the date blinking several times.

Her head was foggy and she laid her head on the steering wheel for a few moments trying to organize her thoughts, but quickly found she was more likely to go back to sleep.

Catherine opened her car door and getting out walked the short distance to the bathhouse. The place was deserted and she made use of the facilities, showering and washing her hair then donning clean new clothes. Refreshed she fired up the auto's powerful engine allowing it time to warm before driving slowly out of the park. Once again headed in a northerly direction Catherine stopped at the same group of stores, hotels and restaurants where she had seen the agents. Using the same pay phone as before she called Kevin, the phone rang once.

"Catherine?" Kevin sounded sleepy.

"It's me." she affirmed.

"We, ah, I had hoped to hear from you sooner, I was worried."

"More than usual?" Catherine queried. "And who is 'we'?"

Alarms sounded, Kevin startled, "Catherine!"

"Yes Kevin, where are you, those alarms..." the phone went dead, Catherine stared at the dead receiver, a shiver racing up her spine. 'Where was Kevin?' she asked herself. She feared he had been arrested.

Kevin stood, still holding the receiver in his hand, to watch the huge crash doors close over the cathedral windows in At'r's chambers. At'r had responded to the blaring alarms by calmly going to his desk/console and activating his view screens to monitor the bridge, gaining information without interrupting the crew doing their jobs.

"A large fleet of Zerion craft are entering this solar system." he looked to Kevin, "They are still out past the asteroid belt. We will be ready for them." he said confidently, "They are not aware that Tos-hawk Two is one hour behind them." At'r smiled, one of the few times Kevin had seen him do so, "Since we have moved Tos-hawk One closer to Earth your people on the planet below should get a spectacular show tonight." he grew serious again, "I only wish I knew where Izadra was."

Darkness grew from the east to cover the highway and surrounding prairie, hues of red, fuchsia and lavender arrayed the setting sun in brilliance, soon the stars began to blink on and the sky turned to indigo. 'Another night on the highway' Catherine thought, one more day and she should cross the boarder and be safely in Canada. A meteor streaked through the clear night sky, then another and another. Now the meteors weren't just streaking they began to maneuver at odd angles some falling burning through the atmosphere. Traffic pulled over, stopping altogether until the interstate looked like a long slender parking lot. Catherine too stopped, got out of her car and stood staring up at the now obvious battle being fought there. Some of the observers were excited, some were crying, others were shocked into silence, but Catherine knew. The Zerion fleet had arrived and were engaged in a deadly battle with the Creasions for control of Earth. Catherine held no doubts that the Zerions would loose, but she was worried for the friends she had made on Tos-hawk One. She prayed they would not be killed, and she pondered what At'r was doing in all of this.

After an hour and half of intensive battle the arena overhead started to clear, now only an occasional explosion brightened the night, but there were still many small craft zipping across the heavens. As the skies cleared so did the traffic.

CHAPTER 21

Long awaited by the construction crew of the now destroyed bases, the Zerion supply ships and military men to staff them arrived too late. Instead of tired workers preparing to return home waiting to greet them, they found all of their bases destroyed and the personnel dead or scattered among the populace to hide. Before discerning what had happened the Zerion found themselves trapped by a Creasion battle-station that did not register on any of their instruments until moments before it fired. At'r had waited, baiting them through the captured communications relay station on the Moon. The Creasion's presence had come as a total and devastating shock to the Zerion.

Already heavily engaged in battle with one Creasion Tos-hawk, the Zerion Commander lost heart when a second appeared, moments later his ship was badly damaged and he instructed the self detonate sequence started. But it never reach zero, instead it received a terminal blow from Tos-hawk Two. With all but six troop transports remaining the Zerions broke off the attack and turned back toward home with Tos-hawk Two close behind. At'r had ordered Commander Delia only to 'escort' the Zerion ships safely home. Troop transports were not heavily armed and At'r considered their destruction, unless necessary, to be murderous. In all the battle lasted two hours causing panic on the planet below.

Night wore on slowly, measured by the passage of the half moon. Stretching before Catherine the gray satin ribbon of interstate seemed infinite and hypnotic, lulling her tired senses to a near euphoric state. Catherine felt sleep overtaking her and fought back, managing to roll down the windows. Breathing in the cold night air she revived, and spotted a cluster of civilization consisting of two gas stations and a store open twenty-four hours a day. Pulling off the interstate at the exit, Catherine filled her car with fuel and checked the other fluids. After going to the ladies room she bought some junk food and a coke.

Reluctant to again conform her tired body to the seat of the sports car Catherine stretched and twisted, working her muscles and getting her blood moving a little quicker. She looked at the car's cockpit and was reminded of the more spacious cockpit of At'r's fighter, the comfortable couches and the auto-pilot that would allow the pilot to rest. Her automobile had none of these things. Resolutely she bent her tired body to fit the space, wearily she laid her head on the steering wheel. Catherine was tired of running and Canada held only minimal hope for security. Starting the engine she put the car in gear and leaving the gas station failed to notice the government car in front of the store across the road.

Agent Brooks spotted the suspect's car as she left the gas station but had to wait for Lutz, who was still inside the men's room. Agent Lutz hated life on Earth, but after the Creasion attack on their bases he knew his stay would be longer. Hearing his unsuspecting earthling partner sound the auto's horn he hurried from the bathroom, his shirttail hanging out one side and his zipper stuck. Lutz, like all Zerion, had never encountered zippers before Earth and he just could not get the hang of them. Pulling on the little piece of metal it suddenly came unstuck momentarily to grab the flesh beneath his fly. Lutz screamed in agony, he rarely wore the underwear most human males wore, they were too restricting, now he wished he had learned to tolerate them.

Managing not to drop to his knees, he freed himself and stumbled to the car much to the amusement of the few other travelers who had stopped at the same oasis. With their laughter stinging his Zerian ears, he swore, hating Earth even more, they accelerated onto the highway. Brooks, with the control of a saint, didn't laugh at his partner.

Behind Catherine, the flash of headlights did not alarm her. She maintained her ninety-mile an hour cursing speed, the radar detector on just in case a highway patrolman waited ahead. Still pondering the space battle she had witnessed, Catherine would not allow herself to believe At'r had stayed to search for her. Remembering with clarity how his presence affected her, her concentration waned. When At'r was near she felt weak, as if he sapped her strength of will. His lovemaking had taken her to yet another world far above the orbit of Tos-hawk. Had she stayed with him longer he would have had access to her mind as he did her body and that frightened her far more than his anger. In her fear Catherine had run from him and her fate, only to obtain the letter from her grandmother confirming what Catherine would not believe before. 'But how could I ever trust a man with my soul if he did not love or care for me?' she asked herself.

White lights glaring into her rear view mirror brought Catherine abruptly back to the present. Obeying a conditioned escape reflex, she depressed the accelerator and the Lamborghini moved ahead of the imposing vehicle for a few moments. With in moments the unknown car move to within inches of her back bumper then swinging over into the right lane to move up next to her. In the dim light she could see it was the two agents. Under her breath she cursed them, looking ahead again she pushed the gas petal to the floor and moved away from the government car like it was stationary.

Having been modified the agent's auto gained but only enough speed to follow Catherine's sports car. Both agents knew their car was incapable of keeping pace over a long period of time.

A piercing sound seemed to engulf Catherine and she prayed the car was not malfunctioning, seemingly on the horizon a red ball was moving toward her. Before it became recognizable an inner sense told Catherine the object that approached was a Zerion fighter, but she could not know the pilot was Stx, intent on killing her at any cost.

A green glow began to illuminate the Lamborghini, Catherine was startled and looked around for the source of the strange light only to realize it was her necklace. The fighter screamed past her just over the roof of the car, and behind her agent Brooks was startled by the obviously alien craft, but not agent Lutz, who knew his home planet's ship. Agent Brooks swerved as the fighter blasted over, the piercing sound fading into the darkness. Brooks lost control of the car and it spun around twice before he could regain control. With shaking hands he accelerated once again, giving chase to Catherine in her quickly disappearing car.

Catherine watched their spin in her rear view mirror and quickly put several miles between them and herself. On the horizon a speck of red light was growing. Shuddering she knew it was the Zerion fighter. Wondering, as she drew nearer the now hovering object, how it had escaped At'r's scrutiny. Behind her the two agents were closing the large gap she had opened between them. Ahead, no longer hovering, the fighter closed the distance firing lazzers and burning the pavement, making the asphalt a flaming trap.

Out of desperation Catherine flung her car to the right gripping the steering wheel tightly to keep it from being ripped from her hands. She rode out the course she had chosen going through a ditch to fly up in the air and crash through a fence coming to a stop in the middle of a cow pasture several yards from the highway. Overhead the Zerion fighter circled to line up on Catherine's stalled car and destroy it and her.

CHAPTER 22

At'r had insisted one of Doctor Trentos' special sensors, used to override the Royal Necklace, be installed on his fighter, with it At'r hoped to find Izadra. He had grown impatient waiting for their agents on Earth to locate his wife and had searched most of the general area they had tracked Izadra to without results. Growing more concerned about her by the moment he hoped the Earthmen did not find her first. At'r still had not decided what he would do with her when he found her. In trying to envision what punishment he would extract from Izadra he would remember the feel of her lips and the softness of her body. His anger would leave only to be replaced by a gnawing anxiety for Izadra's safety. An alarm sounded, At'r jumped, unnerved, the alarm announcing the presence of a Zerion fighter.

At'r guided his fighter toward the Zerion ship, he monitored the firing of the enemy's lazzers, directed toward the ground. A cold feeling swept over At'r and he pushed the thrusters further in, accelerating the ship. Seconds later he could visually see the Zerion ship closing on what the Earthmen call a car. Another alarm began to sound, the medical scanner telling him he had found Izadra.

Bright light bathed the area casting ominous shadows over the attacking Zerion fighter. Dazed by the rough ride in the car and from striking her head on the roof, Catherine tired to focus on the fighter. Numbly she tried to move but could not, Catherine knew the Zerion was about to fire on her, but she could not get out of the car. The she recalled her buckled seatbelt. With trembling fingers she touched the button on the seatbelt, releasing it. Pushing the door open she stumbled out, looking up at the Zerion fighter Catherine's eyes moved further skyward, following the white light coming from above her attacker.

Catherine froze, amazed, At'r had returned for her. A green beam emanated from beneath At'r's fighter, radiating toward the now retreating Zerion fighter, upon impact the beam exploded the fighter, lighting the area for miles as the burning wreckage fell in the near by fields.

Luminescent light from the other two Creasion fighters, now visible and the burning wreckage of the Zerion fighter changed the area from a farmer's field to an errie unearthly landscape. At'r's ship descended while Catherine steadied herself against the car's fender. Appearing in the doorway At'r scanned the area, his eyes resting admiringly on the Lamborghini, then on Izadra.

Angry eyes met frightened ones. On shaking legs, Catherine slowly stood away from the car. She felt her blood race and her breath grew short. Catherine wanted to run from him, so wrathful was his look, but she had run from her destiny for too long and she was tired. Fate had decreed she would be his wife, Catherine knew it, and felt it in her inner self to be true.

Compelled by a force Catherine could not resist she started the long walk toward At'r knowing she must now go back with him and fulfill her destiny. Suddenly she was halted by screaming brakes and skidding tires as the two agents finally caught up with her, their car blowing steam and oil all over the two agents. At'r also watched the two, one hand on his lazzer pistol.

At'r knew a Zerion no matter what clothing they wore, and he knew one of the agents was a Zerion. He heard Izadra scream and an explosion, then fire in his right shoulder. Aware a primitive earth weapon had shot him he took careful aim at the Zerion who had pulled the trigger and returned his fire.

Izadra watched in terror as the man melted, dying horribly before her eyes, at last she pulled her eyes away to stare wide eyed at At'r who now stared at her, lazzer still in hand. Resolutely Catherine walked toward him, stopping just short of touching him; she glanced down at the lazzer now held loosely in his hand, then at the darkening stain around the bullet hole in his right shoulder.

"At'r, milord," she managed to say, just above a whisper, "you are hurt!" concern filled her voice.

"And the Zerion responsible is dead." At'r returned.

At'r holstered his weapon then looked back at Izadra who seemed to sway slightly. Pain radiated through his chest and Izadra's form faded then reappeared before his eyes. At'r knew he was loosing blood.

Seeing his condition Izadra moved in to support him but he straightened working hard to overcome the pain. "I trust," At'r bit out through tightly clenched teeth, "that you are prepared to return with me!" he stated pulling her against himself on his left to glare menacingly down into her upturned face.

Swiftly Izadra's fear of him renewed, but her pride caused her to react, "Do you offer me a choice?" already she could feel her blood heat.

"No!" he all but growled, "You are mine and you will return with me." then he roughly pushed her toward his fighter.

Izadra turned back on At'r, an enraged snarl on her pretty lips, only to again find he would need her help to re-enter the fighter. Overhead Captain Kara was observing her leader's condition and she was well aware of the friction between the Royal couple. Tari smiled, she could understand Lady Izadra's pride and she knew positively of her Emperor's.

At'r was losing blood and Izadra eased him onto the couch inside the fighter. Panic threatened to rule her actions as she scanned the technical nightmare of the ship's controls. "Think!" she said aloud and remembered where the communications panel was from the trip At'r had taken her on the day before her escape. That trip now seemed a lifetime ago.

Flicking on the audio she spoke aloud to the ship's interior, "Creasion fighter—can you hear me?" all this while she kept constant but gentle pressure on the wound in At'r's shoulder.

"Yes Lady Izadra, I am monitoring you, this is Captain Kara."

"You saw what happened?"

"Yes milady, how badly is Lord At'r injured?"

"He is losing blood and unconscious," there was a pause, "and I can not fly this damn ship." Izadra said fearing being trapped, already other travelers were stopping outside, and form a large circle about the Creasion fighter.

"Milady will be returning to Tos-hawk One?"

"Yes Tari." there was silence, then "I have stopped the bleeding."

"How did you activate the communications?"

"I was in this ship before. Remember the Zerion ships we caught between Mars and Jupiter?"

"How much do you recall?" Tari asked.

Izadra was quiet, remembering what At'r had shown her, "I can begin the start sequence, I can operate the defense panel and communications, but the flight controls," she sighed, "I have only flown a small jet."

"It is a start," and step by step Tari instructed Izadra on how to lift off the spacecraft, but just as Izadra made final adjustments At'r regained consciousness and sat up, surprised to see Izadra at the controls.

"Izadra!" he called and struggled to stand.

"At'r," she said startled, "At'r you must stay still, the bleeding wil…"

At'r managed to stand and motion Izadra out of his seat, "I will fly her back." he eased himself down in the pilot's seat as she vacated it.

Drawing a deep breath he contacted Captain Kara that he was lifting off.

"Sire, there are five Air Force fighters closing on this area quickly." she informed him.

"Thank you." At'r told her and lifted the fighter off the ground much to the amazement of the gathered crowd below. Five F-16's rocketed past him unable to turn before the two alien spacecraft blasted out of the atmosphere.

Once safely in space At'r turned to look at Izadra who sat apprehensively on the couch. "You should buckle your seat belt." He told her casually, then turned back to the controls.

Fastening her seatbelt as At'r had instructed her, Izadra pondered her situation. At'r had appeared furious before he had been shot, now he was so nonchalant, what punishment he would extract? Did Creasion men beat their women, or would he drug her into obedience as he had threatened to do before the wedding ceremony. Izadra only pondered these things for a few minutes before Tos-hawk One came in view. It surprised her that At'r had left his prize ship in such a low orbit around Earth.

"At'r," she ventured, "do you know Earth's defenses are capable of monitoring Tos-hawk One in her present orbit?"

"Yes, but after the Zerion bases destruction and the battle earlier, I doubt they are unaware of us. However, Earth's defenses have nothing that can reach this far out in space before we could leave orbit or destroy what they fired at us." He drew a slow deep breath careful not to make the wound worse, he sagged a little.

"Milord?" she unbuckled her seatbelt and went to his aid.

For a long moment At'r contemplated her, surprised at her concern, wondering how genuine it was. "I will be fine, now please go back to your seat, we will land in a few moments." Setting the controls, At'r turned his fighter for the final approach to the hangar. Again he turned to Izadra, "Only lords Betus, Trentos, Commander

Kron, and Captain Kara know of your escape, the others believe you were on a mission. It is better they do not see dissension between us."

"Yes, milord." Izadra answered just before she was pushed back against the couch as the fighter touched down inside the hangar.

Behind them Captain Kara landed emerging from her fighter to see Emperor At'r being attended by the physician lord Trentos. She approached bowing to her Lord and Lady, and saluting Kron.

"May I inquire as to milord's condition?" Tari asked respectfully.

"I will be fine, Tari." At'r addressed her as a friend, "Thank you for your assistance."

"My pleasure, sire." Turning she followed Kron to give him her full report on the flight. At'r was taken to sickbay.

Sometime later Doctor Trentos joined Izadra in the sickbay waiting area he noted the concern clearly visible on her face. "I see you ignored my orders to wait in your chambers," Trentos began gruffly, "There is nothing you can do here, and from what I can see you're not in much better shape than At'r is." Trentos gestured toward the treatment room behind him.

"Doctor," Izadra said resolutely, "I have been pursued on Earth and shot at by Zerions only to see," her voice grew soft, "At'r almost killed because of my…ah," she paused, "As angry as I know Lord At'r is with me I cannot rest until I know he will recover."

"I assure you Lady Izadra he will recover, now," he became stern, "your health also concerns me and my monitors tell me you are exhausted, you will go with my nurse to your chambers, she will see to your comfort." Trentos could clearly see the rebellion in her eyes. "So! You have decided you are the heir?" he croaked at her, "about time, but around here you do not disobey your doctor." Still she would not be moved, "I will release His Highness in about an hour, he will need rest but otherwise he will be fully recovered by this time tomorrow. Please milady, go get a bath, change your clothes and At'r should be waiting for you." He smiled, "Go on before I call one of the bodyguards to carry you."

"All right, Trentos," she conceded, "I will go." Izadra followed the nurse from the room and with her help did as the Doctor ordered. After she was comfortably settled, dressed in the peach gown she had worn the first night on Tos-hawk, the nurse left her alone.

Time dragged, Izadra's apprehension grew. She could not guess what path At'r's anger would take. She shivered.

Gathering her courage Izadra walked to the living room, to At'r's desk where she had placed the letter from her grandmother. In fear of loosing the document, Izadra had kept it safely tucked away inside her jacket on Earth.

Pacing before the windows, Izadra stopped at last to rest her weary head against the cold glass like barrier. Tears slipped from beneath her closed eyelids which Izadra quickly wiped away, only to jump abruptly as the door hissed open and At'r strode in.

They looked at each other for a long time, Izadra feeling the heat of his stare melt her, she braced herself against his desk chair as she felt the touch of his consciousness in her own mind. At'r did not press.

"Your shoulder?" she asked softly as he joined her behind the desk.

"I will be nearly healed by morning." He assured her, the anger and fire in his eyes was petrifying.

At'r's presence made her breathless, she wondered again what retribution he would extract from her for her escape. Tension hung heavy in the air, Izadra knew she was at his mercy and did not depend on his leniency, she saw none in his blazing green eyes.

At'r regarded her through piercing green eyes. He recalled his anger when he first heard she had escaped and the various punishments he had considered for her defiance. An escapade no other had ever dared. At'r remembered the worry and the danger involved in her 'rescue', the pain in his shoulder fresh in his mind. For the first time in his life he had not thought of his people, only of getting Izadra back. At'r resented her for making him forget his duty and his people. His look became fiercer, with his left hand behind her neck he pulled Izadra to him, seeing fear clearly in her beautiful eyes. "Perhaps I should strangle you for all the trouble you have caused." He told her viciously, all the while lightly stroking the racing pulse in her throat with his thumb, "Or leave you to evade the authorities on that backward planet below."

Izadra closed her eyes, she had no strength to fight him, she remained still, what At'r would do, he would do. There wasn't any place to run and her legs were to numb to carry her anyway. If he wished to kill her, Izadra knew he would.

At'r could not resist any longer, slowly, though he fought against it, his lips crushed Izadra's, demanding she submit. She lay weak and panting against him.

"Why?" he demanded hoarsely, "Why did you leave?"

Izadra found the courage to bravely look at At'r, masking little of the panic she felt. From the fury she saw in his eyes Izadra wondered if she should have taken her chances on Earth. How could she explain why she had left. Izadra could not tell At'r how close to penetrating her mind he had been and how she feared losing her identity if he did. How, if At'r did not love or care for her, could she tell him. Slowly she looked down to the desk where the letter lay, the seal declaring the document's importance.

"Milord." she finally found her voice, "I had to retrieve the letter my grandmother left in my lawyer's keeping, I," she paused, "I had to have it…"

At'r, already aware of the letter had a general idea of the contents, "What?" he asked, "did it tell you?"

"She confirmed what you and lord Betus have told me."

"And now you believe what you have been told is true?" At'r asked, Izadra nodded slightly. "Had you told me of the letter, I would have had one of my Earth agents obtain it. There would have been far less risk."

"My lawyer would not have turned it over to the agent, he was instructed not to give it to anyone but me. Kevin can be stubborn—I had to go myself." again she looked at the letter.

"I have a feeling," At'r said turning Izadra's face back to his, "there is another reason for your escape." he felt her shiver and gently he touched her temple.

With his touch came a powerful surge from At'r's mind to Izadra's, his telepathic powers were strong, but she pushed him out.

"No!" Izadra all but screamed, her hands pressing her temples as she move back from At'r, bumping the windows. Dazed she looked up with glazed eyes. "You have taken my body, but," she spat out, "you can not force your way into my mind. My thoughts will remain my own!"

Trapped against the window At'r pressed Izadra against the glass with his body and roughly tilted her head back. Their eyes met. He looked deeply in her eyes but made no further attempt to press into her mind, instead he told her through telepathic thought, "Yes, Izadra I can; however, it would leave you," he caressed her cheek, "damaged, so I will enjoy what I can, and soon you will relinquish all." Emphasizing his domination of her, At'r's mouth closed hard over hers with such vigor Izadra resisted him until he pinned her arms behind her.

Releasing her suddenly At'r pulled her by her wrists, jerking Izadra brutally, drawing her with him to the bedroom. Dropping her arms At'r turned to look upon Izadra's flushed face. Izadra stood before him proudly, defiantly, her eyes level with his, her chest heaving from exertion.

A cruel smile touched his lips, her defiance irritating him. At'r wondered how long her pride would overrule her fear. Leisurely he sat in a chair near the bed where he had left Izadra standing. His fiery ogle sweeping slowly over her, heightening her blush. At'r would see how long her pride would sustain her, then he would have her, totally.

"You have caused me much concern and time with this, escape. You jeopardized our attack plans and kept Tos-hawk One in orbit around Earth far too long. For your actions I could extract any punishment I desire from you." he watched his words effect on her, "However," he smiled again the same cruel smile, "you are my wife, so I will be lenient, this time!" he paused studying Izadra, knowing it made her uncomfortable. "I will expect to see some improvements from you. Your performances in public as 'my loving wife' have been only adequate—" he refused to give her praise although she appeared the perfect Creasion wife, "also, I grow tired of your resistance in bed—I want no more of it, Izadra!" he all but growled and fell silent, watching. Izadra said nothing. "Now my wife," his tone sarcastic, "remove your clothing, and to bed with you." he commanded.

Izadra could not move, her arms were frozen at her sides, her feet rooted to the thick carpet beneath her feet, her knees felt numb. Surly she had not heard him correctly. Never had he demanded she strip before him.

"Shall I assist you Izadra?" he growled and leaned forward.

Izadra took a step back, her face suddenly ashen, her hazel green eyes round with fright as she watched At'r stride toward her. She took another step back, widely glancing around the room, more fearful of him now than on her wedding night. On that night, his demeanor had been gentle.

Reaching her, At'r laced his fingers in her long hair and forcing her head back savagely kissed her again. Izadra felt his hot hands on her shoulder then his hands grasped either side of her gown. Though lessened by the injury, the satiny material yielded with a loud rip to At'r's strength. He released the fabric and it slid down Izadra's rigid body leaving her in only brief underpants. At'r stepped back to brazenly view a shivering Izadra, allowing her to see the growing passion in his eyes as he scrutinized her.

Izadra crossed her arms over her full breasts, obeying an age-old drive to cover herself in her embarrassment. Catching her eyes At'r held them easily, "Drop your arms, wife!" he commanded her as he removed his loose fitting black silk shirt, "Down Izadra!" he commanded more sternly, and she dropped her arms as he dropped his trousers.

Izadra's stare fell on the clear bandage that covered the nearly healed bullet wound in his right shoulder. Suddenly he grasped her arms tightly, his eyes glowering down, holding hers.

"So! You did not think I would come after you?" he shook her, remembering again how he had felt when Kron had told him of her escape. "You were mistaken!" At'r bit each word out and pushed her onto the bed.

Izadra rolled away as he joined her, but At'r pulled her back across the silken sheets by her ankle until she was under him. Wildly Izadra fought him, trying to free herself from his grasp, knowing she was losing. She swung at him fiercely, striking his cheek, her hand numbing from the blow. At'r's retaliation was swift, to Izadra's surprise he struck her back.

Infuriated, Izadra swung again, this time he stopped her assault catching her by the wrist and holding her to the bed. Roughly he kissed her, Izadra struggled beneath him but could not stop At'r from penning her to the bed. Closing her eyes in defeat she lay still as he caressed her tense body, but she could not still the unbidden tears that stole from beneath her eyelids.

"Izadra!" At'r said sharply and she hesitantly opened her eyes to be entranced by his. "I will always come after you and I will always find you, no matter where you run or hide. Remember that if you choose to leave again." Then he took her, swiftly and roughly.

To Izadra's shame her body responded to his, At'r controlled her, compelling her to match his passion.

Suddenly Izadra gasped, "Please..." she begged looking up to see a triumphant smile on At'r's face.

"Soon, he commanded, prolonging the intense pleasure he alone controlled until Izadra thought she would faint from the ecstasy. "You are mine Izadra," At'r told her ferociously, "and I will—never—let—you—go!"

Izadra cried out from the sensations At'r drove through her body, her cry soon joined by At'r's victorious one. Long moments passed and At'r held her tightly, hesitant to release Izadra, unable to admit to himself why he was so reluctant to let her go.

Shaken and appalled, Izadra scrambled to cover her nudity in the sheets when he did release her. Beneath the bed covers At'r's arm went around her waist, pulling her to him.

"Sleep now." he told her and ordered the lights off.

Slumber was long in coming for Izadra, her muscles ached and she longed for the soothing waters of the whirlpool but dare not attempt to leave the bed for fear of waking At'r.

Many unfinished items clouded her mind, Izadra would always wonder about Kevin, she hoped he was safe, she dare not ask At'r to find out for her. At last sleep came, but it was far from restful, the events of her fearful journeys on Earth haunted her and she tossed fitfully in her sleep.

CHAPTER 23

At'r knew Izadra's sleep had been restless, she talked feverishly in her sleep, tossing and turning. Each time At'r had drawn her near, whispering softly to her that she was safe now. A pang of conscience that his rough treatment had caused her distress was quickly squelched. Her escape had given him nightmares too, when he could sleep. Upon waking the third time At'r rose from bed, dressed and went to his desk.

Contemplating the letter, he ran his fingers over the seal, then as if drawn, he sat and withdrew the papers.

After reading the letter At'r turned his chair to stare out at open space. Considering what he had read Izadra should not have any doubts, she appeared to now accept the truth. Absently he rose and paced the room, why did she still refuse him passage to her thoughts. Somehow, he felt her refusal had in some way motivated her escape, but she would not confide in him her reasons. On Creasion it was expected for married couples and a must for the Royal Couple.

For the first time in his life space travel irritated him, he longed for his palace on Creasion and to see Izadra in her new home. Nevertheless At'r had purposely ordered the return voyage to be at minimum speed, giving him time to ensure Izadra would be carrying his child when they arrived on Creasion. A slower return would also give Izadra time to learn their customs and become comfortable with them. He walked quietly through his apartment to the bedroom and gazed on Izadra's sleeping face, she looked so vulnerable. Vividly the previous night came flooding back again. He had been so rough with her, and she had fought him savagely. At'r felt his blood warm at the memory of her passion and how she had come close to matching his. Resolutely he turned and pushed those disturbing thoughts from his mind, he must not allow himself to be distracted by her again. Izadra would perform her wifely and official duties and that would include their minds uniting. She would learn to do as he told her and she would be content. At'r turned and walked back to his desk, pushing the button to summons Kins.

"Yes milord." came and almost immediate reply.

"If Commander Kron, lords Betus and Trentos, Captain Kara and Mr. Bonnett are out of their sleep periods, I would like to see them in the outer receiving room in one hour. If one or all are not awake let me know." he released the button on the desk panel and Kins' image faded. At'r sat and read the letter once more, then ordered his breakfast, showering before it arrived. Finishing, he instructed the crewman who brought his meal to instruct the galley to prepare Lady Izadra's breakfast when she woke. As he left Kins entered, bowed and informed At'r of the arrival of the people he had summoned, then followed him down the hallway connecting his private chambers to the receiving room.

Scanning over the assembled group, each bowed, even Mr. Bonnett, At'r wondered what reaction Izadra would have to his presence.

"Thank you all for coming." At'r said politely, "You may consider this a de-briefing of the past twenty-four hour period of time and Commander after this will switch back to the twenty-five hour day of Creasion. Please be seated." At'r indicated the chairs around the table.

"Sire."

"Yes, lord Trentos?"

"I would like to check your shoulder."

"As you wish." At'r told him.

"You are fine, my Lord." Trentos returned to his seat.

"Commander, your report first please."

"On board Tos-hawk One repairs preceded as needed, most damage from the Zerion fleet was minimal, from near-misses or power surges, after your departure for Earth sire, all went as planned. The last report from Commander Delia was an hour ago, the transcript is ready for you."

"Lord Betus?"

"Little to tell, news of our victory has been transmitted back to Creasion, our people are anxious for our return and to welcome Lady Izadra. They view her presence as a portent of future security from the Zerion."

"Lord Trentos?"

"Injuries among the ship's crew have been minor. We lost two fighters pilots and six are injured." He glanced up at At'r. "Your Highness was brought to me last evening, er," he glanced at his watch, "eight hours ago with a wound to your right shoulder, a bullet wound, I believe they say on Earth. Your condition was at the time stable, but you had lost a great deal of blood." he cleared his throat. "Thanks to Lady Izadra, you did not bleed to death. Currently your condition is greatly improved, the wound has healed with the assistance of the Quon-two process of tissue replacement."

"Captain Kara."

"All went as planned until you were shot, the other Earth agent did not move after the impostor, Zerion, agent was killed. I believe he was too frightened. Lady Izadra helped you back to your fighter, closed the hatches and activated the force shield, then requested assistance from me. After she informed me your bleeding had stopped I began instructing her on lift-off procedures. Lady Izadra was about to implement those procedures when you awakened."

"Mr. Bonnett, do have anything to add?"

"No Your Highness, but how is Cath…ah, Lady Izadra?"

"She is still sleeping, later you may see her if you wish." At'r told him then turned to the others, "Anything any of you have a question about?" he saw none. "Good. We have a long voyage before us, about three weeks. Between here and home I want scanners active at all times recording data as it is taken. If there are any more Zerion out posts I want to know it. Commander, if you detect any further indications of Zerions please let me know at once."

"As always, milord."

At'r stood, followed by the others, "Oh, lord Trentos, Captain Kara." At'r called them aside.

"Lady Izadra stopped my bleeding?" he questioned.

"Yes my Lord." Captain Kara assured him, Trentos nodded, "She helped you back inside the ship, and I asked her if she was returning to Tos-hawk. She said, 'yes.'"

"And I had to force her to leave my office while you were inside, then only after I assured her you would be fine."

"Thank you," At'r dismissed them, a perplexed frown wrinkling his brow. 'Why?' he wondered, had she returned so willingly, 'the letter? Still why would she care what happened to him.' Alone in the room he went back to his private chambers, finding himself once again in the bedroom staring down at his slumbering wife. At'r did not understand her, she stubbornly refused to complete their marital tie as was customary on Creasion, she fought him in bed, yet she was frantic with concern for him.

Izadra stirred, her muscles stiff, opening her eyes to see At'r, wearily she yawned.

"Good morning." At'r greed her casually.

"What difference out here?" she retorted sitting up and pulling the sheet with her for cover. At'r handed her his robe he left across the foot of the bed. "Thank you." Izadra slipped the heavy garment on trying to show as little of her naked body to At'r as possible. With him watching her every move she got out of bed hoping he would not notice how stiff she was. "How is your shoulder?" Izadra inquired.

"Lord Trentos has declared it healed." He said moving around the bed to the side Izadra had gotten out of, trapping her in his arms, for a long time studying her face before slowly kissing her. "You are lovely in the morning." he told her.

Confused by his gentle mood Izadra answered caustically, "As I said before, what difference out here?"

A scowl covered At'r's face and he released her, causing Izadra to sit abruptly on the bed, jarring her stiff body painfully. Drawing a slow breath, and gathering the robe around her, Izadra stood and again made toward the bath. At'r's voice stopping her.

"When you have dressed, join me." he commanded her as he returned to his desk, there taking the time to re-read the letter once more.

After a hot shower Izadra felt more alive and stood wrapped in a towel pondering her limited wardrobe. She contemplated ordering a few more garments from Roberta, more pants and shirts instead of long sensual gowns, Izadra at last choose the yellow gown from the closet and dressed. Brushing her hair she steeled herself and joined At'r. He did not hear her enter the living room, and Izadra halted just inside the room scrutinizing At'r for a few moments. Memories of the previous night made her blush, At'r looked up.

Izadra showed few signs from the preceding evening's wear, the yellow gown she wore had long sheer sleeves that hid the bruises of her upper arms, he regretted causing them.

"I have read the letter," At'r told her, Izadra nodded, "it appears authentic. Lord Betus has requested to read it, that is your decision Izadra."

"As it was to make it available to you." she paused, "I haven't any objections, my lord great-uncle is welcome to read it."

"I have ordered your breakfast," At'r said ignoring the first part of her statement, "afterwards there are a couple of people who wish to see you." he stood, "I have duties to attend, Kins will see to your needs and your visitors." So bidding her, he left.

Confused by his change in attitude she mechanically ate the huge breakfast At'r had ordered for her. When she had finished and the dishes had been cleared, Kins escorted lord Betus in.

"My Lady," he bowed slightly.

From the moment Betus touched the envelope, a peaceful expression came over his face and he closed his eyes. After he had sat unmoving for several minutes Izadra gently touched his arm, concerned he was ill.

"Uncle, shall I call Trentos?"

Betus' eyes fluttered open and Betus smiled most joyfully. "No my dear," he said, "I have not felt this young in years." Seeing Izadra's bewildered expression, he explained, "Iza knew you would allow me to read her letter, so she left an ingrained physic message for me, a physic recording."

"Your people communicate telepathically a great deal," Izadra commented, "I find it most disquieting and invasive."

"Hasn't uniting with Lord At'r eased your fears of this?"

"We have not...I will not allow his entrance. My thoughts will remain my own." she told him quietly, then asked, "Can he force me?"

"Izadra, there is nothing to fear, you will cause yourself more problems with Lord At'r if you refuse him."

"Can he force me?" she demanded.

"Yes." he said solemnly, "but he will not take the chance of damaging you. But why do you refuse him?"

"I cannot!" was Izadra's firm reply. She wanted to scream at him. How could she trust a man with her private thoughts when he cared nothing for her. To At'r she was a necessary encumbrance, when he felt magnanimous he was kind to her, otherwise she was but his duty to his people.

Izadra cleared her throat and changed the subject, "It has come to me uncle that I am ignorant of the people of Creasion, their history and customs, not only that, but I fear though I have been to college on Earth, that I am painfully behind in an academic sense. Is there any way I can learn some of these things before we reach Creasion?" she paused, "I do not wish to appear stupid or embarrass At'r."

"I was hoping you would show an interest. Tomorrow we could begin working together on these things and there are one or two here who could coach you also, but I have things to teach you first that your grandmother wanted too, but could not. You have suppressed your mental powers too long, now you must learn to use them, tomorrow we will begin."

"I believe they have already been at work. On Earth I seemed to be pre-warned before the Zerions appeared. It was very strange, but" she paused, "I had no idea At'r would come after me." her voice trailed off.

"You knew." Betus told her, "But you would not allow yourself to believe. I must go now, there is another who wishes to see you." the old man stood, so did Izadra and he hugged her. Then looked deeply into her eyes, "One thing you must learn my niece," he said telepathically, "is to mask your stronger thoughts. Believe me, you are more than duty to His Highness." he kissed her cheek and left her pondering his powers.

Unknown to either lord Betus or Izadra, At'r was monitoring their conversation from a hidden vantagepoint only he and Commander Kron knew existed. At'r was pleased with their meeting, though he wondered what thought message had passed between the two. He found himself jealous of their communication.

Next came Kevin Bonnett, the Earthman. At'r hoped their relationship had only been platonic, if it was not he would, most reluctantly, arrange the Earthman's return to Earth. At'r liked the alien from Earth. He knew within a short span of maybe twenty Earth years that he would need the Earthman as a diplomat to his home planet. Watching Izadra alone in the room waiting for her next visitor At'r could only wonder at her reaction.

Nervously Kevin walked down the now familiar hall leading to At'r's private chambers, he was unprepared for the vision that awaited him when the doors slipped open. Kevin starred admiringly, his mouth open as Izadra turned toward him, the open windows of space behind her.

She was dressed in a long yellow gown, never had Kevin seen her wear anything like it. Swirling around Izadra, her long auburn hair framed her composed face, she look like a goddess.

"Catherine?" Kevin asked astonished.

"Kevin!" she shirked, smiling, "Oh, Kevin, I was so worried about you!"

"And I about you," he said hugging her, "That is until I knew you were safe with Lord At'r."

Izadra pushed him away suspiciously, "How long have you been on-board Tos-hawk?"

"Since the night you left me. Lord At'r was in the room when you called."

"And you did not tell me?" Izadra asked, anger in her voice.

"I could not." he sat in the chair, "Catherine, you are wrong about him."

"Kevin," her voice was edgy, "you must not call me Catherine, not even in private."

"As you wish. Are you happy now that you are back with him Izadra?" the name sounded hard on his tongue, "Do you love him?"

Izadra glared at him, "You ask questions I have not yet asked myself," she turned toward the windows, "what brought you here, did At'r force you?"

"His Highness did not force me, and had I wished to return to Earth I could have." he drew a deep breath, "I wanted to come. To make sure you were all right and because I wanted to see space." he laughed, "You should have heard my partner's voice when I told him.

I think the only thing that convinced him I told the truth was the recent confirmed sightings of U.F.O.'s and he knew a bit about you."

"And did you tell Don, did you tell him where his car was?" Izadra smiled again herself, caught by his light mood, amazed at how comfortable Kevin seemed with his alien surroundings.

"Yes, just after you arrived on Tos-hawk One."

Her smile faded, once again suspicious of his easy demeanor, "None of this," she swept her hand around the room, "seems alien to you? You are quite—at home here?"

"Lord At'r has been most generous and hospitable, good heavens Cath—ah, Izadra, he saved me from that Zerion posing as a government agent."

Running her hands through her hair the loose sleeves of the her gown fell onto her shoulders revealing the blue bruises on her upper arms for only a moment, "I grow tired of others telling me how great he is." Izadra mumbled barely audible as Kevin reached her side.

"Did he beat you for you escape?" Kevin asked in alarm, pushing up one sleeve to stare at the hand marks.

"No! He did not!" she pulled away the sleeve falling to cover the marks, "I am glad you are safe Kevin, though amazed to see you here, I hope you find you have made the correct decision."

"I believe I have. You must be filling the role well, Lord At'r seemed at terms with the universe when I saw him this morning."

"Lord At'r is always at terms with the universe, I have little to do with it."

Kevin shrugged, "Not so, while you were gone, he was most ill at terms. I don't think the man slept two hours the entire time."

Without warning the chamber door slid open and At'r strode in. "Ah, Mr. Bonnett," At'r greeted him cordially, "As you can see Lady Izadra is safe and well."

"Of that I had little doubt, sire."

"You will join us for the late meal?" At'r asked.

"As you wish, now I will leave you." Kevin bowed slightly and exited.

At'r turned to Izadra, "I am sure you are relieved to see your close friend safe."

"Why did you bring him?" Izadra demanded, suspicious of his motives and resentful of his familiarity with her friend.

At'r turned to consider her, then turned back and poured himself a glass of the green juice he liked and drank if before answering her, "In a few years Earth will be advanced enough, and I will send a diplomatic representative. Mr. Bonnett knows Earth laws and history, now he may learn ours and in a few years will become a good advisor and ambassador." his eyes swept over her, "I do little without a purpose."

"So I am learning." Izadra absently ran her hand over the desk's smooth wood, "Lord Betus has consented to instruct me in Creasion history and customs, with your permission of course." she added, "I do not wish to embarrass you when we reach Creasion."

"I am happy you have an interest in our people." At'r informed her, "They are very interested in you. From what lord Betus has told me, our, ah—adventures, are becoming legendary." He went to his desk and pushed several buttons. "Come here please." he told her.

"It is time you learned how to use the ships computer. On Creasion the palace's computer works on a like basis." Seeing her interest peaked, At'r continued, both becoming engrossed in the functions the device was capable of. At'r found Izadra intelligent, her quick mind absorbing what he taught her. After explaining the basics they changed places, and that is how Kins found them, At'r leaning over Izadra, when he to announce dinner. Excusing herself Izadra changed her attire, donning the newly produced garment Roberta had finished. Izadra hoped At'r did not object to her wearing pants.

Surprised by her outfit, At'r was pleased at her selection of style. Long fawn linen pants with loose fitting legs that resembled a skirt, and a cream silk, button down shirt with loose sleeves gathered at the wrists and open at the throat. Thin strapped, golden sandals with a slight heal gave her a little more height. At'r smiled his approval and offered her his arm to escort her to dinner.

Commander Kron, Kevin, and Captain Kara greeted lord Betus and lord Trentos moments before the Royal couple arrived. At'r and Izadra welcomed them casually and dinner turned out to be a light hearted affair, both Izadra and Kevin finding themselves plied with questions about Earth. After dinner drinks were refilled and consumed twice before the evening came to a close. With a warm glow the group returned to their chambers for their sleep periods.

Feeling the effects of the strong brandy-like liquor she had drank, Izadra tripped slightly just as they reached their living room. At'r caught her in his arms saving Izadra from landing on her bottom, she giggled against his chest, then straightening, a smile still playing at the corner of her lips.

"Sorry m'lard." she said in a Scottish brogue, and giggled again, ashamed, she looked shyly up, her amusement fading as she read the heat smoldering in At'r's eyes.

"Since the Metos brandy seems too strong for you," he said lifting her high in his arms, "I will carry you." surprised when she put her arms around his neck, he slowly touched her lips, kissing her gently then carried her to their bed.

Reluctant to tear her clothes from her again, he deftly undid the buttons on the shirt and her pants and rolled Izadra over to remove her garments. Standing he removed his clothes and joined Izadra who had moved to the far side of the bed, all of her merriment gone.

Izadra knew she had drank too much, but it had felt so good to be free, even with the assistance of the brandy, now she was becoming sober quickly. Averting her eyes when At'r joined her, naked under the covers, now hating the brandy for dulling her senses and reactions. With out resistance At'r pulled her to him, looking down to capture her eyes with his.

"I should allow you strong drink more often." At'r said softly in her ear as he nibbled on the lobe, enjoying the shiver he felt race through Izadra's unresisting body. He planted hot kisses on her neck and breasts only to cover Izadra's lips as she moaned in pleasure. All the anger from the night before had fled as At'r slowly awakened Izadra's body. There had been other women, but never had At'r hungered for a woman the way he did Izadra, he found his control strained when she was near even in a roomful of people.

Izadra could not fight, or deny At'r, her body was no longer controlled by her mind. Instead of force, At'r coaxed, knowing Izadra could not resist. It was late in their sleep period before they slept, Izadra resting comfortably in At'r's arms.

CHAPTER 24

*I*n space, the days began to run together, passing with days of intense study and nights of intense pleasure. Betus, and other selected tutors filled Izadra's days and At'r filled her nights. Izadra became completely absorbed in the depth of new knowledge, and with lord Betus' help the further awakening of her mental powers. Izadra found she could now remember many of the mind controls her grandmother had taught her as a small child. Betus was patient with her and did not try to push too far into her private mind, as he called the inner circle of thought where, as he explained, reside the essence of one's being and the sub-conscience. Still unknown to either Izadra or lord Betus, At'r observed them occasionally, pleased with Izadra's progress.

Now less than two weeks to Creasion and a frenzy of activity gripped the crew. Izadra felt it and a glow seemed to radiate from her. She was pounding Betus with what seemed endless questions about the world she would live in when At'r joined them.

"Lord Betus," he addressed the priest, "could I borrow your student for a few hours?"

"Yes of course—but I warn you," he said good naturally, "her questions are like the sands of Zerion, infinite."

"Yes," At'r agreed smiling, "I know." Betus left them with a bow, At'r turned to Izadra, "Please change your attire, we are joining

Commander Kron's patrol." seeing her excitement he added, "Hurry, the patrol leaves in ten minutes."

Izadra went to change remembering her last flight with him and her promise to herself to ask him to allow her to fly the space fighter. Secretly she had used her necklace to gain entry through the security locks to the fighter simulators, since becoming adept at how to use the necklace to over-ride the security devices she had learned many things At'r had forbidden her. He had no idea she was so clever.

It was only a couple of minutes until she returned still buttoning the sleeves, "I am ready," she announced.

"Shall we?" he motioned her ahead of him allowing her to set a quick pace, her exuberance clear on her face.

They passed many crew personnel, most bowing or saluting, gratified to see Izadra so eager to accompany her Lord. Ahead, coming toward them was Captain Kara, seeing her monarchs she bowed until At'r addressed her."Off duty for the period?" he asked.

"Yes milord." she answered. "Milady," and bowing again they each continued their separate ways.

Entering the hangar, Izadra found the intense activity and excitement intoxicating, upon their entrance it all stopped, each crewmember saluting their sovereign, then it all began again. Izadra went directly to their craft, encountering Commander Kron waiting at the bottom of the stairs of At'r's fighter.

"All is ready sire," Kron told At'r bowing slightly, "when you are." turning to Izadra, "Good to have you along milady." he welcomed her.

"Lead the way Commander," At'r told Kron and they both went to their ships, Izadra settling comfortably in the passenger seat of At'r's fighter.

At'r turned to her, "Ready?" he asked."Always," she replied, he hit the launch button.

Catapulting into space they obtained light speed with the other patrol ships after clearing Tos-hawk One. Izadra watched At'r handled the fighter with ease, wondering if it felt like the simulator had. Izadra's hands itched to take the controls. Never having asked At'r for anything before now, Izadra summoned her courage.

"Milord?" she hesitated, "Sire, would you allow me to fly the ship?" she paused, "Please At'r?"

At'r turned slowly to stare at her. 'Why,' he asked himself, 'would she want to fly the fighter?' Another escape attempt flashed in his mind, but this far out in space At'r knew she would not know her way back to Earth.

"Please." she asked again.

"Very well Izadra." he agreed reluctantly, marveling at the smile that rewarded him as they traded places. Taking the control Izadra found they did feel like the simulator's only a bit heavier. Thrilled by their touch, she guided the ship in formation with the other five of the patrol. Finally Tos-hawk came back in their view, and reluctantly Izadra returned control of the fighter back to At'r.

"Thank you, At'r." Izadra told him quietly, going back to her seat. Sitting she watched him wait his turn to land. Suddenly Kevin's voice rang in her head asking her if she loved At'r.

Izadra had fought the answer for so long, refusing to admit the magnetic pull she felt toward At'r was more than physical. Izadra now knew she loved At'r, she would fight him again to keep him from knowing, for if he knew, he would control her totally, including her thoughts, but Izadra could no longer deny the truth to herself.

A warm feeling tingled through her. A happy smile on her lips and for the first time since her capture she felt some hope for the future. Izadra was going to a new world, she had a new found family, and the people of Creasion seemed eager to love and accept her, she could hope At'r would someday love her too.

Watching At'r, Izadra remembered him telling her he would never allow himself the luxury of love, except for his duty and his people. Resolutely Izadra hid the love away, not sure how long she could maintain her cover. Suddenly she was pushed back in the seat as the ship landed, seconds later they were back on board Tos-hawk One.

Feeling light headed and dizzy Izadra undid the seat belt, before she could stand At'r noticed how pale she was and assisted her to stand, commenting on her pallor. Shrugging, Izadra told him she had not eaten lunch and competently maneuvered the stairs from the ship. Drawing a deep breath when her feet were again on Tos-hawk. Taking the post flight checklist from the awestruck crewman who handed it to her, Izadra smiled and thanked him for it. Turning she assisted At'r in the post flight systems check then excusing herself went to their quarters to change for the late meal.

At'r joined her as Izadra was brushing her long hair, for a few moments he stood to one side watching her, contemplating. Roberta, present as always to assist Izadra, gave her the gold band, which she placed on her head before turning to At'r.

"Izadra," his voice had an edge to it, "where did you learn to control a fighter in that manner?" he came to stand before her as she rose from the vanity stool, they were very close.

"I have a pilot's license on Earth," Izadra began uneasily, knowing she would have to tell At'r of her time in the simulator, "and when you were unconscious on Earth, Captain Kara gave me some instruction."

"That does not account for your knowledge or skill, only flying time or simulator experience would." he pulled her closer, "Which is it?" he demanded looking fiercely down into her eyes.

Once again she felt his mind touch hers, but now her mind control was greater and At'r's power was not as frightening. Concentrating on the first time she entered the simulator she projected that picture to At'r.

Not expecting such a reply or her mental power, At'r stepped back slightly when Izadra relayed it. His look became stern and Izadra paled.

"Your uncle has taught you well." At'r said referring to her use of telepathic thought, just a touch of envy in his voice. "But how did you learn to override the security scans with your necklace?"

"You milord taught me how to operate the ship's computer and how many times have you used your necklace to gain entrance to high security areas when I have been touring the ship with you." Izadra smiled slightly, "I meant no harm, milord, but I have been fascinated since my first flight."

Amazed at her advancements At'r had to suppress a proud smile, "From now on, madam, when you wish to use the simulator, you will consult me first."

"Yes, milord." Izadra replied, repentant, relieved At'r had not forbidden her use of the simulator.

Some of his sternness dissipated, "Your progress is pleasing, you have done well in the small amount of time you have had."

"Give the credit to the instructor." Izadra shrugged.

At'r's look was consuming, she felt bathed in the heat and feared she might melt, "Do not sell yourself short, Izadra." he pulled her into a passionate embrace that made her cling to him weakly.

Izadra drew a slow deep breath, she wanted to return his passion, to tell him she loved him, but she managed to remain in control. "You are too kind." she said a little breathlessly.

A signal announced the arrival of their dinner, and together they enjoyed the simple fare that had been prepared. Conversation was quiet, At'r telling Izadra a story about his childhood. In like manner they passed the next week, falling into a comfortable routine, each playing their roles before the others.

CHAPTER 25

*I*zadra woke in darkness with At'r's lips touching hers, in her dream like consciousness she slipped her arms around his neck drawing him closer.

"I must go Izadra." At'r smiled her at response, "I am going on a recon mission of our outer solar system's planets, Kins will wake you when Tos-hawk nears the first planet." Kissing her again he was gone, Izadra turned over pulling his pillow close and slept again.

An hour later she woke with a start to stare blankly around the dark room, she was drenched with sweat and a haunting but fleeting vision lingered vaguely before her eyes. "Light!" she said aloud to the monitoring computer and covered her shocked eyes to hide them from the brightness. "Dim!" she commanded the monitor, slowly she uncovered her face.

Rising from bed Izadra was assaulted by a wave of nausea that chased the remainder of the dream from her mind. Making her way to the shower she stood under the warm water for several minutes before feeling recovered. It had been the same yesterday, nausea and dizziness when she woke. Drying, she wrapped her hair in a towel and donned her heavy robe, feeling a weird chill in the room. Kins had been alerted to her rising and awaited her in the living room. Izadra asked for only a light breakfast of juice and dry toast.

While dressing a dark feeling came over her, returning fragments of the dream she had awakened from. Going back to the living room she found Kins already had returned with her breakfast.

"Milady seems a little tired this morning, are you well?" Kins inquired, concerned.

"Still a bit sleepy." she made excuse, "Can you fill me in on where Lord At'r has gone?"

"Yes milady, of course." he seated her at the breakfast table and directed her attention to the viewer screen. "His Highness will be with an advanced security scout several light years ahead of us, we do not expect them back for about eight spans. They will check this area of our solar system," he indicated a series of six planets, small in size and close together, "Zerions have been known to hide in these plane-toids and ambush ships coming through."

"But with the shroud?"

"These six create an electrical field and here our sensor block will not function." he saw the troubled and distant look in her eyes, "Milady, are you sure you are well? Should I call lord Trentos?" for a moment she was silent, her face ashen, then with a distraught look on her lovely features she turned towards Kins.

"No! Call lord Betus. Now!" she commanded him.

Kins was quick to do her bidding, then turning told her, "He will be a few moments milady, he has only just risen."

"Tell him we are coming there, his state of attire is not important." she gave Kins only seconds to inform her grand-uncle of her visit before Izadra left the room, Kins hurrying to keep up, wondering what had taken possession of Izadra.

Coming toward them Izadra saw Kevin, a grin on his face. "Kevin!" Izadra said in a very strained voice, "I haven't time to talk, please come see me later."

"What is wrong?" Kevin asked turning and keeping pace with her, Kins also listened intently as he all but ran to keep up.

"I have to see Betus, Kevin, and I cannot explain now, but At'r is in danger."

"But how would you know?"

"Later Kevin, please, I will tell you later." she disappeared through the door to lord Betus' rooms, leaving Kevin and Kins to stare in confusion after her.

"Uncle," Izadra called from the small outer room. Betus joined her as he was adjusting his outer tunic, "Betus, I have had a vision! At'r is in danger, there is a Zerion base, you must make Kron warn him." Izadra was becoming frantic.

"Easy child, sit down." he gently nudged her into a chair, "Now tell me what has happened." hurriedly she explained, then allowed him to see the dream she could barely remember. To Izadra's surprise she could now see the entire dream.

A Zerion outpost located on the second planet after entering the six planetoids. Tos-hawk Two, having come in earlier, passed before the cluster of little planets' orbit brought them around. Now Tos-hawk One would be in jeopardy and the patrol At'r had gone with in even more danger.

"Please uncle," she pleaded, "you must tell Commander Kron, I fear they will kill him."

Betus regarded her for a moment, after seeing the vision himself, he knew it to be authentic and knew Lord At'r would be in real danger, the ending had been clouded.

"I will inform him to meet us in your chambers," which he promptly did, then turned back to Izadra, "so much concern for His Highness, do you love him my niece?"

Izadra blushed bringing some color to her pale face, "You embarrass me uncle." she stood, together they walked from her uncle's rooms, Kins and Kevin had waited and joined them.

Commander Kron had arrived when they reached the Royal apartments, and Izadra explained in depth to Kron what she had seen. Knowing Izadra had never seen the six planets, and knowing of a possibility of telepathic powers he believed her and his father, but remained cautious.

"Milady, I will dispense back-up squadrons but even with His Highness' life in danger I can not jeopardize this ship or your life, Your Highness." he explained, "Lord At'r has given strict orders to that effect. He suspected trouble."

"How?" Izadra asked him boldly, unafraid of the fearsome Commander Kron, "Could you let him go Commander?"

Kron studied her momentarily, she had the rank to ask that question and the right, and she had saved his life. "Milady," Kron said dejectedly, "I could not stop him. As when he came after you, he would not listen to my council and allow someone else to go."

"I know Kron," she said apologetically, "forgive me. But why? Why did he go?"

"One moment milady," Kron excused himself long enough to order the back-up patrol departure. Returning he explained, "His Highness goes on regular patrols. As you know he will not shrink from a scheduled flight, regardless of danger."

"But I flew a mission with him only yesterday?"

"That was unscheduled, he wished to check out his ship and knew you would enjoy the trip."

"Oh Kron," Izadra said a little sickly, "he is in such danger and I have an awful feeling, when will we have a report?"

Kron cleared his throat uncomfortably, "It is over due."

Izadra sank down in At'r's desk-chair, "Do what is necessary Kron," she told him, "and please keep me informed."

"Your ladyship may monitor the bridge on this screen." He pushed the desk button, "You will see it as it happens."

Bowing again, Kron left to return to the bridge, moments later alarms sounded and the protective doors slid across the windows, closing Izadra's view of space, now she must rely on the viewers.

Lord Betus, Kins and Kevin had remained with her and they sat in silence for a long time, finally Izadra spoke, "The vision is still unclear, Betus, why can I not see how it will end? Why, do I see only danger?"

"Your powers are still new and you do not have full control." he paused, "Had you joined with At'r you would be capable of seeing as he sees what is happening."

"I cannot?"

"Izadra," Kevin asked, "You have the power to keep Lord At'r from seeing into your mind?"

"Yes Kevin, you haven't?"

"Not I." Kevin admitted.

"Few do Kevin," Kins informed him, then looked to Izadra, "I tell you honestly my Lady, there is nothing to fear."

"Thank you gentlemen, I will keep my own thoughts." she told them firmly.

"Tell me, niece, what is it you do not want him to know?" Betus asked, the only one who would dare.

Izadra did not answer, Betus didn't press further.

Two hours crept by before the back-up squadrons reached the second planetoid and what remained of the Zerion base. But the battle had taken a toll on the patrol. Izadra viewed the transmission of the wreckage with dwindling courage. There were no Creasion ships remaining in flight from At'r's patrol. The Zerion base was not functioning, but small groups of Zerions remained. Searching the area the teams found three downed Creasion fighters, two pilots were dead, the third in critical condition. At'r and another fighter pilot were still missing.

Excusing herself, Izadra made her way to the bathroom before the tears flowed down her cheeks. Over and over she saw the dream without an end. She wished she could see the end. But she would not allow At'r the freedom of her mind if he was found alive. If he was gone? Tears streamed down her face, Izadra could not accept that either. Gathering her wits about her, Izadra forced herself to stop crying and rejoined the others in the living room.

Kron had ordered the search expanded to cover the nearest plane-toid, the others were incapable of supporting life, and this one could not for long. In the normal orbit of these six only the one the Zerion base had been on could support life continually without pressure domes. The planetoid they now searched would be in winter season within several hours, the temperature going from a tolerable hot one hundred ten, to sub-zero in a matter of hours. Finally unable to tolerate her rooms any longer, Izadra informed her guests she was going to the bridge and they were welcome to stay or accompany her as they wished.

Kins remained, but Betus and Kevin joined her and together entered the bridge just as the second search team was leaving Toshawk One. To Izadra's amazement, all attention on the bridge was on her each member on duty as well as Commander Kron bowed.

"Please," she admonished them, "continue with your jobs." Instantly the bridge was a hub of activity again. A seat was quickly provided for her next to a back-up console of monitors, one of the crew taking a little time to explain the simpler workings of the instruments. "Thank you." Izadra smiled slightly.

"Do not worry, Your Highness," the technician assured her, "we will find him." the girl blushed and returned to her console.

Izadra turned back to watch the telecasts from the search fighters looking for At'r. After a time Kron stood before Izadra and she looked up.

"Madam, you grace our company." he said cordially.

"Thank you Commander, I could not have stayed another minute in our chambers, I had hoped you would not object to my unannounced visit?"

"You are always welcome on my bridge." he assured her and returned to the con.

It was becoming increasingly difficult to conceal her feelings of dread. Izadra feared At'r was dead but would not allow herself to dwell on the possibility, instead she concentrated on the screen where she could see wreckage coming in view. At'r and the other missing pilot had been found.

With relief Izadra saw At'r's royal fighter still in one piece, seemingly undamaged; however, sitting next to it was a badly burned, crashed Creasion fighter.

In a survival shelter made from items from At'r's ship the rescue team found their sovereign and a badly injured pilot.

Izadra watched the viewer as At'r waved lord Trentos, who had insisted on going with the rescue team, away. "I am fine Doctor, see to Major Dhor, he needs you more right now." Lord Trentos ordered the pilot taken to Tos-hawk One at once and returned with him.

Hot and dirty, but most of all tired, At'r returned with the rescue team, joking with them about the destruction of the Zerion base. Then sadly, praising the fallen pilots who would not be going back to Creasion. Izadra watched from her telecast vantagepoint, appreciating the scene of camaraderie At'r shared with his people.

Slipping unnoticed from the bridge and hurrying to the hangar bay where At'r's rescue ship would be landing, Izadra arrived well before the ship landed. Like it had been on the bridge all activity stopped when Izadra entered the hangar until she returned the crew to their duties. Captain Kara approached her, having just landed from a patrol she had lead, and bowed. Then turned to say hello to lord Betus and Kevin who accompanied Izadra.

"His ship is the next to land milady." Kara told her. Together the group watched the vessel enter the hangar and Izadra moved to stand closer when the engines stopped, Captain Kara and the other close behind her.

Izadra held her breath until At'r came through the door, drawing a relieved breath when he appeared. His eyes were instantly on her. With agility despite his exhaustion At'r descended the steps to crush Izadra in a passionate embrace, releasing her as suddenly as he had taken her.

He whispered, "Were you worried about me?" At'r asked expecting a curt reply despite the details Kron had given him of his rescue.

"Sick," Izadra answered him seriously, "please At'r," she begged, "do not put yourself in such peril again."

Surprised by her sincerity his fierce countenance softened and he turned to the assembled people, who were still bowing, commanding them to rise, slightly embarrassed at having left them so standing.

Thanking the crowd for their concern and patience At'r rested his arm around Izadra's shoulders and left the hangar with her, still pondering Izadra's concern.

Making their way back to their chambers became a slow trek as the crew they passed greeted them warmly. At length the Royal couple found themselves in the solitude of their chambers. At'r wrapped his arms around Izadra and looking solemnly down, studying her face asked, "You were concerned?" his manner cool.

Izadra blushed and lowered her eyes, unsure of how to reply, unsure of her own feelings. "I had a premonition," she said softly, then looked up at his face again, "I saw a fighter crash in a dream, then woke to find you gone." Feeling drained by his proximity and the past few hours she tiredly rested her head against his shoulder, "I feared for you." Izadra said in a low voice that he heard more from telepathy than sound.

Taking a deep breath Izadra drew away slightly from At'r, "Come, get in the whirlpool and relax, I will order our dinner then bring you something to drink." Izadra accompanied him to the bath, but left quickly as he began to undress stopping only to lay out a large warm bath towel for him. After Izadra left a slight smile played at the corners of At'r's mouth, marveling at Izadra's mood, perhaps the girl was truly concerned.

Lazing back in the hot swirling water he heard the door open to admit Izadra with a cold glass of Zarka juice, "Dinner will be about ten minutes." she told him leaving him to lounge in the water. Izadra could be molded to make a good Creasion wife, At'r thought, then reprimanded himself mentally.

'I must not allow myself to love her.' he told himself silently, drained the glass, and rose from the tub to enter the shower. In cold water he washed his hair and body, then dried quickly, chilled in the cool air. Tying the belt on his robe At'r emerged from the bath as Izadra was dismissing the steward who had brought their meal.

At'r admired her manner with the servant, she addressed him with respect thanking him for his thoughtfulness of placing silk flowers on the table.

Dinner passed, At'r telling Izadra about the space battle he had been involved in and the crash. Izadra listened intently. After dinner At'r explained that their arrival on Creasion would be delayed due to the Zerion base, now they would arrive on Crea in six days instead of five.

Bedtime came too quickly. Izadra slid under the covers, At'r's arm slid around her waist and he drew her close. She felt his breath on her neck and swallowed hard. Gently he kissed her ear lobe.

"Tonight we sleep." he whispered and kissed the nape of her neck. Almost at once his even breathing lulled Izadra to sleep.

Toward the last hour of their sleep period Izadra drifted upward on the waves of a storm washed ocean. Opening her eyes to the blackness of eternal night seemed to smother her making Izadra feel like she could not breathe.

"Low light!" she said aloud to the room monitor, the lights came up. Moving slowly away from At'r she reached the edge and sat up, nausea washing over her. Valiantly Izadra fought the urge until she made it to the bathroom. Ten minutes later she managed to splash her face with cool water. Turning off the water she heard At'r calling her from the locked door, Izadra did not have time to reply until At'r had overridden the computer lock and entered the bath.

Upon seeing Izadra weakly supporting herself on the edge of the basin, At'r rushed to her and scooped her into his arms.

"Why did you not wake me? If you are ill I wish to know." he told her firmly, carrying her from the bath, Izadra too faint to protest. He put her to bed and called Trentos.

Trentos arrived it seemed almost before At'r had switched off the intercom.

"She is in bed?" Trentos inquired as he hurried through the door, not bowing but going directly to the bedroom before At'r could answer his question. At'r remained in the living room waiting for Trentos to complete his examination.

"Lady Izadra." Trentos said crossly, "How long have you been experiencing this?" he finished the examination.

Izadra looked at him questioningly, "Trentos what is wrong with me?" One thought prevailed in her mind, what if she carried a virus that would infect these people.

"Do the women of Earth not get morning sickness when they are pregnant?" Trentos asked.

Izadra stared at him the thought had not entered her mind, now it made since, "Four," she said stunned, "I have been sick four mornings, and I have been faint several time in the last few days."

"You are going to be a mother," Trentos smiled patting her hand, "Lord At'r will be thrilled."

Sighing Izadra looked to Trentos, "Please, allow me to tell Lord At'r." she asked, unsure of how she would tell him.

"Of course Lady Izadra, I do have a few instructions I will expect you to follow." he explained, then giving her a mild tranquilizer to settle her stomach he left her alone in bed.

Trentos encountered At'r sitting patiently at his desk reviewing ship's data, "My lord," Trentos bowed.

"How is she?" At'r asked without looking up.

"I will allow her to tell you sire." Trentos explained.

At'r looked up, "Is it serious?"

"Lady Izadra begged me to allow her to tell you, sire. "Trentos bowed again "by your leave." he said and departed.

Rising, At'r paused at the desk's edge to ponder one of the reports on his screen, then drawing a deep breath went to the bedroom.

CHAPTER 26

*I*zadra did not remain in bed, she preferred to meet At'r standing. Sighing she pondered his reaction to his impending fatherhood, Izadra decided he would be pleased.

"Izadra," his voice caused her to jump, "it would seem if you are ill, you should be in bed." he admonished, moving to stand next to her.

"Milord," Izadra began, "I am not ill."

"You seemed to be earlier," he said confused.

Nervously Izadra glanced about the room until At'r took her by the shoulders and sat her down on the couch.

"Now. Tell me what lord Trentos found wrong?"

"I" Izadra's voice faltered, "I am pregnant, At'r."

He saw the uncertainty in her eyes and the questions there, "Good! I had hoped you would carry an heir before we reached Creasion! Excellent!"

Izadra's face flushed, "Is that all a child will be to you? An heir? You have made it clear you will not love me, but I thought your own child."

At'r stood stiffly to stare coolly down at Izadra. Now that she carried his heir, his responsibility was filled, "The child will, as all our children will, be trained to put their duty first. Give them all the love you can, my dear, I will see to it they know their duties well." At'r turned sharply leaving her alone, amazed at his mood change. Looking out at the stars she yearned to see the sun again. A deep sadness filled her, before Izadra could halt them, tears flowed freely down her cheeks. With a great amount of effort she still them.

For the first time since her arrival on Tos-hawk, Izadra ate dinner alone. She ate little, her mind troubled by At'r.

Trying to busy her mind with some of the learning tapes Betus had given her, their sleep period drew closer and Izadra hearing the door open and close, looked up expecting to see At'r. Instead a young nurse had brought the medication Trentos had prescribed for her, taking the pill Izadra thanked the girl and dismissed her.

Izadra felt the emptiness of their quarter's closing in on her and she knew At'r would not come, absently she wondered where and if he would sleep. Now that she carried his child he had no further need for her except an occasional appearance before his people. Idly Izadra again wondered if she should have stayed on Earth.

Had she stayed At'r's child would have been born there. From Trentos' sensitive monitors he had pinpointed her conception date as her wedding night. Shaking her head Izadra knew Earth would not have been the place for his child. It wasn't any longer the place for her.

She yawned, and stretched out on top of the covers on the bed, the medication making her sleepy. Without At'r's presence the room had a chill, and climbing under the bed covers Izadra drifted into a restless slumber. Sensing her slumber the monitoring computer lowered the lights.

Because of the unexpected events as they passed the six planetoids, their arrival on Creasion had been delayed by a full day. Creasion had appeared first as a large blue ball bordered on either side by two moons of different sizes the third moon was behind the planet.

Similar to Earth but slightly larger, Izadra's heart leaped to see a planet so much like her birth world.

Izadra turned her attention to the star Tos, around which this solar system orbited, looking forward once again to feeling the sun on her skin. She found herself hoping At'r had a garden, then chided herself for worrying about such petty matters. Feeling alone, Izadra turned to the desk monitors, switching the screens to different locations she could watch the crews and officers work. To her surprise she found Kevin and Tari in the recreation hall, they too watched their approach to the planet.

Gathering her daring, Izadra left her chambers and found her way to the spacious hall where the crew spent their leisure time. Izadra's entrance was marked by the normal manner and after returning the company to their activities she joined Kevin and Tari who stood before a viewing window.

Comfortable with the two, Izadra began to enjoy their conversation comparing Earth customs with Creasion customs. Izadra recited a nursery rhyme she remembered from her childhood, laughing, Tari thought a moment.

"There was one old Creasion nursery rhyme." Tari said, "How did it go…" she reflected, "Oh, yes."

'Silver and Gold, Silver and Gold.

Only a Creasion would be so bold.

Turn Mercury to Silver and Lead to Gold.

A Creasion secret never to be told.'

They all laughed, their merriment mixing with the others until the room was suddenly silent, all persons on their feet and bowing. At'r entered the room and it seemed to shrink, Izadra turned to him a smile lingering as she curtsied.

"As you were." he bade them watching Izadra as she rose to greet him with a smile he decided was genuine and not just for the benefit of the crew. His anger at finding their chambers vacant quelled a little.

"You found the message I left on the desk screens?" Izadra asked, not trying to hide how happy she was to see him.

"Yes," At'r answered her and after a short polite conversation with Kevin and Tari he escorted Izadra back to their quarters.

"Finding our quarter's empty upon my arrival was," he paused to look up from the screen he was studying on his desk, "alarming." his pleasant tone from the recreational deck had changed to one of disdain.

Izadra was vexed with At'r, he had left her alone for the last five days with the brief exception of a daily visit to shower and change his clothing. She turned to answer him from across the room.

"Considering how little time you have spent here in the last few days, I am surprised you noticed. Still, that is why I left you the note on the screen." her tone did little to hide the hurt she felt at his neglect.

"Next time," he said firmly, "if you require company you will invite them to join you." he sat back in the desk chair. "Which reminds me of an item lord Betus has brought to my attention." He waited until Izadra stood before his desk. "You will need to choose five ladies of my, ah, our court to serve as your assistants."

"But At'r, I do not know the ladies of your court." Izadra said evenly.

"Lord Betus will assist you after you are settled on Creasion." he ignored her tone.

"May I choose anyone I wish?"

"Yes Izadra, anyone you wish, as long as they are not Zerions."

"So much for my first choice!" she said sarcastically, "Then I guess my next choice would be Captain Kara."

"She would be an excellent choice." At'r again ignored her tone. She seemed to be baiting him. "One of your ladies should be from the military, she will act as the head of the group and your personal bodyguard. I thought you might ask her, she is a good officer." As if to dismiss her he returned to study the reports he brought up on his viewer. Turning Izadra went to their bedroom, At'r looking up as she left, watched her retreat with interest.

Izadra's announcement several days past did not surprise At'r, indeed, he had planned for this. He should be pleased, but At'r did not feel overly joyous. Since Izadra's discovery his life and duty had become increasingly more difficult. He could not purge the memory of her soft lips and body, and the glimmering fire of scarcely controlled passion in her eyes. Now that she was pregnant, and his duty to produce an heir filled, he could resume his life as it had been. Izadra would fill her role as wife and mother he would not allow her to further complicate his life. He would not allow himself to fall in love with her.

A disturbing thought entered his tired mind and he clearly saw the dead bodied of his parents and betrothed after the Zerion attack that had killed them. Having once loved and known the pain of loss he had sworn never to become vulnerable again. He would remain aloof from Izadra, taking her when he needed her. Otherwise, she would only be a pretty addition to his court. Resolutely At'r rose and walked to the bedroom to find Izadra. He found her clad only in underwear, laying out the clothing she would wear for the short journey from the space station where Tos-hawk One would dock, to the planet below.

Izadra sensed his presence and quickly donned her robe then looked up. "Sire?"

"Are you nervous?" he asked casually.

A little wistful smile tugged at the corners of her mouth, "A little." she said. Then added, "A great deal." she admitted.

"Our people will be impressed with you. You have nothing to fear." his tone changed, becoming more sarcastic as he continued, "The tales of our adventures and of your bravery and rescue of Commander Kron are told in every meeting place, I am told." he added.

From the edge his voice had taken on and his suddenly stern countenance Izadra drew back slightly. "I apologize if I have done anything to displease you." she said flatly, determined not to let know how he hurt her. "Next time shall I allow the Zerions to shoot Commander Kron?" she added acidly.

"Next time you will stay where you belong." he all but growled.

"By your leave, Your Highness!" Izadra bowed stiffly and swept past him going to the bath, dropping her robe as she walked past, "I must prepare for our departure."

At'r turned and went back to the living room, the scent of her perfume following him. He had not intended to be so angry with Izadra. It amazed him how quickly she could vex him, her temper flaring as quickly as his. With some effort, he pushed her to the back of his thoughts, he had other matters to concern himself with. In three hours, he would be back on Creasion, drawing a deep breath he could almost smell the fresh air.

Waiting until At'r left Izadra cautiously exited the bath. Sadly she looked around once again aware of At'r's absence, sorry for her own lack of control but she was nervous and more than a little frightened. A frown crept over her face, like it or not, At'r would have to accept what she had done when she had escaped. With a last look at the planet Creasion she gathered up the hair clips she had left behind and went to finish her toiletry.

Izadra had relaxed for about five minutes in the whirlpool when the admittance buzzer sounded, pushing the intercom button she inquired who was there. Captain Kara answered.

"May I enter, milady."

"Of course Captain." giving Tari time to enter the living room Izadra again said into the intercom, "Tari, I am in the bath." a moment later Tari cautiously appeared, Roberta tagging along behind her with Izadra's robe and a warm towel.

"I though you might enjoy some company before you departed." Tari explained.

"Thank you, I am glad for your company." she hesitated for a moment, "can you tell me what to expect when we land?"

Tari smiled, "I have been in contact with a couple of friends on the planet, the people are anxious to greet you." As Izadra began to dry herself Tari told her what she knew would take place. They migrated to the bedroom where Tari helped Izadra as she began dressing. After slipping on the silken undergarments, Izadra faintly sank down on a chair. Remembering how little she had eaten and her condition she rested for a moment.

"Are you ill, Izadra?" Tari questioned.

"Just a little light headed Tari."

"Did you eat lunch?"

"No, Tari I was too, ah," she remembered her words with At'r, "nervous to eat."

Tari immediately ordered a snack for both of them. "It should be here in a few minutes."

"Tari can I tell you something in confidence?"

"Of course Izadra, you have my word nothing you tell me will ever go further."

Izadra briefly wondered if that would include At'r, "It is not really a secret, but is not common knowledge, yet."

Izadra was silent, unsure if she should tell Tari.

"When you feel comfortable about telling me, tell me." Tari said genuinely, they looked up to see a steward had brought their food.

They ate and Tari talked again of her childhood as did Izadra until she was silent, thoughtful for a moment. "Tari, what I was going to tell you." she blushed, "I am pregnant."

Tari's face lit up, "Oh how wonderful!"

Talking as Izadra finished dressing eased Izadra's nerves and after eating she felt less faint.

"I must go now milady, be sure you eat a little something before you depart, you will feel better when you meet your new people."

"I promise, Tari." Izadra agreed.

After she had gone, Izadra stood before the full-length mirror, unaware that At'r had entered and stood watching her from the hall. Izadra smoothed a hand over the light mint green jumpsuit she had designed and Roberta had produced. The silk like material made Izadra appear thinner than she was, the loose long sleeves held at the wrists by tight cuffs, the loose legs disappearing down emerald green boots and a wide tight belt of matching material around her waist. Leaving the front zipper open to show her necklace she placed the gold band in her loose shinning tresses.

"You are beautiful." At'r said, Izadra startled and turned toward him.

"Thank you." and she stopped to admire how he was attired. Beneath his emerald green flightsuit he wore his formal military uniform, "You look nice yourself." she returned lightly.

"This is for you." he handed her a flight suit similar to his, "it should compliment what you are wearing."

Izadra slipped the garment on adjusted it over her other clothing and straightened her collar. Pleased with her appearance At'r guided her from their quarters.

Commander Kron himself piloted the Royal shuttle from Toshawk One down to Crea. Izadra occupied the navigator's chair and At'r sat in the co-pilot's chair. Silently each watched as Kron expertly guided the craft down, the planet dominated the cockpit windows and now landmasses were visible. Noticeable at once was the lack of land, although larger, Creasion had only one third of the landmasses of Earth.

Entering the atmosphere was as Kron had explained, similar to Earth re-entry, Izadra felt almost like she was coming home, she smiled, in a manner she was.

At'r gave Kron an unnoticed signal and Kron orbited the planet at low altitude coming to the capital city of Crea last. Awed and amazed, Izadra said little trying to soak up all she viewed.

From a far distance Izadra saw it, her eyes becoming transfixed to the glowing green structure. Managing to speak her voice barely above a whisper Izadra asked slowly, speaking as though she were under a spell, "What is that?"

At'r turned to look at her, "It is beautiful."

"That is the Diamerald Tower, your grandfather built it after the war that followed Lady Iza's kidnapping." At'r explained, "It began to glow again the day you were brought on board Tos-hawk One."

"Amazing!" she said in the same tone.

At'r and Kron looked at each other, concerned at the Tower's effect on Izadra. After they passed the building the effects diminished as if they had never occurred. At'r knew lord Betus would want a detailed report on her behavior, most of the legend of the Diamerald tower had purposefully been omitted from Izadra's education so that her reaction, if any, could be observed.

Ahead was the landing platform and below them, cheering, were thousands of Creasions happily welcoming home their Emperor and his new Lady. Izadra, upon seeing the crowd grew lightheaded until she felt At'r's hand on hers.

"Are you ill?"

"Only nervous." she replied.

"Please Izadra, do not faint before them." At'r asked.

"I will not fail you milord." Izadra assured him, incensed by his reproach.

Studying her closely At'r contemplated what Izadra had said, "No, I don't think you would." he said sincerely, taking her hand in his.

Kron sat the craft gently down and began shutting down the shuttle's systems. Finishing, he rose from his seat, "I will announce you." he said and strode to the exit.

At'r stood and assisted Izadra in taking off her flightsuit, then he too slipped out his. Looking at Izadra he beckoned, "Come, wife!"

Drawing a deep breath Izadra took his hand allowing At'r to lead her from the shuttle onto the platform outside floating above the

roaring crowd. Trentos had given them all a pair of shaded contacts
to wear, Izadra found out why when, after three weeks out of natural
light she stepped into the bright Creasion sunlight. Following At'r's
lead she waved to the mass and smiled widely.

They began to shout At'r's name, then Izadra's, until their names
alternately became a deafening roar, brought to a halt only when At'r
stepped to the podium to speak. Then silence fell as still as the air
before a storm.

"Thank you for your welcome." he said smiling. "It is wonderful
to be home." they cheered, he held up his hand becoming more serious, "As you know our recent victory over the Zerion will allow
another planet to evolve normally. And we were fortunate to find
another Zerion outpost among the six planetoids. Commander Kron
and the crews are to be commended for their success in destroying
the Zerion's bases." Cheers for the crew were wild and lengthy. "As is
Commander Delia and Tos-hawk Two crew for arriving in time to
destroy the Zerion fleet and help protect Tos-hawk One." More
cheers. "But! Had it not been for the woman who is now my wife,
none of this would have been possible. She is the granddaughter of
our lost Empress Iza. Izadra, heir to Iza, is a courageous woman, as
was Iza. I am honored," At'r turned to Izadra, smiling, "to have her
as my wife and the mother of my children." The crowd cried her
name. At'r turned to Izadra and extended his hand to her.

Wishing At'r really felt that way about her, Izadra was compelled
to move forward and take his hand, he drew her forward to the
podium. At'r placed his arm around her waist, her name echoed on
their lips and with whispered urging from At'r, short of a command,
she spoke to them.

"Thank you." Izadra said sincerely, "Your welcome makes me feel
at home already, never was I so greeted on planet Earth." She glanced
to At'r, and smiled, turning back she continued, "I will try to make
your welcome deserved. Thank you." she concluded moving back
from the sound equipment. Waving at the people, they turned and

were escorted from the platform by six of At'r's bodyguards to the waiting shuttle tubes.

Settling comfortably in the seat, the tube shuttle sped At'r, Izadra and Kron to the palace.

Tos, Creasion's sun, had slowly eased from the sky, turning the deep emerald waters to blazing yellows, oranges and reds. Illuminated by the light from two of the three moons, Izadra first saw her home. Surrounded by a high wall of white polished stone the spiraled towers of their castle resembled a city, and were much like one. Behind the complex stood the Diamerald tower, off to the right was a white sand beach and open sea, to the left a landing pad large enough for several fighters. At'r and Izadra emerged from the tube car to be greeted by the palace staff and a few close members of the court. Their greetings were brief and the Royal couple was finally able to go to their chambers.

Izadra had expected the palace to be impressive but she was unprepared for what her new home comprised. Entering purposely through the formal receiving halls and Throne room followed by At'r's official offices, all decorated in a style unique to Creasion. At'r's offices' decor were of heavy woods from the Moon Konas, the forest moon, At'r's family's home. Leaving these they traveled down a private hallway entering the court dining area. Shortly afterward Izadra lost track of the many salons and apartments for dignitaries and guests all equipped to alter the chamber's environment to suit the occupant. Coming finally to their private apartments.

A large salon for guests waiting to be summoned was comfortably appointed with sofas and chairs, they walked through this room and through a smaller office.

"This is Kins' office," At'r told her, "he has another, larger one next to my official office." Continuing on At'r opened a door and they entered their private living room. Glass paned doors opened out to reveal a dense, green garden, the scent from many alien flowers filling the room from the open windows on either side of the doors.

Izadra stared, "Oh At'r, it is lovely." she walked through the room.

"You may make any changes you wish, Izadra," At'r told her, try-ing not to soften his resolve toward her. Opening the door set in the right wall, directly opposite it in the left wall was another door. "I thought you would be more comfortable here." At'r said and moved back from the portal to allow Izadra to slowly enter.

Covering her dejection, Izadra turned to face At'r from inside the room, she knew the obviously feminine room was only for her occu-pancy.

"My sleep room is across the salon, the door will always be open should you become ill or need me." he explained. "Tonight, however; I will be in a debriefing meeting for a time." He left her, alone and bewildered.

Feeling the toll of the day's events, the more recent causing her to sink onto the bed in despair. It was clear to her, now that she carried his child, an heir, At'r had no further interest in her. Izadra shook her head sadly. Stretching out on the bed, dismissing the food the maid brought, forgetting the medication lord Trentos had prescribed to prevent morning sickness and still dressed in her lime green jump-suit, Izadra fell asleep. The monitoring computer, as on Tos-hawk One, dimmed the lights, and an eerie green glow replaced it, but Iza-dra slept soundly on.

CHAPTER 27

$\mathcal{A}$fter becoming accustomed to the darkness of space the first rays from the morning sun streamed through the pane glass terrace doors and woke Izadra. She sat up, puzzled, the covers falling away from her still dressed form. Before she had time to notice her loosened wrist and ankle cuffs a strong wave of nausea washed over her and she ran to the bathroom. Many minutes later Izadra emerged from the lavatory extremely pale, shaken and weak. Midway back to the bed she stopped to lean on the back of a chair for momentary support, her hand came to rest on the wide belt that matched her jumpsuit. Puzzled, Izadra remembered falling asleep across the bed and on top of the covers. She pondered who had put her to bed. Deciding it had been At'r she moved to scan the salon from her doorway, Izadra saw no one. At'r was not in their chambers, if he had been there he was gone now.

Yawning Izadra lay back down and slept for short time feeling almost herself when she woke.

Stretching as she rose, Izadra looked around the room more closely than she had the evening before. Dark, richly grained wood furniture comprised the furnishings of her apartments. Peach and cream hangings, rugs and other accessories combined to produce a warm comfortable effect.

Izadra located the closet and found it filled with many gowns and other garments that would suit different occasions. Drawing a bathrobe from the collection Izadra also chose a pair of mauve broad wasted, loose-legged pants and a lighter sheer blouse that matched.

She made her way through the necessary part of the bath and going through a curtained entrance found herself in an indoors garden bath. Undressing she stepped down in the pleasantly warm water of the pool and swam laps before going to the shower cubical. As on Tos-hawk, the shower operated on voice command.

Izadra passed the remainder of the morning alone, her only company was the maid who brought her lunch, which she picked at with some interest. Mid afternoon brought a messenger from At'r. His aid Kins bowed before her.

"His Highness will not be able to join you for dinner this evening, Lord At'r suggests you ask Captain Kara or your uncle to join you."

"Thank him, but I believe I will dine alone this evening." Izadra smiled and explained, "I have not even been out in the gardens yet, I am not really up to company." she tried to sound sincere knowing Kins would report back to At'r.

Smiling at Izadra knowingly, Kins assured her, "I understand Your Highness, a long space journey can prove disturbing especially for a lady in your condition. Do not trouble yourself, I will see that His Highness understands." he bowed again, "Your servant milady." Leaving Izadra alone again, Kins wondered why At'r was treating her so.

Still considering At'r's aid, Izadra opened the pane glass doors and stepped out to gaze with glee at the manicured and intricately landscaped Creasion garden. A dark grassy path lead her deeper through the garden and Izadra followed it entranced by the lush vegetation and exotic flowers. Overhead the trees were filled with birds and large and odd shaped butterflies. Feeling almost at home in the garden Izadra lost track of time and how far she walked, at last rounding a geometric shaped shrub Izadra discovered a beach.

Blowing off the fresh water-sea a light breeze lifted the strands of her hair. On the distant horizon Izadra could see black clouds building, flabbergasted she watched how fast the storm was growing. Even though the storm was many miles away, Izadra saw a great flash of lightning, serving to remind her of what her grandmother had written about storms in the letter and what At'r had said about the storm's intensity and how violent they could quickly become. Turning Izadra rounded the shrub once again to find herself in the midst of a garden she had become lost it.

"Oh boy!" she said aloud, then stood still looking around, Izadra shivered. She felt eyes watching her but saw no one. Calmly, though she did not feel calm, Izadra retraced her steps following the path as well as she could remember, knowing all the time she was being observed. A dark, foreboding, sensation past through Izadra and she shivered again.

Coming to a crossing in the paths Izadra stopped, unable to recall which path she had traveled. Looking up, the sky had begun to darken and the wind was rising. In the distance, she could hear thunder, even on Earth Izadra hated thunder storms and from what she had seen on the horizon, she did not want to be caught in this one.

Hearing a rustle of underbrush Izadra turned to see the bushes move but too late to see who had been watching her. They had disappeared, lost in the maze of greenery. A peal of thunder reminded Izadra she was still lost. Resolutely she stood where the paths crossed and concentrated hard.

Another crack of thunder sent her running down the path she had seen in her mind. Rounding a planter of tall shrubs she saw her chambers' door, and hurrying Izadra closed them as the rain began to fall.

Breathing a little quickly Izadra sat on the foot of the bed and watched through the windows and doors as the storm's intensity grew more violent. Rain pounded against the class like material of the windows, the thunder was deafening and the lightning came in

fireballs. One ball crashing in the courtyard just outside her bedroom door sent Izadra fleeing to the salon common to both At'r's
and her rooms.

Outside the storm raged, still frightened and feeling no more
secure in the salon, Izadra dared to venture into At'r's room, hoping
he would be there. But the room was vacant. Izadra's eyes traveled
around the chamber, the decor had a masculine feel and was larger
than her room. Dark furniture also graced the room, but his color
was the color of the royal house of Crea, Diamerald. Silver was used
to accent the chamber as were many objects that At'r must have
brought back from other worlds. Suddenly feeling very much the
alien in his room, Izadra retreated back to the salon. Outside the
storm continued to vent it's savage furry, but now only one thought
rang inside her head; she was just like one of his ornaments from
other worlds, he admired, toyed with them for a time and then
placed them on a self.

Behind her the door to the salon opened, and Izadra turned, ready
to meet At'r but found it was the maid with her dinner.

"Would this storm," Izadra asked the servant while she arranged
Izadra's dinner setting, "be considered mild, or severe?"

"Mild, milady, a severe one would cause the city controllers to
drop the city underground. Those rarely come in land, this one only
affected the coast."

"How long will it last?" Izadra questioned further.

"Possibly two hours." pausing, the girl stopped what she was
doing, "Would you like me to stay with you for a time?" she asked
genuinely.

"Thank you, but it is not necessary, I am sure you have other
duties." Izadra told her, knowing she should appear strong before the
staff.

"Did Your Highness know," the girl asked, "you can access the
current weather reports on the viewer?" Going to the viewer the

maid activated the screen and explained to Izadra how to change to different programs, including the weather.

"Thank you so much," Izadra said, glad for something distracting to occupy some of the evening. "What is your name?"

"I am called Lana." she smiled, "I am assigned to Your Highness, call me when you need something."

"Again thank you, Lana." Izadra told her as she bowed and left the room.

That evening the sunset was lost in heavy cloudbanks over the sea, gradually the storm abated and the stars came out. Rising out of the north the moon Tross rose first. In the moon's normal orbit it was so far away that it looked more like a distant star than a moon. Izadra only knew it was Tross because Betus had told her what to look for. Tomorrow night it would not be visible.

An hour later Metem rose from the east. This was the moon Izadra's family had claimed as their home after the planet's civil war. Tonight the moon Konas would not appear, Izadra would have to wait until after the formal reception tomorrow night before she would see the moon At'r's family had claimed as conquerors. In the gardens Izadra could hear the songs of the nocturnal insects and creatures and she breathed in the fresh clear air enjoying the their natural music. At the height of their symphony silence overcame their serenade and Izadra again had the uneasy felling she was being watched.

Slowly, turning full around, surveying the dark gardens with not only her eyes and ears, but her telepathic mind; someone was there, just outside her sensitivity range and in the garden's deep shadows, watching. Izadra wondered if At'r had assigned a guard to watch her. Then shrugged, he would watch with cameras; however, she would mention it to him anyway. She remembered how her grandmother had been kidnapped and shuddered. As suddenly as it came the feeling departed and the night was again alive with sound, Izadra walked back toward the garden doors, stopping she turned to gaze at the

Diamerald Tower. Last night she had not noticed it, but flowing out from the Tower like a glowing Green River, the luminous light seemed to flood the courtyard and bath Izadra in its cool warmth. Izadra was not alarmed enjoying the soothing feel of the mysterious light. Spinning around when she heard her name called, she saw no one. Again she heard the voice and it seemed far away. Going inside to her bedroom Izadra closed the doors and activated the lock, but the ominous voice and eerie light penetrated the very walls.

"Who are you?" Izadra demanded. Abruptly the light disappeared and the voices ceased. Izadra sank onto the bed, 'this was an interesting place,' she thought, shaking her head. Rising tiredly she chose a nightgown and robe from the dresser drawer then made her way to the bath.

CHAPTER 28

❀

L ater in the evening At'r entered their chambers after twenty hours of inspecting Creasion military bases and outposts. Half of those hours he and Kron had spent in their fighters between locations, the other half inspecting the installations. Upon his arrival back on Creasion At'r had ordered the surprise inspections, the Zerions' latest exploits had made him uneasy and he wanted to be positive his forces were in top form. At'r sighed, Kron had been satisfied, but he had not been pleased with what he had found. Beginning in the morning he and Kron would continue to plan the new renovations At'r wanted implemented.

At'r also wanted to keep busy, to give himself time away from Izadra, time to push her to the back of his mind where he could place her in a neat well ordered place in his life. Being around her was far too distracting.

At'r found his chambers as they always were, comfortable, but now they did not seem as warm since his return. Shrugging he bathed and prepared for bed as was his habit. Stretching out between the sheets was luxury, drawing a deep breath At'r closed his eyes, but after long minutes he found he was wide-awake. At'r opened his eyes to a room flooded in the green light from the Tower, swearing lightly under his breath he rose from bed and closed the heavy drapes that covered the windows. Returning to bed he tired again to sleep.

Now he could smell Izadra's perfume drifting on the air and with the fragrance came bold memories of her. Closing his eyes did not help he only saw images of her. Rising from bed, he drew the curtains back to look out, still restless he walked back to the salon. Feeling drawn to Izadra's room, his tired mind could not control his feet.

As the night before, At'r quietly entered Izadra's room and stood looking down at her face. She was dressed in a turquoise gown, the matching robe lying over the foot of her bed. At'r ran his hand over the sheer garment. At times like this he was not sure he could exile Izadra to the back of his thoughts, or if he could continue to ignore her as he had.

At'r wondered if the storm had frightened Izadra, she had told him once Earth storms terrified her, Creasion's storms were worse. At'r watched her for a long time, until exhaustion reminded him of his need for sleep. Temptation to join Izadra in her bed haunted him and At'r wished he had not assigned her a separate room. Calling upon all his will power he walked back to his own bed and slept.

"Milord," he heard Izadra's voice, "At'r," her soft voice caressed his unconscious mind. "At'r, Commander Kron is in the salon, you have slept late." At'r opened his eyes to look at Izadra's face so close to his, still half asleep he gently touched her cheek and would have kissed her had he not heard Kron's voice speaking in the intercom to his second in Command. Now awake he sat up in bed and Izadra drew away, returning to the salon.

"How have you been Izadra?" Kron asked, concerned at At'r's recent neglect of her, not understanding his changed attitude, either with her or his concern with the system's highly efficient defenses.

"Well Kron, and you?" Izadra managed a smile for him.

A strange look passed over his face, "Your Highness knows I am always at your command." he assured her, "If you should need…"

At'r had finished dressing and joined them. "Commander," he coolly greeted Kron, Izadra could only guess at the reason, "Lady Izadra," At'r said to her in the same cool and formal tone, "Tonight is the reception we spoke of while on Tos-hawk One. You will meet our court this evening as well as many dignitaries, and tonight would be a good time to announce the appointment of your first Lady in Attendance. Your friend Kevin will also be there. Kins and Kara will explain any questions you may have." At'r spoke, giving her instructions as he would any servant.

"Milord," Izadra said carefully, injured by his manner, and seeing the embarrassed look on Kron's face, "I have not yet asked Tari, ah Captain Kara…"

At'r considered her for a moment, "Why not? Have you changed your mind?"

"No, sire, I have chosen her."

"Madam! Must I tell you how to do everything? You must summon her this morning and tell her. The sooner the better." At'r turned and signaling Kron left the room. Kron bowed quickly, smiled at her encouragingly and followed At'r.

Never, never, even when they had fought had At'r spoken to her in that manner. Izadra could not decide if she was angry or hurt. She stood in the center of the empty salon thinking in bewildered silence.

When At'r had awakened he had been so gentle, almost kissing her, but suddenly he had become a different person. Izadra did not understand. Hearing the door she turned just as Kins was entering, a nonplused look on his face.

"Good morning Your Highness." he said in a slightly dumfounded tone, he too had been given instructions by At'r and did not understand his Lord's changed demeanor.

"Good morning Kins." Izadra returned distractedly, "Could you do a favor for me, please." she asked.

"Yes of course."

"Would you summon Captain Kara for me?"

"Consider it done, what time would you like to see her?"

"About an hour, and I will need her for the rest of the day and evening, if it is possible?"

"My Lady, if you wish it, it is possible." Kins assured her and was off to summon Captain Kara. Kins had come to admire Izadra and he could not understand why At'r had pushed her away.

An hour after Kins left, Captain Kara was bowing before Izadra.

"You have summoned me, milady, and I am here." she smiled.

"Good." Izadra smiled, happy to see her friend again. "Please sit down Tari, do you wish anything to drink?"

"No, milady, thank you."

"Do you know why I called you?"

"No, Your Highness."

"Tari, as I asked you to on board Tos-hawk One, when we are alone, please all me Izadra." she reminded her. "I called you here to ask you to be the first of my ladies. His Highness and my great-uncle, lord Betus, have told me this is expected, to choose several ladies for companions."

"I am honored." Tari said amazed.

"You will have authority over the others, when they are chosen, most of all you will guide me. That is why I wanted you for the remainder of the day. Tonight is the reception and we both will need time to get ready."

"Thank you, my Lady," Tari said sincerely, "I will serve you faith-fully."

"I know." Izadra said.

Together they went through Izadra's wardrobe, "But how could they all fit so well?" Izadra asked after she had tired on several gowns, and remembered how well the pants, blouses and undergarments fit.

"Your measurements as well as your body impression were trans-mitted from Tos-hawk, I was on duty when His Highness ordered them sent and your clothing prepared." Tari explained, "but" she hesitated, "not until he had chosen the styles and materials to be used himself."

"Figures," Izadra murmured, trying to see the back of the pale lemon gown she had tired on.

"You are beautiful, niece." Betus said from the doorway.

"Uncle!" Izadra said cheerfully, "Come in." she hugged him, then stepped back, "But how did you get in unannounced?"

"I am an old man Izadra," his eyes twinkled, "but not yet ready to reveal all of my secrets."

"You remember Captain Kara?" Izadra asked.

"Yes, of course," he turned to Tari, "how are you Captain?"

Bowing slightly, Tari replied "Well milord."

Betus smiled at the two, "I have brought you something Izadra," he drew the heavy wooden box from beneath his arm, laying the coat size box on the bed. Carefully Betus opened the ornately carved, hinged lid revealing a crystal box which he lifted from the wooden one lined with green satin.

"This is a very special box," he said to explain, "it was made from natural crystal from Metem, and etched by artists of Creasion after it was shaped by the mind powers of the High Priest and Priestess, who are now dead." Betus sighed, "But this is just the wrapping," he lifted the lid, "Here is the gift. This was made from gold mined on Tross, and spun by the weavers of Konas, the Diameralds were added on Metem. It was given to Iza by your grandfather. She never had a chance to wear it, and I thought you might like too this evening." he smiled warmly, "I am sure you will look lovely in it."

Awed by the spun gold vision Betus held up, Izadra gently touched the misty gold lace that had been made and crafted into a flowing cape with a large hood. Each golden lace flower had a tiny Diamerald cleverly inset in the center. Sunlight from the widow caught on the fabric and it set the room aglow.

"It is." Izadra searched for words. "Magnificent. I would be honored to wear it."

"Then it is yours, be careful to always place it back in the crystal box then in the wooden one, that way it will remain as it is. Outside of the box for more than a few days and it," he paused, "will change."

He concluded mysteriously. Looking from Tari back to Izadra he asked, "but what will you wear with it?"

"A very special gown." Izadra answered thoughtfully.

"Until this evening then." Betus said quietly and was gone.

Izadra turned to Tari, "Although all these are beautiful, I have a special dress in mind. An Earth style gown." Izadra smiled slyly, maybe this gown would tempt At'r, she blushed at the thought causing Tari to wonder what her Lady was thinking.

"Tari," Izadra called going to the computer terminal, "you are faster at this than I, please set it up so that I may draw on the input screen." Tari quickly complied.

Izadra sat at the terminal after Tari had finished, sketching the gown she had designed in her mind. Pushing a yellow button on the console gave the screen animation and the appearance of a three dimensional form, making an adjustment here and there, some contributed by Tari, they created an original gown that would enhance the unique beauty of the cape. Nodding in agreement, Izadra pushed the button to activate the mechanism.

An hour later after Izadra and Tari had eaten a small lunch the gown was completed. Carefully Izadra laid the special dress out on the bed marveling at how fast and efficiently the computer had finished the garment.

Made from a rich black material a little heavier than satin with a higher sheen it was tailored to fit Izadra very tightly. The back of the sleeveless gown was low and draped from each shoulder forming a drape just below her waist. Similar, but not as low, the front draped across her full breasts provocatively. A long slit up the right front of the strait skirt allowed her legs to show well past her knees with each step.

Satisfied with the gown Izadra turned to Tari, "You must go and prepare yourself for this evening, tonight your appointment will be announced. What are you going to wear? Perhaps we should design a gown for you also, there is still plenty of time."

"Thank you Izadra, but I will wear my formal uniform.'

"Can you wear a gown if you wish?"

"I could, but it is proper to wear my uniform."

"Go and prepare, we will meet as planned just prior to the beginning of the reception." Izadra told her friend.

"Before I go, promise me that you will eat before the reception, there will be refreshments but you need more."

Izadra smiled, "As the day we arrived, I promise." She contemplated Tari as she exited. Izadra had not had friends on Earth, she had never seemed to fit in, but this girl seemed to be genuinely concerned for her.

Izadra walked outside and drawing a deep breath of fresh air found a relaxing bench shaded from the late afternoon sun.

At'r weighed on her mind, he had been so brusque this morning she wondered if she had inadvertently done something to anger him. She shrugged coming to the conclusion her mere presence angered him.

Sadly looking skyward her eyes caught the top of the Diamerald Tower, there it settled and she wondered about the builder and the Tower's occupant. How long Izadra sat looking at it she did not know, but her maid Lana appeared in the garden, bowing she informed Izadra she had only two hours to prepare for the reception. Izadra rose to ready herself to meet the court.

"What are these?" Izadra asked once back inside.

"Those are called Trittles, they are made from fruit combined with purple sugar and baked into these confections."

"Oh, they're delicious." Izadra said popping the third one in her mouth. "I'll bet they're fattening."

The maid's eyes twinkled, "Very." she told Izadra.

Izadra stood before the mammoth doors to the main audience hall, too nervous to notice these doors rivaled those to the entrance to At'r's quarters on Tos-hawk One.

Behind her, Tari was carefully arranging the flow of Izadra's golden cape to trail behind her when she walked. Inside the hall that would comfortably entertain a thousand, Izadra could hear the noise of the ladies and lords anxiously awaiting the arrival of their Emperor and his new wife.

Izadra had a strong memory of accompanying her father to Buckingham palace when she was fourteen. She had watched the Queen and wondered if she ever felt tense meeting her court, Izadra did.

"All is ready, milady." Tari told her, "His Highness has signaled."

"Very well." came Izadra's only reply.

A loud voice, Izadra recognized as Kins, rang over the excited crowd's chatter they quieted as he announced the imminent arrival of the awaited couple. After a lengthy oration she heard their names echo from the walls and the huge doors opened.

Propelling her feet forward she glided across the polished crystal floor to poise on a landing above a flight of thirty steps leading down to the bustling room. Across the room on another like landing stood At'r. Their eyes met across the lengthy expanse. Izadra was drawn to him as they slowly began to move toward each other.

At'r had worn the Royal Crown and chosen his garments in black and sliver, his stern countenance making Izadra's knees shake and dampening her proud posture, though, for the sake of the gathered court she hid it well.

At'r stared, disbelieving the vision he knew was his wife. She seemed spiritual. Light danced around the gold cape deflected by the many inset Diameralds and by the Diamerald necklace and earrings he had given her, combining together to give Izadra a green fire halo.

Meeting in the center of the room, At'r took her hand as Izadra sank down in a deep curtsey. He greedily feasted his eyes on the display of her décolletage, remembering well the smooth softness of her breasts. Izadra rose to look At'r in the eyes, blushing at the desire she saw there. Silence reigned as the two regarded each other. Then guided by At'r's hand she walked the length of the hall, down a long corridor of subjects who bowed as they passed.

At'r seated her at his feet on a large, dark green velvet cushion next to his Throne. Pausing momentarily to whisper in Izadra's ear.

"Madam, that dress is near to indecent, take care you do not embarrass yourself by coming out of it."

Izadra smiled inwardly, the dress had done the job she had designed it to do and gained his attention. The lecherous gleam in his eyes was unmistakable.

Kins began the introductions of the court, which proved to be a long procession of Creasion lords, and ladies as well as the assembled diplomats and their mates from other worlds. Some so different in appearance to a human, that Izadra was hard pressed to conceal her surprise. Finally the formalities ended and the room began to buzz with the laughter of the assembled company.

At'r had said little to Izadra in the time she sat next to him while they received their court, only what was required in polite conversation. Now he turned to her as the last of the guests left the dais.

"Madam," he said stiffly, "you may join the others." he indicated the court, "Kron and I have things that must be attended." Leaving Izadra as hostess to a large gathering of dignitaries she did not know, At'r bid Kron follow him.

Tari, now that her appointment was announced, was never far from Izadra. Having overheard the cold words At'r had said and the manner he was treating Izadra, was for the first time in her life irritated with her sovereign, not understanding his manner with his wife.

Shaking her head Tari remembered how difficult it had been to fly escort to At'r when he had gone to Earth to rescue Izadra. But her concern and her duty were now to Izadra. Gathering several of the people, she thought Izadra might enjoy talking with, Tari brought them to the dais and joined Izadra on the steps leading to the Throne. Soon the small group grew to include many of the young lords and a few of the ladies in attendance. They questioned Izadra about Earth and she retold some of her adventures both before and after the Zerions came. Izadra's laughter mixed with theirs and the court hummed in merriment.

Among the many people Izadra met during the evening she could feel one staring at her with such intensity and hate that it made her shiver. Izadra's gaze stopped on a side door to see it slowly swing closed, to late to see who went through it, but the sensation stopped as the door closed.

Stopping in mid conversation, Izadra scanned the room, a strange look in her eyes, not knowing her jewelry had begun to softly glow.

Blushing, Izadra turned back to the people around her, the Diam-eralds around her throat still retaining some of their glow. "Excuse me, my friends," she made apology but did not offer an explanation.

Ba-lyn quietly left the reception while Izadra scanned the crowd for her. In her haste she missed the warning glow of the gems around Izadra's neck. Walking slowly back to the small room she had recently been given next to the temple, Ba-lyn considered what her next step should be. Lady Izadra did not seem to have strong mind powers, probably, Ba-lyn thought, because Izadra was a half-breed; also, Ba-lyn noticed At'r did not seem overly fond of his wife. This she found reassuring. Perhaps if she could find a way to dispose of Lady Izadra she could catch At'r's eye after all.

But Ba-lyn knew she needed to be closer to the situation before she could do anything. Watching Lady Izadra in her gardens was dangerous and told her little.

"I need to be one of her ladies." Ba-lyn told herself and considered how she could accomplish this as she entered her room. Before closing the door she glanced skyward, Konas was rising and Metem was high, suddenly Ba-lyn was uneasy, unable to determine the reason, she shrugged and closed the door.

After the strange experience, Izadra was not as cheerful but kept her guests from seeing, only Tari knew something was amiss. Time passed more slowly and Izadra grew tired.

"Milady," Tari addressed Izadra, "it is late and many of the guests would like to retire."

"I also Tari," Izadra agreed, "but is it not customary for His Highness to adjourn the evening?"

"It is traditional." Tari agreed.

"I should ask him?" Izadra asked softly, dreading interrupting At'r in his current mood.

"Yes." Tari answered, Betus, who had come to stand next to her agreed.

Rising resolutely, Izadra made her way to the office where At'r and Kron were discussing planetary security. Izadra stood quietly until At'r finally looked up, well aware of her presence from the moment she entered his office.

"What is it?" At'r asked abruptly, looking back at the data he was reading.

"Sire," Izadra said, her voice tired and uneasy, "many are requesting permission to retire for the evening."

At'r looked up again and considered Izadra, "I do not need you to remind me of my duty." he growled and bushed past her. She could hear him smoothly dismiss the court and wish them a goodnight. Casting Kron a weak smile, Izadra turned to leave the small room and bumped into At'r.

"Excuse me." Izadra said simply, stepping aside and pulling her cape with her.

"You also have my permission to retire." he said in passing.

"By your leave." Izadra said caustically, dropping into a deep curtsy, adding as she passed through the door, "Your Highness."

At'r returned to stare down at the plans they had been working on until Kron handed him a glass of Metem brandy. At'r looked up at his friend's worried face.

"Get it out of your system, Kron." he told him, accepting the drink.

"What has she done to cause you to loathe her so?" Kron asked seriously, "If she nettles you so, place her in her own palace away from here."

"I do not loathe her Kron." At'r told him looking back down at the plans.

"Then why do you treat her as you have, especially the past few days? When Izadra escaped you and fled to Earth you were like a madman to get her back."

"Of course," At'r replied coolly, "she must be the mother of my heirs, it is that simple."

"And now that you have gotten her pregnant she is only a necessary means to an end?"

At'r did not reply, he only glared at Kron, who continued undaunted.

"The girl cares for you At'r, it is cruel of you to treat her this way."

"She will survive and become accustomed to her role. In time she will concern herself with other interests."

"Possibly one of the lords of your court?" Kron asked and found his shirt grabbed in the fists of his Emperor, "You will not accept her love, will you live with her hate? For that is what will happen."

"You go to far Kron. How dare you suggest such a thing?" At'r growled.

"She is a beautiful, young woman, alone in a strange world, how many of the men of our court would be happy to comfort her. Frankly At'r the way you've treated her, I can see why she has not allowed you the freedom of her thoughts."

"Kron, you are on dangerous ground." At'r released his tunic.

"I only speak candidly because you are family and my friend, and because she too is my family. I am responsible for her being here. I could have returned her to Earth before you saw her and little would have said about it."

"You come close to treason!" At'r warned him.

Kron stood stiffly at attention. "I am at your disposal." Kron bowed formally. "Sire." Then left his monarch alone to consider the harsh words he had said. Never had he known At'r to act in such a manner, Kron could only conclude that At'r loved Izadra and would not admit it even to himself.

At'r could not believe Kron's tenacity. Only because Kron was his friend had At'r allowed his words. He tried again to loose himself in the security plans, but he could not rid himself of what Kron had said. Quietly he moved to stand behind the throne in a place he could observe the dwindling crowd. Izadra had stayed, being a good hostess, to say goodnight to the last of the guests Tari stood next to her. Much to his chagrin most of the stragglers were the young unmarried lords of his court. Angered, At'r watched until the last had gone.

Izadra turned to Tari and Kevin, who had also remained, and they all laughed at something she said. Walking away the three giggled until At'r could hear them no longer.

With the weight of Kron's words in his mind At'r went back to the office and sat down removing the Royal Crown. A light knock at the door drew his attention away from what Kron had said. Hoping it was Izadra, At'r instructed the visitor to enter.

Betus bustled into the room, a cross look on his face. "Milord." he said bowing only slightly.

"What is it Betus." At'r asked tiredly.

Betus considered At'r for a moment before he spoke, "I am an old man, At'r." he began. "And have lived many years, but I cannot understand why you have placed your wife, the woman you risked so much to reclaim, in another bedroom."

"Lord Betus!" At'r began not wanting another lecture.

The High Priest dared to interrupt At'r, "Now At'r I have known you since you were but a boy running free on Konas, and I am as fond of you as I am of my own children. However, Izadra is my grandniece and I do not like your treatment of her. Not only that, but others have noticed as well. What has she done," he asked "to cause you to change your attitude toward her?" At'r did not answer Betus continued his assault. "Is this because she will not share thoughts…"

"I am sorry," At'r began, cutting off the last of Betus' words, "that you do not feel I am treating her well." for the first time at odds with Betus. "It is true she will not share her thoughts with me. Nevertheless, that is not why I placed her in her own bedroom. Now that she is carrying my child there isn't a reason for us to sleep together."

"Perhaps," Lord Betus said becoming angry with At'r, "I should have opposed this union." he shook his head. "I had hoped." he stopped and looked to At'r, "Do you really care so little for her, that you cannot see how you hurt her? What will you do when she grows to hate you for it?" Abruptly Betus turned and left without asking permission or bowing. He was disappointed with At'r.

At'r looked around the room feeling trapped, he paced. Kron and Betus were right. How long before she would hate him. "Damn!" he swore, unconsciously using the Earth word. He had not wanted it to come to this. The sight of Izadra standing amid the young lords earlier came to mind. 'How long' he asked himself, 'before one of those struck her fancy, perhaps even the Earthman.' At'r could have hit Kron when he had suggested it, but now he knew it was because he feared it himself and could not bare the possibility. At'r was not blind, he saw how the men watched her.

Unable to remain in his office any longer he went to the intercom and depressed a button. Kron's face appeared on the screen.

"Have my fighter readied, I will pre-flight it myself." At'r switched off the device and headed for the hanger where his fighter was stored. In space At'r could think clearly. A short flight and maybe, he thought, he could find a solution.

Immediately Kron ordered At'r's fighter readied and assigned one of his own crew to pre-flight the craft. Knowing At'r was a bit distracted he did not want to take any chances with the Emperor's life. At'r would not know the craft had been checked.

Kron cared deeply for his friend and Emperor, because of this and not duty he guarded At'r's life, frequently with his own, but he could also remember many times At'r had saved his life. Kron hoped his friends could work out their differences. Barely finishing before At'r entered the building Kron watched the efficient crewman scurry to his normal duty station.

"Your Highness," Kron said bowing formally as At'r approached.

"Well, Commander, is my ship ready?" At'r asked coolly.

"As you commanded, sire." Kron assured him stepping aside as At'r began his list of pre-flight checks on the ship.

"By your leave?" Kron said bowing and At'r dismissed him.

At'r blasted off the planet a few minutes later after completing his checklist. Inwardly At'r smiled knowing Kron had already had one of his men go over the craft, which reminded At'r that Kron was probably his best friend. It was reassuring to know Kron was so loyal.

CHAPTER 29

*U*naware of the turmoil At'r was experiencing Izadra sadly dressed for bed, still unable to understand At'r's manner toward her. She had tried so hard and still he was not pleased. Yawning, Izadra sat on the bed until she looked out the windows. Konas and Metem were at opposite points, Konas one quarter up and Metem three-quarters down. In the center, forming a triangle stood the glowing Diamerald Tower.

Suddenly the double doors blew open, the wind stirring the curtains in the room. Izadra walked over to close them again and her eyes fell on the Tower, now it glowed brighter than the nights before. A triangle of green energy seemed to be forming between the tower and the two moons, the Tower becoming the bottom point in the triangle. Izadra's white night gown billowed around her feet.

Izadra found herself bathed in green light as she had been the night before, but now she could feel the energy of the beam. Again the voice called her name, now loudly. Izadra looked around but saw no one. Unable to fight the will of the Tower and soaked in the cool warmth of the green light Izadra felt herself lifted off the courtyard stones and drawn toward the structure. She was not afraid. Instead she felt peaceful and secure, all her worries gone.

Joined with the two moons, the Tower's power was awesome. It carried Izadra over the ground and any obstacles that blocked her path to deposit her gently before the entrance.

Both Royal guards were in a hypnotic state and did not see her, but stared straight ahead. Fearfully she looked through the now open door up the stairs that disappeared in the swirling green mist. Swallowing hard, the euphoric feeling gone, Izadra drew a deep breath and entered the building. Trying to fight the compulsion she felt to climb the stairs was a losing battle. What ever it was that had called her and brought her here now demanded Izadra walk the last steps herself. Slowly she climbed, never looking back, soon the mist surrounded her and her only choice was to finish climbing the stairs.

Izadra emerged from the mist to find herself in the large room at the top of the Tower. Through the green crystal of the walls she could clearly see the city, the palace and the sea. Other than a glowing crystal platform the spacious room was bare.

"Welcome!" the same voice that had called her, said.

"Thank you. Who are you?" Izadra dared to ask.

"Please, daughter, stand on the platform and all will be explained to you."

Izadra stared hesitantly at the glowing platform. Concern for her unborn child rang loud in her mind.

"I have brought you this far but I will not force you to stand on the platform, though I could compel you. You must do this yourself. Rest easy, no harm will come to you or the child you carry."

"How did you know?" Izadra covered her still flat stomach with her hands.

"I know many things."

Izadra approached the platform and gingerly placed a foot on the first step then the next until she stood on the top. A peaceful feeling came over her, deeper than before, and Izadra became a part of the emerald beam emanating from the clear crystal platform. She could feel the power pulsating through her as the walls faded from sight, vanishing to leave her standing high above the city.

Then the city was gone and beneath her Izadra saw only the planet. She floated in the light unafraid and alone in space. Only the voice guided her.

"I am the essence of the past and the viewer of the future, with me you will experience the past to learn what you will need to know to shape the future. I will teach you about your powers and your history." Time became meaningless and space even less as she followed her teacher through the cosmos.

CHAPTER 30

*I*n space flight At'r's spirits soared, his mind cleared and he felt himself again. Unwilling to return to his problems he allowed himself to be entranced by the rhythm of the stars. However, after such a long time in space on the Earth expedition he needed to feel the ground under his feet. Changing his direction he re-entered the planet's atmosphere to land on an island far out in the Blue sea. Long ago his father had secured this ten square mile paradise as a retreat. It had been one of the few things he had done for himself. As a small boy At'r had spent many hours playing in the sun at his mother's feet as she sunbathed on the white sand.

Walking in the moonlight he skipped stones across the still waters. At'r looked to the horizon and beheld a green glow in the direction of Crea, his eyes moved skyward to the two moons, opposite each other and he thought of his wife. 'Izadra would like this island.' At'r thought. 'Perhaps he should bring her here.' At'r could almost see her walking in the moonlight like one of the Astral women that visited Crea in their early myths. Sitting on the sand he sighed. After a time taking off his boots, he undressed and went into the warm surf.

Leaving the water At'r felt refreshed but chilled in the cool air. As he dressed he heard the distant cry of a Watercat leaving for her nightly hunt. It was a lonely cry, and At'r felt privileged to have heard it, Watercats were rare animals.

Izadra was still heavy on At'r's mind, he could no longer deny how he felt about her. He remembered how Izadra had looked when she had first come to him. Battered and dirty, she had stood bravely before him not bowing or showing any fear or pain. At'r re-lived their time together and through all of it she had found a place deep in his heart. Now At'r knew what had motivated his actions when Izadra had escaped to Earth, why he had gone himself and risked his life against all warnings from Kron.

At'r had set aside his duty because he loved the beautiful Earth captive who had turned out to be a lost princess. Sadly he smiled. Now he knew that had she not been a princess he would have taken her anyway, he knew too that he would never let her go. He loved her!

With new resolve he entered his fighter and flew home in a light mood, a smile on his full lips. Soon Izadra would wake from her sleep, dawn would be in just a few hours. Then he would tell Izadra of his plan to take her to his island. There he would tell her of his love. Together, just the two of them, no servants or guards. No longer the alien Lord who conquered her. No longer would she be his captive, only two people alone, a man and a woman. At'r felt his blood heat, he and had to concentrate hard on controlling his fighter through landing.

Kron waited patiently at the landing site, "Did you enjoy your flight?' he asked as At'r descended the stairs.

"Yes, thank you Commander." At'r said in an annoyed tone but softened his demeanor. "Thank you, my friend for your honesty, please forgive me my harsh words, I have never doubted your loyalty."

Embarrassed, Kron said nothing and At'r slapped him on the back jovially, "I will see you later. I've got to see Izadra. You, my friend should take tomorrow off."

At'r walked through a little known entrance to his private gardens, enjoying the smell of the air blowing in from the sea. Rounding the last shrub he found himself in his courtyard and to his alarm Izadra's garden doors were open. A numbing feeling overcame him and before he entered her rooms he knew she was not there. In despair At'r walked back out in the gardens, she had gone again. He wondered where she had flown, he hoped she had not tried to return to Earth.

Looking up his eyes caught on the Diamerald Tower. A curious stare turned to a reassuring feeling. The Tower had stopped glowing with the exception of the top room, he now knew where Izadra was. Running as he had not done since his youth, At'r covered the three-quarters of a mile to stop, gasping just short of the door.

Both guards stood straight as statues with dazed looks on their faces, they were oblivious to At'r's presence. At'r surmised they were hypnotized by the green aura that surrounded each one. Between the two hypnotized guards stood the open door to the Diamerald Tower. Looking in At'r could see only green mist covering the stairs and most of the entranceway. With hardly more than a glance at each guard he bolted up the steps, fearless of the mist.

At'r was halted at the top by a spectacle that made him stare in fear for Izadra. She stood before him on a raised crystal platform that emanated a green light. Her eyes were closed and a peaceful smile was on her lips. At'r moved slowly forward trying to think of a way to get her out of the beam. As he examined the aura a mechanical but male voice seemed to speak in his mind.

"Do not attempt to touch her."

Immediately At'r blocked his thoughts, disallowing any intruder entrance.

"Who are you?" he questioned verbally.

"I am the essence of Emperor Tor, nephew."

"What have you done to my wife?" At'r demanded.

"Your wife and unborn son are well, do not fear for them."

"What have you done to her?"

"My grand-daughter will explain to you why I called her," there was a pause, "and you, to this Tower after she awakens." At'r's silver necklace glinted in the light and the presence of Tor noticed it. "I see you still wear the silver necklace."

"Yes," At'r answered him and the room began to fill with the green mist, swirling around At'r until he could not see Izadra. A chorus of seemingly ancient voices echoed through the Tower, their voices flowing from the walls and singing in their ancient language. At'r began to feel drawn into their song, the mist tranquilizing his will.

At'r fought the numbing effect of the mist to no avail, the voices had reached a deafening level. Suddenly the silver necklace around At'r's throat slid from his neck to shatter in a million particles upon impact with the crystal floor. Amazed At'r put his hand to his throat expecting to find the necklace gone, instead he found a gold necklace replacing the silver.

As the mist cleared Tor's voice came again in his mind, "I have watched you lead our people to a more safe future and it is time that necklace took it's rightful place. Wear it with honor nephew. In a moment I will return you wife to you, she will sleep for a while, do not wake her, allow her to awaken naturally."

At'r stood at the foot of the platform ready to catch Izadra when the beam released her. Gathering her in his arms he drank in each detail of her pale face, gently kissing her before he descended the steps, Izadra held lovingly in his arms.Dawn was just breaking over the city when At'r stepped through the open Tower's door. Both guards were alert and had alerted Kron of the Tower's unsecured condition, neither knew what had happened and both sank fearfully to their knees when At'r, carrying Izadra, came through the door. Before At'r could speak to absolve them, Kron and a contingency of At'r's personal bodyguards were on the grounds.

"My Lord," Kron addressed At'r after bowing, "Are you unharmed? Her Highness?"

"We are well Commander. Her Highness seems to have held the key to the Tower. Please secure the area then report to me in my chambers." He started to leave but again saw the two guards still on their knees. "You may rise." He told them. "Commander Kron," he indicated the two. "These men could have done nothing more than they did, take no disciplinary action against them." At'r glanced down at Izadra's sleeping face then strode down the path through the gardens and back to his chambers.

Trentos came immediately, Betus was in the inner room of the temple and no one, not even his son Casso, would disturb him there.

Trentos had finished examining Izadra when Betus arrived. At'r ushered him to the bedroom where Trentos gave At'r and Betus his diagnosis, which was the same as Tor had instructed At'r.

"Allow her to sleep until she is ready to wake, possibly until tomorrow at this time. Other than needing sleep she and the baby are doing well."

"At'r?" Betus asked informally, "What happened?" his voice a mixture of emotions and concern.

Motioning them out of his bedroom they followed At'r to the salon and he explained the events of the past few hours. In the dim, early morning light neither Betus or Trentos had noticed At'r's new gold necklace. Now that he explained, the two marveled at it as they closely examined the medallion.

"I am anxious to hear Izadra's account of her experiences in the Tower, when she wakes would you notify me?"

"I am sorry to disappoint you, lord Betus, but when she wakes I am taking her to the Island for two days. We, ah," he hesitated, "have many things to straighten out."

An understanding glimmer came to Betus' eyes, "When you return will be fine."

"That should not be a problem." At'r assured him as Kins entered the room and Betus and Trentos left.

"Good morning Kins." At'r greeted his aid.

"And to you also milord." Kins returned, "How is her Ladyship? Captain Kara and Mr. Bonnett seem most concerned after Her Highness' experience."

"Sleeping," At'r told him. "Please explain to them she will not wake before tomorrow morning." At'r paused, "How did they know?"

"Most of the palace knows sire." Kins informed him.

"What else do they know?" At'r asked himself, but Kins heard him and replied.

"Gossip travels fast, Milord, I know you are aware."

"Yes Kins, I know," he drew a deep breath, "Kins I want you to have Lady Izadra's clothing moved into my closets."

"Milord, there is not room." Kins said in exasperation.

"Then Kins, you have three days to remodel my closets as well as dismantle her room, you may pack her clothing in storage until the work is complete, have Captain Kara pack Lady Izadra enough clothes for two days on the Island first."

At'r could read the relief on Kins' face, "Sire?" he questioned.

"When we return, Lady Izadra will sleep in my room.

While you dismantle her room, please keep in mind it will become a nursery in a few months time."

"Yes lord." Kins smiled as he left the room.

Calling Kron on the intercom, At'r asked him to come to his quarters. When Kron arrived At'r told a servant to serve breakfast and together they enjoyed the meal.

"I see you haven't taken the day off." At'r chided him.

Kron shrugged, "Perhaps the afternoon."

"I called you Kron because I want the Island secured for tomorrow noon, I am taking Izadra there overnight, we both need the rest. You need only have the beach house opened and on automatic please, we will not need servants, or guards."

"I am glad to hear it At'r." Kron told his friend.

"I hope it isn't too late." At'r said unsure of himself.

"Go easy with her At'r, she does not trust you."

"I know, Kron."

Rising Kron excused himself to attend to the day's business. At'r began feeling the exhaustion of not having slept in many hours and knowing he could not for many more. He went to the shower and discarded the clothing he still wore from the reception the evening before. At'r's spirit reveled in the cool water helping him to prepare to meet the diplomats of other worlds and his own people needing his decisions on local matters. After re-dressing he checked on Izadra and assigned one of the chambermaids to check on her periodically with instructions to alert him should she awaken. Knowing people awaited him, At'r left his chamber and his slumbering wife.

Thanks to Kins' ability to efficiently arrange his schedule, At'r took care of the important matters by dinner. At'r and Kins dinned together in At'r's office between visitors as was their custom, afterwards working until moonset.

Entering his chambers, At'r went first to check on Izadra. She lay sleeping peacefully. The maid he had left to watch over Izadra bowed and departed. Seeing her condition unchanged At'r went to Izadra's now dismantled room. He was pleased with the work his craftsmen had accomplished, tomorrow they should start rebuilding and enlarging closets. Satisfied, At'r returned to his bedroom.

Izadra's even breathing reminded At'r how tired he was, he shook his head. Crossing the room he eased his weight onto the bed, 'just for a minute,' he thought, and stretched out on the bed next to Izadra.

Hours later Izadra stretched and rolled over, bumping into At'r. She came slowly awake, opening her eyes to gaze across At'r's chest, his even breathing telling her he slept soundly. She was disoriented and puzzled. Sitting up Izadra looked around At'r's rooms amazed to find herself here, in his bed. Trying hard to recall the events of the past night and the reception she could only remember going to close the windows in her room.

Slipping out of the bed she donned her robe and ventured to the salon. Outside it was a picture perfect day, but her eyes went to the Tower. Now it stood, no longer glowing but glistening in the rising sun, her memory of the events there returned and she sank weakly onto the couch. From when the Tower had called her, until Emperor Tor told her to sleep, she clearly remembered all. However, how she got from the Tower to At'r's bedroom Izadra did have a clue. Scratching her head she realized her need for a bath.

Going to her bedroom, Izadra halted in mid-stride when she opened the door. Everything had been removed from the room, Izadra wondered where her clothing was and why At'r had ordered this done. Turning in amazement, Izadra speculated how so much could have been done in one night and without waking either herself or At'r. Closing the door she went back to At'r's bedroom where he still slept, and entered his bath.

Feeling refreshed and her appetite sharpened she could not recall the last time she had eaten, and depressing the button on the communications panel Izadra summoned Kins, in only moments he appeared.

"Milady," he bowed, "I had not expected you to call me...His Highness?"

"Is still sleeping. Could you tell me where my clothing has been moved?"

"Of course milady." he quietly led her to the small storage closets that were temporarily housing her garments and waited while she selected. They returned to the salon.

"Kins would you also order my breakfast, I feel as though I haven't eaten in days."

"You haven't!" Kins exclaimed, 'Milady you have been asleep for twenty-eight hours."

Izadra stared at Kins incredulously, "What happened Kins?"

"His Highness found you inside the Tower and brought you back here. You have slept since. I will see to your breakfast Milady."

"Mine also, Kins." At'r's voice called from the bedroom.

"Yea Lord," Kins answered on his way out.

At'r had gone to the bath leaving Izadra holding the garment she intended on wearing without a place to change. Her room was out of the question, already Izadra could hear workers carrying out whatever orders At'r had given them. Still pondering what those orders were, Izadra hoped At'r would be in the bath long enough to allow her to change. Shedding the robe, Izadra slipped the sheer undergarments on.

Startled by the bathroom door opening she jumped, grasping the shirt she was about to don before her, her heart pounding in her temples. Seeing her, At'r stopped in mid-stride appraising her. He wanted to take Izadra in his arms and love her, but without interruptions, there were many things they needed to talk about first.

"Good morning, my dear." At'r smiled slightly, a here-to-fore unseen smile that left her more puzzled and apprehensive.

Nervously Izadra finished dressing and joined At'r just as their breakfast arrived. Sitting down together they shared their first meal together in several days. Izadra's appetite was demanding and she said little as she ate.

"Izadra," At'r said, "I have never seen you eat like this." he noticed, "I must warn you, in two hours we are going on a flight in my fighter, you might want to keep that in mind." he said watching as she put her fork down.

"Milord," she began hesitatingly, "At'r," she looked up, "did you find me in the Tower?"

"Yes," he said standing, having finished his breakfast, "I will be back in an hour, have your flightsuit on and be ready to leave." he left her sitting alone unwilling to say more about how he had found her.

Sighing, Izadra rose from the table trying to understand At'r, shaking her head in turmoil, nothing Tor had taught her had prepared her to understand him. Going through the storage closets Izadra dug through the hastily hung garments.

Withdrawing her mauve flightsuite and pushing her legs through the openings Izadra drew the garment over her daily clothing. She styled her hair back in a loose braid and twisted it in a loop at the nape of her neck, after applying a few cosmetics Izadra placed the gold band on her head. Ready, she returned to the living room to wait for At'r.

Minutes seemed to drag by out of boredom she switched on the computer and began testing her newfound knowledge.

At'r had become involved in reviewing a set of reports that had just arrived from one of their agents. Realizing the time, he asked Kins to escort Izadra to the flight hanger where he would meet them.

Izadra followed Kins through the palace and toward the Royal hanger, on the way they met Captain Kara, and Izadra stopped to talk for a moment.

"Milady," Kara said bowing.

"Tari have you been on patrol?" Izadra questioned seeing Tari's flightsuite.

"Yes, just routine, oh, by the way I put your suitcase onboard the fighter yesterday." then she asked more quietly, "What happened to you?"

"I will explain later Tari," Izadra said hugging her friend, "see you later."

Before her the doors to the hangar swung open. Izadra saw At'r waiting for her across the expanse, she walked toward him. Stopping a little in front of him, she curtseyed slightly.

"I am ready milord." Izadra informed him but did not inquire about their destination.

"So you are." he looked her over from head to toe, "Go on up and get comfortable, we leave in a few moments."

Doing as she was told Izadra contemplated what At'r had in mind. 'Why had he dismantled her bedroom, why would he have Tari pack her suitcase, why had he placed her clothing in portable storage units, and why had he placed her in his bed?' Puzzling questions that

Izadra could not fathom answers for, nor did she have the courage to ask At'r. Having become aware of At'r's dissatisfaction with her, she avoided displeasing him, if possible.

Since discovering her pregnancy, At'r had set her aside, only requiring her presence on official occasions. Sighing, Izadra thought, 'This isn't an official occasion, so why?'

"You would tell me if you were not well enough to travel, wouldn't you?" At'r inquired.

"Yes At'r." she answered, more puzzled by his tone.

"Good." At'r turned and sat in the command chair. Going quickly through the starting sequence the engines roared to life.

They lifted off in silence adding further to Izadra's suspicion of his motives. 'Where was he taking her?' Repeatedly the question tortured her mind. Clearing the planet's atmosphere Izadra observed At'r set course for Metem, her family's moon, perhaps he was going to leave her there. Izadra had come to the conclusion that At'r could no longer bare her presence and was taking her into exile. Izadra knew he would not harm her, but he could move her away form him. Still, why had she been in his bed, Izadra could not silence the question.

At'r broke the cold silence, "We are approaching the moon Metem, your ancestral home, it is not our final destination; however, I thought you might like to see it."

"Thank you." Izadra said quietly, now even more perplexed.

At'r guided the ship down to within several hundred feet of the moon's surface.

Izadra was awed by the industry, the mines, and the clean cities, someday, maybe, At'r would allow her to visit. Izadra was not overly optimistic.

After several low orbits At'r reset the controls and the ship turned back toward Creasion. Their return trip seemed quicker in the strained and electrified atmosphere of the ship's cabin. Izadra fought hard to still the trembling tears that threatened to fall from her eyes,

fortunately At'r kept his attention on the ship. Once again in Creasion's atmosphere At'r began slowing their speed and Izadra knew
they were preparing to land, but where? From her vantage Izadra
could not see land, only crystal blue water. Suddenly fearful, her concentration broken, two tears slipped from her eyes and she quickly
wiped them away. At'r was watching much closer than Izadra knew,
and he puzzled at her mood, but then he knew pregnant women
sometimes were teary. Still he watched her closely, but with out her
knowledge.

CHAPTER 31

※

*A*ppearing on the horizon was a sandy beached island, the high inland mountains were covered with lush thick green plant life and it reminded Izadra of a Caribbean island on Earth. At'r circled the island revealing a large house on a hill several hundred yards off the beach and on the beach, a bungalow.

Reducing the ship's speed further, Izadra knew At'r was landing here. Conceivably this island was her new home, isolated and many miles from Crea, At'r would not have to be near her. Gently At'r sat the craft down on the sandy beach then opening the door the fresh air flooded the ship's interior.

"After you." At'r motioned Izadra first. Hesitating, she unbuckled her safety belts and preceded him from the craft, half expecting to hear the door slam shut after she had exited.

Had Izadra's heart not been so heavy, the feel of the warm sand beneath her boots would have been thrilling but not today. Looking out over the massive ocean Izadra stood with her back to At'r, over and over asking herself, 'Is this where At'r will leave me?'

Tears still smarted in her eyes, Izadra jumped slightly when At'r placed his hands on her shoulders, the feel of his strong hands causing her blood to ignite. At'r turned Izadra to face him, but Izadra would not look at him, not wanting him to see her tears.

In one fluid motion At'r moved his hands slowly from her shoulders to raise her chin, Izadra would have to look him in the face but she kept her eyes tightly closed, tears slipping from beneath her long dark lashes.

Occasionally At'r had seen an uncontrolled tear slipped past Izadra's strong will, never like this. "Open your eyes, Izadra, look at me." he commanded.

"Please, At'r." she murmured feeling weakened by his nearness, "Leave me if you must, but with some dignity."

"Obey me Izadra." his voice was low, even gentle but still commanding. Amazed by the glistening tears he saw in her eyes, he stopped the descent of one that streamed down her face. "Why do you cry?"

Izadra was silent, unable to answer him. How could she tell At'r why she cried when he cared so little for her.

Abruptly Izadra pulled free of his grasp, angered that he should treat her so gently just before leaving her.

"Let me go!" Izadra yelled, turning from him. Wanting to run but knowing she could never escape him.

"Tell me what is wrong with you?" he half begged, half commanded, turning her back to him.

"Why so concerned?" she questioned harshly "After you have left me here in exile it really will not..." her voice trailed off. Izadra looked away, out to sea, "I trust, for the child's welfare, you will allow me a maid?"

"Exile? Exile? What are you talking about?"

"From the beginning I have known how you felt about me." At'r heard the pain and anger in her voice. "This morning I find my clothing packed in storage, my room dismantled and a suitcase awaiting my departure. I can only conclude..." Izadra's voice broke, her breathing suddenly constricted by the ache that grew in her throat. "Now that I carry your child," she managed to say, "you no longer desire my company." Izadra looked up, anger clear in her turbulent hazel green eyes.

At'r pulled Izadra to him. "I desire you!" he stated only to have Izadra interrupt.

"Of course, that is why you gave me a separate room, and..." Izadra's pride stopping her from saying more.

"Now I have moved you back."

Again, Izadra interrupted her anger past discretion. "My sincerest thanks. My Lord." she bowed formally, "Why At'r?" Her eyes flashed, "Have our separate sleeping arrangements filtered out to the people? As you have said, you do nothing without a purpose."

At'r's patience was wearing thin. Izadra appeared intent on provoking his anger. "Take care Madam," he warned, "I am still your master and your husband."

"I have not forgotten!" Izadra said with a sneer, "My Lord Emperor." she added.

Looking deeply into her eyes At'r knew he could not tell Izadra he loved her tonight. Studying Izadra's face he knew she would not believe him and At'r knew why. Trust, he must gain her trust. It had not mattered to him before, now he knew it was his only hope.

"While our chambers are being renovated." At'r said stressing the later word, "I thought a couple of days here would be relaxing after our experiences en-route to Creasion and more recently, the Tower." Tenderly he drew her nearer seeing the suspicion in Izadra's hazel green eyes.

Izadra studied At'r's face wondering at the real reason he had brought her here. No servants or guards, complete privacy. Shaking her head slowly, Izadra could think of only one reason At'r would bring her to such an isolated place. Here, on this beautiful Earth like island, through either seduction or force At'r would enter her mind. At'r would finally see what Izadra feared him learning. She loved him.

With this knowledge, he would control her totally. Izadra knew she could not fight him any longer. She did not have the will to resist any more. Slowly she looked away.

"What I am to you," she said quietly, "but your duty to your people? That is what the child will be too. This you have already made clear."

At'r numbly released Izadra, afraid she might never trust him. Here was someone whom his power could not influence.

"I am sorry, Izadra," At'r said sincerely, "that you are suspicious of my motives. Come now, this fighting is not healthy in your condition." He escorted her silently to the bungalow. Once there he insisted she rest. "I will be outside on the beach." he assured her, and seeing doubt in her eyes added. "Do not fear. I will never leave you." Turning At'r went through glass pane doors that opened onto the beach.

Still doubtful of At'r's motives, Izadra did as he instructed her, quietly accepting his concern and assurance. Izadra could not sleep. Instead, she lay contemplating her husband, watching as he walked outside.

She did not understand or trust him, but somehow she must live with him. Izadra's head hurt from trying to find a solution.

At the edge of the jungle grew an ancient Vartee tree, in the unusual trunk and root system At'r found a comfortable and worn seat used since childhood when he needed to think in solitude.

He could not fault Izadra for the way she felt. She had cared for him. At'r hoped she still did. He remembered her obvious concern for him when he had been shot. Her relief from anxiety clear in her eyes when he had been found on the planetoid. Despite her regard, At'r had pushed her away. 'How many times!' he thought had he seen Izadra's fear of him in her eyes and done nothing to assure her. At'r swore to himself, he would be careful not to frighten her anymore.

Quietly At'r entered the double glass doors to the bungalow, Iza-dra appeared to be sleeping. Cautiously Izadra viewed At'r from beneath her lashes, opening her eyes when he sat on the bed.

"How was your nap?" At'r asked, his eyes warm and hungry.

"Fine." Izadra replied watching him closely.

"Would you care to go swimming?" he asked her.

"Did Tari pack a swimsuit?"

At'r smiled down at Izadra, "Here you do not need one. We are alone." At'r could not resist any longer, gently he kissed Izadra, his lips caressing hers. "Come." he commanded softly, reluctantly Izadra followed.

"I will await you in the water." he told Izadra leaving her and his clothing behind.

Finding a light robe in the closet, Izadra undressed and covered herself in the robe, dropping the garment at water's edge and enter-ing the water as At'r dove. Izadra was thankful he did, surfacing after Izadra was shoulder deep. At'r swam to her.

"Feels good, don't you agree?"

"Yes," Izadra nodded as At'r came to her, "the water is not salty."

"Nicer than Earth's salt oceans," he said proudly,

Izadra shrugged, "Tomorrow, if you are up to it, we can explore the island."

"As you wish, milord."

Both fell silent watching the sunset. Leaving the water first At'r built a fire, Izadra went to dress in the bungalow. Returning with At'r's robe and a blanket, Izadra spread the blanket on the sun warmed sand as At'r bade her.

Still cautious, Izadra did not sit until At'r pulled her down next to him. For a time they sat quietly together, Izadra tense, waiting. At'r noticed Izadra's trembling and pulled her into his arms.

"Are you cold?" he inquired.

"No." Izadra admitted honestly.

Looking in Izadra's eyes At'r's lips found hers, the heat of his kiss stilling her trembling. Not to invade, only to communicate At'r gently touched Izadra thoughts, drawing back in amazement at the lack of barriers.

"Why?" At'r asked.

"I will fight with you no longer, my Lord." she said simply and quietly.

Gently At'r touched Izadra's face, his instincts warning him not to press too far into her open soul. Izadra's fears, At'r wanted now to erase, but her luscious body he could not resist. Drawing her once again to him, At'r kissed Izadra passionately.

"For now your beautiful body is what I desire, when you are ready, you will give the rest." he told her telepathically.

Totally amazed by At'r's response Izadra's mind was in turmoil. For weeks, he had tried to enter her thoughts, not caring that she did not want him. Now that she would not block him, he did not press.

Under the moon and star's light At'r kissed her neck slowly traveling down to her breast, his hand caressing Izadra's legs and back. At'r said nothing while he placed light kisses on her slightly rounded stomach and with skilled hands he firmly parted Izadra's legs. Running his hands up her smooth legs, At'r gently moved Izadra's hands as she tried to cover herself. There, At'r concentrated his exquisite lovemaking.

Moving slowly upward he returned to kiss Izadra's trembling lips only after he had propelled her to her own paradise. His eyes shown triumphant at the depth of her pleasure and lightly he settled his weight on her. Tenderly and slowly At'r penetrated Izadra's aroused body.

Completely under At'r's command Izadra knew he could have taken possession of her thoughts as well at this point, but he did not. At'r loved her instead with restrained passion, Izadra pulling him closer. So sweet was the ecstasy Izadra found herself absorbed in that tears slipped from beneath her tightly closed eyes to be kissed away by At'r.

It had only been a few days since At'r had last loved Izadra body, but it felt like years. Beneath him, At'r could feel Izadra's body responding to his. Finally when At'r thought he would cry out from the exquisite ecstasy/torture of propelling Izadra to the summit of her passion, Izadra called out his name and At'r, unable to push his control further released into her throbbing body.

For long minutes, they lay entwined together before either was willing to let go. Izadra, not knowing how At'r felt about her, attributed his gentleness to concern for their child. Still confused by his behavior and why he had brought her here Izadra did not hear when At'r spoke to her.

"Izadra," he called again.

"What?" Izadra said, "I did not hear you."

He smiled slightly, "Come wife," he pulled her up, "let's go for a swim." still holding her hand, they entered the surf.

Later, lying on the blanket enjoying the still burning coals of their earlier fire, they enjoyed a simple dinner At'r had brought with them, and the clarity of the night. Izadra began relating the details of her visit to the Tower, and At'r added in his experience. Their conversation was cut short as the sky above them became alive with meteors.

"At'r look!" Izadra drew his attention to the astral display.

"This was not predicted." he murmured watching the spectacle. "Last time," he said rising, "I saw anything like that was on Tross. As boys" he explained, "Kron and I were on a survival trip when we came upon a forbidden sect of what on Earth you would call sorceress, here they are called Troscoss. They are evil individuals and their practices have long been prohibited."

"At'r," Izadra said breathlessly, awed by the phenomenon, "they must be powerful." remembering what Tor in the Tower had said about these people, "Lord Tos mentioned them while I was in communication with him."

"I am going to call Kron," At'r rose from the blanket and ran to his ship, switching on the viewer as Izadra entered the craft, Kron's face appeared on the screen.

"Yes milord."

"Kron have you monitored the meteor shower in progress over this area?"

"Yes sire, it is not a natural occurrence, we are trying to pin point the center of the disturbance."

Izadra who had stood in the door called At'r's attention from the screen, "At'r, it has stopped."

"Kron did you get the location?"

"Close, it is near you milord, just outside the protective barrier, I have dispatched several fighters and two water-fighters to the area, do you wish to return to the palace tonight?"

"We are safe here Kron, at this point I see no reason to change our plans, if something should occur, contact me."

"By your leave, milord." Kron signed off.

At'r rose from the control seat and turned, joining Izadra they walked back to the bungalow, but the night had changed since the meteor shower. At'r was distracted and he slept lightly and restlessly as did Izadra.

Her dreams became a changing scene of what Tor had taught her about the evil cult. Suddenly a face she hoped never to see again invaded her dream. Quar, the Zerion Captain was again chasing her, then dragging her away. Izadra could hear a baby wail, the sound filling her with such fear and sadness that she cried in her sleep. At dawn Izadra finally wrenched her captivated sub-consciousness free and woke with a terrified scream.

At'r was next to her immediately, sitting on the bed and watching her intently, drawing Izadra close he encircled her in his arms and kissed her.

"Tell me." he said reassuringly, "Tell me what you dreamed that has frightened you so. Before you screamed you were crying in your sleep, I was about to wake you." he said persuasively, laying Izadra back among the cushions and covering her. "You are sweating," he told her, concerned because of the cool morning breezes floating in from the sea.

Izadra studied At'r closely before she spoke, "I recalled all the Tower told me about the events we saw last night." she said.

"That is not what made you scream."

"No," Izadra admitted.

"Then what?"

"I was being," she paused, wondering why she had dreamed of the Zerion, "chased by Captain Quar, the Zerion, but I was not on Earth."

At'r, aware of her awakening powers of sight did not dismiss her dream as quickly as he reassured her, "It was only a dream, Izadra, brought on by the strange meteor shower last night. The Zerion Captain is safely in freeze sleep on board a penal station orbiting Tross. He can not harm you, nor would I allow that." He made a mental note to double-check the security around the Zerion. "Would you like to return to our palace this morning? I can not guarantee our chambers will be completed, but after the meteor shower..." he shrugged.

"If you wish to return At'r, I will dress. Last night's astral display has disturbed me also." she agreed.

Both dressed and with a last look around walked together toward the fighter. Izadra still confused about At'r's reasons for bringing her here. At the foot of the steps up to the fighter At'r turned and took Izadra in his arms kissing her.

"I will bring you back here one day, under better circumstances." At'r promised, Izadra did not reply.

Turning toward the fresh water sea, she gazed out over the wind blown white capping and angry ocean so different from the night before.

A strange high pitched sound met her ears and she listened intensely to the wind trying to hear it again. At'r noticing the distant look in her eyes and strain on her face, he searched the horizon for what she saw, but saw nothing there.

"Izadra, what is it?"

"Oh At'r," her voice was soft, and so sad, "it is the strangest sound…" she answered slowly, again she heard the call, "did you hear it?"

"No, can you tell from which direction it is coming?"

"Ahead, on the beach past the fighter." she said beginning to walk in that direction.

After walking a hundred yards down the beach, At'r too could hear the high scream. He quickened their pace, rounding a rock out-cropping that had been submerged until low tide.

"Can you tell what it is?" Izadra asked.

When At'r had first heard the sound he had known the origin and the closer they came the more he dreaded finding it.

"Yes." he said then was silent, remembering the rare sighting he had two days ago of the Water Cat.

Lying on the edge of the next rock formation, half in, half out of the surf was a mortally wounded Water Cat.

Stopping a good distance away, At'r bid Izadra stay where she was. He knew the big cat could be dangerous both in and out of the water and if what he suspected was true, the animal would be a gory sight.

Cautiously At'r drew close, the scream now a loud moan. A great sadness settled on him as he gazed down at the animal. She had been caught obviously at sea, probably hunting for food, by the Troscoss. At'r felt Izadra's presence beside him.

"I told you to stay back." he said firmly.

"I could not," she said her voice barely loud enough to be heard over the roar of the wind. "Did the Troscoss do this to her?"

"Yes, but they did not succeed in sacrificing her." he grew quiet. "That explains why the meteors stopped so suddenly last night, they must have been at sea when they tried. She got away." he said amazed.

Izadra moved closer to the dying cat amazed at what she saw. As big as a tiger but with a coat that was camouflaged to blend with the water, a changing blue color. Her paws were webbed, the back ones resembling padded paw-sized flippers, and she was panting from the stress of her injuries allowing Izadra to clearly see her large teeth. Around her, the sand was stained a deep purple from the wound, which was not visible, because she lay on that side. Izadra stepped yet closer suddenly feeling the animal's pain in waves as it emanated from the cat. Izadra drew back looking bewildered to At'r.

"I can feel..." she said.

"I know," At'r said, "Water Cats can communicate with some people, the fact that you heard her from such a distance in this wind suggests you did more than hear."

Izadra looked into the cat's glowing blue eyes allowing her mind to open to the cat's, "At'r she has a baby." she paused, "She is calling it."

From a din deep inside one of the upper caves on the beach came a six-month old cub. Because of the kitten's bright blue fur, she was wary, vulnerable in the open as she approached the humans. Only last night she had watched her mother leave to bring them food. During the night the cub had heard her mother fighting with humans, but she knew these were not the same people. The cub came close, nuzzling her mother's face, listening while she explained.

Izadra listened too, as the mother told the cub through primitive telepathic communication to go with At'r and Izadra, knowing they would care for her baby after she had gone.

At'r watched as tears streamed down Izadra's face, the cub licked her mother's face one last time and came to sit on Izadra's foot, he knew the cub would return with them.

Izadra viewed the cub as a baby, not a wild animal and she reached down to stroke her silken baby fur, At'r watched holding his breath in fear the cub would scratch his wife. Instead the baby Water Cat purred and rubbed Izadra's legs, then trotted after them down the beach, stopping once to look back at her mother.

Entering the fighter At'r apprised Kron of what they had found and ordered a proper burial for the dead Water Cat. Then lifting off the island At'r guided the fighter skyward passing an in-coming patrol craft that would secure the island.

"It is well the Troscoss did not finish their black ceremony. After they had killed the Water Cat they would have next come looking for the cub. That would have lead them to our island and the security patrols that have circled island since before our arrival." At'r told her.

"Had they found this cub," Izadra paused, closing her eyes and allowing the knowledge to flood into her conscious thoughts, "and their ritual completed. At'r!" she gasped as her psychic warned her. "Someone, one of the Troscoss would have used the power to, kill me." her face was ashen when At'r turned to stare her.

"There is evil on Creasion as well as good, as it is on Earth. At'r told her. "We shall have to be more careful in the future." he became quiet trying to control the anger he felt toward the Troscoss. This cult he had tried to abolish now dared to threaten the life of his wife and unborn child.

Crea came into view, then the Tower, followed by their palace and their private landing pad. At'r sat the fighter carefully down. Izadra rose and proceeded At'r from the craft followed by the cub. Outside they greeted the gathering of relatives and friends explaining how the cub came to be with them. Shyly the cub hid behind Izadra and At'r, never having seen so many people before.

Kins and Tari waited in the crowd until they could get to the Royal couple. Kins drew At'r aside as did Tari with Izadra, each having matters for their monarch's perusal.

Kron soon joined At'r and Kins presenting him with even more pressing problems. Turning back to Izadra, At'r kissed her cheek, telling her he would see her later in their chambers. Kron and Kins followed At'r, neither missing the regretful look At'r gave Izadra as they parted.

CHAPTER 32

"*I* have comprised a list of possible candidates for your remaining ladies." Tari told Izadra, "His Highness instructed me to do so before you left and as he expected there have already been numerous requests on your time."

"I have weeded through those also; however, if you wish to look through them, I have prepared a short summary on each organization requesting your presence."

"Thank you Tari, but for now do you know someone who is knowledgeable about Water Cats? I think she is getting hungry."

"I have sent for a veterinarian, Doctor Shi will be joining us in your chambers." Tari looked sadly down at the sky colored cub, "We heard what happened only minutes before your arrival or I would have had the doctor join us here." With the cub trailing them, they walked toward the Royal chambers, talking as they went.

"Tari, please compile a report on the Troscoss activities since my arrival on-board Tos-hawk One, I learned many things about them in the Tower, and I want to keep track of their ceremonies."

As they completed the walk Izadra briefly explained what had happened the night of the reception. Tari shook her head, "You have a strenuous destiny, Izadra." she said quietly, her Lady's name still feeling a little too informal.

"I know," Izadra agreed, "and you are part of it also."

They smiled at the entrance guards expression as the forty-pound cub rubbed between their legs in house cat fashion, then bounded behind Izadra and Tari.

"Was that fear I saw in their faces?" Izadra questioned, amused.

"Probably, Water cats are known to have nasty tempers even at this age." Tari explained.

Izadra looked at the cub a little differently. Before, she had been just a cute, cuddly orphan.

Inside the receiving hall waited the veterinarian. Izadra cordially greeted the woman, who bowed slightly, more interested in the cub than formalities. The doctor was a handsome woman, about forty, sturdy in build but not fat. Her brown eyes sparkled at seeing the Water Cat, and unafraid she knelt down, resting on her heels and called the cub to her, but made no move toward the cub.

After a few moments of coaxing and after Izadra assured the cub, she gingerly moved toward the woman to take the small tidbit of cheese the doctor held out to her.

Rising, the woman introduced herself and bowed more respectfully, "I am Shi, Your Highness, thank you for calling me."

"You may thank Captain Kara. She assures me you are knowledgeable about Water Cats, it seems she is correct." Izadra smiled warmly.

Bowing again Shi returned to the cub, using a scanner similar to the one Trentos used, she checked the animal's physical condition and was pleased to report a healthy six month-old female Water Cat.

Pleased with the Vet, Izadra bid her stay and attend the cub. Leaving the Doctor in the salon, Izadra and Tari entered the private chambers. While bathing Izadra arranged her schedule for the next few days. Because Tari was efficient and had prepared files on the more suitable candidates for her court, Izadra could begin interviewing the applicants the next day.

These ladies, under Tari's supervision, would comprise her court of advisors and secretaries. They would handle many of the duties Izadra could not personally attend. Knowing she would need help but not over anxious to share her world, Izadra looked skeptically at the stack of dossiers she must read through by morning. Following Izadra back to the living salon, Tari brought the stack with her.

"Yuk!" Izadra grumbled humorously, "I thought college was bad."

"I know," Tari agreed, "here on Creasion students hate homework too."

"Best to get to it, ladies," both turned in surprise at the male voice to find At'r standing behind them, Tari began to stand, but At'r waved her to remain seated.

At'r's eyes devoured Izadra as he explained, "I will be here only briefly. I know you and Tari need to begin going through those." he indicated the files. "Tonight we will be having guests for dinner, the sovereign protector of each moon and their wives. You met them at the reception, but then," he smiled, "you met half the realm that night. Have Tari show you the information in the computer on each and Kins has prepared a short visual for you." For long moments At'r looked down into Izadra's eyes forgetting the matters he had come to discuss with her. Unable to deny the urge to kiss Izadra, At'r bent and briefly their lips touched.

He glanced up to see Tari discreetly engrossed in the stack of files; smiling at her manner At'r turned his attention back to his wife. Much to her surprise he again covered her soft lips hungrily with his.

"Until later, Izadra." he said after he released her and turning returned to his office.

Izadra and Tari worked through lunch, not noticing the time until the door guards announced Kevin.

"Enter." Izadra ordered and a minute later Kevin bowed before Izadra.

"Good heavens Kevin, stand up." she commanded a little annoyed, "You do not have to do that in private, and if you call me Your Highness, I'll sock you." Izadra laughed, "Where have you been since we arrived?"

"Lord At'r assigned me to the law school here in Crea, the elders there have left me little time to visit. They are very curious about Earth law, history and culture. I wish I had thought to bring my law books." he paused to smile at Tari, "and the ladies here," he sighed, still looking at Tari.

Izadra looked from Kevin to Tari and back, a little amazed at the attraction between the two and the scarlet blush that covered Captain Kara's face. Izadra took on a stern facade.

"Are you dallying with my ladies, sir?" she demanded.

Kevin was confused as was Tari, her face paled and Kevin's reddened, but before either could speak Izadra giggled.

"Only one." Kevin conceded.

"That is all I have right now." Izadra informed him, "relax you two." She said. "So you have come to see me, or is it Tari you came to see, and how did you manage to get time off?"

"I took it. And I hoped to see both of you. How have you been Izadra?"

"As always At'r is correct, you will be a good diplomat and Tari and I are fine."

"You know, Izadra, you've become a bit of a legend, word of the Water Cat is the latest gossip." Kevin said nothing of the other rumors concerning At'r's attitude toward her.

"Is it true?" Kevin asked as the door from the formal salon opened and the cub bounded in.

Spotting Kevin she came to an immediate halt and crouched, sizing him up. Relaxing, the cub decided Kevin was acceptable and rubbed around his legs in greeting.

"I am sorry Your Highness," Shi explained, "she opened the door herself before I could stop her."

"Do not concern yourself, Kevin likes cats." Izadra turned to see Kevin stroking the cat's fur. "And it seems she likes him."

"She is beautiful, a Blue Tiger with webbed feet." he admired the cub.

Izadra invited them to sit and their conversation turned from the cat to other matters until a growl from behind the desk alerted Izadra to the cub's mischief.

Out of the stack of files the cub had chosen one to rip apart. Now the printouts were in shreds, the applicant's name barely visible on one sheet that Izadra had to pry from between the Water Cat's teeth.

"Shi, did you feed her?"

"Yes milady, until she was full." Shi responded.

"No, No!" Izadra scolded the cub handing the paper to Tari, "Whose file, can you tell?"

"Ah, her name," Tari said trying to read the ripped papers, "is Balyn, she is the daughter of a Konas diplomat, her mother, the daughter of a Tross official." Tari recalled from memory.

"Can you reproduce her file?" Izadra asked.

"Of course, my Lady."

"Shi perhaps during working hours you might take full charge of, ah…" Izadra stopped, "I will have to choose a name for her." Izadra bent to stroke the cub's fur, "What will you be called little one?" she asked looking into the cubs eyes.

"Call me Nemsis, after my mother." she told Izadra telepathically.

"She wishes to be called Nemsis," Izadra told her company.

Izadra turned to Shi, "Take Nemsis with you, have a large enclosed run built for her inside the gardens. Better still, have the gardens secured and she may roam them as she pleases." Izadra like the idea of Nemsis guarding her gardens, she remembered the feeling of being watched. Now no one would dare enter her gardens.

"Now if you will excuse me, I must prepare for a formal dinner this evening." Izadra explained, and Shi left with Kevin and Nemsis, Tari staying behind to assist her in dressing.

At'r arrived to escort her to dinner. Watching while she put the final touches on her toiletry, he sat stroking Nemsis' fur. The cat had followed him back in and sat purring contentedly. Ready at last, Izadra walked with At'r hand in hand to the dining room.

CHAPTER 33

*B*a-lyn weakly eased onto her bed. After the failure the night before last of the power ritual, she had barely made it back to her room before her leave expired at dawn. Sighing she angrily remembered the events and disappointments of the entire excursion. Had the Water Cat not escaped she would be reveling in her new powers, instead she mourned her brother's death. Still firmly pictured in her mind was the sight of her brother in the jaws of the mortally wounded Water Cat as it slipped under the surface of the turbulent sea.

Disgusted, she rose and went to her bath to soak before starting her daily duties. To further Ba-lyn's aggravation, upon her return she had learned of the return of the Emperor and his consort who had brought a female Water Cat cub with them after finding the mother dying on the beach of their island hide-away.

Allowing the heat of the water to soak out her aches she shook her head. 'This Izadra from Earth must have a strong Karma.' Ba-lyn thought. 'Now she has the cub that would have given me enough power to rid myself of the impure half-breed who has taken what should be mine.'

A knock on the door and a call from one of the other girls brought Ba-lyn back to the present.

"I will be there in a few minutes." Ba-lyn called answering the summons to breakfast.

Strangely silent, Ba-lyn's subdued mood did not go un-noticed by the others or by the girl's chaperon.

"Ba-lyn," lady Tosna addressed her, "are you ill?"

"No lady Tosna, I did not sleep well last evening, but I am fine." she answered.

"I am pleased to hear it," the chaperon said sharply, you have an audience with Lady Izadra at two this afternoon." Tosna watched Ba-lyn's reaction, she did not trust the girl but could not put her finger on the reason.

Ba-lyn didn't try to suppress a smile she could not believe her fortune. If chosen, she would be in a comfortable position to rid Creasion of the half-breed wife of the Emperor, then she would catch At'r's eye and her plans would be back on course.

"I am honored." she managed to say humbly.

"As you should be." Tosna admonished her charge. "You will be excused from you duties one hour before the appointment, that should give you sufficient time to freshen."

"Thank you." Ba-lyn replied, even more humbly than before, again thanking her benevolent spirits who were obviously watching over her with great care. Silently she thanked them.

CHAPTER 34

$\mathcal{T}$ ari and Kevin stood hand in hand watching from the space controller's viewing windows as Commander Delia docked the sleek Tos-hawk Two in the orbiting space hanger. Watching from spaceport high above the planet was thrilling and Kevin observed the impressive sight with interest.

"How long have you known Commander Delia?" Kevin asked.

"She was my mother's best friend and has watched over me since a Zerion attack left me an orphan."

"There are a great number of orphans on Crea, I have noticed."

"Too many, thanks to the Zerion attacks, since Lord At'r became Emperor they are more rare." Tari's face was solemn.

Kevin pondered Tari and this New World he found himself a part of. Unlike Earth there was little dissension here, only the shadowy Troscoss and the apparent threat of the Zerion. Crime was minimal and swiftly punished. Here the people were genuinely more interested in enjoying life and securing their safety from the Zerion, they had little time for social disruptions. There was no slavery and with the exception of At'r and the moon's family of governors the remaining officials were elected. And on Crea political indiscretion was not tolerated. Kevin was very comfortable here, and he knew he was falling in love with Tari. He hoped she felt the same.

"Come on Kevin." Tari's voice brought him out of his revere, "We will miss her, she does not know I am here."

"Sorry," Kevin said hurrying behind her as they moved through the disembarking crew, Tari greeting others she knew.

Delia had just entered the reception room when Tari and Kevin caught up to her "Tari!" she said amazed to see the young friend who was more like her daughter, "How are you?" Delia hugged her tightly.

"Well and you?" Tari laughed, "Out chasing Zerions home with their tails between their legs, you sure showed up at a good time back in the Sol system." Tari teased, then pulled Kevin closer, "I have someone to meet you. Delia this is Kevin."

"Pleased to meet you Commander," Kevin extended his hand to find it firmly grasped in the Commander's gloved hand.

"And I you. You are Lady Izadra's Earth friend?"

"Yes."

"Come to my quarters." Delia said cordially. "We will have dinner and get acquainted." Delia escorted them to her on board quarters. When they were comfortably settled Delia asked Tari. "So now you are one of Lady Izadra's attendants."

"Her first." Tari replied.

"Then you are to head the group?"

"Yes,"

"A big responsibility," Delia commented, "guarding her life. Has she chosen the others?"

"Not yet, but Lady Izadra has narrowed the group down to eight. It has take us two weeks of interviews to accomplish this."

Their conversation turned to Kevin, and Tari enjoyed her day off spent with friends, the first day off since Izadra had begun the interviews.

Today Izadra was reviewing the final eight with At'r and enjoying a slower paced day herself. Outside in the garden Nemsis played among the gold and red leaves that were falling from the trees, the air had turned cold and At'r warned Izadra of the approaching winter. She shivered, amazed at how fast the season had changed. Two days ago it had been a warm summer's day. That night as the Meteorologist had predicted a major winter storm rolled in from the sea causing the city controllers to drop the city beneath the surface of Creasion. For this Izadra had been grateful and for At'r's company that night. When they had surfaced the air temperature had dropped fifty degrees and the garden showed the wear of the storm's fury.

At'r laughed at Nemsis' antics outside, drawing Izadra's thoughts away from the files, looking out the glass door again she too laughed at Nemsis. Izadra was tired of the files and put them aside to enjoy the show Nemsis was putting on.

CHAPTER 35

Standing on a secluded Creasion mountaintop, before a high Troscoss altar, Ba-lyn raised her arms to the heavens, beseeching the evil gods she worshipped. A cool breeze stirred her long hair and the blood-red cape she wore revealed her naked golden-tanned body beneath.

"Hear me Oh spirits of my Troscoss ancestors, your humble and loyal slave begs your assistance." she implored, "Help me rid Creasion of the half-breed that has beguiled the Emperor." Standing on the high peak, Tross was directly above her, to her right Konas was visible in the last quarter, and on her left Metem was visible in the first quarter. Dark clouds moved over the heavens and only the light from Tross penetrated the mists. Beneath Ba-lyn's feet the ground shuddered while the spirits she summoned gathered to aid her.

"Lady Izadra is well protected by the necklace and her heritage." a whispered choir of voices informed her. "Her Scottish ancestors spawned from the same stock as Creasion, and her karma is strong."

"Are we not stronger?" Ba-lyn asked bowing her head respectfully.

"Perhaps…" the voice answered, "Why should we assist you?"

"I wish to be Empress and your servant." she said kneeling on the hard sharp rocks around the altar, "I will restore the practices of your worship."

Silence fell over the altar, Ba-lyn held her breath in anticipation "For our assistance we will ask much of you."

"I am your servant," Ba-lyn assured them.

"Very well, leave the flask you have brought and return at dawn." the voices instructed her.

Rising from her prostrate position, Ba-lyn placed the flask in the center of the timeless altar. Above her the clouds erupted in an electrical display. With lightning flashing and striking around her, Ba-lyn walked from the mountain calmly and unafraid, the tingle from the electricity confirming her success. At dawn she would return and retrieve the flask of poison she had left to be touched by the spirits and soon she would be Empress.

Because Ba-lyn had only been chosen as first alternate she had little contact with Lady Izadra. It had taken her four months to have an opportunity to be in Izadra's company. Tomorrow Ba-lyn would attend a luncheon with Izadra, then she would remain one more night on Creasion and a pawn would be chosen to carry out her evil plan.

Once again safely inside her small room Ba-lyn marveled at how easily she had slipped past the guards. Ba-lyn smiled, happy with the evening and the prospect of tomorrow. Entering her shower Ba-lyn reveled in the hot water.

CHAPTER 36

*I*zadra opened her eyes wearily to the low-ton buzzer of their wake-up signal. Through blurry eyes she stared at the top of the curtains around their bed, At'r stirred next to her, stretching his muscles and yawning. Rising he leaned over her supporting himself on one elbow and gently kissed her.

"Good morning." he said softly.

"At'r," Izadra murmured, "I am so tired," she saw immediate concern in his face.

"Are you ill?"

"No, just tired, I dreamed…" a puzzled look spread over her face, "A high mountain top, and lightning." she was quiet. "I wish I could go back to sleep."

"Is there a reason you can not? Your luncheon is not for several hours."

"But I have other appointments," Izadra managed to sit, the child within her kicked several times, "I will be all right." she said unsure.

"I will call Trentos." At'r rose from the bed.

"No, please At'r," Izadra stopped him, "he is due here after break-fast anyway for a routine check-up."

"Why don't you stay in bed until he arrives?" At'r suggested.

"I must get dressed." Izadra said in a determined manner, swinging her legs over the bed's edge. Lovingly she placed her hands on her rounding tummy, looking at At'r who was watching her closely, she smiled, "Your son is awake also." At'r joined her and placed his hand on her stomach to feel the movement of his child, who quickly reacted to the heat of his touch by kicking.

Shared moments like these were scarce and At'r treasured them, biding his time until he felt he could convince Izadra of his love for her.

After breakfast At'r wished Izadra a pleasant day and with a light kiss on her lips left her to begin her schedule while he went to his court and council to conduct the business of Creasion.

Trentos could find nothing wrong with Izadra her progress was normal for a late five month pregnancy. Increasing her vitamins, and ordering her to rest more, he hoped would minimize her tiredness. Shaking his head as Izadra told him the small amount of the dream she could remember. He made a mental note to confer with lord Betus when he returned from Metem.

Tari arrived shortly after Trentos left her and together they prepared for the luncheon for the four other ladies and two alternates of Izadra's inner court.

Izadra dressed in a stylish maternity gown, and Tari brushed Izadra's hair until it glowed with a sheen then placed the gold band on her mistress' head.

Izadra had ordered the informal dining room prepared, and she received the ladies in the garden salon next to it. Tari stood next to her as the other six filed in, paid their respects to their lady then began to enjoy each other's company, until Nemsis pushed the garden door open and bounded in.

"Nemsis!" Izadra called sharply and the cat immediately came to her, "Say hello to the ladies then return to the garden." she instructed. In turn Nemsis did just that. With the exception of the alternate Ba-lyn, who had excused herself only moments earlier. Nemsis stopped before the chair Ba-lyn had been sitting in and sniffed picking up her fragrance. Growling, Nemsis recognized the scent and turned to look at Izadra with concern. Not understanding Nemsis' behavior, Izadra dismissed her into the garden where the ninety-eight pound kitten disappeared in the bushes, settling herself just out of sight where she could watch Ba-lyn when she returned.

All through the luncheon Nemsis watched. Ba-lyn knew she was being observed but she did not know by whom. Despite the blessings she had received last night she was uneasy, but by the end of the luncheon Ba-lyn had chosen her pawn.

Out of the five chosen ladies was one of her old classmates, lady Contena of Konas. She was a shy lady and Ba-lyn found Contena more receptive to her will. At the luncheon's conclusion Ba-lyn dropped a small white pill in Contena's wine. Later when Ba-lyn called her to the altar, she would come.

Ba-lyn bathed by moonlight in a spring at the base of the altar, donning her red robe she brushed out her long blond hair. Reverently she walked the rocky steps bare footed calling Contena's name on each step until she reached the top where the sacrificial table rested. Continuing to chant the victim's name, Ba-lyn built a small ceremonial fire on the time and element worn stone.

Angry clouds developed over the shrine and again lightning flashed around the evil sanctuary. The malevolent spirits that inhabited the site joined Ba-lyn's voice and soon Contena appeared at the foot of the steps.

Entranced by the pill and spellbound by the voices, Contena removed her clothing and naked entered the cold spring. With the frigid water dripping from her body she slowly climbed the steps until she was at the top and stood before the altar. Contena looked into Ba-lyn's eyes mesmerized by the spell she was under.

"You have summoned me, mistress?" the girl asked.

"I have. You are my slave and will do as I command."

"I am at your command, mistress."

"Reach out your hands," Ba-lyn commanded, "surely they are cold, warm them in the fire."

Slowly Contena extended her hands, the fire burning her delicate hands.

"Remove them." Ba-lyn commanded and was obeyed. Contena felt no pain, but the skin was singed.

Ba-lyn knew Contena was completely under her control now, "You will take this gift to Lady Izadra." Ba-lyn ordered.

"I will take this gift to Lady Izadra." she repeated and accepted the box of poison Trittles Ba-lyn had prepared from the flask of blessed poison.

"Give it to her after I leave tomorrow at mid-day." Ba-lyn further instructed and sent the girl back to her apartments in the palace.

Ba-lyn danced in merriment around the altar fire she had built. Since Izadra's pregnancy she had craved the sweet fruits known as Trittles and the box Ba-lyn had prepared was strong with poison. So potent was this poison that should a man eat one he would die, should it only touch his lips he would become extremely ill. But if a pregnant woman even touched one she would miscarry and die. Ba-lyn's laughter echoed across the mountaintops. Again the evil gods made their presence known, intensifying the already occurring electrical storm.

CHAPTER 37

Izadra tossed and turned all night, causing At'r to become concerned. Trentos had found nothing wrong with her and had expressed concern that the problem might not be medical. At'r decided to ask Casso to visit that afternoon. If Betus had been on Creasion he would have asked him, but the High Priest was resting on Metem, his son Casso was handling his duties.

"Sleep in Iza," At'r said to her as she woke, "I will cancel your appointments for the day."

"I must get up At'r…" Izadra began.

"Must I command you?" At'r half teased, "And place you under guard. One of the luxuries of your position affords you a morning spent in bed." he smiled reassuringly down into her sleepy face, "I will send Tari to you in a few hours."

"Thank you milord." Izadra conceded and turning on her side went back to sleep. Finally finding peaceful sleep as the sun rose.

At'r breakfasted and checked on his wife before leaving for his morning duties, on the way he passed Tari as she was going to Izadra.

"Oh, Tari," he said stopping her, she bowed politely, "Izadra had a restless night and needs to sleep in. Cancel her morning appointments and wake her about noon, you may have the morning off after you have canceled her appointments."

"Thank you milord, but if you do not object I will remain with her, their are several other matters I can take care of for her."

"As you wish Tari, Casso will be by after lunch, her sudden tiredness concerns me, lord Trentos could not find a medical problem, perhaps Casso can help."

"I will watch over her." Tari assured him and they went their separate ways.

At'r worried most of the morning and dismissed court early to check in on Izadra at lunch. He found her up and feeling better, she and Tari sitting in the low winter sun on their terrace.

Joining them he asked, "How did you clear the ice?" indicating the terrace stones normally covered with ice this time of the season.

"Tari zapped them with her lazzer." Izadra explained.

At'r inwardly smiled at Tari's obvious discomfort, "Captain," he said becoming serious, "Your weapon is to be used for defense." he said sternly.

"At'r!" Izadra protested, "The lazzer was used for defense...against the ice, I needed the fresh air."

"Very well," At'r agreed and winked at Tari then placed a light kiss on Izadra's lips, he lingered a moment.

At'r stayed through lunch enjoying his wife's company and that of Tari's. Regretfully as the servants cleared the table he returned to work.

Tari suggested they walk in the garden, the paths having been cleared by more conventional methods. Nemsis tagged along after them, her long fur turning to the darker blue of an adult, but her still playful nature kept her chasing ahead of them. Occasionally the cat stopped to eat one of the multitudes of icicles that hung from the dormant plants.

Izadra and Tari talked as they progressed, not noticing the cat's disappearance until they neared the garden salon. Both caught sight of Nemsis running from the salon and upon investigation found one of the garden salon chairs ripped to shreds.

"It must be a stage," Izadra commented, "Yesterday she acted strangely at the luncheon and today this." she indicated the chair.

"Wasn't that the one she was growling at?"

"You know it was! Now that is curious." Izadra agreed, neither remembering who had occupied the chair.

Returning to her private salon just as Casso arrived, Izadra saw a box of Trittles that had been left for her, she assumed by one of the servants. Casso also loved these sweet morsels that Izadra craved.

"May I Your Highness?" Casso asked.

"Help yourself Casso, I will join you in a moment." Izadra said turning to Tari.

Casso drew one of the confections from the box with a napkin, and just as Nemsis came in from the garden he popped one in his mouth. Nemsis' nose, sensitive to poisons, picked up the smell and acting with animal speed pushed the remaining candies off the table, scattering them on the floor as Casso spit out the candy and collapsed.

Izadra rushed to him, but Tari stopped her from touching him or the fallen plate of confections.

"They are poison Izadra." Tari half shouted, "do not touch them."

Izadra's face grew ashen, she knew those had been meant for her. With numb fingers she pushed the button on the desk console and summoned Trentos, sounding his private emergency alarm. She returned to watch in horror as Tari carefully removed the last traces of the Trittles from Casso's mouth with a cloth napkin. He was not dead, but if Trentos did not arrive quickly he would be. Having done all she could for Casso, Tari secured her Lady's chambers, ordering the suite sealed off by the Royal bodyguards. Trentos arrived as the guards did.

Izadra watched Tari competently take control of the palace security without alarming the court, not an easy task. She oversaw security until Commander Kron could be reached. It happened that he and At'r were together, putting in time in their fighters to retain the

hours needed for continuing certification. Even At'r had to be certi-
fied to fly. Landing together on At'r's private pad, they rushed
through the garden, the guards quickly allowing them passage to the
Royal chambers.

At'r's face was stern as he entered his private salon, but upon seeing Izadra safe he joyously gathered her into his arms and kissed her
deeply, heedless of the others. His show of emotion surprised Izadra,
and he released her to appraise the situation, listening intently, along
with Kron, to Tari's report.

Casso was conscious due mainly to the efforts of Tari and Trentos
acting so quickly. At'r ordered him taken to the treatment room
reserved for himself and Izadra. There, Trentos could watch over
Casso condition. Turning to Kins who had just entered the room he
instructed him to summon lord Betus from Metem.

Dinner came and went, Izadra unable to eat and At'r was too
angry. It was clear the poison Trittles had been intended to be eaten
by Izadra and clearly the type of poison used had been Troscoss. At'r
could not understand why they wanted to kill Izadra, she was not a
threat to them. Perhaps it was the son she carried that they were
after. Nemsis rubbed against At'r's leg, he patted the cat's head and
remembered her mother. Why did the Troscoss want Izadra dead?
He shook his head.

Tari and Kron had stayed with their friends neither had been able
to eat, so dinner had gone untouched. Kevin had joined them afterward, entering the room in a happy mood. Kevin as well as the
remainder of the court and the Creasion people did not know of the
attempt.

Seeing their serious faces his smile faded and he looked from face
to face. "What has happened?" he asked. "Izadra, are you unwell?" he
noticed her pale face.

"I am well, Kevin." she told him.

"Kevin," At'r said hesitantly, "the Troscoss tried to…" he paused, a sick feeling washing through him, "they tired to poison Izadra this afternoon." he managed.

"Oh!" Kevin sat down abruptly. Nemsis trotted to him, placing her head in his lap. The two had become close friends. Quickly Tari explained the details to him and he sat solemnly quiet afterwards, asking the same question At'r had "Why?"

For a short time they talked but as the evening grew late the group made their excuses, Kron leaving first and Tari and Kevin shortly afterward. At'r thanked Tari once again for her quick action and command of the situation.

Izadra had walked outside enjoying the cold of the winter's evening and stood gazing skyward. Her figure had changed to accommodate his child but her beauty seemed to double despite the tiredness of the last two days and the scare she had just had. Coming up behind her, At'r placed his arms around her hugging her close.

"You will catch a chill in the cold night air." he said softly in her ear.

"I suppose," Izadra returned, "but the room felt like it was closing in."

"Come back in, we will go to bed." At'r told her, "You must be tired." he added reassuringly, "We both need to sleep."

Izadra shrugged and allowed At'r to escort her back inside. "I do not think I want to sleep, and neither does our child." She placed his hands on her stomach, with tears glistening in her eyes Izadra looked to At'r "Why?" she asked with a sob, "Who here have I caused to hate me enough to kill me, and an innocent babe?"

"It may have been only because you carry my child." he explained gently, "Do not worry, Iza," he shortened her name in private, "Captain Kara has been relieved of her other duties and will be your full time body guard now, unless I am here. I have ordered the garden and palace guards stepped up plus Kron will upgrade the sensors in the garden. I will not let them harm you, Izadra."

Izadra regarded At'r for a moment, wondering if his true concern for her was only because she carried his heir. Since their night on the island he had been more attentive, and less moody. Izadra long ago decided this was for appearances. Turning she absently ran her hand along the back of the sofa, then felt At'r's hands on her shoulders. He turned her to face him and raised her chin, placing a lingering kiss on Izadra's lips. Searchingly she looked into his emerald eyes, but her unspoken questions remained silent as At'r drew her toward their bedroom.

Cautious of her condition, At'r had lessened his lovemaking, but tonight his passion was obvious in his eyes. Izadra did not resist him, since their night on the island she had denied him nothing he requested.

Tenderly he cupped her face in his hands, "You are beautiful," he told her quietly, "and very brave."

Before Izadra could reply, he encircled her in his arms and though his kiss was gentle, Izadra was certain of his desire for her. Carefully he laid her down on their bed joining Izadra and pulling her once again close, secure in his arms.

Izadra's head was reeling, amazed that he was still aroused by her body in her present condition. Soon she was lost in his lovemaking, his hapless captive.

At'r's fear of losing her had come so close to realization he needed the physical contact of lovemaking and the warmth of her touch to dispel the almost overwhelming fear he felt. The complete awareness of her true importance to him had hit like a shock wave when the alarm had first reached him. Now holding her close after their exquisite lovemaking, At'r felt compelled to tell her of his true feelings but the sound of her gentle snores as she slept told him that was impossible. Kissing her forehead tenderly, he too slept.

CHAPTER 38

✿

I zadra's ladies began to arrive just after breakfast, Tari appearing before At'r left.

"I am relieved to see you feel better," At'r told Izadra gently, "it is easier to leave knowing Tari is with you." he kissed her good-bye. On his way to his offices At'r passed four of Izadra's ladies, they bowed and At'r wished them all a good morning, glad that the poisoning attempt had been kept quiet and had been so well handled by Tari. At'r had already ordered her rank increased from Captain to Sub-Commander, his wife's bodyguard should be higher ranked than Captain and she had earned it.

An hour after the appointed time, Contena still had not arrived. Normally the girl was early. Izadra, becoming concerned about her, questioned the other ladies and none could account for her absence. Fearing she might be ill, Izadra sent one of the other to see if Contena was in her apartments. Moments later Rozi, the aid Izadra had sent was calling frantically from Contena's room.

"Stay there," Izadra ordered Rozi, "I will send lord Trentos to her room." Izadra would have liked to go herself, but looking at Tari, she knew Tari would not permit it. Izadra knew, as did Tari, that Contena was entranced. "Lena," Izadra turned to another aid, "Please inform my Lord At'r of what has happened, inform lord Casso also, if he is well enough, I know he will want to see her."

"At your command, my Lady." Lena left to fulfill her orders.

All the events of the previous evening had been kept guarded, only the immediate concerned personnel knew about the near poisoning, not even the other five ladies had been told. Izadra, suspecting Contena was an unwilling victim now told her court of the attempt, swearing them to secrecy.

They were astonished, angry, and very concerned. Already Izadra was more a friend than a superior.

A little later, Trentos entered Izadra's working salon and greeted the group grimly.

"She is in a deep psychic induced trance. Physically she is healthy, except for the traces of the same poison used in the Trittles last night. It absorbed through her burned fingertips. Interestingly enough the amount is so minimal." Trentos stopped, "She was not the one who put the poison in the Trittles, lady Contena was a pawn in this, had she handled the poison the trace amount would be greater."

"I agree lord Trentos," Casso's voice was weak but he entered Izadra's salon and bowed, settling in a comfortable chair quickly at Izadra's bidding. "I left her just after you did, doctor, she is not responsible for her actions."

"Can we get lady Contena out of this trance, perhaps she could tell us who is behind this?" Izadra asked.

"I will try," Casso said, "it will not be easy or quick." he rose having rested, "By your leave my Lady." he said managing a bow.

"Of course Casso, please keep me apprised of your progress." Turning to her bewildered ladies Izadra gave them their daily assignments and sent them to their separate tasks. Moments later At'r entered accompanied by Kron and Kevin, passing the ladies and Casso as they left.

Izadra explained to them what had happened. At'r placed his arm around her waist protectively. Having dealt with the Troscoss before, Kron and At'r were not surprised, but Kevin was astonished.

"I cannot believe this!" he said shaking his head, "You brought Izadra from Earth to be threatened by these, ah, devil worshipers?" he turned to At'r with the question, forgetting At'r was Emperor, "This seems like a horror story."

"Kevin!" Izadra said sharply, before At'r could respond, "You forget yourself, this is not Earth!" Izadra reminded him, "And to whom you speak! Believe me, I came with Lord At'r willingly," Izadra turned to gaze into At'r's eyes, then back to Kevin, "and I remind you, the Troscoss are responsible for this."

At'r said nothing, amazed at Izadra's reaction to Kevin's words. Kevin, realizing his blunder, turned to At'r, "I beg you indulgence, I am only concerned…"

"I too am concerned Kevin," At'r interrupted, "she is my primary interest." At'r smiled down at Izadra.

Lunch came and went in a solemn mood, At'r and Kron returning to their work and Kevin to the elders and recorders of Creasion law. Izadra turned to Tari and instructed her to notify the first alternate, Ba-lyn, that she would now be needed to serve. After Tari had arranged to send a messenger to Ba-lyn on the moon Konas, she returned to Izadra for further instructions.

"Rest yourself." Izadra said indicating a chair, drawing her thoughts together. "Tari, I have a favor to ask.

"Anything Izadra." Tari assured her.

"Speak to Kevin, should he again make such a mistake, At'r might not be so forgiving. I do not wish to see that happen."

"I will speak to him, but Lord At'r has never been a vindictive ruler, he understands Kevin's concern for you."

"Thank you Tari," Izadra said, wondering if At'r really did understand Kevin's concern, or if his only care was his heir.

CHAPTER 39

$\mathcal{B}$a-lyn knew her plan had failed. Had she succeeded the entire system would now be in mourning. She had no idea of what had gone wrong. Lady Contena had been discovered she knew, Ba-lyn felt the loss of control over her entranced victim. Since the attempt, Ba-lyn had been too worried to sleep. She was glad she had taken leave to come home after the luncheon, here she could come and go as she pleased.

Outside her window she had a view of her families landing port and Ba-lyn stopped short as she passed the window and saw a Royal messenger's craft landing. Her pulse quickened and she feared her plot had been discovered. As the messenger, whom four honor guards escorted neared the house Ba-lyn quickly dressed and dusted a little make-up on her face to cover her tired features. Soon a maid knocked on her door to summon Ba-lyn, the messenger awaited her.

Ba-lyn entered the receiving hall calmly with as much composure as she could muster, the messenger bowed slightly.

"Lady Ba-lyn?"

"I am she."

"Her most gracious Lady Izadra requests your presence at the palace as one of her attendants, I will arrive here tomorrow morning to escort you back to Creasion." the messenger bowed again and was gone.

Ba-lyn breathed a sigh of relief and made her way back to her room where she set her maids to packing and preparing for her living in the palace on Creasion. Although her attempt was again foiled, she found herself in even a better position to claim what she felt was rightfully hers. With her evil god's help the palace would be her new and permanent home.

Ba-lyn's father was announced and her maids left allowing them privacy. He was an older man, having married Ba-lyn's mother late in life. Grozier was a diplomat and had served his Emperor's well, he hoped his daughter would do so also. Embracing Ba-lyn before he spoke, Grozier remembered her mother, he had been saddened when he had returned from an assignment to find she had taken ill. Ba-lyn had been fourteen and her mother's loss had greatly effected her, shortly afterwards she had gone to the temple on Creasion to study. Grozier realized he did not know his daughter.

"Congratulations, daughter." he said drawing away, "I am proud of you Ba-lyn."

Ba-lyn smiled, thinking how proud he would be when she married Lord At'r, "Thank you father."

"Are you nervous?" he smiled, "Is there anything you need to ask me?"

"Not now, but later," she paused, smiling at her father sweetly, "I am sure I will need your council." They talked for a little while and Grozier left Ba-lyn to attend a meeting, sending her maids back to her as he left. Ba-lyn instructed them to wake her at sunset and she went to bed feeling much relieved and very tired. Later tonight she would go to her secret altar high in the near-by mountains to thank her evil gods for their protection and pray for another chance. Her first attempt had failed, but now she was in a better position to destroy Izadra. With a smile on her face she slept soundly.

Ba-lyn woke as the sun set on Konas, the maid entering the room to wake her when she sat up. Ordering a light dinner and sending the maid to the kitchens, Ba-lyn rose and dressed warmly before she returned. Dismissing the servant for the evening and instructing her to allow no one to disturb her Ba-lyn herself closed and locked the door. Donning her fur lined coat and hiking boots she carefully placed her ceremonial robe in her backpack along with several other items and slipped out a secret entrance her mother had shown her. Since Konas was a moon, tonight the planet was fully visible and dominated a third of the night sky, lighting her way. Ba-lyn feared none of the wild animals that stalked the mountains. None dare harm or even approach her they sensed her powers of evil.

Ba-lyn rested after two hours of walking and before she started the steep climb to the top of the ridge. Above her, she could see the shrine she and her mother had built.

Following the stream that flowed down from a pool that formed twin falls just below the altar, Ba-lyn made her way to the pool. Stripping off her heavy winter clothes after laying out her ceremonial robe Ba-lyn slipped beneath the icy waters. Regardless of the weather, before Ba-lyn summoned her protectors she was required to bathe in a natural, flowing stream.

Rising from the frigid water Ba-lyn dried herself in a large towel then slipped the black robe over her head. Black was to show her repentance at her failed attempt, but Ba-lyn was confident, her gods had already given her another chance. Reverently she walked to the top of the altar and laying out the items she had brought with her, began the ceremony. Soon the spirits were whispering to her.

"You have failed!"

"I beg your forgiveness." Ba-lyn said prostrating herself in a sacrificial position across the altar.

"Perhaps," silence and a long interval reigned, "do you still wish to be Empress?"

"Yes!" she said falling to her knees on the hard stone.

"We will forgive you. But understand now, we want the child Lady Izadra carries, a Royal child will give us great energy. And, we will send one to direct you." they paused, "A sacrifice will also be required of you."

"I am your servant and slave, the child is yours as am I. What must I do?"

The evil gods whispered their dark plan Ba-lyn smiled occasionally until the gods again told her they would send a mentor to guide her. She did not argue, but Ba-lyn resented that type of assistance. Wondering what sacrifice they would require of her she descended the steps, redressed in her normal clothing and began the long trek back to her family's estate, it would be dawn before she arrived, then she must leave for Creasion.

Izadra welcomed Ba-lyn warmly giving her the day off to adjust to her new quarters and surroundings. Instructed by Izadra, a maid escorted Ba-lyn to her rooms and helped her get settled.

"Report at nine in the morning with the other ladies, then you will be given your new duties." Izadra said and watched her follow the maid from the room.

Tari was now Izadra's constant companion where ever she went as well as several guards who discreetly mingled with the other court people. Only when she was alone with At'r did Izadra find privacy. In an effort to still any gossip about the attempt on her life, Izadra ordered Ba-lyn not told about the event. Perhaps later after she had proven herself trustworthy, Izadra would tell her.

Beginning the next morning Izadra observed Ba-lyn and found her to be bright and intelligent but some yet unknown fault made Izadra leery of the girl. Nemsis did not like her and would not come in the room if she were in it, Izadra found this strange, but she assumed a wait and see attitude.

CHAPTER 40

$\mathcal{P}$reparations for the arrival of the Ambassador and his life mate from the neighboring solar system of Cu'gon were completed. Several hours after their morning arrival a formal dinner was planned. Izadra, escorted by At'r arrived at the banquet hall before their guests and politely awaited their presence in the ante-room enjoying the varied conversations of their court and other honored guests from distant worlds. Izadra was radiant in a long Earth style empress gown of a warm coral color and accented by the Royal Diameralds.

At last the court crier announced the Ambassador and his wife and an isle cleared down the center of the room. Cu'gons were humanoids, but their ancestors spawned in a different primordial soup from the Creasions and Terrains.

Their skin bore a distinct purple hue and their eyes were an alarming bright yellow color. Although they could breathe the atmosphere of Creasion, to be totally comfortable each wore a small tube that boosted a small amount of Potassium Permanganate into their nostrils, and in an attempt to make them even more comfortable a tiny amount had been added to the food they would consume.

Both were in their middle years for their species and the wife, even by Creasion standards, would be described as exotically beautiful.

Her skin was smooth lavender, her eyes more of a golden color and her long dark purple hair fell well past her knees.

At'r and Izadra welcomed them warmly and soon found they had much in common. Dinner passed cordially and afterwards the entertainment was well enjoyed. For Izadra the evening would have been perfect except for Ba-lyn.

This was Ba-lyn's first occasion to publicly attend Lady Izadra and although her manners were flawless, Izadra did not approve of the daring gown Ba-lyn had worn. Izadra made a mental note to discuss it with her later. As the evening wore on Izadra became aware that Ba-lyn was brazenly flirting with not only Commander Kron and Kevin, but also the Ambassador. He ignored her. This Izadra would not tolerate, nor did she approve of the coy glances cast in At'r's direction. At the end of the affair Izadra coolly said goodnight to Ba-lyn affixing her with a cold stare when she curtsied, displaying most of her bust to the Emperor. Glancing to Tari and back to Ba-lyn, Izadra wondered what measures she could take to halt such conduct. Later in her chambers she would consult with Tari.

At'r escorted Izadra back to their private salon and left her in Tari's care until he could retire an hour later.

"I'd like to send her back to Tross." Tari said aggravated, "Kevin is quite taken by her. I do not trust her."

"You are jealous Tari," Izadra laughed then sobered, "I must admit that in this condition." she indicated her stomach, "I too feel much the same way."

"I think it will take more than Ba-lyn to turn milord's eyes from you." Tari said reassuringly.

"I hope so," Izadra said suddenly quiet, then smiled at Tari, "thank you my friend, I needed to hear that. Now," she drew a deep breath, "let's find an assignment on one of the moons for her, a long one, I do not want her here when the baby is born." Izadra stopped, "I just can not quite put my finger on it, but I do not trust her."

"We could send her to Earth." Tari commented dryly.

"Do not tempt me." Izadra returned and they laughed, both falling silent, thinking.

On the moon of Tross was an orphanage, traditionally supported by the Royal family. Each year an envoy was sent to ascertain the needs of the youngsters. This was the mission they sent Ba-lyn on. Nothing could have pleased Ba-lyn more, though she did not show it. Humbly and a little dejected Ba-lyn bowed to Izadra and left to pack for the assignment that would keep her on Tross two or more months.

Ba-lyn was aware of the reason Lady Izadra was sending her on this trip, but she mused, 'you could not have sent me to a better place.'

Her guardian spirits truly must be powerful to have influenced Izadra to send her to Tross. On Tross were the roots of her ancient religion. Here Ba-lyn had learned about the Troscoss ways and the power of being favored by these gods. Suppressing her enthusiasm, Ba-lyn did not want to seem elated at her isolated destination.

Later as she packed her clothes for the journey a knock at her door revealed Kevin sadly waiting to escort her to the star shuttle that would carry Ba-lyn to Tross. Ba-lyn plied her sweetest smile on the Earthman, enjoying her hold over the friend of Izadra. Possibly she could use him to aid her in Izadra's destruction.

"I will not be gone that long, do not brood so." she touched his cheek, "You could come visit me."

"I will try Ba-lyn," Kevin promised as they walked the short distance where she left him with a kiss on the cheek.

Tari watched their parting from an observation deck above the boarding platform, a scowl on her pretty face.

Tari was glad to see Ba-lyn leave, all her instincts warned her against the girl. Absently Tari's fingers caressed the hilt of her dress sword, her eyes transfixed on Kevin. So deep was her concentration that Tari did not hear Kron and Delia approach until they called her name for the third time.

"Tari!" Delia touched her shoulder.

Tari turned a little startled, saluting her Commanders, "Your pardon, I did not see you."

"No I guess not," Kron commented, "You saw nothing other than Kevin. Why is he here?"

"Kevin saw the lady Ba-lyn off on her first off planet assignment for Lady Izadra." Tari explained a little embarrassed.

"Oh, I see." Kron said with a smile knowing Tari was jealous, and remembering Ba-lyn at the Ambassador's dinner he could understand her concern.

"Come, Tari," Delia said putting her arm around Tari's shoulders, "we are on our way to lunch, join us?"

"No, I can not, but thank you, I must get back to Iza…ah, Her Highness." Tari said and saluted them again, "By your leave." they went their separate ways.

Kevin turned as the three parted in time to see Tari's sad face as she left. He suddenly realized he had seen little of Tari in the last few weeks, Izadra kept her so busy, and he wondered why she looked so upset. Thinking Izadra might be ill he made his way to Izadra's business salon where he found Izadra sitting alone at her desk studying the computer screen before her.

"My Lady," he said bowing as he entered the room, "how fare you?"

"Kevin," Izadra smiled having not seen Kevin in a while, other than at the length of a dinning table, Izadra rose and met him at the front of the desk.

"My God, Izadra," Kevin exclaimed, shocked at how big she had become.

Izadra giggled, "In a little less than a month, I should be getting back to normal."

"I am pleased to find you well, I saw Tari earlier and she looked so," he paused, "well, sad. I thought you might not be well."

"I am fine, where did you see Tari?"

"At the space center, Ba-lyn left today on her Tross assignment, I saw Tari at a distance, she was with Kron and Delia." Kevin explained. Izadra knew Tari was at the spaceport, she had sent her there to observe Ba-lyn's departure.

Nemsis pushed open the garden door and sauntered in. She went to Kevin, but stopped short, picking-up Ba-lyn's scent. Turning, the big blue cat went to Izadra, ignoring Kevin who she usually liked. Tari came in and Nemsis ran out the door as she entered.

"My Lady," Tari said to Izadra, then nodded to Kevin, and turned back to Izadra, "I am sorry to be gone so long."

"It was not a problem," Izadra looked between the two knowing what Tari was upset about. "In fact I was just about to ask Kevin to stay for lunch."

"Oh." Tari said a little dejected.

"I am going to freshen," Izadra said walking toward her private chambers, "I'll be back, Tari, order lunch, please, she left the two alone."

"I saw you this morning." Kevin said moving to stand close to Tari, she shrugged.

"You were talking to Commander Kron and Commander Delia." she shrugged again, "Tari, what is the matter with you?"

"I must order lunch!" she said gruffly and depressed the Communication's button, "Are you staying?"

Izadra returned and sensing the tension still between her two friends ordered a flask of light wine. Lunch was quiet with little conversation, Tari excusing herself as soon as she politely could.

"I do not understand what is wrong with her." Kevin said exasperated.

"Kevin, to be so intelligent, you have your moments."

"What have I done?" he asked innocently.

"Ignored Tari, and devoted yourself to lady Ba-lyn. Now that she is gone, you are noticing Tari again."

"You have kept Tari pretty busy the last few weeks, and Ba-lyn is just a child." Kevin explained.

"No, Kevin, Ba-lyn is not a child." Izadra told him firmly.

"I must go," Kevin said in a disturbed tone, "I've got to talk to Tari." Kevin hurried off, leaving Izadra alone, save the two body-guards who were just outside the doors. Izadra again began studying the screen she had been using before lunch.

CHAPTER 41

Ba-lyn received a friendly welcome on the moon Tross. Her uncle, her mother's younger brother, met her at the spaceport despite the blizzard that had gripped the moon for a week now. Tross was at the furthest point away from Tos, the sun, and it was extremely cold. Ba-lyn shivered even though she was inside the glass receiving area. Looking out on the frozen landscape Ba-lyn marveled at the improvements that had been made since her last visit as a child. Emperor At'r was a good ruler to have accomplished all this, he put the ancient city of Ross under a protective, invisible field that kept out the cold, snow, and rain. The field absorbed Zerion attacks, and only a massive attack would penetrate the barrier.

After a small reception Ba-lyn was escorted to her apartments, allowing her to unpack before the evening's celebration, given to honor Lady Izadra by honoring Ba-lyn.

Ba-lyn did not waste her time resting, she required little. Going over the guest list she acquainted herself with the guest's occupations and positions. Ba-lyn was pleased to see the name of the penal station's Commander Cy'r included in the list. If her plans were to be successful she would need to get on board the orbiting jail as the Commander's guest. After that she must contact the Zerion Captain who had found Izadra on Earth.

An hour before Ba-lyn should dress she finally laid down on the couch and closed her eyes. Not to sleep, but to concentrate on the actions she would take this evening to put her plan into motion, and what the fruits of her actions would hopefully bring. An hour later a maid entered and spoke her name, Ba-lyn opened her eyes, stretched and rose from the couch feeling refreshed and prepared to meet the evening's adventure.

To accent her blue eyes Ba-lyn chose a gown of the same color, her long tanned legs showing through the high slits of the skirt with each step. She wore her long blond hair down and loose about her shoulders with only a silver pendant around her slender neck. Ba-lyn was a beautiful girl and she was aware of the effect she had on men, many times a smile did more than her powers.

Entering the humming hall of waiting guests she enjoyed the hush that fell over them when she entered and her name was announced as the lady Ba-lyn, a Royal envoy of Her Highness, Lady Izadra. 'Soon,' Ba-lyn thought, 'I will be Her Highness.' Smiling graciously she entered the room.

Ba-lyn danced with many different partners until her feet felt numb, finally she found herself in the arms of Sub-Commander Gerin. She was readily aware of the strength in his arms and felt a thrill from it. Ba-lyn smiled coyly up into his gray eyes.

"Tell me Commander, Oh, sorry, Gerin, what is it like on your orbiting jail?" she smiled sweetly seeing a flash of anger in his gray eyes.

"Not a jail, milady, a penal station." he corrected.

"I am sorry, but what is it like?" she questioned.

"Come," he said and drew her from the dancing area through a short hall and out of the building to an enclosed garden. "Here we can talk," he sat on a bench pulling her next to him, "Do you really want to know what it is like? he questioned, most do not care to be told.

"Yes, or I would not have asked." Ba-lyn assured him.

Gerin told her many stories about the prisoners and the programs to help them re-enter society, his final story about their last, but most notorious inmate, Captain Quar, a Zerion.

"He is the one," Ba-lyn asked, "that found Milady on Earth?"

"Yes he is, and he is on ice, as we call it."

"What do you mean?" she questioned.

"He is in freeze-sleep, quite harmless, we bring them around every two months to check them."

"That I would like to see."

Gerin considered her for a moment, "Possibly next time we thaw him you can be present, but I do not think you will like it." They rose and walked a while in the garden until they reached the limit of the enclosure, where they talked for some time, Gerin explained why Commander Cy'r was not present. In the fashion of an officer he escorted her back to the gathering which was beginning to diminish. Assuring Ba-lyn he would see her again, Gerin left her safely in the company of her uncle.

Later that night slipping discreetly out of her rooms Ba-lyn made her way through the city to an outer portal, here she charmed the guards, persuading them to allow her to go outside the protective dome. Journeying the two miles on foot through the now calm winter night Ba-lyn made her way to the most ancient of Troscoss altars. This was the High alter of the Troscoss where the spirits were omnipotent. Here Ba-lyn paid homage to her deities and while deep in thought felt herself no longer alone. Coming alert, Ba-lyn turned slowly, her ceremonial robe swirling around her otherwise naked body. Dressed in the robes of a Troscoss priest stood Sub-Commander Gerin. Their eyes met, Ba-lyn hardly able to believe hers.

"How dare you follow me and to this place!" Ba-lyn demanded, "What right..." she halted mid sentence, the cold stare from his gray eyes cutting through her.

"I, am the protector of this place." Gerin said authoritatively, "That, mistress Ba-lyn, gives me the right." His voice was commanding and cold, all traces of the former officer vanished. "I have been instructed to assist you as needed, guiding you at all times, as I feel warranted." he smiled, a cold smile that sent shivers over her. "You failed in your first attempt, they," he explained, "want no further failures, they too want rid of the Lady Izadra and the child she carries."

Ba-lyn closed her eyes for a moment then gazing skyward stretched her arms outward, imploring her guarding spirits. "Why?" she questioned.

"We informed you one would be sent to aid you. You will do as Gerin instructs, all that he instructs." the choir of familiar voices whispered.

Ba-lyn looked at Gerin, she hated to be instructed, by anyone, by him even less. She had looked forward to using him in her plan, but not him using her.

"Come here, Ba-lyn." he told her and hesitantly she obeyed. "When our plan is met you will soon afterwards be Emperor At'r's wife. That you were promised, but a sacrifice was also required from you."

"And what do you gain?"

He did not answer for a moment, "I become High Priest of the Troscoss, and I get partial payment now, and you make your sacrifice."

By the look in his eyes Ba-lyn was afraid to ask what his payment and her sacrifice was, but she felt compelled.

"What…"

"You! Now and when ever I want you hereafter, even after your Royal marriage. You see, the son that inherits the Throne of Creasion will be our son, not At'r's."

Shaken by what Gerin had just told her and needing to think Ba-lyn stepped back from Gerin. He roughly pulled her back into his powerful embrace.

"How will?" she tired to question.

"Quiet!" Gerin commanded.

"Please Gerin, not here." Ba-lyn protested trying to buy a little time.

"Yes here, and now!" he lifted her onto the altar and laying full on her kissed her lips cruelly, bruising them. "You do not like to be told or forced to do anything, do you Ba-lyn." he felt her struggle beneath him, he kissed her again and pulled back suddenly as Ba-lyn bit his lip. Laughing at her struggles he kissed her, sadistically forcing her to taste his blood, enjoying the feel of her supple, half naked body writhing beneath his.

Panic stricken, Ba-lyn fought him until the whispered voices returned and she felt her bruised limbs being restrained by unseen forces, above her Gerin looked triumphantly down at her.

"Now I will have you." No part of her body went unexplored as Ba-lyn lay helpless to stop him. Moans of pleasure escaped her lips as he caressed her lissome body. At last Gerin came to lie full on her again, now she needed no restraints, but was held tightly anyway. Gerin looked down to enjoy her beautiful face with it's enlarged blue eyes as he merged with her body causing a piercing scream to wrench from Ba-lyn's throat.

"So!" he said, an evil smile on his lips, "you were a virgin, now you are mine to do with as I please." his body moving rapidly within her. Ba-lyn's body responded to his, and she felt the restraints lifted, her arms wrapped around his neck to pull him closer.

"I am yours Gerin." she said quietly as he burst inside her.

CHAPTER 42

*D*espite the cool temperatures, Izadra made it a habit to walk in her gardens for an hour after lunch Tari was her constant companion. Today was much like the one before, earlier they had reviewed Izadra's ladies progress on their individual assignments and had been satisfied with their accomplishments. Even Ba-lyn, who had been on Tross for four weeks, was doing well. Tari informed Izadra, Ba-lyn's work would keep her another month. Izadra was pleased, she did not want the girl near the child she carried, but could not explain why, only that her inner intuition warned her.

Since her size had greatly increased Izadra kept mainly to her apartments seeing only close friends, relative, her ladies and At'r.

After their argument on the island, At'r had treated her gently and with consideration. Izadra found his more congenial manner agreeable and she dared to hope that At'r might come to love their child if not her. She steeled herself, knowing his kindness was motivated by duty only. Sighing Izadra sank onto an inviting bench.

"Tari, my stamina isn't what it was." Izadra said turning to her friend.

"Do not apologize on my account." Tari shrugged.

"How are things with you and Kevin?" Izadra asked adjusting her position on the bench.

"We are seeing each other," Tari said hesitantly, "he is strange."

"No, just different. You should go with him and visit Earth one day, it might clarify his attitude for you."

"You have told me many things about Earth, I must admit that I am fascinated. My short visits previously gave me little chance to become acquainted with the people."

"Perhaps a longer visit could be arranged, I would be more content knowing my affairs there were properly handled. Lord At'r might allow Kevin and you to visit for a few weeks."

"It will be sometime yet before I would want to leave you..." Tari said quietly.

"And sometime before I am willing to allow you to go." Izadra smiled, "Let's go back inside, there are a few more items I want to finish before At'r arrives for the evening meal." With tired steps Izadra walked back halfway to her chambers, then sank onto another bench. "As I said, I do not have the stamina I use too."

Tari had begun to worry about her mistress, Izadra's face had become pale and Tari had noticed her tiredness long before it had been mentioned.

"Izadra," Tari said concerned, "maybe I should call Trentos, you do not seem well."

"No, just tired." Izadra told her friend more confidently than she felt. Rising she told her, "I will be fine." But as they reached the garden doors and entered the salon Izadra knew she was more than tired.

A strong tightness began to build into a surge of pain, which left Izadra gripping the back of the nearest chair for support. Tari rushed to offer assistance, supporting Izadra until the pain subsided.

"I am calling Trentos!" Tari told Izadra after easing her lady unto the sofa.

Izadra said nothing, marveling at the pain she had just experienced. Tari returned from the communications desk to sit next to Izadra, covering her with a knit blanket.

Trentos arrived in only moments. Izadra judged he had run, as he was out of breath, but he began examining her immediately. Finally after several moments his brows knit and a worried expression covered his face, he looked up to Izadra's pale face.

"You are in labor, milady." he informed her, then he hesitated, "the baby is turned the wrong way, he is in a breach position, we will have to turn him." Izadra's face became even paler.

"How?" she asked in an unsteady voice.

"This procedure has been done many time with great success and with little risk to the child, however, it is uncomfortable for the mother."

"Do you not do a cesarean section?"

"Only in the most extreme emergencies, we only use that method as a last resort.

"Very well Trentos, His Highness must be notified. I would prefer you to do this." Izadra paused, "Where will you do this, procedure?"

"In the weightlessness of space." Trentos watched Izadra closely for any sign of panic, he saw none. "I will go now and inform Lord At'r and to prepare the medical shuttle. I should return in about thirty minutes, in that time you will probably have at least two more contractions, try to relax and rest as much as possible." he smiled, "and do not worry."

"Yes milord." Izadra answered primly, then smiled. "I will try not too." Moments after his departure another pain gripped her, she sighed as it passed.

"Tari will you accompany me please."

"Of course, Izadra, is there anyone else you wish to go

"No, I am sure Trentos will bring more than enough medical personnel."

As they waited neither spoke, Izadra was worried and Tari knew it, but could give her little comfort. At'r burst through the doors and rushed to Izadra. Lovingly he tenderly kissed her then drew back to search her face.

"How fare you Izadra?"

"I will be fine, my Lord."

"Tari," At'r turned to Izadra's friend, "would you excuse us for a few moments."

"By your leave." she bowed slightly and left the room.

"I am accompanying you on the shuttle." he told Izadra, then stopped to look deeply in her eyes.

Suddenly Izadra closed her eyes as another contraction surged through her causing her to grasp the sofa cushions tightly in her hands. At'r watched her intently despising himself for not telling her on the island that he loved her and making her believe it. Since then the atmosphere between them had been better, but not what he wanted. Gently he took her hand, kissing the wrist. Izadra opened her eyes and managed a smile as Trentos came in followed by Tari.

"The shuttle is ready to go and fully staffed." the doctor drew a deep breath taking in the tender scene he had interrupted.

At'r rose from the couch where he had been sitting next to Izadra, "Then we will go." he stated, carefully lifting Izadra in his arms.

"Sire, we have a float-chair ready." Trentos told At'r.

"Thank you Doctor but I will carry her." At'r told him. Izadra placed her arms around his neck and the group made their way through the gardens to At'r's private landing pad where the medical shuttle waited.

As they approached the shuttle Nemsis bounded out of the gardens causing the medical staff that waited lined up next to the shuttle to draw back in fear of the famous Aqua-fe. But Nemsis was not interested in the staff. She sauntered up to At'r, who held Izadra firmly in his arms, and looked up, At'r met her appraisal and the cat's eyes.

"Nemsis," Izadra said, "Come." and falling in behind Tari followed them through the shuttle door, past the amazed and apprehensive staff.

Piloting the craft was a highly trained medical pilot who lifted the shuttle off with such ease Izadra hardly knew they were racing toward space. During the brief flight Izadra had reclined on an adjustable bed and now that they were in stable orbit Trentos made At'r leave her and sealed the chamber Izadra was in. With a touch of a sensor switch on Trentos' control panel the chamber became weightless.Izadra felt the light feeling over take her and she found it relaxing. Trentos' control monitors told him this and he spoke quietly through the intercom.

"My Lady you will feel a slight vibration, do not be alarmed." Trentos explained.

Slowly, Izadra turned to look at him through the glass window of the chamber, "I won't be." she said positively, though she was more frightened now than when the Zerion had captured her. As Trentos had warned, the vibration seemed to ripple through her as Izadra floated. She felt the child kick, then felt him slowly turn, a groan came with the next contraction and Izadra fainted.

At'r's was the first face she saw, his face grim with concern, he studied her strained features.

"How is my child?" Izadra demanded, fearful of what At'r's answer might be.

"Our child is well Izadra." he told her reassuringly, "The child turned and your labor should now be easier."

"But" Trentos interrupted, "We are going to stay out here in space at half gravity until the child is born. "Trentos further instructed Izadra to rest as much as she could, his monitoring instruments indicating a long labor.

At'r sat with Izadra for a while, monitoring her condition closer than the monitors could. The staff of nurses kept Izadra comfortable and one young, timid nurse offered to sit with Izadra for a while so At'r might walk around in the spacious shuttle. Hesitantly At'r consented, but only after Izadra, seeing his tired state insisted.

Once Claudina got over her shyness she had a marvelous gift of story telling, giving Izadra time to forget, between contractions, how frightened she was.

At'r needed to stretch, he was grateful to the observant nurse who had suggested he take a break. In the dimly lit waiting area he gazed out the small windows at space, enjoying the light feeling of half gravity. In the time that passed he found he was increasingly aggravated with himself than he had been for sometime. Because of his pride he could not be the comfort to Izadra that he should be at this time.

When he had taken Izadra to his island so many months ago, At'r allowed Izadra's surrender to stop him from telling her he loved her. Now and since then he had felt the same frustration. Izadra had told him she would not deny him passage into her mind, she said, she could no longer fight him. However, it had been a weak victory, and he had known his declaration of love would not have been believed.

"Damn." he swore aloud, "Why didn't I just tell her, then she would not have to go through this alone." With an oath that he would tell her now, At'r returned to Izadra's side. Entering the chamber he heard the nurses light voice as she told Izadra one of the old Creasion myths.

"Oh!" Izadra gasped, "Another one," her laughter gone, Izadra grasped the nurse's delicate hand tightly trying not to break the girls hand but Claudina seemed unconcerned. Looking up, panting, Izadra watched as At'r thanked the nurse and his strong hand replaced her delicate one.

"Squeeze as hard as you like Izadra," At'r told her sitting next to her bed in the chair provided. Watching her closely At'r gathered his courage. Never had anything scared him, but this admission made him weak. As he was about to speak Izadra moaned and her water broke. Instantly Trentos was next to his patient, monitoring her condition and that of the child to ascertain their condition.

"Not much longer milady." Trentos told her, "I would like to give you a pain sedative."

"No!" Izadra stated firmly, "I can handle this. I want to be conscious when the child is born."

"It will not knock you out." Trentos explained.

"No!" Izadra insisted, fearful that in a drug induced insensibility she would betray her true feelings for At'r. She was convinced his main concern was for his duty and the heir she was struggling to give life. "No." she repeated.

Trentos looked to At'r, knowing that he could not help Izadra as so many Creasion men did at this time. The Royal couple still had not shared their psyche. Turning away, Trentos finished preparing for the imminent birth.

Through out the ordeal At'r was beside her holding her hand but, not once did Izadra tighten her grip, instead she dug the nails of her free hand in the cushioning of the medical couch she lay on.

Trentos was ready as the child's head crowned, marveling at how quiet Izadra had been. Finally after several contractions Trentos delivered a normal, healthy, screaming baby boy, and although the princes' birth was several days early he was robust. Gently Trentos laid the child on his mother's stomach allowing them a few minutes to form the bond so important between mother and child.

Claudina then took the new prince and cleansed him, giving Trentos time to make Izadra comfortable before he examined the baby. Soon the child was returned to his parents, first to At'r who placed him in Izadra's waiting arms.

During the birth, Tari had taken over the controls of the craft to allow the pilot to assist with the medical chamber controls. Normally the pilot would set the craft in an automatic position orbiting the planet, but due to the patients they carried, Tari piloted the craft. When the medical pilot returned to take over, Tari hurried back to Izadra.

Izadra was sleeping when Tari arrived, the chamber vacant of medical personnel, At'r, still sitting in the chair with his head down on the mattress, also slept.

Consoling herself, Tari looked down at the little baby who stared back with questioning eyes. Nemsis came up next to Tari and for a moment she was alarmed at the cat's proximity to the prince. Nemsis sniffed the baby, then looked to where Izadra slept turned and sniffed the baby again. Grasping this was Izadra's child Nemsis lay down protectively next to the cradle.

"Good girl." Tari said quietly and At'r's head jerked up. Nemsis, seeing he was awake, padded over to him and licked his face.

"Thanks for the bath." At'r smiled and rubbed the cat's head then rose to join Tari in admiring his son.

"He is beautiful." Tari confirmed.

"I know." At'r returned proudly.

"We should land in a few moments," as she spoke they felt the craft ease onto the planet's surface, "correction, we have landed."

"Milord," Trentos addressed At'r, "The Communicators are requesting information about Lady Izadra and the child."

"I will handle them milord." Tari volunteered, "What shall I say you have named him?"

"Izadra," At'r turned to gaze at his sleeping wife, "has requested he be named Ry-tr, meaning child of prophesy, and I agree."

"I will meet you back at the palace later to attend to Lady Izadra." Tari said bowing.

"Thank you Tari." At'r said gratefully, he was tired, unkempt and did not feel like dealing with the waiting Communicators, known as Reporters on Earth. At'r escorted the medics as they took Izadra to their chambers, Claudina stayed to look after the prince.

Exhausted, At'r stretched out on the bed next to Izadra only to be awakened several hours later by the loud wails of his son demanding to be fed. Sitting up blurry eyed he found Izadra sitting next to him, freshly bathed, her hair combed and braided, her arms out stretched to receive her son. After routing for a moment Ry-tr found Izadra's nipple and latching on began kneading Izadra's heavy breasts contentedly.

Izadra's gaze traveled from her son to look into the consuming eyes of her husband. He placed his finger gently beneath her chin and tenderly kissed her with closely restrained passion. Drawing away he found Izadra blushing but her eyes were as warm as his.

"Thank you for a beautiful son Izadra, I am sorry he was so difficult for you. Next time," At'r paused, his uncertain manner causing Izadra to wonder at it's cause, "it will be different."

Leaving Izadra to feed his son, At'r went to the bath, enjoying the hot water of his whirlpool. Feeling refreshed and rested he dressed and rejoined Izadra as the nurse laid the child in his crib. At'r picked up the infant confidently, he had held many children.

Quietly At'r talked to his son as he walked out the doors and entered the garden, immediately Nemsis joined him and followed close behind. They were gone a few minutes and Izadra was getting concerned when At'r came back through the door, Ry-tr sleeping soundly in his arms. Tenderly At'r lay his son back in the crib. Looking around the room he saw only Izadra, no servants, nurses or friends. He went to sit next to his wife on the bed.

"Izadra," he began, "I wish too..." the door opened and Trentos entered, had it been anyone else he would have told them to leave. Moments later lord Betus also joined them.

"I must go, there are many things to which I must attend." At'r said rather disconcerted and left, Izadra worried after him, he had been about to tell her something, she wondered what.

CHAPTER 43

*P*rince Ry-tr's birth was celebrated through out the realm. Emperor At'r wasted nothing on making the child's birth remembered. Ba-lyn and Gerlin celebrated too, but for different reasons. The prince's birth meant their plans were closer to reality. In six weeks when the child would be acknowledged by At'r's family on Konas their plan would be activated. Until then Ba-lyn bided her time and though she tried to avoid Gerlin he made his demands on her body, but always at times he knew she would not conceive. They were not yet ready for that part of their evil plan. Ba-lyn hated having to submit to him, she did not like losing control, never had anyone controlled her as he did.

In order to win the trust of the Zerion Captain Quar, Gerlin arranged for him to be released from freeze sleep and put on a light work team. Gerlin then instructed Ba-lyn to visit Quar and gain his confidence. After several visits she had told him a small amount of their plan.

Later Quar was called to Gerlin's office and questioned about what Ba-lyn had told him. Quar did not know that Gerlin had arranged his release from freeze sleep, Ba-lyn had not told him that. Keeping Ba-lyn's confidence, he told Gerlin that Ba-lyn only wished to check on his condition for Her Highness. Quar passed his test.

Gerlin smiled, so the Zerion was trustworthy, he thought, at least to a point. Gerlin explained to the Zerion he was in safe company and they talked freely. Gerlin told him little more than Ba-lyn had, but promised to explain in full before his escape.

"There is just one thing I want." Quar said with an evil smile, "I want Ba-lyn." he saw the warning look in Gerlin's eyes, "Just one night. You can spare her that long, you Troscoss priests are known even on Zerion for your collection of women and perverted habits."

"Ba-lyn is meant for higher things." Gerlin said.

"I am sure she is, but I don't want her to bear my children," Quar assured him, "take what ever measures you wish, but I could die in this endeavor, I would like to at least..."

"Very well." Gerlin agreed, interrupting him. "But when I say."

"Agreed." Quar said and returned to his work.

CHAPTER 44

During the weeks following Ry-tr's birth At'r proved to be an attentive father and husband, but either servants, visitors, or official duties made their private moments non-existent. Izadra was generally asleep when At'r came to bed and she was up before him in the mornings. Nemsis was always underfoot where ever Ry-tr was, like a loyal dog she guarded the prince.

Frustrated by the lack of privacy, At'r resolved to set aside a couple of days after the child's presentation to his family for a small vacation. Set high in the forest of Trur on Konas was the ancestral home of At'r's father, now a family retreat. After informing Kron to prepare the security for the trip, he asked about the special fighter he had ordered built. Kron informed him it was ready and At'r excitedly took it on a test flight. In a light mood he landed the craft on his private pad.

Entering his chambers from the garden doors At'r found Trentos giving Izadra the last of her post-natal check-ups. Prince Ry-tr was one month old.

"You are back to normal my lady." Trentos informed Izadra and then examining the prince, also gave him a clean bill of health.

"Good." At'r stated drawing Izadra's and Trentos' attention.

"By your leave milord." Trentos said, "I must attend lord Betus, it is time for his yearly physical."

As Trentos left the room At'r turned to Izadra, "Come with me Madam." then to Tari who had joined them, "Tari please sit with Ry-tr." He took Izadra's hand and led her through the gardens, stopping before they reached the pad. He drew her to him and kissed her heatedly.

"For giving me such a beautiful child, I had this designed for you." At'r smiled like a child hiding a big surprise, then drew her onto the pad.

Izadra could not believe the sleek fighter sitting on the pad was for her. While she was pregnant she had trained in the simulator and was qualified to solo but she had not dared to hope At'r would allow her to do so. Now before her was her own craft.

"It is really mine?" she questioned.

"Do you doubt my word?" At'r questioned with an amused smile.

"No, but…"

"She handles like a normal fighter, similar to mine but she has been programmed for your impulses and I think you will find she handles better than a simulator."

"You have flown her?"

"Yes, now it is your turn. You will find your new flight suite inside with the helmet." he guided her to the fighter.

Excitedly Izadra donned the flight suite and sat in the control chair expecting At'r to settle himself on the second seat. Instead, he kissed her lightly on the lips and stopping at the door told her.

"See you when you get back."

Izadra was astounded. Staring at the now closed door she wondered at At'r, amazed he trusted her alone to fly.

Finally, turning she started the sequence of systems to give the fighter life. Almost timidly Izadra switched on her video monitor and the control tower's interior filled the screen. A young man answered her request to lift-off, by quickly clearing her. Izadra eased the controls in and the craft gracefully ascended up through the clear lavender Creasion sky.

Streaking through the inner atmosphere she achieved the darkness of outer space and found it exhilarating. Izadra expertly performed all the maneuvers needed to obtain her certification, and with the fuel tanks still reading three-quarters full Izadra used another quarter of that thrilling to the response of the fighter. Never had she felt so free.

Below, At'r watched Izadra on the space monitors. When she had first lifted off, At'r worried she might attempt another escape, that fear haunted him and he knew this was the test. Watching her competently maneuver the ship he could not suppress a proud smile at her abilities. Izadra was a fine pilot, with time and experience she would equal any pilot in his fleet. Turning toward the communications officer as he heard his wife's voice requesting landing clearance, At'r drew a sigh of relief. Hurriedly he made his way to the landing pad as Izadra expertly settled her fighter on the pad. After shutting down the engines she stepped from her craft.

Joyously Izadra threw her arms around At'r. "Thank you, At'r, thank you." she said kissing him briefly in her joy. Finally Izadra drew away, embarrassed at her loss of control and reveling in the fire she saw in At'r's eyes. Together they walked back to their chambers.

A week later they were preparing to leave for the moon Konas, tomorrow prince Ry-tr would be welcomed as a new member of his father's family, lord Betus had welcomed him into the house of Metem the day he was born.

Aware that At'r had planned a quiet two days at the secluded family home deep in the forest Trur, Izadra packed extra clothing for herself and the prince. As she supervised the packing Izadra wondered what she would do with herself for two days alone with At'r, she shuddered remembering their last vacation on the island. This time he was permitting several servants and Tari to accompany them, as well as Nemsis.

Izadra had requested to be allowed to fly her own fighter but At'r had denied her request. He explained her fighter was undergoing a refit with a new blocking device to confuse the Zerion instrumentation even more than the Tos-hawk device had.

"But Why?" Izadra had asked him. "You will never permit me to fly in combat."

At'r had looked seriously down at her, noting her stubborn look, "It may happen that I will have no control over the matter. I have ordered the device installed and it is being done." He stood close in front of her, absently he ran his hand over her arm, "I would prefer your company in the Royal shuttle anyway." bidding her finish her packing he left.

In high spirits the next morning Izadra picked up her son from his cradle, "Good morning Prince Ry-tr." she said teasingly and kissed his chubby hand, Ry-tr watched with clear green eyes. "Such a handsome young man, all the little girls will be after you before you are out of diapers." Izadra giggled and Ry-tr managed one of his first toothless grins. "You like that idea?" Izadra laughed.At'r watched the exchange between mother and son unable to clear the sudden tightness in his throat. He strode in the room intent on telling Izadra on the spot that he loved her and had for sometime. But as it seemed to always happen a servant hurried in the room just as he did. The maid curtsied and signaled several young boys to take the luggage to the shuttle.

"You are ready to leave?" he asked instead.

"Yes milord." Izadra answered still holding the child.

Placing his hand dominantly on her back they left the nursery.

Konas was a beautiful moon. Forests covered what farmland did not, and as At'r explained, in those forests roamed a varied multitude of game from birds and flying reptilian to a species of plant life that had mobility. At'r had instructed their pilot to make several low orbits around the moon as he explained that his family had ruled Konas for twelve generations, their history and a few of the sites.

Landing the shuttle on a small pad near the village, At'r ceremoniously lead his wife, who held their son, from the shuttle to greet the gathering of people that waited. After a glorious greeting from his people they were taken, in a slow procession, through the clean wide streets of the village.

With all the modern and advanced technology, these people had managed to keep their values of home and family very much alive.

"Then you are pleased with my family?" At'r asked.

"They can not all be your family." Izadra said, "But yes, I am pleased."

"Yes Izadra, each person you see is either a distant or close cousin, they are all family." Impressed, Izadra smiled and did not further question her husband.

Leaving the crowds behind they entered the courtyard of his ancestral home. Here his remaining aunts and uncles waited to greet them, the oldest of the clan being his Uncle Morin, At'r's father's youngest brother.

Taking his son from Izadra, At'r gazed down at the awake infant, kissed him gently on the forehead then placed him in the arms of his Uncle.

Morin held the child with ease as he had when At'r was the same age. "I began to wonder, At'r, if you were going to marry and produce a new generation to rule this system." He was stern, but his face changed to a smile as he too kissed the child's forehead, a gesture of acceptance.

For the remainder of the day they stayed at Morin's home, enjoying his hospitality and his company. Morin had attended their reception but that night had been hectic Izadra had had little time to become well acquainted, now she found Morin's kindness and understanding comforting.

At'r spent the day with Morin's only living son, Qy'n. After settling several family matters they returned from the hike At'r and Qy'n had taken through the woods of their estate. Later, long before sunset, they were guests at a large family dinner given in their honor.

Afterwards At'r Izadra and Ry-tr flew to the family retreat in the dense forest of Trur.

Trur, meaning Sea of Trees, was over a thousand square mile of heavily wooded forests, lakes and hot springs, with the Konas family's home sitting in the center. Because of the heavy forest the Zerion attack forces had never touched this castle. Here during the early Zerion raids the Royal family had taken refuge. Here At'r felt safe.

Telling Izadra to dress for hiking, At'r rummaged through the unpacked clothing for the pants and shirt he required. Moments later he heard Izadra telling Tari to watch after Ry-tr while they were gone. At'r entered the anteroom to find his wife dressed in Earth style blue jeans. Her Creasion knee boots covered the lower part of her pants so that the entire boot was visible, though this was not the proper way to wear the boots, At'r decided he preferred them in this manner, he also decided he liked her tight jeans. Perhaps Izadra would start a new fashion on Creasion.

Izadra turned from Tari and the child to see At'r ready and resting against the door jam watching them.

"I am ready milord." Izadra announced picking up the heavy pull-over sweater she would wear over the heavy blouse she was already wearing. "Do I look, Ok?" she asked hoping he would approve of her jeans.

At'r's eyes fixed on her, the fire in his eyes answering her question, "Since only the forest animals and I will see you, yes, look very nice." Together they walked from the room, the cool air made At'r feel so alive. Izadra jumped as At'r slapped her on her tightly clad buttocks.

"At'r!" Izadra shrieked in surprise and exasperation.

He laughed, "Does that not happen on Earth?"

Izadra replied, rubbing the abused spot with an alluring smile, "Well sometimes." She laughed too, but noticed the sinking sun.

After an hour of walking At'r lead her to a pool beneath a waterfall where they rested with their feet in the warm water. At'r explained that this stream was fed by a spring that was thermally heated deep inside the volcanic mountain that had been dormant for thousands of years. By the time it covered the distance to this pool it had been cooled by other springs that joined it along the way.

"Have you swam in it?" Izadra asked, wishing she had brought a swimsuit and remembering their skinny-dipping on the island.

"Many times." he looked at Izadra and was silent for a time. Drawing her to him at last he kissed her, holding her close.

Izadra did not resist him, neither did she encourage, though she longed too. At'r's slightest touch caused unbelievable commotion in her body and his kiss evoked a slight trembling.

"Are you cold?" At'r asked, looking deeply in her eyes.

"No." she answered him and did not look away, Izadra knew she could not hide her love much longer. She yearned to tell him all.

"Izadra," At'r began searching her eyes for a clue of how she felt, he could feel her mind open to his as it had been since their stay on the island.

"Milord?" Izadra asked, "What troubles you?"

"You."

"Me, sire?" Izadra's voice became tense, immediately she was suspicious of his motives. At'r remained quiet, pensive, causing Izadra's worst fears to surface. She swallowed, but her mouth was dry.

"Have you come to like the people of Creasion, do you feel at home here?"

"Yes At'r, I really had little family on Earth."

"Good." At'r said and was once again quiet, behind them the sun was setting.

"Are we going to stay here after dark?" Izadra asked after a few more minutes passed.

"We may stay here forever." he told her breathlessly, "Here we have privacy," he laughed, a cold mirthless sound, "at my palace we have none, an Emperor with no privacy."

"Milord," Izadra began, "I know you have something you wish to tell me." Izadra drew a deep breath, "Please, do not keep me in suspense." nervously she looked away, afraid still he would send her from him and now their child.

Turning her face to meet his, At'r felt a strong surge of her fear, "When Kron brought you before me, dirty, your clothes torn," he touched her face, his eyes roaming over her, "and beautiful. That gold necklace boldly declaring your Royalty, I wanted you. Had you been just an unlucky Earth girl I would have taken you that night."

Izadra watched At'r, having little difficulty remembering how he had looked at her their first meeting, her face flushed.

"But you were not. You were the heir of Empress Iza and as such I was duty bound to marry you." his gaze moved to look deeply at the steamy waters. "Before our departure from Creasion on Tos-hawk One's maiden voyage, my council members were putting pressure on me to marry, I did not wish to. Especially since my bride would have been much younger or older than I, again thanks to the Zerions. You filled the need very conveniently." He drew a deep breath, enjoying the smell of the evening air. "In the last war with the Zerions I lost most of my family, my parents, my betrothed. I was twenty when I became Emperor and swore that the Zerions would never again surprise attack us. After having lost most of my family I dedicated myself to my people, afraid," he looked back at Izadra who was listening intently, "to love. I convinced myself that love was distracting to decision making and would interfere with my duty. When you were brought to me I was determined not to fall in love with you. You would still the council's demands for an heir and discharge my duty." He was quiet for a few moments watching Izadra's face. "When you fled and returned to Earth I ignored all warnings from Kron of possible danger and went to find you myself. Tos-hawk One and her entire crew I placed in peril to get you back and still you were but, my duty. I have fought how I felt for you since the beginning. First denying my love, then after we fought on the island I suppressed it. I had intended to tell you then." his lips were close to hers, "Now I know I can no longer deny or suppress what I feel for you."

Wanting to kiss her but afraid, he turned and walked to the waterfall leaving Izadra speechless and amazed.

He turned to look back at Izadra, who watched him closely, "I, of course, can not force you to care for me, I can only ask and hope…"

Remembering how she had vented her anger at him on the island she marveled, Izadra had no idea what he would have told her. Raising her eyes to meet his troubled ones she stood, her legs wobbly, unsteadily she walked toward him. Stopping close but not touching him, words could not express how she felt.

Not knowing Izadra wanted to tell him she loved him, but thinking she meant to refuse him, he did not touch her.

After studying his face for a long while she finally spoke, but with her mind. "Oh, Mighty Emperor At'r, House of Konas," she began formally. "Milord, my husband." she smiled sadly, "After these many months as your wife, your lady, your play thing." his face paled visibly as her thoughts echoed in his head, "Do you not know?"

"But on the island?" his mind answered hers.

"At'r you frightened and hurt me," she admitted. "Many times I have regretted…"

"I too have regretted," he paused, "many things. It was not what I wanted."

"What did you want, my Lord?"

"At first, to control you, then to hurt you for defying me when you escaped, none has ever dared that! At last only to love you and hope you could still love me, I have not been kind…"

"I do love you At'r, I have for a very long time." she sobbed slightly, he pulled her to him and covered her in his arms.

Lost in their passion and love they sank to their knees onto the soft blanket of generations of colored fallen leaves.

Pulling away At'r contemplated Izadra, "Why did you not tell me?"

"I was afraid, that is why I would not share my thoughts with you, how could I when you did not love me?"

"I do love you, Izadra." he paused, "Shall I climb the mountains of Metem and sing it from the peaks?" He asked her looking intently in her eyes. "Shall I brave the cold deserts of Tross to show you how hot my blood becomes when I think of you? Or shall I make love to you amid the forests of Konas, and make you my Empress on the next *Three Moons Rising*?" he kissed her briefly, "Which is four days hence?"

"Mountain tops are too high, but sing to me of your love. A cold desert is no place to fan a burning passion, our bed is much warmer. Make love to me here, if you please."She smiled, her eyes merry, "I am content as your wife." The warmth in his eyes was mirrored in hers.

"In my most optimistic hopes, I did not think you would say those words." his voice was low and broken, "I…"

Izadra covered his lips with her fingers, "No more talk, we can talk later." for the first time At'r felt her lips close over his, searching, demanding, equaling his passion. They made love among the leaves, the sound of the waterfall blending with their whispered words of love.

Later they lay next to each other and At'r pointed out the stars, naming the ones that had life on the planets that orbited them.

"Where is Earth?" Izadra asked a bit timidly.

"You can not see your sun from Konas?" he said gently.

"Oh," they were quiet for a time, "Can we swim?"

"Yes, if you want to."

Standing they strode hand in hand until the waters covered them. Together they played like children until late in the night. Stopping in their play, At'r contacted the house to reassure Kron's security teams that he and Izadra were well and would return when Creasion rose to illuminate their way. Shortly afterwards the planet rose to show itself through the trees, rising like a full harvest moon on Earth and lighting up the forest. Donning their clothing they walked the several miles back to the ancient castle.

"Tomorrow," At'r promised, "We will explore more of the moon's streams."

"In like manner, I hope?" Izadra inquired, laughing.

CHAPTER 45

Ba-lyn had received a summons from Gerlin to meet him at the altar of Tross at mid-night. Carefully she prepared herself, drawing all the power she controlled inward. Somehow she must resist him and convince the spirits she did not need him, for she hated his control over her body.

Sneaking out of her rooms, Ba-lyn went to the private altar she had prepared in a secluded spot of her families home. Here Ba-lyn summoned the spirits she knew to favor her.

"Why," she asked humbly, "have you commanded me to obey this Gerlin. Have I displeased you?"

"We are not displeased." The whispers emanated from the atmosphere, "He is but a pawn, do as he commands. All he commands, until you carry his child. On the night you bring us the Royal child you will conceive Gerlin's child. Then you may sacrifice him also."

"But, I must be wed with Lord At'r first."

"It will not matter, with-in a week of Lady Izadra's death you will wed Lord At'r. We will insure this with out newly gained powers."

Graciously Ba-lyn thanked them, swearing her obedience to them. Then rising from her kneeling position she hurried to meet with Gerlin.

Ba-lyn reveled in the cold of Tross, wearing only the ceremonial robe she ascended the ancient steps toward the altar. Gerlin stopped her almost at the top. Ba-lyn jumped, lost in the euphoria of the ritual trance's beginning and startled by his sudden appearance.

"You are late!" he said sternly, "You have put the entire plan in jeopardy."

Looking at Gerlin, Ba-lyn envisioned how she would kill him, "You worry too much. What is it you require?"

"Tonight we release the Zerion." Gerlin said, "He has but one condition for his cooperation."

"And this is?"

"He wants you."

"Me?" Ba-lyn's face was incredulous. "Well he can not have me. I am meant for other more important men."

"Right now he is the most important man in your life." Gerlin told her. "If he does not consent to our plan then how will we dispose of Lady Izadra without drawing attention to ourselves?"

"Is his freedom and a chance to return home as a hero with the Emperor's wife as a prize not enough for him?"

"As he put it," Gerlin said, "I could die in this endeavor." he smiled, "You will go to him this evening as soon as I help him escape from prison."

"No!" Ba-lyn defied him.

"You were commanded to do all I bid. Are you disobeying?"

Ba-lyn glared at him for sometime, "Very well I shall await him. Mayhap the child I will bear His Highness will be half Zerion."

"Do not dwell upon that possibility." Gerlin told her, "Measures have been taken, the Zerion does not know, but, he has been sterilized." Gerlin laughed, "Permanently. I gave him a drug in his last meal on the prison ship."

Ba-lyn did not trust Gerlin, and after he had promised her to the Zerion even less. Now he had done this to the man and stood before her to boast and laugh about it. Ba-lyn was thankful she had been given permission to do away with him. She could never trust him. "Where am I to meet Quar?" Ba-lyn asked with a resigned sigh.

"Next to the altar is a door that leads down inside the mountain, follow it and at the bottom you will find a comfortable room. Wait there. I will bring him to you soon."

"I await." Ba-lyn said and climbing the remaining steps to the altar found the door and disappeared through it.

Gerlin had, through use of his power entranced the prison station's Commander. By Gerlin's command he would now help Quar to escape. All went well until they climbed the stairs to the escape shuttle and the Commander began to come out his trance. Captain Quar's solution was a simple one. He ruthlessly snapped the Commander's neck before Gerlin could prevent it.

"That was not necessary." Gerlin told him incensed.

"What does it matter, now you are Commander." Quar laughed, the scar on his cheek whitening, "What do you think the final fate of your Lady Izadra will be?"

"That does not concern me."

"Then this," Quar pointed at the dead Commander, "should not either." Setting the ship on auto Gerlin dragged the Commander's body in an airlock and closing it pushed the button to open the outer hatch. The body floated out, drifting in space. Returning to the controls he piloted the craft to a hidden landing site near the altar.

Gerlin explained how to find the hidden room where Ba-lyn waited. After the Zerion disappeared down the hatch, Gerlin made his way to the view-room above the room where Ba-lyn waited, Gerlin would not take chances with Ba-lyn's life, if the Zerion harmed her Gerlin would intervene. Besides, Gerlin was a voyeur at heart.

CHAPTER 46

*A*t'r and Izadra had been awakened the next morning by the loud roars of Nemsis, closely followed by the howls from their son demanding his breakfast. Putting the infant to breast, Izadra laughed as At'r opened the garden door to admit the cat. A little later while Ry-tr took his mid-morning nap his parents enjoyed their Breakfast, reviewing with amusement the report they had been given from Nemsis' handlers. It seemed Nemsis had objected to being left behind the night before when At'r and Izadra had taken their hike. Today she would be permitted to go and was pacing anxiously before the doors. Leaving the nurse attending Ry-tr the couple followed behind Nemsis who race ahead, then raced back in her exuberance, chasing the birds that dared to fly over her and roaring at anything that was too quick to be caught. She was still just a baby at heart.

Walking through the dense foliage the two lovers talked, unmindful of their surroundings. Sooner than At'r remembered they came to the lake where he had planned to spend the day.

A thermally warmed lake was just what Nemsis wanted to see. Without a second glance back she dove in the warm water and soon came up with a large legged fish, immediately settling down to lunch. At'r and Izadra were amused by her fierce antics as the fearless hunter.

"When I was a small boy," At'r explained, "my father brought me here and taught me the beginning techniques of survival training." He busied himself gathering limbs from the rubber like trees that made up this part of the forest, "One of the first things he taught me was how to make a shelter." After only a few minutes At'r had constructed a comfortable hut of the branches of the same tree. They gave off a light musk scent that proved to be slightly intoxicating and radiated enough heat to keep the little room comfortable even without their clothing.

At'r held out his hand to Izadra drawing her inside the cozy interior, soon they found themselves entwined in each other's arms. Breathless, Izadra purposely drew away, leaving At'r a bit perplexed.

"We are alone here?" she asked.

"Completely," he assured her.

"Then it is time." Izadra saw the questioning look in his eyes. She returned to kiss his lips and to his amazement he felt her consciousness touch his. "Come milord, I am ready and gladly share not only my body but my soul with you." her thoughts told his.

Slowly they began to follow the intricate paths through each other's memories. Each saw from the other's eyes their first meeting and all other events they had shared. They ventured through the other's childhood and back to the present, themselves once again. Resting in each other's arms and sleeping for a short time.

They were awakened by Nemsis' roar, followed by the deeper roar of another Water-cat. Fearing for her friend's safety Izadra rushed from their primitive abode, At'r closely behind her.

"Nemsis!" Izadra screamed in her fear for her when she saw the other cat.

"No!" At'r grabbed her arm or Izadra would have run to her cat, "That is a male, he will not hurt her."

"But…" Izadra tried to protest.

"No!" At'r roared, and Izadra turned to stare at him, "That cat would; however, kill you."

At'r kept his hand tightly on her arm, as they watched the cat emerge from the lake and approach Nemsis who stood her ground bravely. This was the males' territory and he did not give ground, even to a female, but he had been known to allow a few to remain. He approached Nemsis slowly to circle just outside her reach, she snarled savagely and swung at the male, he swung back and Nemsis went rolling in the soft underbrush.

A little cry escaped Izadra's lips, At'r now held her with both hands, restraining her.

Moments later Nemsis returned, unshaken, to roar loudly at the male who stood watching her every move. Slowly she cautiously walked to him, roaring again ferociously then hit the male with all her strength. He went sprawling in the mud of the lakeside. Pulling himself up he raced back to Nemsis to stop short, her fierceness causing him to halt, then he saw the humans.

He looked closely at Izadra, then side stepping Nemsis slowly walked toward them, At'r slowly drew the lazzer he had worn. His eyes intent on Izadra, the cat stopped a few feet away, suddenly he turned and sauntered back to Nemsis.

"They are discussing us." Izadra said, and At'r had to agree. Face to face, no longer fighting, the two cats now made low mummer sounds, stopping they both looked at Izadra.

"Nemsis," Izadra called the cat telepathically, "Who is your new friend?"

"He is now a friend. He calls himself Conir. This is his territory—he says you are welcome here and that he has heard of you." Nemsis paused, "I will return soon." Nemsis raced away with her newfound friend.

At'r laid the pistol down, relieved for the reprieve.

"Will Nemsis be safe with him?" Izadra asked.

"Safer with him than us." At'r assured her before he silenced her questions with his lips.

Later in the afternoon Nemsis returned. Tired, and a little dirty but seemingly fine in all respects. Making the trek back to their villa they made the final preparation to leave in the morning.

Creasion was but a short flight from Konas and it was good to be back, especially now. Izadra could not believe her happiness. 'At'r loves me' she felt like shouting from the pinnacle of their palace. Ry-tr was a merry child, and was great source of love for both parents. Nothing could have made her happier.

Still she felt a shadow lurking behind her. Ba-lyn crossed her mind, she shivered. A servant entered announcing lord Casso presence in their outer chambers, he was requesting an audience immediately. At'r nodded to the servant and he ushered Casso in.

Casso's face was ashen and drawn. His eyes were red rimmed and he bore a grim expression.

"What is wrong?" At'r questioned seeing his condition, "Is it Betus?" At'r's voice was full of alarm, and Izadra eased Casso back in a chair.

"Yes. He is visiting Metem and last night he became, well, ill."

"Do you know what is wrong with him?" At'r asked, handing Casso a brandy, he downed it, thanking At'r.

"No. None of the physicians can determine what is wrong, but he seems to be dying." Casso shook his head. "Actually, his symptoms point to a Troscoss energy drain. But who would be powerful enough to effect my father?"

At'r and Izadra shared a glance at each other, their minds thinking along the same paths. Now that they had shared their essence, At'r knew of Izadra's concerns about Ba-lyn, and he agreed with her.

"The same individual that poisoned you, Casso." Izadra said gently.

"He is asking to see you Lady Izadra." Casso told her with a sigh, "He feels you can help."

"I will go immediately." Izadra said without question, "Milord, is my fighter operative?"

"You will have to take a shuttle, your fighter is still being updated, besides, I want you take a guard, you may be the Troscoss' real target. Perhaps Captain Kara."

"As you will it, but I must hurry," Izadra stopped, "I can not take Ry-tr."

"No." At'r agreed.

A sick feeling came over Izadra, dark feelings, she looked to At'r, he had not picked up on her foreboding thoughts.

"Sire," Izadra entreated At'r, "I will take another guard, I can not trust anyone else to care for Ry-tr but you or Tari, the lady Jelsa will accompany me."

"Very well," At'r was thoughtful a moment, "I think I will cancel my new systems checks on my fighter. It can be done another day."

"No, this is why we returned early, if needed you can be summoned in flight and go directly to Metem." Izadra assured him, "I will go."

Kissing Izadra, At'r left to make the arrangements and taking Casso with him tried to comfort the distressed man.

Still tugging at Izadra was the annoying feeling of impending disaster. Calling Tari she explained the situation. "If anything strange begins to happen," she noticed Tari watching her closely. "Tari, I have had a bad premonition about this, but I must go and can not take Ry-tr. Please if anything happens guard him, Nemsis will stay with you."

"I will guard him with my life." Tari assured her, "but also I fear for your safety, lady Jelsa is a good warrior but..."

"I understand Tari, try not to worry. You have taught me much about defending myself in the last few months."

"You did well at that before I taught you." Tari smiled remembering the badly wounded Zerion Captain. Hugging Tari, Izadra left for the launch pad and the moon Metem.

CHAPTER 47

❀

*U*sing an unmarked shuttle Gerlin had stolen from the prison fleet he, Ba-lyn and Quar carefully landed on the Moon of Metem. Here Gerlin and Quar departed and using forged passes made their way near Izadra's shuttle. With Gerlin's help the Zerion gained control of the Royal shuttle. Quar killed the Creasion pilot in a particularly bloody Zerion method.

"That was not necessary." Gerlin objected.

"Why do you care?" Quar said harshly, "This way they know it was I that took the shuttle, and I want your Lord At'r to know who has his wife." Quar laughed, "Now get out, before I leave your body behind also."

Gerlin returned angrily to Ba-lyn who waited in their shuttle, he did not tell her of Quar's departure.

'Tonight,' Ba-lyn thought in her most guarded thoughts 'tonight Gerlin, you die.' She almost smiled as they neared Crea, the contemplation of how she would sacrifice Gerlin, then the Prince was almost to savory to quell.

Preparing to land near the palace, Ba-lyn informed the controller who she was and that she was returning to the palace, they cleared her at once. Gerlin this time stayed with the craft. Ba-lyn made her way to the palace, noticing the security was unusually heavy but she did not have difficulty gaining entrance to the Royal chambers. Once inside she cautiously entered the nursery to find the child not in his crib. Carefully she peered through the door to the brightly decorated interior of the playroom. Sitting in an Earth style rocking chair Tari sat holding the Prince. 'So' Ba-lyn thought, 'Our Lady has left you to guard the Prince.' Ba-lyn would have to be clever, Tari was also from Tross, and although she did not have the training Ba-lyn did, Tari could protect and defend herself against mental attacks.

Ba-lyn's thoughts turned to Kevin and how easily she had influenced his mind. She hurried to his section of the palace and finding him home, knocked on the door.

Surprised evident on his face he gladly welcomed her in. "I did not know you were coming back tonight."

"Lord Betus is quite ill on Metem, Lady Izadra flew there this afternoon."

"So I found out, but I wanted to see the new Prince and I couldn't get near him."

"Really, who was with him?"

"Captain Kara." Ba-lyn said casually.

"Then she was left to insure his security instead of going with Izadra." Kevin said a little alarmed. Why was Ba-lyn so curious about the Prince, and why was she back un-announced? "I doubt she would even allow me in."

He had begun to feel strange as Ba-lyn began entrancing his mind. Kevin's glass slipped from his hand and crashed on the floor but he did not hear it. He only heard Ba-lyn's voice telling him to take her to Tari. Deep inside his mind he fought the compelling urge to do her bidding but she was already too strong for him. Arm and arm they walked to the nursery. Once past the outer guards Ba-lyn told Kevin to go ahead and leave the door ajar. Like a zombie he obeyed. Tari seeing only him opened the door. Kevin fought what Ba-lyn was telling him to do with all his strength, but her will was powerful. With one quick blow he knocked Tari unconscious, only to stare disbelieving down at her. He was vaguely aware of Ba-lyn's presence, she picked up the Prince but found Kevin blocking her exit. He had regained some control.

"What are you doing?"

"When you wake," she began to tell him the lie he would believe true and there-by cover her, but she heard a low growl and turned to stare into the cold eyes of Nemsis.

"I will kill you." Nemsis told Ba-lyn through her mind, "Leave the child and you may live."

"You will not harm me while I hold him." Ba-lyn returned then turned back to Kevin, who was totally out of her control now. Slowly she backed from the room, Ry-tr in her arms. Gerlin appeared behind her as she backed out the garden door. He fired at Nemsis barely missing her as she ran for cover. He did not miss Kevin who had rushed toward Ba-lyn to try and take the child. Kevin lay badly wounded on the grassy path. Despite Ry-tr's crying, Ba-lyn and Gerlin made it back to their shuttle, killing two palace guards in their escape.

Kevin managed to crawl to Tari who was beginning to wake, Nemsis had returned to lick her face and moaning loudly she finally came too. Kevin told her what had happened and Tari alerted the space controllers as the shuttle lifted off. At the same time she ordered her own ship readied and a squad to accompany her.

Izadra was greatly distressed about her Uncle, for the length of the life span of a Creasion he was not really old, but for no apparent reason his health was failing. As she and lady Jelsa approached the shuttle bay after her visit Izadra's mind was pre-occupied with worry for not only her Uncle but also the continuing anxiety about Ry-tr's safety. As soon as she reached space she would call Tari.

"My Lady," Jelsa stopped her, "there are no guards around your shuttle."

Izadra looked around, Jelsa was correct, "that is peculiar," Izadra said and they turned back toward the closed hangar doors only to find they did not open. Jelsa immediately drew her lazzer pistol and stood before Izadra, standing still they waited.

From the outer side of the door came the loud voice of the base Commander, "Lady Izadra! Are you all right?"

"Yes." she answered calmly, "However, the door appears to have jammed."

Rending the air, the sound of a lazzer pistol echoed in the enclosed space of the shuttle bay. Izadra turned to find lady Jelsa at her feet, not dead but heavily stunned. Her eyes froze as she looked up, the Zerion Captain Quar stood less than ten feet in front of her. Never had she expected to see him again. He smiled, the scar on his cheek whitening, Izadra straightened and glanced down at Jelsa's lazzer next to her hand.

"Do not think of it, milady." he sneered and firing again destroyed the gun.

Behind them a security team was vainly trying to get through the doors, the Commander having just received word of the Zerion's escape and the events on the planet.

"Your shuttle awaits," Quar bowed slightly, "I can stun you and carry you in, if you prefer." he smiled.

"I can walk Zerion." she said with contempt.

Their lift-off was fast and rough, a squad of fighters hot on their tails. Quar quickly told them to keep their distance. Ahead in his path he saw a Royal fighter and what was obviously Commander Kron's ship.

"Lord At'r," he teased over the communications system, "I have your wife," he laughed, keeping his eye on Izadra who also watched him.

"I am taking her to Zerion, my Emperor will be so pleased with her." he taunted before breaking off transmission.

"Quar if you think I would allow you to take her to Zerion then you are mad. Harm her and your life is forfeit."

Izadra's image appeared on the viewer, Quar's arm around her waist and his other hand holding her head back against him by her hair he had ripped her flightsuit and the garments beneath, reminding At'r of their first meeting. Suddenly her mind touched At'r's and he opened his thoughts to her.

"At'r, I beg you do not allow him to take me to Zerion, I would rather...die." she said to him. He could feel her grief, "Our son At'r, he is in danger, destroy this shuttle and go save him. Please!" At'r could feel her tears, and her fears.

"Never!" he told her, somehow he knew he must work fast and try to save them both. Their happiness had been so short, her time with him had been hard for her, was this to be confirmation that who ever he loved was destroyed by the Zerion? A desperate idea came to mind, signaling Kron to be ready he touched Izadra's mind.

"My love," his voice seemed to caress her mind, "listen well, can you get in the escape pod?"

"Possibly," she returned, "if you can distract Quar."

"Be ready." he told her telepathically, then to the Zerion "Quar, I will make you a deal." no response, "QUAR!" At'r yelled.

Quar released Izadra, soon he would enjoy her as he had planned when he had captured her on Earth, but for now, he would play with At'r a little longer. Then he thought, 'I will take Izadra before the viewer so At'r can watch.' Quar laughed to himself.

"What?" Quar said sharply, "Please At'r," he said informally, "I am busy." he smiled a lecherous smile.

At'r's face clouded, "I will make you a deal."

"A deal? I hold all the cards. What will you deal with."

"Riches Quar, I will make you the richest man in the galaxy if you will return Izadra to me, and tell me who has helped you."

"I do not believe you." Quar switched off the viewer and turned to find the shuttle empty. A sudden release of air pressure alerted him to the escape pod's launch. With in seconds of the launch At'r and Kron directed their stun cannon toward the shuttle. At'r wanted

Quar alive, but when the beams touched the shuttle's skin the entire craft exploded, disintegrating in a flash and leaving only tiny space debris hurtling through space. Someone had not wanted Quar taken alive, so they had planned for this contingency, stun beams set off the explosion.

Docking with the pod, At'r secured the lock and opened the air chamber between the two crafts. On shaking legs Izadra climbed out of the pod and threw her arms around At'r.

"At'r they have him, I know they do, please, we have to hurry, Dawn…"

Breaking through the normal controllers chatter came the special bulletin confirming what Izadra knew from intuition. Tari's voice was strained and she was in pursuit of the kidnappers. They were bound for Tross, this too Izadra already knew.

"How far ahead of you are they." At'r questioned.

"One hour." Tari replied. "My E.T.A. is just under an hour, they are probably landing at this moment. I do not know why they took him, but I will find him." she said confidently. Tari blamed herself for not preventing the abduction. Kevin had been a good choice for Ba-lyn to use in her abduction plans, Tari had not suspected him.

"We will be only minutes behind you, activate your tracers so we may follow you." At'r instructed. Ending his transmission he turned the ship toward Tross. Kron peeled off to attend to the planetary defenses just encase a Zerion attack was brewing.

"Why?" At'r said aloud, "Why?" hearing a sob from behind he turned, "Do you know?"

"Yes. It came to me in the escape pod. And I know for sure who." At'r had never seen Izadra look so frightened, even in the beginning after her capture, "They plan to sacrifice him to the pagan Troscoss gods, at dawn on Tross."

"Who?" At'r demanded, as he expertly controlled the fighter.

"Ba-lyn and a priest name Gerlin."

"Gerlin, that is the sub-Commander of the prison station." At'r said and now he too became alarmed, he didn't tell Izadra but dawn on Tross was only two hours away, they did not have much time.

CHAPTER 48

Ba-lyn and High Priest Gerlin thought they had lost Tari in the side trip they took through the asteroid belt. Nevertheless, Tari had out guessed them and followed at a distance. She now landed her fighter close to the Troscoss High Altar on Tross. In awe she and Nemsis, who would not be left behind, watched from a short distance until they could gain advantage:

Ten young girls emerged from the icy waterfall and dried their supple young bodies in the light of Creasion. Lastly Ba-lyn emerged, they dried her and placed a white satin robe over her head. Then brushed her long blond hair until it reflected the light of Creasion. Following her example the ten girls donned thin robes of white gauze and walking before Ba-lyn the girls ascended the ancient steps followed by Ba-lyn who looked slightly entranced. She carried the Prince.

At the top waited Gerlin in a robe of blood red. Chanting as they scaled the steps to the top, the girls then surrounded the Altar and knelt on the sharp stones. Ba-lyn approached and handing the Prince to the closest girl knelt before Gerlin.

Raising his voice to the heavens Gerlin proclaimed, "I will take this woman on the High Altar of Troscoss so that our child may serve you and have your blessings."

"What have you brought for us in exchange for our favor?" a whispered choir of voices inquired.

Tari almost gasped as Ry-tr was raised before the Altar.

"Proceed." said the choir, "But first take the Royal child down from here until it is time for us to receive him." a slight breeze rose, "He is a distraction to us."

Chanting the ten girls rose, blood ran from their knees punctured by the piercing rocks, High Priest Gerlin gave the child to the same girl and they descended from the Altar. At the bottom they waited, guarded by several large male Troscoss.

Tari watched as Gerlin drew Ba-lyn up from her knees and kissed her roughly. Laying her back on the stone altar he began a brutal assault of her body, Ba-lyn did not protest, instead she to revel in the brutal passion.

Using this time Tari and Nemsis reduced the population of male Troscoss by four before they heard the chant begin and hurried back for chance to save the Prince. As the young girls picked up the chant from Gerlin and began their slow ascent of the steps with the Ry-tr, At'r's Royal fighter screamed overhead and woke the sleeping child.

Ry-tr began to howl at the manner he was being treated.

Turning back to the Altar Tari was shocked to see Ba-lyn draw a knife from Gerlin's chest just as he emptied his life force into her body.

A look of pain and shock distorted his face and he lived long enough to hear Ba-lyn beseech the gods favor in their ancient tongue. Tari did not understand until Ba-lyn parted from Gerlin's body and it disintegrated.

At'r quickly took in the scene below, he knew what would happen next. Turning and using his stun lazzers he strafed the Altar area then set the fighter down next to Tari's.

Before he could stop her, Izadra was out of the fighter and running toward the Altar, At'r close on her heels did not try. He shot the other two guards that Tari had not been able to take out and Izadra raced to the top of the Pagan Sanctum. At'r noticing a green aura beginning to surround Izadra. By the time she reached the top it was diamerald in color and very strong.

When At'r had strafed the area Tari had seized the opportunity and grabbed Ry-tr, who was beginning to calm down in her arms. Just as Izadra reached the top, Ba-lyn grabbed the baby from Tari and stabbed her at the same time with the Ceremonial Knife, Tari sank to the ground. Turning Ba-lyn then saw Izadra who stood emanating green with such rage in her eyes that Ba-lyn faltered, but she still lay the Prince on the Altar.

"Since before you came I was meant to be Empress. Had you not come I would be already, but with his blood comes the fulfillment of my promise." Ba-lyn declared madly, and laughing raised the knife over the child.

Instantly some of Izadra's aura left her to surround her child, as At'r lazzer took the knife from Ba-lyn's hand.

She stepped back in awe and fear, never had Ba-lyn thought Izadra could be so powerful.

Suddenly Nemsis jumped protectively on to the Altar, "I warned you," she said to Ba-lyn, both Izadra and At'r were also tuned in the confrontation. "I told you I would kill you if you took the child. What you did to my poor mother is enough to kill you." she took a step off the Altar and closer to the terrified Priestess. Ba-lyn stepped back, again Nemsis stepped closer, Ba-lyn backed up, suddenly finding herself teetering on the edge of the cliff.

A wrenching scream broke the stillness, and try though she did to regain her balance, Ba-lyn could not stop herself from falling from the edge. A thousand feet down, after hitting the mountainside several times she finally stopped. Her body instantly carried away by the raging and freezing surf below.

At'r and Izadra, cuddling Ry-tr close, gingerly looked over the side.

Ba-lyn was gone, no trace remained.

Shaken, Izadra drew away from the cliff's edge and spotted Tari, badly wounded but trying valiantly to stand. At'r saw her too, and calling for the medical team that was racing up the steps eased Tari down admonishing her to rest. Nemsis sided up to her and lay down, providing her body heat to help warm the injured Tari.

At'r hugged Izadra and Ry-tr close. The medical team stabilized Tari's bleeding, placed her on a hover stretcher and began the slow trek back down. Izadra, holding Ry-tr close with At'r's arm around her waist accompanied them.

Tari recovered in a room adjoining Kevin's both under the constant supervision of Trentos. Betus' recovery on Metem was immediate with the death of Gerin and Ba-lyn, his condition was the direct result of a Troscoss energy drain.

Izadra and At'r both allowed Nemsis to sleep in their quarters on a permanent basis. They felt more secure with the alert cat guarding their precious son and she took her duties seriously.

CHAPTER 49

$\mathcal{A}$ ll of Creasion celebrated. A holiday had been declared to mark
the occasion and diplomats and ambassadors had been sum-
moned from the reaches of Creasion influence. Historians were busy
recording this great event as well as those that had taken place just
three days before.

Today the Lord Emperor of Creasion would crown his Empress.
Their story had become a legend, still fresh in the mind of all and the
topic of most conversations.

Since early morning the masses of people had been gathering outside the Royal city of Crea, and those who could not be in the city
watched via tele-monitors that transmitted to over a thousand different worlds.

At'r had spared nothing to make this occasion unforgettable.
Food and drink had been provided to the hundreds of thousands of
people who crowded the capital city of Crea. Entertainment had
been provided for them as well as the viewers on other planets. But
underneath all the merriment, security was tight. System defenses
were placed on their highest alert and these selfless individuals gladly
gave up their holiday to provide a safe holiday for the others. The
stage was set.

As the last lavender hues of Tos disappeared from the cloudless
sky, and the three moons, Konas, Tross, and Metem rose to shine

down on Crea, trumpets blared through out the city. Silence fell on the massive crowds gathered and all eyes turned to the high Plexiglas platform that hovered, suspend a hundred feet up.

Lord Betus fully recovered after Ba-lyn's and Gerlin's death, and lord Trentos stood in attendance on the platform, as did Tari and Commander Kron. Trumpets sounded again, their high notes announcing in a fan-fare the arrival of Lord At'r. He rose on an anti-gravitational elevator to stand in the center of the flower bedecked platform.

His robe was of a heavy satin, dark Diamerald green in color, the cape billowing gently in the slight breeze that stirred. On his head was the Gold and Diamerald Royal Crown of Creasion and on a golden pedestal next to him rested the Empress' Crown.

Yet another blare of trumpets announced Izadra's arrival. Majestic and elegant, she had appeared on the bottom step of the clear escalator stairs.

At At'r's request she had dressed in a dark green satin gown and her grandmother's golden Diamerald cape. Drawing on the light from the three moons of Creasion blazed the Diamerald necklace around Izadra's throat and on her ears the matching earrings. Beneath these her Ankh-Angle necklace clearly proclaiming her Royalty.

Slowly the stairs carried her upward toward At'r. Still the crowds were hushed, none daring to speak for fear of breaking the spell that seemed to engulf the entire realm. Reaching the top Izadra and At'r's eyes met, they stared deeply into each other's eyes. After a brief moment Izadra sank before him in a deep curtsey, her head bowed in respect. At'r lifted the Empress' Crown and placed it upon Izadra's head. Offering Izadra his hand, assisted her to rise. Only then did he address the multitude.

"My people." he began. "Many years ago the Zerion stole from us the Empress Iza. As the prophecy has foretold they have now returned her heir. Empress Izadra.

The silence was broken, the people cheered wildly.

At'r raised his hand for quiet, "Empress Izadra has on many different occasions proved herself worthy of her Crown. And so to show my respect, gratitude and most of all my love for her I have crowned her my Empress. Only my command precedes hers, in all matters." He turned to her and took her hand, "She was not only fated to be my wife and the mother of my children, but, she is my chosen Empress."

Under the *Three Moons Rising* At'r drew her forward to the cheers of their subjects, then turning and beholding the brilliant smile on her face, and the tears of joy and love that glistened in her eyes, he kissed her. Not just a token kiss, but one that lengthened, leaving no doubts in the minds or hearts of any who beheld them of the love and passion shared by their Emperor and his Empress.

THE END

Glossary

Anke-Angle—Symbol of the Royal House of Creasion—An Ankh with an inverted Pyramid set with three round Diameralds symbolizing each moon in the system and a teardrop Diamerald symbolizing the main planet.

Creasion—The main planet in the System of Creasion orbited by three inhabitable moons. Konas, Metem and Tross.

Diamerald—(dia-merald) A gem stone only found on Creasion having the properties of a Diamond and an Emerald. Known to be the conductors of mind powers. The purest stones set in the Royal Emblem necklaces of the Emperor and Empress of Creasion.

Diamerald Tower—The Mystic Tower constructed by the Emperor Tor, after the abduction of the Empress Iza by the treacherous Zerions. Emperor Tor sealed himself inside just before his death. Opened mysteriously when Izadra, Iza's heir, was returned to Creasion in order to instruct her about her heritage and powers.

Lazzer—A weapon similar to a laser but more powerful. Designed on Creasion.

Symaka—An ancient Creasion ceremonial weapon.

Tos-hawk—(Star Hawk) A star class Battle Station designed to keep the war like Zerion (the natural enemies of Creasions) from attacking the planet Creasion.

Troscoss—An evil cult who's practices were long forbidden on Creasion. Practiced in secret by the beautiful but evil priestess Ba-lyn, she plotted to kill Izadra and take her place as Empress.

Vartee Tree—A huge tree that grows on tropical islands on Creasion. The root structure forms above ground sometimes produces comfortable seats.

Water Cat—A rare and unusual cat the size of a Tiger but blue in color and striped to blend in with water. Water Cats are known to have nasty tempers but are telepathic. They have webbed back feet and are reclusive barring one cub every two years, the female dens alone after mating. One exception was Nemsis, the female cub Lady Izadra and Lord At'r rescued after her mother was killed by the evil Troscoss in a failed sacrifice.

Zerion—A desert planet in the Creasion system. Inhabited by humanoid a species that are sadistic and war like.

0-595-22487-3

Printed in the United States
16179LVS00003BA/19